A Sydnee Marcola Adventure

AGU: BORDER PATROL

CITIZEN X

Book 1

BY

THOMAS DEPRIMA

Vinnia Publishing - U.S.A.

AGU:™

Citizen X

AGU:™ Border Patrol – Book 1
Copyright ©2011 by Thomas J. DePrima

ISBN-10 : **1619310171**

ISBN-13 : **978-1-61931-017-9**

1st Edition

Amazon Distribution

Cover art by: Martin J. Cannon

Appendices containing political and technical data highly pertinent to this series are included at the back of this book.

To contact the author, or see information about his other novels, visit:

http://www.deprima.com

Dedication

This book is dedicated to David Pomerico, the Del Rey editor who requested I develop a new trilogy that would occur in the story universe I created for my A Galaxy Unknown series. Although all parties believed the spin-off series I pitched had great potential, contract negotiations with Random House failed to produce an acceptable agreement. I didn't wish to see the series wither on the vine, so I've developed it as an Independent publication.

Acknowledgements

I always seem to have too many irons in the fire and as a result I tend to brush past self-imposed deadlines like a waiter brushes past hungry patrons in a busy restaurant. So I would be seriously remiss if I didn't express my heartfelt appreciation to my copyeditor at Independent Author Services, Myra Shelley, who puts up with my failure to complete projects in a most timely fashion and who always comes through for me in a pinch.

And last, but certainly not least, my thanks to Michael A. Norcutt for his suggestions, proofreading, and for acting as my military operations and protocol advisor.

This series of novels includes:

A Galaxy Unknown™...

A Galaxy Unknown ™
Valor at Vauzlee
The Clones of Mawcett
Trader Vyx
Milor!
Castle Vroman
Against All Odds
Return to Dakistee
Retreat And Adapt

Other series and novels by the author:

AGU:™ *Border Patrol*...

Citizen X
Clidepp Requital

AGU:™ *SC Intelligence*...

The Star Brotherhood

Colton James novels...

A World Without Secrets
Vengeance Is Personal

When The Spirit...

When The Spirit Moves You
When The Spirit Calls

Table of Contents

Chapter One
~ April 5ᵗʰ, 2282 ~

Sydnee Marcola leapt to her feet and began screaming for all she was worth. All around her, others were doing likewise. Admiral Jenetta Carver had just finished delivering her speech, and as she stepped back from the podium, the NHSA Corps of Cadets went wild. All were clapping, most were stamping their feet in unison, and many were cheering, screaming, or whistling. The Admiral had already received several standing ovations, but now the building literally shook from the noise and stamping feet as the cadet corps attempted to express their admiration of the speaker in the only way possible on this occasion.

Lightheaded with exhilaration, and with hands that stung from clapping too hard, Sydnee just couldn't stop. Jenetta Carver was her idol, and this was the first time the Admiral had returned to the Northern Hemisphere Space Academy in the twenty-six years since her graduation. Now in her senior year, Sydnee couldn't believe her good fortune in still being here for the Admiral's speech. In two month's time she would have missed it. She wished she had an excuse, any excuse, to speak directly with the Admiral, but cadets didn't rush up to one of the most senior officers in Space Command and beg an audience.

Besides— Sydnee knew she probably wouldn't be able to articulate a single coherent sentence if she suddenly found herself face to face with Admiral Jenetta Carver, Commander of the Second Fleet and Military Governor of Region Two of the Galactic Alliance.

At that moment, every cadet in the hall was ready to drop everything and follow the Admiral back to Region Two where she faced the challenges of settling a vast, lawless territory, but there were still educational requirements to fulfill. Following graduation in May, Sydnee expected to travel to the GSC Warship Command Institute in Australia. She hadn't received her orders yet, but it was a done deal unless she screwed up royally in the next two months. She was determined that *that* wasn't going to happen. Oh sure, she had received a number of demerits during her Academy years, but all were for minor infractions, such as failing to properly stow some small item prior to a room inspection. She'd received no more than the average cadet and had always performed the punishment duty that would wipe the slate clean. Scholastically, her grades were not only good, they were excellent. Her math and science grades were not as outstanding as Admiral Carver's grades had been while she was at the Academy, but then nobody had ever managed to surpass the academic marks set by Cadet Jenetta Carver. In fact, only eight students had received the Admiral Matthew Tissdell Award for Excellence in Mathematics in the twenty-six years since Admiral Carver had received it, and none of those award recipients had math grades that surpassed, or even rivaled, Carver's.

Where Sydnee had really outshone most other cadets was in Command and Control exercises. With scores that consistently ranked in the superior range, her career path was established. Following the anticipated two-year program of intensive study at the Warship Command Institute, she would be promoted in rank to Lieutenant(jg) and assigned to a warship as a line officer. When the appropriate time came during the next three decades, she would receive orders to proceed to the Space Command War College, where two years of intensive study would prepare her for command of a ship of the line. Only Admiral Carver and two other line officers in the history of Space Command had been exempted from attending the WCI and the War College. The other two were the Admiral's sisters.

Sydnee's C&C scores were the only area where she had been able to surpass Admiral Carver's record. While she knew the Admiral's scores had been surprisingly dismal, she had never been able to learn why. She'd heard persistent rumors that Cadet Jenetta Carver had been a prankster who delighted in harrying her instructors, especially Professor Hubera, now a member of the Admiralty Board. If any other cadet had done that, it was said, they would have been dismissed from the Academy. But Cadet Jenetta Carver had always gotten away with it, and had then gone on to scale heights only dreamed of by most other cadets and officers. Since C&C scores could be quite subjective, Sydnee subscribed to the commonly held belief that a few irked instructors might have misused the scoring mechanism in retaliation for the pranks.

Following her last class for the day, Sydnee stopped into the Cadet 3rd Company HQ office where she picked up a data wafer containing the speech by Admiral Carver. Upon entering her dorm room, she slid the paper-thin wafer into the special slot in the picture frame on her dresser, then powered on her stereo and entered the frequency to pick up the audio signal broadcast by the picture frame. After touching the spot on the frame that would play the file, she quickly hopped onto her bed. With her back against the wall, she focused her hazel eyes on the photo frame to enjoy the speech again.

"Oh, you've got it bad," she heard from the door. "You heard that speech just a few hours ago."

Sydnee had already identified the speaker by her voice, but she turned her head to look at Cadet Katarina Somulowski, leaning against the doorframe, and smiled. "Shush, this is the best part," she said, and returned her attention to the picture frame.

Katarina came in and closed the door, then took a seat on the bed next to her best friend to watch the speech. When it ended and the cadet corps rose to their feet in applause, Katarina climbed off the bed and turned the volume down to minimum. The speech would morph to the beginning and replay until Sydnee cancelled the function.

Sydnee sighed. "She is just so amazing, Kat. She's beautiful, brilliant, a full Admiral at just forty-five, and looks as young as us. Most people say she'll become the Admiral of the Fleet when Admiral Moore retires in a few years."

"What a depressing thought," Katarina said.

"Name someone better," Sydnee said defensively.

"I didn't mean it like that. I meant, 'Ugh, who wants to be Admiral of the Fleet?' I bet Admiral Moore hasn't been off-world in decades. He probably spends all his time running back and forth between Galactic Alliance Council meetings and Admiralty Board meetings. I suppose it's okay when your career is winding down to retirement, but look at Carver. As you said, she looks as young as us. Would you like to be stuck in an office all day, reading reports and attending meetings?"

"You know the answer to that. I'd go crazy in a week."

"Yeah, me too. Hey, let's go to the gym for an hour before dinner." Facetiously, she added, "We can do a little kickboxing to help you prepare for the day when you have a chance to spar with Admiral Carver."

"Okay," Sydnee said with a grin as she jumped up and began pulling a brush through her collar-length brown hair. "Give me two minutes to get ready."

* * *

As she'd anticipated, Sydnee Marcola received orders to proceed to the WCI following graduation from NHSA. Her friend and fellow cadet, Katarina Somulowski, received similar orders, so they traveled together via a sub-orbital shuttle that set down at the WCI landing pad southeast of Perth just two hours after lifting off from Nebraska, USNA.

That ensigns are the lowest of the low in the officer corps couldn't have been made clearer as they moved through orientation and indoctrination. Four years of hard work had earned them steadily increasing privileges and standing at NHSA, but it was as if that had never happened. At the WCI, they were returned to the bottom of the pecking order. It was disconcerting, although not unexpected, to again be considered less astute than a garden slug.

While all cadets at the Academy are taught to pilot a shuttle, WCI students learn to handle every small ship currently in use by Space Command and the Space Marine

Corps. Sydnee, like most of her classmates, quickly adopted the FA-SF4 Marine Fighter as her favorite and spent as much time in the simulator as possible. The small deadly ship handled like an extension of her body. Her least favorite ship was the MAT-12A, the new Dakinium-sheathed Marine Assault Transport ship. While tugs typically behaved like a brick during sub-orbital flight, the MAT-12A behaved like a deep-dish baking pan filled with water. As long it was kept straight and level when landing, it was fine, but allow the glide path to get the least bit sloppy, and it was a real fight to regain stability before suffering something between a hard landing and a controlled crash. Assuming the pilot lived through that, they might then find forty pissed off Marines lining up to express displeasure with their flying skills.

The MATs were 'opposed gravity' ships and could hover like a butterfly, but every LZ was to be considered 'hot.' One must be able to get the ship down fast so the Marines could deploy, thus minimizing exposure to enemy fire. With each class of ship, Sydnee started with simulator practice and then moved to the real thing for her final grade. Flight training was the best part of every day.

The worst part of every day was the Alien Anatomy class. The Academy had covered the sentient species in GA space, so the WCI had responsibility for introducing every other known species of animal the cadets were likely to encounter. To Sydnee, there seemed to be millions. Almost as bad as AA were the studies in Protocol. As a representative of the Galactic Alliance who would have substantial contact with races from every world while performing interdiction activities, a line officer had to be aware of most social customs and mores. Somewhere between AA/Protocol and Flight Training were the classes in GA Interdiction Law, Shipboard Command and Supervision, Ancient and Modern Warfare Studies, and a myriad of other important courses. Looking forward to the day she would join Admiral Carver's fleet in Region Two, Sydnee applied herself to her studies with the same intensity others reserved for flight training.

* * *

The days, weeks, and months seemed to stretch on interminably, but finally classes were over and graduation was just two days away. All but two of the cadets who began the training with Sydnee and Katarina completed the two years. One was excused from classes following a serious accident in his second year that saw him unable to complete flight training. The cause of the accident was ruled mechanical failure, so he would return next year to complete the required work. The other cadet had mysteriously vanished overnight. One day he was there, the next he was gone. No one knew why he left or where he'd gone. He had maintained excellent grades up to his disappearance. Neither the Institute nor his family would respond to inquiries from students.

Sydnee and Katarina raced to pick up their new orders in the Company HQ upon learning they were available. They already knew their final grades and class ranks. Sydnee had finished near the top of the class in every subject except Alien Anatomy. That was no surprise since she'd hated the class. Although not in the top five percent of that class, she had at least made it into the top ten. Her class rank overall was seventh. Katarina wasn't quite the scholar, but she had finished with a very respectable class rank of seventy-two in a class of four hundred fourteen.

Both young women were in a celebratory mood and raced to a table where they could view their orders. Katarina made it ahead of Sydnee, dropping her data ring over the spindle. The face of a Space Command officer filled the screen and announced her posting.

"I've been posted to the *Pholus* in Region Two," Katarina screamed out to everyone within earshot. The others called back their congratulations. Sydnee and Katarina hugged and wept happy tears.

Wiping her tears, Sydnee said, "Let me check my orders. Maybe we'll be together on the *Pholus*."

As Katarina picked up her ring, she said, "That would be wonderful, but it's unlikely they'll need two new bridge officers. At least we'll be together in Region Two. We can keep in touch and see each other occasionally.

Sydnee dropped her ring onto the spindle and the face of the same officer appeared on the screen. As he announced the name of her assigned warship, the happy look on Sydnee's face froze, then turned to one of shock and dismay.

"It must be a mistake," Katarina said. "You're number seven in the class. They wouldn't assign you to *that* ship."

Sydnee was too shocked to respond.

"You should go see the Commander," Katarina said. "He'll be able to clear it up and get your orders corrected."

Sydnee nodded and began to walk cheerlessly towards the door with Katarina right beside her. She could feel a cold numbing sensation spreading through her abdomen.

"The Commander is busy right now, Ensign," Commander Collins' aide said. "Perhaps tomorrow."

"But, sir, I have a serious problem. I received my new orders and there seems to be a mistake."

"That hardly seems likely, Ensign."

"But sir, I've been assigned to the *Perry*, GSC-DL423."

"The *Perry*? I thought that went to the scrap yard thirty years ago. Are you sure of the designation?"

"Yes, sir. DL423. It's listed as a *Jones* class ship. I read that they stopped *making* them sixty-eight years ago."

"Let me check," the aide said, keying his computer interface. After a few seconds, he said, "It's listed as an active-duty warship, alright. Your orders require you to report aboard as quickly as travel arrangements can be made after graduation. It appears they're shorthanded."

"But, sir. My rank is number seven in the class. This has to be a mistake."

The aide sighed. "Let me see if the Commander can find time to see you." He turned to his com and said, "Commander, I'm sorry to bother you right now, but Ensign Marcola is here. It seems she's been posted to the *Perry*,

GSC-DL423, and feels sure it's a mistake. Can you spare her a couple of minutes?" After a few seconds he read a message that scrolled up on his com unit. "Go ahead in, Ensign," he said to Sydnee, "but keep it brief or you may find yourself posted to a reclamation ship."

That might almost be better, Sydnee thought, but only said, "Thank you, sir," and walked quickly to the Commander's door.

"What's the problem, Ensign?" Commander Collins asked brusquely as Marcola braced to attention in front of his desk. "Did you misunderstand your orders?"

"Um, no, sir," Sydnee said. "I just felt there has to be a mistake."

"Because of your class rank?"

"Um, yes, sir."

"You feel that you should receive special privileges because you finished near the top?"

"Um, not *special*, sir."

"What would *you* call it, Ensign?"

"I've, um, always believed that the better students received postings more consistent with their abilities and attitudes, sir."

"Have you?"

"Um, yes, sir."

"Stop *umming* me, Ensign."

"U— yes, sir."

"Are you *refusing* to accept this posting, Ensign?" Collins asked in an accusatory tone.

"NO, sir. Absolutely not. I just believed that a mistake may have been made and that it should be cleared up without delay."

"There's no mistake. You're to report the *Perry* as soon as transportation can be arranged."

"Yes, sir," Marcola said smartly.

"Was there anything else, Ensign?"

"No, sir."

"Dismissed."

Sydnee saluted, then turned on one heel and retraced her steps out of the office. As the door slid closed behind her, the aide asked, "All cleared up?"

"Perfectly, sir."

"Good. Good luck, Ensign."

"Thank you, sir."

"Well, did you get it straightened out?" Katarina asked as Sydnee emerged from the Headquarters building.

"Commander Collins said that no mistake has been made."

"What? How could he say that? What else did he say?"

"That I was dismissed."

"And you didn't press him to check on it?"

"No way. He was in that 'How dare you question the decisions of Space Command HQ' mode. I was afraid that if I said anything, I'd find myself posted to a reclamation barge."

"Yeah. Well, as soon as you reach your post, apply for a transfer. They can't shunt you off to a rec-lam if you're following SOP. Want to go to town?"

"Yeah, I need a drink— maybe two— maybe even three."

"Two is about your limit. We haven't graduated yet, you know."

"So what. Everything is finished except the final ceremony. I'm finished too. I've busted my backside for six years, only to wind up on the worst ship in the fleet."

"Try to look at the positive side."

"You see a positive side?"

"You're bound to be the best damn officer on that ship. You might make captain before any of us."

"I'd rather be a lieutenant on the Battleship *Pholus* than the captain of the Light Destroyer *Perry*."

* * *

"Ohhh, my head is killing me," Sydnee moaned to Katarina, who was doing her best to hold the five-foot eleven-inch cadet upright, fully clothed, in the shower. "What time is it?"

Katarina, an inch and half shorter, was having difficulty supporting Sydnee's full weight. "It's almost 0800. I've been trying to wake you for an hour. You have to get ready for graduation."

"I don't have anything left to do until tomorrow. I'll worry about it then."

"Graduation is in two hours."

"Two hours? No, it's tomorrow."

"Today is tomorrow. You slept all day yesterday."

Sydnee came instantly alert. The burden on her sodden, auburn haired friend was immediately relieved. "What? What did you say?"

"Graduation is today. You slept all day yesterday. You're still wearing the same clothes from two days ago."

"Impossible. I couldn't have slept an entire day away."

"It's not impossible for someone who tossed down a dozen Canberra Coolers."

"A dozen?"

"I couldn't stop you. I got you outside the bar three times and you ran back inside and ordered another round. I had all I could do just getting you back here without the MPs picking us up."

"Oh, my aching head."

"You deserve it."

"Don't say that, Kat. You're going to your dream job aboard the *Pholus*. I'm going to hell— ohhh, if I live that long."

Chapter Two
~ Aug 24th, 2284 ~

Sydnee made it through commencement conducted on the school's largest athletic field, but at the conclusion of the graduation ceremony when everyone cheered, screamed, whooped, and tossed their hats into the air, Sydnee barely made it to a waste receptacle on the sideline where she could toss her cookies instead. Fortunately, her stomach was empty so there was no disgusting mess. All she accomplished was to make pitiful retching noises as her body tried to expel non-existent contents. By then everyone knew of her posting, so no one faulted her condition. They were grateful beyond words that they weren't the one going to the *Perry*. Even her classmate with the distinction of being ranked number four hundred fourteen of four hundred fourteen students had managed a better posting. She was going to the Destroyer *Tokyo*, currently on patrol out in deca-sector 8667-1844. It was also in a backwater sector, but at least it was a decent ship, not a bucket from a bygone era.

The parting with Katarina and her other close friends was a tearful one, all the more so for Sydnee because the others were going to great posts. She couldn't have been more miserable if she had been sentenced to a dark cell on the prison colony of Saquer Major.

* * *

With the advent of travel at Light-9790 speed, transportation between commands in the same region could often be measured in weeks or months instead of years, but the war currently raging in Region Two meant that all new Light-9790 warships were being sent to Admiral Carver's fleet. Sydnee's posting was in the opposite direction, so it might well have taken her two years to reach the *Perry* if not for the new Quartermaster ships now supplying the outer sectors of GA space.

The *Tafton*, a single-hull Quartermaster ship of twenty million tons, was Light-9790 capable. It not only ferried ordnance and supplies to distant bases but had also taken over the task of ferrying personnel, a chore previously performed mainly by the older and slower warships. Sydnee would have been perfectly content if it had taken two years to reach her new ship, but the *Tafton* made the trip to Simmons Space Command Base in just fifty-two days. The *Perry*, currently scheduled to arrive at the SCB base to resupply, would arrive soon after the *Tafton*.

Sydnee contacted the station housing office to have her things moved to the BOQ as soon as the *Tafton* docked. From there she would morosely await the arrival of the *Perry*.

Lieutenant(jg) Sydnee Marcola was at a dockside viewing monitor when the *Perry* arrived a few days later. The helmsman did a credible job with the dock-and-lock maneuver, and the ship was moored and accessible within twenty minutes of the dock master certifying the seal in the forward cargo bay ramp tunnel. Sydnee was anything but anxious to go aboard, so she headed to the shopping concourse to have a light lunch first.

She couldn't delay the inevitable forever, so at 1400 hours Sydnee walked out the airlock pier to report to the ship. A lieutenant(jg), functioning as officer of the deck, stood on the pier at the entrance to the airlock tunnel. Two armed Marine sentries were standing at the other end of the tunnel just inside the cargo bay. She handed the data ring containing her orders to the OD and waited while he touched the ring to his viewpad's spindle. The computer confirmed her identity and posting, so he activated his CT by touching the index finger of his right hand to his Space Command ring. When the carrier wave was established, he notified a Commander Bryant that the new lieutenant(jg) was reporting aboard. After a few seconds, he said, "Yes, sir," and added "Carstairs out," to terminate the connection.

All SC personnel had a miniscule device implanted subcutaneously against the exterior of the skull just behind their left ear when they entered the service. The CT provided two-way communication for officers, in addition to providing a confirmation of identity for many devices on bases and ships. Enlisted personnel received an ID chip for receive-only communications, but it provided identification like the CT.

"Lieutenant Milton will be down shortly," Lt. Carstairs said to Sydnee. He'll show you to your quarters."

"Aye."

The two Marine sentries were out of earshot, so Carstairs, after looking at Sydnee for several seconds, asked quietly, "So, what'd you do?"

"Do?"

"To get posted to the *Perry*. Did you crash a ship or something?"

"Is that the usual reason for getting posted to the *Perry*?" Sydnee asked.

"Just one of many. Some have merely said something embarrassing to a senior officer or diplomat, or perhaps fallen asleep during their watch. We had one guy who was a helmsman who brushed his ship against a freighter while leaving port. He's gone now. He left the service after he fulfilled his educational requirement. So what did you do?"

"I'm still trying to figure that out. The only time I strayed from the straight and narrow was the day I got my orders to report to the *Perry*. I went out and got blasted. I slept for a day and half, but it was all downtime."

"There must be something you did. There always is."

"What did you do?"

"I repeated a story about my Captain's lovemaking technique that someone learned from a whore on Earth Station Two. He recorded my retelling and it got back to the old man. The next thing I know, I'm in the Captain's briefing room listening to the recording. I couldn't deny it. I found it hilarious that the old man couldn't get it u— er, couldn't get excited enough to have sex until after his partner had spanked him hard a dozen times while telling him he'd been a bad boy. Anyway, he didn't want the story entered into the official records, so he couldn't bring charges or anything. But he could arrange to have me posted to the *Perry* with a 'pestiferous' in my file. Now no one will take me, even if a transfer was possible."

"So the rumors are true?" Sydnee said.

"What rumors?"

"That everyone aboard the *Perry* is either a screw-up or a jerk."

Carstairs stood a little straighter, obviously upset about the comment. "I don't consider myself either. I just repeated one little story to a fellow officer I trusted. It turned out he wanted my job."

"Did he get it?"

"Yeah, the SOB managed to get it. And I was sentenced to the *Perry*."

"So what does it take to get transferred off the *Perry*?"

"Transferred off? It'd be easier to grow a pair of wings and fly off."

"I'm serious. Space Command permits officers and enlisted to request transfers. There must be a way."

"Only through an act of God."

"Come on. I'm serious."

"The war in Region Two has drained the officer complement of all ships in Region One. Even the ones who made it to other ships are still in this Region; they only filled positions vacated by people needed in Region Two. But we're at the absolute minimum complement now, so you can forget transfer as a way off the ship."

"What's left?"

"Death, or Separation from the service. I don't recommend the former."

"Funny," Sydnee said with a grimace.

"Come on, tell me. What did you do? We'll learn anyway. It always comes out."

"When it does, let me in on it."

"You're serious? You really don't know?"

"Haven't a clue. I was ranked seventh in my class at WCI. I expected to be heading to Admiral Carver's command. Instead, I was sent here."

"Seventh? Wow. I was only four hundred two. Congrats."

"Yeah, you can see it really did me a lot of good."

"Maybe it wasn't you at all."

"What do you mean?"

"Maybe someone high up wants to get back at a family member and they're doing it through you by pulling some strings."

"Doubtful. My dad died at the Battle for Higgins, and my brother and sister aren't in the service. My mom has wanted nothing to do with Space Command since my dad's death. She's remarried now— to a toy company exec."

"Action toys, like vid games or military items? They frequently have a lot of contact with the military."

"No, he's into dolls— for little girls."

"Did your dad have any enemies that would hold a grudge for a very long time?"

"Who doesn't? But he died sixteen years ago."

"Some people hang on to their hate for a long time."

"Like the way you feel about the officer who landed you here?"

"Yeah, except I'd never take it out on his kids. I'm not a heel. But if I ever get a chance to return the favor to him…"

"That's another reason I want to get to Region Two. I want to be as far from the bureaucratic bullshy as I can get."

"Well, you can never get away from it completely. But on the front lines I guess it doesn't seem quite as important. You're too busy worrying about other small matters, such as,

'Will I still be alive for breakfast tomorrow?' Ah, here's Milty."

Lieutenant Milton strode down the ramp with purpose. "You Marcola?" he asked Sydnee as she stood straighter and saluted. The gentle tone of his voiced belied the exhibited stride.

"Yes, sir."

"Come with me, Lieutenant."

Sydnee nodded to Carstairs and followed along behind Milton, who didn't seem inclined to talk any more than necessary.

The trip through the *Perry* was an eye-opening experience for Sydnee. She recalled a movie where a character had talked about an old oh-gee vehicle being held together with spirit gum and prayers. While that description may not have applied to the *Perry* exactly, it was obvious that the ship was a collection of incongruous parts from a time long past. Milton spotted the appalled look on her face.

"He's better than he looks. Proper replacement parts haven't been available for a long time, so the engineers have had to use whatever they could find. Some they have to make. But everything works; that's the important thing."

"An officer at WCI was under the impression that the *Perry* had gone to the scrap yard decades ago."

"He was scheduled to go twice, but he got a reprieve both times. First they turned him into a training ship for the War College. When he got too old even for *that*, they mothballed him. When war with Milor broke out, he was restored to service, without any upgrades, so the newer ships could be sent to fight the Milori. He's fine for simple interdiction work. We're not likely to come under fire."

"Um, *Jones* class ships are said to be a little light on armor."

"He ain't a *Prometheus* class battleship, if that's what you mean, but his plating isn't all that far from spec for pre-

Dakinium Light Destroyers. His main handicap is his speed. He's only rated for Light-162."

"162? That's not much faster than an old freighter."

"Not much, but enough. Most freighters with homeports in Region One can't exceed Light-150, while freighters coming in from the Clidepp Empire are pretty much limited to Light-75. Their government ships are mostly rated at Light-150 and they haven't wanted to invest in newer military ships with higher speeds, so they restrict private ownership of faster vessels."

"How can they enforce that?"

"They can't, which is just one more reason why things are heating up over there. The government can't catch smugglers and pirates who have faster ships, so things are falling apart faster and faster every year. Here're your quarters, Lieutenant."

Sensors normally opened a door automatically when anyone entered the area immediately in front of the door and stopped while facing the door. The exceptions were quarters and private offices, hazardous materials areas, and restricted access locations. Since these were Sydnee's assigned quarters, the doors should have opened immediately.

"Computer, acknowledge the presence of myself and Lt. Marcola at her quarters," Milton said.

Through her CT, Sydnee heard, "Acknowledging the presence of Lt. Mark Milton and Lt(jg) Sydnee Marcola at her quarters."

"Computer, why isn't the door opening?"

"The door is open, Lieutenant."

"Computer, the door isn't open. Open it."

"The door is open, Lt. Milton."

"Computer, the door is not open. Override sensor data and open the door."

"Overriding sensor data and opening door," the computer confirmed.

"Computer, the door still isn't open," Milton said a second later.

"The door is open, Lt. Milton," the computer said.

"Good grief," Milton said. "Try the bulkhead sensor, Lieutenant."

Sydnee reached out and waved her hand in front of the sensor. The door remained closed.

"Whack the bulkhead just beneath the sensor," Milton said.

Sydnee hit the bulkhead just beneath the sensor with the flat of her fist. The door slid noiselessly open.

"I saw a specialist from engineering do that one day. He said the sensor board is located there and sometimes a circuit switch hangs. A healthy whack frees it."

"There are *mechanical* switches on the circuit cards?"

"The *Jones* class was designed a century ago, and you probably can't find an original electronic part anywhere on board. Who knows where they get the replacement sensor boards for the doors. Maybe they come out of those buggy old twentieth-century computers they used on wet navy vessels."

"I can't imagine how this ship escaped the scrap yard."

"A question we've all asked ourselves at times. The Captain will see you in his briefing room at 1530. I suggest you not be late. He's a stickler for punctuality."

"I don't know my way to the bridge."

"You can find the ship layout maps on your computer. It's all set up with the ID and passwords you used at the WCI. You can change them if you want. Good luck, Lieutenant."

"Thank you, sir."

"Outside of protocol situations, I'm just Milty, unless you've screwed up and my tail got caught in the wringer for not stopping you."

Sydnee smiled for the first time in days. "I'm Syd," she said, extending her hand.

"Welcome aboard, Syd," Milty said, taking it and shaking it lightly. "I know the *Perry* isn't anything like the new ships, but this old bucket will grow on you if you give it half a chance. It's never let its crew down."

"Thanks, Milty."

"See you later Syd."

Sydnee entered her quarters as Milton headed back the way they'd come. So far, the two officers she'd met had seemed like decent types. Maybe the *Perry* wasn't the worst place she could have landed after all. It had to be at least a step above a reclamation ship.

* * *

"Just what the hell are you doing on my boat, Lieutenant?"

Sydnee, standing at attention in front of the desk, stiffened even more as the Captain practically spit the words at her. "I don't understand the question, sir. I was posted to the *Perry*."

"I know that, Marcola. I want to know why. I've read through your file several times and examined every entry. You graduated twelfth in your class from the Academy and seventh from your class at the WCI. Your file is full of comments from your instructors that contain glowing praise for your hard work and dedication. You've never been in any trouble, and there's not a single use of 'pestiferous' anywhere in your history. So why are you on the *Perry*?"

"I was assigned here, sir. That's all I know."

Captain Lidden grimaced. "That's not good enough. I want to know what you did to wind up here. Who did you piss off enough to be sent to my ship?"

"Sir, I honestly don't know why I was sent here. I expected to receive a posting to a warship in Region Two. My posting here came as a complete surprise."

The Captain came out from behind his desk to face Sydnee and stare into her eyes. Not too long ago, he would have been in the final months of his years in space, but since the mandatory age for space duty had been increased from sixty-five to eighty-five, he would be able to spend another twenty years on the *Perry*. That is, if he wished to remain on the *Perry* for twenty more years, or until someone screwed up even worse than he had and hadn't been booted from the service, thus freeing him to receive a posting to a better ship.

"I don't buy it, Lieutenant," he said, his face just inches from hers. At five-ten, he stood a full inch shorter. Sydnee could feel his hot breath on her face and smell a hint of garlic with each exhale. "Space Command doesn't send bright young officers to the *Perry* unless there's something in their past to justify it. Now, I'm asking you again. Why are you on my boat?"

"I'm sorry, sir. I know of nothing I've done that would justify assignment to other than a top-caliber vessel."

Lidden exhaled noisily and walked back behind his desk. As he plopped into his chair and brushed his hand over his curly black hair, he said, "At ease, Lieutenant."

Sydnee relaxed noticeably but continued to stare straight ahead.

"I hate mysteries when they have to do with my crew," the Captain said, "and your being here is a mystery. The last time I had such a mystery, it turned out the officer was from Intelligence. They had done a very credible job with his file, but something didn't smell right. I didn't learn he was SCI until after he was transferred off the *Perry*."

"I'm not SCI, sir."

"Perhaps not, but something doesn't ring true. We'll find out what it is, eventually. You'll be on third watch with Lieutenant Milton, whom you've already met. Normally, watch commanders hold the rank of Lt. Commander, but we're at minimal complement at present. Report to the armory to pick up your personal battle armor, then get some sleep. That's all."

"Excuse me, sir. Did you say personal battle armor?"

"I did."

"Um, may I ask why sir? Don't the Marines go in first and ensure that everyone is disarmed?"

"That's what they teach at the WCI, but we don't have any Marine pilots on board so we have to provide the transportation. Your file says you're shuttle, fighter, and MAT certified. Besides, *all* my people wear personal battle armor when boarding other vessels during interdiction activities. I'm never losing another officer to some crazy with a lattice pistol who wants to shoot it out. This is the last stop for me. Another incident, even a minor one, and I'll be flying a desk on some god-forsaken planet no one ever heard of and doesn't want to hear of. Don't make that happen or, if you survive, I promise you'll regret it for the rest of your life. Do I make myself clear?"

"Perfectly, sir."

"Dismissed."

"Yes, sir."

Sydnee came to attention, saluted, turned on her left heel and exited the room. All hands on the bridge looked in her direction as she crossed from the briefing room to the exit corridor. Sydnee smiled weakly at them and continued without stopping. This wasn't the time to try to establish new friendships.

Rather than ask someone how to locate the armory, she returned to her quarters and used her computer to find it on the ship's layout. She hurried to reach it so she could return and get some sleep, but she got turned around somehow. She knew the frame number and deck but couldn't find a path through the labyrinth of corridors. She kept encountering bulkheads that blocked her path no matter which way she tried. She finally backtracked most of the way to her quarters and discovered where she had gone wrong. As she began her trek again, she put aside all the thoughts that had been crowding her mind and concentrated on finding her way to the right section and deck.

When Sydnee entered the armory, the door closed behind her and she found herself enclosed in a cubicle of transparent polycarbonate. She was required to perform a retinal scan for identification before the Marine on the other side of the bombproof barrier would allow her to proceed further. The armory was the one place she'd seen so far that looked to be the equivalent of what she'd expect on a new ship. Of course, that was because it was just a room full of weapons and support gear. They couldn't very well outfit her with outdated weapons, so everything there was state of the art.

"What can I do for you, Lieutenant?" the Marine Staff Sgt. asked as she stepped up to the counter.

"The Captain sent me down to get personal battle armor."

"Gonna join our guys and gals on a mission or two?" he asked with a chuckle as he checked his computer monitor.

"That would appear to be the situation, Sergeant."

He already had her ID info from her log-in, so he said, "Be right back," then turned to walk towards a long row of lockers at the back of the armory. He returned a few minutes later carrying a duffel almost as large as he was. He lifted it and dropped it on the counter with a thud.

"Here you go, Lieutenant. Everything was prepared from measurements sent to the ship when you were assigned here. In addition to a complete set of personal battle armor, you're receiving a laser pistol and rifle, both with extra packs and rechargers, two knives, rifle sling, holster, knife sheaths and belt, two pairs of boots, CT signal repeater, and various sundries. You're responsible for all equipment. Lose any of it and it comes out of your pay." He extended a viewpad towards her and said, "Press your thumb here, please."

"We were taught to always check all items before signing for them, Sergeant," she replied instead of simply accepting his word that everything was in the duffel.

"Yes, ma'am," he said with a slight grimace before removing everything and repacking it one item at a time as Sydnee nodded acceptance.

"Satisfied, Lieutenant?" the sergeant asked as he sealed the duffel.

"Completely. Thank you, Sergeant," Sydnee said as she signed for the equipment by pushing her thumb onto the viewpad he was again holding out to her. As she grabbed the duffel, she braced herself for a weight she could barely handle and pulled it off the counter with a jerk. But the duffle was surprisingly light. It couldn't weigh more than fifteen pounds.

"I saw you pack everything with my own eyes, but this doesn't seem right, Sergeant," Sydnee said to the Marine.

"Yes, ma'am. Are you asking because it's so light?"

"Yes."

"The armor is the new stuff. The *Tafton* just delivered it with our ordnance and other supplies. Have you worn personal armor before?"

"Yes, during summer maneuvers in my third year at the Academy we were shown how to put it on. And while at the WCI, everyone was required to wear it for a full day to gain an appreciation for how difficult it could be for Marines to enter and exit an aircraft under a variety of conditions. But the personal body armor on both occasions weighed in at over a hundred twenty pounds, not counting the weapons."

"This new armor weighs just one tenth of that and is said to be impervious to laser, lattice, and lead projectiles. Dakinium, I think they call it."

"Yes, that's the compound Admiral Carver discovered on Dakistee."

"Yeah. Her Marines in Region Two were the first to get it, and I've heard it's saved quite a few lives. As production has ramped up, more and more commands are getting their allotment, but I was surprised to see it listed on our shipping manifest so soon. I thought it would be another year or two before *we* got our first shipment."

"They say it's almost indestructible."

"Yeah. You can still be ripped apart by a grenade landing in your lap or by a rocket that slices your head off at the shoulders, but they claim that shrapnel will never penetrate this body armor. The armor will just go to someone else once the blood is washed off."

"That's reassuring," she managed to say with a straight face.

"Yeah. The rifle and pistol are also made from it. I'm told they can't be damaged. The grips on both are keyed to your DNA, so no one else can discharge the weapons without a complete reprogram. If you're wearing the supplied gloves, they read your DNA and communicate it to the grips."

"Thank you, Sergeant."

"Yes, ma'am, Lieutenant."

Back in her quarters, Sydnee stood the duffel in a corner of the bedroom. It seemed to take up a third of the room, but that was only because her quarters were so small. A century ago, when ships like the *Perry* were being designed, the junior officer staterooms were so tiny that one had to go out into the corridor to change one's mind. Sydnee's entire quarters of bedroom, bath, and office/sitting room would fit into just the bedroom of a junior officer on new ships.

Tiny quarters were largely a holdover from wet navy days when space was at a premium and larger spaces meant larger ships with increased fuel needs. When man moved into space, the cost of lifting material into space for the construction of ships meant that every ounce of weight was precious. But as space travel became common, studies proved there was a direct correlation between the amount of personal space aboard ship to contentment of crewmembers during long voyages where they might not make planet-fall for months or years. Personal quarters had grown in size every decade since then until it was decided that an optimum had been reached. Unfortunately, that occurred many decades after the *Perry* was designed.

There was no immediate need for the personal armor, and Sydnee was due on the bridge at midnight, so she opted for sack time over examination of the equipment. She stripped down and pulled her pajamas on in less time than it took to get the lights turned off because an oral command didn't work. She finally climbed out of her rack and searched until she located the manual override switch. At least the gel-comfort mattress on the bed worked properly. Once she got the temperature and firmness settings correct, it felt like she was sleeping on a cloud. She set a wakeup call with the computer and then fell into a deep sleep. Her ability to fall asleep in minutes had always been a great asset. While others would have tossed and turned in a new and unfamiliar setting, she was quickly cocooned in slumber.

Chapter Three
~ Oct. 24th, 2284 ~

"The Clidepp Empire falls further into disarray every day," Admiral Bradlee said to the nine other admirals sitting at the large horseshoe-shaped table. The regularly convened meeting of the group was taking place at the Admiralty Board Hall at Space Command Supreme Headquarters in Nebraska, USNA on Earth. "Their central government is crumbling. For a long time I've felt they were ripe for another coup d'état, but now I believe a civil war will break out in the territory before a junta can take over. The oligarchy has brutally and systematically stripped wealth from all other planets to support the excesses of the wealthy at home. It's been a formula for disaster throughout the history of many races."

"How soon do you expect hostilities to break out, Roger?" Admiral Platt asked. In her role as Commander of the First Fleet, it would be her job to contain problems at the border.

"We could see a formal declaration of secession any day. We've received reports that people are queuing up daily at embassies to get visas before things heat up too much for them to get out."

"Then we have little time to prepare."

"Our only saving grace is that their ships are so slow it may take years for many of them to reach our territory, if that's their destination. I'm sure many will travel near the Empire's outer perimeter to avoid getting involved in the conflict. The first groups to arrive, those from planets closest to GA space, will come directly towards us and could cross the border into our space within six months. The Galactic Alliance Council must formulate a plan for handling the situation. Do we let them in or not? We can't dictate what action the planets in GA Space should take. It's their decision alone whether to allow or deny access to refugees; however, we can restrict travel by anyone not having either a passport or visa. I don't know how the Aguspod will react to a civil war in a neighboring nation— they're having their own problems— but we can be confident the Kweedee Aggregate will block any ships from entering their space. They normally bar all travel except diplomatic missions, and they only allow minimal contact in that regard. Since we don't share a border with the Blenod, and their nation is too far distant for us to have ever had any direct contact before the new speeds became available, we can't begin to calculate how they'll respond to refugees entering their space."

"We can't possibly prevent a massive refugee migration into our territory," Admiral Hillaire said. "Our resources have been shifted towards Region Two. Until that conflict is settled one way or the other, we can't give the Clidepp border the attention it deserves."

"Once refugees make it to habitable planets," Admiral Plimley said, "we'll never be able to evict them. They'll be so entrenched that the task would be insurmountable."

"As Roger says," Admiral Moore, Chairman of the Admiralty Board, said, "the GAC will have to decide policy on this issue. I'll present it at tomorrow's meeting. Until we know their desires, there's little we can do, but let's start thinking about what resources we can move into place. We can't shift warships from the Region One border with Region Two, but perhaps we can shift some ships in the center of the Region towards the Clidepp border just in case we must address the massive refugee migration Arnold alluded to."

* * *

Sydnee reported to the bridge a few minutes before midnight. Lieutenant Milton was already there, receiving a situation pass-down on new and standing orders. She approached the two men and waited until acknowledged before moving into conversation range.

"Hello Lieutenant," Milton said. "This is Commander Bryant, our XO. Commander, this is our new officer, Lt. Sydnee Marcola."

Bryant extended his hand and shook Sydnee's when she responded with her own. "Welcome aboard, Lieutenant."

"Thank you, sir."

"You'll be taking over as navigator on third watch," Bryant said. "When we engage a ship for cargo inspection, you'll move to a tactical station until it's time to continue as navigator, or report to the flight deck to shuttle people over to the stopped vessel."

"Yes, sir."

"I'm headed to my quarters. You have the ship, Milty. Goodnight, both."

"Goodnight, sir," both Milton and Sydnee said as Commander Bryant stepped away and headed for the corridor.

Milton made an entry in the pass-down log regarding the watch change before taking Sydnee around the bridge and introducing her to the rest of the third watch staff. He then invited her to join him at the Command chair. Even though they were currently docked at the Space Station, regulations required that a full watch be present on the bridge at all times. Since there was so little to do in these situations, most watch commanders permitted the watch to engage in light conversation, but all crewmembers had to remain at their posts unless specifically excused by the watch commander.

As Milton climbed into the Commander's chair, he gestured toward the First Officer's chair immediately to his left. He waited until Sydnee was seated before saying quietly, "Bry says the Captain is pretty upset with you."

"Upset with me? Why?"

"Because he doesn't know what you did to warrant a berth on the *Perry*."

"I'd tell him if I knew."

"Would you? Honestly?"

"Of course. I shouldn't have to though. If I'd screwed up somewhere, it would be in my file."

"That's why he's so upset. Your file indicates that you shouldn't be here."

"Um, why is he here?"

"He was the Captain of the *Santiago* back when the incident happened."

"Um, what incident?"

"You haven't heard of the *Santiago* interdiction tragedy? What the heck are they teaching at WCI these days?"

"I don't recall hearing anything."

"Well, sixteen years ago the *Santiago* stopped a freighter for inspection and sent in a company of Marines to prepare the way for the SC inspection team. When they got the all-clear signal, the inspectors shuttled over to begin checking records and cargo. One of the inspectors discovered a cargo container that was giving some unusual readings. It was supposed to contain an unprocessed, low-density ore, but the densimeter readings were way too high. Two inspectors suited up in EVA gear and prepared to climb down into the container to investigate. That's when members of the freighter crew opened fire on the inspection team with laser weapons. They killed the two Space Command officers and wounded six Marines. The Marines would most likely have been killed as well, except they were wearing personal body armor. They managed to kill all five attackers and lock down the ship, but our two guys were DOA."

"But surely that wasn't the Captain's fault. The Marines were responsible for securing the ship."

"A ship's captain is responsible for *everything* that occurs aboard his ship or during any activities connected with the ship, unless he can prove negligence or intent on the part of a subordinate. The investigative body decided the Marine officer in command wasn't negligent, so that left only the Captain to take the fall. Since the deaths hadn't occurred aboard ship, weren't the result of an order he gave, and he had no direct involvement in the action, they didn't force him out of the service or plant him at a desk dirt-side. However, *someone* had to be punished, so they did the next closest thing. They stuck him here to perform his atonement."

"That isn't fair."

"Perhaps not in the civilian world, but that's the way it is out here. The moral in the service is DNDNW— don't never do no wrong."

"DNDNW? That's a quadruple negation."

"Quadruple? Yeah, I guess it is. But in this case it doesn't add up to an affirmative. You can do a thousand things right, things that will cover your chest with medals and give you commendations up the wazoo, but do just one thing less than perfect and you're likely headed for a fall. So if you screw up, make sure the outcome doesn't leave a negative on the balance sheet. Take a page from Admiral Carver's book and memorize it."

"Admiral Carver? What's she got to do with this?"

"Nothing. She's just an example of screwing up royally but leaving a positive on the balance sheet."

"I don't follow you."

"When Carver was an ensign, she wound up agreeing to take command of a tramp freighter that had lost its captain. Then, while serving in that capacity, she responded to an emergency distress call from a convoy under attack by Raiders. She took her old bucket into battle with a Raider Cruiser, hoping that the convoy would have a chance to escape during the confusion."

"Everybody knows that story. Her heroism is legendary."

"Yeah, and I'm not saying she didn't do something great and wasn't exhibiting bravery of the highest order, but think about the act. She was only an ensign at the time and had accepted responsibility for the lives of everyone aboard that old freighter. What was the name again?"

"The *Vordoth*."

"Yeah, the *Vordoth*. Anyway, she should have headed away from that area at her top speed. She was in a freighter, and an old one at that, not a warship. She lucked out when she destroyed the Raider Cruiser, but the odds on that would have been ten thousand to one in any bookie parlor.

"Then, weeks later, she attempted to learn the location of a Raider base by following some ships involved in reclamation efforts. Instead of staying with her charges and getting them safely to port, she goes off on a crazy mission of her own design. Not only that— for transportation she takes a tug belonging to the freight company and brings two civilians along. You *don't* bring civilians on a highly dangerous mission to infiltrate an enemy base. Anyway, the trio is subsequently captured and winds up as prisoners intended for sale as slaves. There was *nothing* about that mission which was wise or correct. She should have been canned and would have been but for the result. She somehow managed to escape, free dozens of other prisoners at the base, commandeer two stolen battleships for her return to Space Command, and then even destroy the Raider base. The people in GA space loved her. Everyone in Space Command and the Space Marine Corps loved her. Even the Royal Family on Nordakia loved her. The JAG knew she had screwed up and did their best to throw the book at her. They lucked out by trying too hard. They made the court-martial charges too stiff, so the jury found her innocent of all charges. And it was a damn good thing they did. If the jury had convicted her, people on every world in GA space would have been chasing after them— the JAG, the judge, and the prosecutor— with a noose. That's what I mean by leaving a positive on the balance sheet. You can screw up royally, but if everything comes out incredibly great, you don't have to worry about being slammed. If it *doesn't* come out great, your career is probably over."

"You really think Carver screwed up?"

"No more than I think the Captain screwed up. They were both doing their job as they saw it, to the *best* of their ability. Carver was an ensign, essentially fresh out of the Academy, when she was dropped into a position that she was ill-equipped to handle. She made two very bad decisions based on gut-instinct rather than mature rationale. No experienced

SC officer would *ever* have done what she did. They know better."

"She should have played it safe?"

"She should have played it *smart*. She was probably court-martialed because she made some admiral look bad. By knocking the Raiders off their feet in that sector, she did what they hadn't been able to do. Admirals don't like having junior officers make them look bad. Such officers usually wind up on the *Perry*, but instead she was hailed as a hero because the balance sheet was so far into the positive. Our Captain got nailed to the bulkhead and wound up on the *Perry* because his balance sheet was in the negative. But don't ever think he's a screw-up simply because he's on this ship. He's the best there is. I mean that. He's just running scared that he'll lose even this old bucket. His wife has passed on and he never had any kids, so we're all he's got. If you were upset after your meeting today, brush it off. He's a great skipper. He's just afraid of being posted dirt-side for the rest of his years. Okay, Syd, better take your place at the nav console before someone thinks I'm hitting on you over here."

"Yes, sir," she said with a smile. His words would give her much to think about over the rest of the watch and in the days ahead.

* * *

The *Perry* remained docked at the Simmons SCB for thirty days. During that time the ship's complement took full advantage of liberty privileges. All too soon, it was time for the ship to go back out on patrol. It would be another year, possibly more, before their next stop in a liberty port. During the weeks with little to do during the watch, Sydnee had begun to build friendships with other third watch personnel. On her off-duty hours, she had met and befriended numerous officers from other departments. As she became familiar with the ship, she noticed more and more unusual modifications where barely compatible parts had been used as replacements for parts no longer available. The engineering areas would give never-ending nightmares to any engineer only familiar with current-production warships, but Sydnee had grown to respect Milty's word. If he believed everything aboard ship was in good working order and presented nothing to worry about regarding the security of the ship and the safety of the crew, she would accept that until she had proof to the contrary. That would naturally come at the worst possible time.

* * *

"You heard me, Captain," Lieutenant Milton said to the image on the front monitor. "Heave to for inspection."

"I told you we were just inspected," the Nordakian Captain of the freighter insisted.

"Not possible," Milton said. "We're the only Space Command vessel in this sub-sector."

"Not here," the Captain said. "The inspection was at a border-crossing station in Clidepp space."

"The Clidepp don't share their interdiction information with us, so you'll have to go through it again. You know the law, Captain. All ships traveling from other nations must be stopped and checked when we first encounter them in our space."

The skin color of the Nordakian began to take on an orange hue, indicating that he was getting irritated. "Lieutenant, I have a schedule to maintain. I'm already a day behind because of the Clidepp inspectors. Can't you just let it go this time?"

"You know the answer to that, Captain. Now heave to. I do not wish to fire on you, sir."

"You wouldn't dare." The Nordakian's skin color jumped to bright red in an instant.

"The law is very specific. Any vessel refusing to yield is to be disabled by weapon's fire to whatever extent is necessary to accomplish the inspection. The Nordakian Royal family fully understands that and is a signatory to the accords. If said vessel is completely destroyed during that process— well— it'll be a shame."

"Okay, okay, we're stopping."

"A wise decision, Captain. An inspection team will arrive at your ship shortly. I know you'll cooperate fully."

The Nordakian scowled as the signal was cut off and the monitor at the front of the bridge changed to a view of space. There wasn't a nearby star, so the image was being created by sensors mounted on the ship's hull rather than by the *Perry's* cameras, but the image of the other vessel was sharp and clear.

Milton was checking the duty roster when Captain Lidden appeared on the bridge. As Captain of the Ship, he had to be notified immediately whenever a watch commander initiated an interdiction procedure, as if the announcement for GQ hadn't been enough. "Sitrep, Lieutenant," was all Lidden said.

"We're currently at GQ. We detected a freighter in transit and moved to intercept. The intercepted ship, underway from the Clidepp Empire to the freight hub at Arlondis, is named the *Xouadess*. The skipper's name is Kludenseth, and the ship is of Nordakian registry. Both he and the ship are listed in the SC database. No serious violations associated with either in the past.

"The freighter captain was a bit reluctant to heave to for inspection, but after a reasoned discussion he's dropped his envelope. But he's not happy about the delay. We're standing off twenty-five thousand kilometers. I'm preparing to send over the Marines to secure the vessel."

"We've encountered him before. He's always in a bad humor, but he's basically harmless and has a good reputation for thoroughness. He always says he's behind schedule and tries to get you to pass on the inspection, or at least rush through it, but it's never been to cover anything illegal, as far as we've been able to discover. Still, take your time and do it by the book. Who have you assigned as shuttle pilots?"

"I just checked the rotation list and was about to notify Weems and Stiller, sir."

"Weems is okay. Stiller is helm on the next watch, so use someone else. Use Marcola. This will be a good chance for her to get her feet wet in what should be a low-danger situation."

"Yes, sir."

"Carry on, Lieutenant."

"Yes, sir." Raising his voice, Lieutenant Milton said aloud, "Marcola."

As soon as Sydnee had heard the Captain use her name, her ears perked up. When Milton called, she stood up and reported to him at the command chair."

"Yes, sir?"

"You heard the Captain. Go jump into your armor and get down to shuttle bay Three."

"Yes, sir."

Before she could go, the Captain held up his hand to stop her.

"Marcola, this should be a low-risk assignment, but let me make your instructions perfectly clear. You're to shuttle Marines over to the *Xouadess* and then remain in the shuttle until the Marines notify us that the ship is secure. You will not leave the shuttle before that unless authorized by the watch commander or inspection team commander. Is that clear?"

"Yes, sir. Perfectly."

"When you are permitted to leave the shuttle, you will remain in full body armor and join Lt. Weems as he supervises the inspection team. You will do everything he tells you, *when* he tells you. Is that clear?"

"Perfectly, sir."

"Very good. Do it by the book. Go suit up."

"Yes, sir."

Sydnee hurried from the bridge and down to her quarters, where she pulled off her uniform and replaced it with the special padded bodysuit worn under personal armor. Most Space Command personnel only wore the soft-soled boots that were part of the standard uniform, so the armored combat boots would take some getting used to. She'd previously only worn combat footwear during summer field-training exercises at the Academy and on a few weekends at the WCI.

A few days after receiving her armor, she'd read the included instructions and carefully examined each piece. It was so light it was difficult to believe the claims of near indestructibility. She hadn't donned any of it yet, so it took her a few minutes to climb into it and adjust it for basic comfort. When she was set, she activated the control that would inflate certain pads to make the armor precisely fit her body contours. The armor had definitely been designed for her exact body measurements. She felt a little clunky at first, like an armored knight from medieval times, but that mostly wore off by the time she reached the shuttle bay. The designers had done everything possible to make the armor comfortable and flexible, and the fitted contours of the armor left no doubt that she was female. The breastplate of a skinny male Marine would have been considerably flatter.

"Loaded for bear, eh, Marcola?" Weems said as she entered the shuttle bay."

"Lieutenant?" Sydnee said as she removed the helmet.

"A rifle, a pistol, *and* two knives? You look more like a Marine than a shuttle pilot. If not for the SC insignia on your helmet, I would have thought you were one of the jarheads."

"I thought we were supposed to prepare as if it's the most hostile situation in the universe until we know differently."

"That's what the book says, but the books are mostly written by inexperienced rear-echelon brass-polishers who have never been off Earth."

"The Captain told me to do it by the book."

"The Captain has to say that because his instructions become part of the bridge logs. It's a CYA statement. And the Captain has more reason to cover his ass than anyone else on board. For us, being sent to a dirt-side post might be an improvement. I've been on this old bucket for six years. I'm getting tired of telling people I'm on the *Perry* and then seeing their mouths curl up at the edges as they try to suppress a smirk."

"Although we're both O-2, the Captain said you're in com-mand. Are you ordering me to leave some of these weapons behind?"

Weems hesitated for a moment. "No, bring whatever makes you feel safe and secure. Bring a teddy bear for all I care."

"I left him on my bed."

The shocked expression on Weems's face was priceless. "You're kidding," he said.

"Yes, I am," Sydnee said with a straight face, and then smiled.

Weems just nodded a couple of times as he studied her face, then smiled as he got the joke. "Okay, preflight your ship."

"Yes, sir."

"I'm Jerry, when military protocol doesn't require the formality," he said as he extended his hand.

"Syd," she said as she shook the proffered hand.

"Okay, Syd, get your bird ready."

"Roger, Jerry."

Sydnee performed the visual inspection of the shuttle she would fly while accompanied by the head mechanic respon-sible for the ship. The mechanic was ready with answers if she had any questions and with arguments if this newest snot-nosed ex-cadet gave him any grief. An ex-military pilot had once told Sydnee that she always had to find something wrong to complain about during her walk-around or the head mechanic would think she didn't know what she was doing and that he could therefore avoid doing any work he was too lazy to perform, even scheduled maintenance. Sydnee didn't subscribe to that nonsense and would only speak up if she saw something that wasn't right. She loved aircraft and space-craft and knew what to look for and where during the visual inspection.

Everything looked fine to Sydnee, and the mechanic beamed when she grinned and gave him the thumbs up sign.

As she entered the shuttle's flight deck, she stowed her rifle and pistol belt in the locker just behind the pilot's seat. The rifle actually wasn't much more than an enlarged pistol that accommodated a larger power supply to allow a greater rate of fire and more powerful beam. But at double the length of the pistol, it couldn't fit into a holster on the belt, so it clipped onto the chest plate to make carrying easier.

The locker was wide enough to accommodate her helmet as well. When worn, the helmet self-sealed to the neckline of the armor and Simage technology took over, making it seem like the opaque front was made of glass. A HUD provided the armor-wearer with a wide range of information about the suit operations and external conditions, and allowed the wearer to interact with the system using special eye movements and winking only the right eye. A special feature using fiberoptic technology allowed the wearer to actually see 360 degrees around the body without moving the head. Since the helmet appeared to be made of Dakinium, it should be as durable as the rest of the armor. A special Simage plate, bonded to the outside, permitted the wearer to project a 3D image of the wearer's face, numerous other images stored in the suit's computer, or no image at all.

Although not technically an EVA suit, the personal armor was about as close as it came. Outside air was normally circulated inside the armor from vents around the neck, but if the internal sensors noticed a pressure drop or the air quality was judged poor or toxic, the armor sealed completely and a small rebreather unit took over. It could fully sustain the wearer during thirty minutes of extreme physical exertion, such as running, or almost eight hours when the wearer was at rest. Where the surrounding 'atmo' was simply light on oxygen levels, the unit pulled whatever oxygen it could from the surrounding air, or via a gill-like arrangement if submerged in water, to supplement its own supply. The armor also provided limited heating and cooling capability, though the suit's capacities would begin to be overwhelmed if the wearer had to spend more than twenty minutes in extremes such as the coldness of space. Lastly, the armor had a feature that allowed the wearer to blend into any environment by projecting an image of the area behind the suit on the side facing an enemy. When the wearer wasn't moving, it worked almost to perfection, but when moving, the system had difficulty keeping up and an observer could see a slight translucent silhouette in bright light. It was the only time the wearer wasn't completely hidden.

The longer Sydnee wore the armor, the more comfortable it seemed to become. As she went through the shuttle's pre-ignition checklist, she was the happiest she'd been since first coming aboard the *Perry*. The feeling was simply an extension of her love of flying. This would be her first opportunity for real flight as pilot in command since leaving the WCI.

It was her fascination with flight that had first drawn her to the military. At one time, her goal had been to become a Marine fighter pilot, but when she became enthralled by Admiral Jenetta Carver's adventures, she decided on a career with Space Command instead. She'd begun to wonder if she'd made the right choice as she struggled to focus on her studies in Alien Anatomy at the WCI, but at this moment everything seemed perfect, except for being assigned to the *Perry*.

After completing the last checklist, she sat quietly watching the activity outside the ship. While warships never had viewing ports because they represented a potential breach point in the ship, tugs and shuttles had windshields made of a polycarbonate-like material. In hazardous situations, a tritanium cover could be closed over the windshield instantly. As on a warship, a monitor filled the area at the front of the flight deck on a MAT.

As Sydnee watched, the squad leaders had their people line up in preparation for entering the shuttles. And when they began to enter the ship, Sydnee could hear the commotion on the other side of the flight deck door. As the noise settled down, a Marine First Lieutenant entered the flight deck and plopped into the co-pilot seat.

"You Marcola?" the LT asked.

"That's me," Sydnee said.

"I'm Kennedy. You will address me properly as Lieutenant," he said irately, "as I will address you. Although we're both O-2, I am your senior here and you will follow my commands to the letter. Do you understand?"

"Yes, Lieutenant. Captain Lidden has briefed me."

"Then move out. We're all buttoned up in back."

Sydnee glanced over at the instrument panel to confirm the ship was sealed, then fired up the shuttle's oh-gee engine and slowly moved the ship into launch position near the hatch using opposed gravity. As she canceled the oh-gee movement and let the ship settle to the deck again, she engaged the magnetic skids. Hinged bulkheads then folded down from the overhead and sealed an area just larger than the shuttle and hatchway. When vacuum pumps had sucked all the air from the area, the outer hatch opened to reveal space. Sydnee released the magnetic skids and used the deuterium thrusters to pilot the ship out and away from the *Perry*.

The *Xouadess*, sitting twenty-five thousand kilometers from the *Perry*, had activated her exterior lights at her maintenance section roughly four kilometers behind the main ship. Sydnee heard Milton's voice in her left ear as she received the signal via her CT.

"Head for the illuminated maintenance section on the starboard side of the ship, Lt. Marcola," Milton said. "The hatch is open and waiting to receive you. Lt. Weems, use the open hatch on the larboard side."

"Message received and acknowledged," Sydnee said after touching the face of her Space Command ring to initiate a carrier for the signal. She didn't shut the carrier wave down by saying, "Marcola, out," because she wanted to stay in immediate contact.

Shuttles don't have FTL drives because of the enormous power requirements such travel involves, but traversing the twenty-five thousand kilometers to the freighter took less than a minute once the Sub-Light engine was engaged. It took far longer to dock and then wait until the airlock section was pressurized.

As soon as the gauge showing the pressure outside the shuttle entering the green range, the Marines piled out like the small ship was on fire. As the temporary airlock bulkheads began to fold up, the Marines spread out and took up positions behind any available cover while amused mechanics, sitting on or leaning against maintenance equipment, maintained non-threatening positions and watched the familiar show.

Sydnee watched from the pilot's chair, perfectly content to remain inside the shuttle. For her, the thrill was over until it was time to return to the *Perry*. It was a shame the shuttle could carry so many at a time. It would have been wonderful if she had to make several trips each way.

Chapter Four
~ Oct. 28th, 2284 ~

It took several hours for the Marines to secure the freight-er. All crewmembers were required to leave the cargo con-tainer section and report to the ship for identification process-ing. After the ID work was complete, the crew was allowed to go to their quarters where they could sleep or relax until the inspection was complete, but they were not allowed to wander around the ship. The Marines then searched the cargo section for any signs of life. It took time to search ten kilometers of cargo containers for stowaways or illegal passengers, even with state-of-the-art sensors. When at last the Marines were satisfied there was no one hiding out in the cargo section, Sydnee was ordered to join Lt. Weems outside the other shuttle.

The work of checking the cargo was already underway when Sydnee arrived at Weems's position. The inspection team had downloaded the freighter's cargo files and was reading through cargo manifests looking for indications of possible illegal cargo or simply anything out of the ordinary. The *Perry's* computer had already computed container masses based on reported loads and verified its estimates with the freighter's estimates to ensure they were consistent.

When the paperwork was done, the job of actually inspecting the cargo began. Obviously, the team couldn't perform a thorough inspection of ten kilometers of cargo containers on every ship, so the *Perry's* computer prepared a random sampling of cargo containers to examine. Twenty-five percent of the list was from the cargo containers most likely to be in violation and twenty-five percent was from the containers least likely to be in violation. The remaining fifty percent were a random drawing from the remainder. Even the containers on this small list would take hours to find and inspect, so they jumped to it. They wanted to be done just as much as the freighter's captain wanted them to be gone, but they wouldn't do a less than thorough job. If any illegal goods were found, every single container would have to be searched from top to bottom.

When the containers reached their destination port, they would be irradiated to guarantee that no pestilence, vermin, or harmful non-indigenous life forms could reach a Galactic Alliance planet. For shipments within the GA, all containers were irradiated twice, once at the shipping point and once at the destination. No known carbon-based life form could survive the irradiation process. Containers used for shipping certain fresh foods, medicines, and biological products were granted exemption from the irradiation sweep but would be inspected dirt-side in special quarantine facilities before the cargo was released to the customer.

Five hours later, the task was complete. The inspection team hadn't found any cargo violations, but they issued one warning about the condition of a container. The container had to be reinforced before it could be used again, or it had to be replaced. If that container was encountered again, it would be inspected to verify the ordered work had been completed. If it hadn't, the company would be fined ten times the value of a new container. The stiffness of the fine meant that few companies ignored the warnings.

Sydnee was unhappy that she hadn't had a chance to interact with any Nordakians, but there'd been no excuse for her to visit the main ship. At one time, Nordakians had attended the Academies on Earth, but that ended when Space Command built an Academy on Nordakia. It had worked out so well that they added a WCI a few years later in time to take the first graduating class of RNSA. Usually referred to as 'RoNSA,' the initials stood for Royal Nordakian Space Academy. The curriculum was the same as that of the two Earth Academies, NHSA and SHSA, and the testing just as rigorous.

Although it was said that as much as one-tenth of one percent of Space Command was now Nordakian, there had been no Nordakians on the *Tafton* during Sydnee's time aboard, and there were none on the *Perry*. All Sydnee really knew about them was that they were very tall, with the males usually over seven feet and the females almost never less than six feet. Everyone knew they could control their skin color in a way similar to that of the Terran chameleon, but during times of stress or exuberance, they lost control of their chromaticity and color could ripple across their skin like a rainbow gone amuck. Sydnee also knew that Admiral Carver, although a Terran born on Earth, held dual citizenship on Nordakia and was a Lady of the Nordakian Royal House, in addition to being an Azula. An Azula was roughly the equivalent of a Duchess in Earth nobility terms.

Sydnee enjoyed the brief trip back to the *Perry* as much as the trip out. As she maneuvered the ship to its parking location in the shuttle bay and engaged the skid's magnetic locks, she was sad the inspection was over, even if her watch had technically ended four hours earlier. She didn't even feel like eating as she exited the shuttle's flight deck. All she wanted to do was strip off the battle armor and slip into her rack for seven or eight hours of restful slumber.

* * *

Finding vidMails from home and friends in their computer was often the best part of the day for military people. Sydnee was ecstatic when she awoke and discovered messages from her mother, her sister Sheree, and her best friend Katarina in her queue. She decided to save the one from Katarina for last, for several reasons, and played the one from her mom.

"Hello, dear. I don't know why you're so depressed. You got your wish. You're aboard a warship— like you've wanted ever since your father was killed. And I'm personally delighted that you're somewhere where *you* won't be killed. Our family has paid a high enough price for peace and freedom. I'd be just as delighted if they kept you there until you're so sick of the military life that you come back home to live. Your stepfather says that with your education he could get you a top executive job in a minute. And if you have to be involved with the military, you could maybe get a position with a manufacturer that supplies Space Command and the Space Marine Corps. I've heard they're begging people to apply. The situation in Region Two means that the military will be needing enormous supplies for years to come while they try to tame the lawlessness there.

"So you see, you don't have to actually be *in* the military to help out— you can do it as a civilian. Won't you please think about it at least?

"I love you.

"Kathee Deleone, Park Central Towers, New York City, USNA, Earth. Message complete."

Sydnee sighed. Her mother couldn't seem to understand that although she might be depressed over having been posted to the *Perry*, it was still a million times better than selling dolls for little girls and boys— or even selling military supplies to the service. "I'd probably find myself selling emergency food packs or lubricating oil," she said before playing the message from her sister.

"Hi, sis. Mom says you're depressed. So what, there aren't any cute guys out there? I thought that guys were like, three to one in the military. Hey, here's an idea; throw a party in your quarters. That's the best cure for depression. It's what I always do. Speaking of which, you know that guy I met in South Africa last year? The one I told you about who has the little mole on his— well you know. Anyway, he's coming to New York on business this week and he sent me a vid. He wants to get together while he's here. I just got back from shopping and you should see the great dress I got for our first date in the City. Wait a minute."

Sydnee's sister disappeared for a few seconds and then reappeared holding a dress against herself. It was a blaze of colors that reminded one of a fireworks exhibition gone wild.

"What do you think? Isn't this fantastic. It was marked down to eight hundred fifty credits from two thousand. It's gorgeous. I wish you were here to feel the material. It's so soft. I can't wait to wear it Friday night.

"Oops, there's the timer. Gotta go.

"Love ya.

"Sheree Marcola, Park Central Towers, New York City, USNA, Earth. Message complete."

Sydnee chuckled and shook her head a little. Her sister was every bit as intelligent as she was, but all she ever thought about was clothes, partying, and men— and not in that order. She chuckled again when she thought about Sheree's suggestion that she throw a party in her quarters. If one person stayed on the bed, she might be able to fit two others in the room.

Lastly, Sydnee played the message from Katarina.

"Hi, hon, how's it going? I hope your life is better than mine. I thought life at the Academy and the WCI was rough. All we ever do out here is train, train, and train some more. After I get done with my watch, I hit the sack, but I have to be back up at 1600 for an hour of training. Then we get a half hour for dinner before we start training again. At 2000 we get an hour for ourselves, then more training. As soon as that training is over, it's time to go on watch. I'm exhausted by then and happy just to sit, stare at, and dream about Quesann on one of my monitors. It's incredibly beautiful. It has thousands of kilometers of pristine beaches, mountains, lakes, and everything. They tell us we'll get a day off next week, but I don't know if I want to sleep in more than I want to go to the beach.

"Keep this under your hat, but it seems like something big is going on. They haven't told us anything, but I expected to see action by now. We know that the Tsgardi, Gondusans, and Hudeerac have surrendered unconditionally, but the Uthlaro are still holding out.

Admiral Carver returned months ago and additional ships keep arriving all the time. The Space Command fleet here is massive. It has to be assembling for a reason. I guess that when all the ships arrive, we'll go to meet the Uthlaro forces. I've also heard the Ruwalchu are involved, but I don't know if there's any truth to that.

There's the timer. Gotta go. Message me."

"Katarina Somulowski, Lieutenant(jg), aboard the GSC *Pholus*. Message complete."

Sydnee wanted to jump up and down, stamp her feet, scream at the top of her lungs, and throw something against a bulkhead— all at the same time. Something big was going on in Region Two and *she* was stuck aboard the *Perry* studying shipping manifests and checking the contents of containers. How could life be so unfair? She had worked hard and earned a place aboard a battleship, but she was stuck here dealing with bored and belligerent freight haulers.

* * *

"Yesterday, the rebels transmitted a declaration of secession from the Clidepp Empire," Admiral Bradlee said to the other admirals sitting at the large table during a regularly convened meeting of the Admiralty Board. "They claim to represent all planets outside the central core where the Empire's power is concentrated, but we have no idea how many local governments on planets and moons are actually involved, if any. The rebels may not have any real support, even though they say they speak for everyone other than the powerful families of Yolongus."

"What's your best estimate, Roger?" Admiral Hillaire said. "How many people do they really represent?"

"I wouldn't even hazard a guess at this point. It could be a thousand or it could be ten trillion. Since this is an autonomous nation outside GA space, SCI has a very small footprint there. We know there's widespread dissatisfaction with the central government, but we have no idea how many citizens are actually willing to support the secession and fight to end rule by Yolongus, or what resources the rebels control. We know that the Empire's military is fanatically loyal to Yolongus because of the generous pay and benefits they've received since the triumvirate came to power, but we won't begin to know how this thing will shake out until their military takes some action. If the rebels have any sort of power base, they'll have to fight back when the military starts placing systems under martial law."

"We should notify our warships on patrol along the Clidepp Empire border to be alert for the possibility of hostilities spilling over into our territory," Admiral Plimley said.

"The GA Council has prepared a resolution regarding the situation," Admiral Moore said. "It will come up for a vote very soon. Essentially, it restates the GA policy regarding travel through our space with the intention of visiting or settling on a planet by persons without a passport, visa, or approved immigration papers. It also redefines Space Command's required response when encountering such ships and individuals."

"So we continue to detain them and then return them to their origin?" Admiral Platt asked.

"No, now we'll turn the entire ship back. That'll make the captains and their shipping companies take responsibility for screening the passengers in advance. It should dramatically reduce the number of illegal aliens we'll have to deal with."

"And if the ship won't turn back?" Admiral Bradlee asked.

"Then we destroy its FTL generator, push it back across the border, and contact the Clidepp military. It's their problem."

"The first time we do that, the media will go absolutely crazy," Admiral Ahmed said. "They'll accuse us of being insensitive to the needs of people displaced by war."

"I know. They'll do anything to sensationalize the news and sell more advertising space, but it's what the GAC is ordering. Remember the uproar with the Dakistee clones? We were only talking about increasing the population density by seventy-nine people. How crazy will people act if we talk about letting billions in? It's a 'damned if we do, damned if we don't' situation."

"In fairness," Admiral Woo said, "the seventy-nine people in question were clones. With the refugees, we're talking about sentient beings forced from their homes because of war. It's quite a different matter."

"That will only be acceptable for the first million or so. After that, people will begin demanding we put a stop to it. It's better if we never let it start."

"We may not have a choice," Admiral Platt said. "I have just twenty warships operating in the sectors that cover most of the seven hundred sixty-two light-years of border with the Clidepp Empire, and the ships are the oldest and slowest in the fleet. The situation in Region Two has reduced our resources there to *far* less than what I would call the bare minimum. We estimate that we only happen upon one ship in twenty that crosses into our territory. And if a border patrol ship encounters more than one ship crossing at a time, our captain has to decide which one should be stopped if they both run."

"If this civil war, or revolution, escalates before things in Region Two are resolved, we could completely lose control in those border sectors," Admiral Hubera said. "We must take action now."

"What kind of action are you proposing, Donald?" Admiral Hillaire asked. "We have no additional ship resources we can spare."

"I don't know, but we have to do something."

"That's helpful, Donald."

"I know what you'd like to do. You'd like to bring Carver into this."

"*Admiral* Carver has enough on her hands right now," Admiral Hillaire said, "or yes, I would suggest we consult with her. We need an innovative thinker right now and I know of no one more qualified to offer a possible solution to this problem. I admit that *I* can think of nothing at the moment."

"I doubt that even Admiral Carver could come up with something this time," Admiral Woo said. "We have neither the ships nor the personnel we need to do the job, so there's nothing we can do right now except stand helplessly by and watch the situation deteriorate. I don't like to admit it, but that's the way it is."

"We didn't have the ships or personnel needed to fight the Milori invasion, but Admiral Carver found a way," Admiral Hillaire said. "Twice."

"I fear this problem is beyond even Admiral Carver's imaginative strategizing," Admiral Moore said. "In any event, she's occupied with the situation in Region Two and I wouldn't even consider distracting her from that monumental task."

* * *

"Who is this Citizen X that he believes he can declare secession?" Gustallo Plelillo, Premier of the Clidepp government, said vehemently. "What power does he have? Is he a planetary leader, a military man, or simply some nutcase?"

"We've been unable to learn much about him in the months since he first came to our attention," Weislis Danttan, the Minister of Intelligence said. "We know that he's been part of the Freedom movement for some time and that he's methodically climbed through the ranks as they grew and now heads the organization. But the leadership always wear hooded cloaks when meeting with others in the group to keep their identities a secret, even from each other. So far, we've been unable to penetrate beyond the lowest levels. We believe that fully half of the organization is dedicated to watching the other half. I've lost over twenty agents— good agents— agents who have been highly successful at infiltration in the past."

"These secession declarations began showing up all over the planet yesterday," said Kurrost Mewaffal, the Minister of Public Information and third spoke in the triumvirate. "And I've just received word that they're appearing on many of our other worlds. Whoever this Citizen X is, he has a highly organized team under him. To have kept this so secret while synchronizing a coordinated dissemination proves that. I could use him on my own team."

"This is no time for foolish statements of admiration for an enemy's organizational skills. This Citizen X represents the greatest challenge to our authority since we came to power. We have to crush him and his followers without delay.

I've put the military on alert. Our troops will begin deploying to every planet in the empire to round up the leaders of this so-called 'Freedom' movement."

"I've just finished saying that we don't know who the leaders are," Danttan said.

"Then we'll begin at the bottom and work our way up until we find out. Everyone in the organization has to know the name of at least one other. I want every individual associated with this group taken into custody and interrogated until we wring every last drop of information out of him. See to it."

"This is hardly the best time to be making enemies," Mewaffal said. "We need to win the minds and hearts of people, not torture and kill their friends and relatives."

"To the devil with winning minds and hearts," Plelillo said. "We've been too soft already. It's what allowed this Citizen X to consolidate his power. We have to crush him and his organization *now*. And if that means opening up the camps that our predecessors once used, so be it. The system worked well for them for over half a century."

"The issue of the camps is what allowed us to come to power," Mewaffal said. "If you travel down that road, we may wind up where General Roppalo and his followers are. And a berth in that overcrowded cemetery doesn't appeal to me."

"We won't make the same mistakes he did," Plelillo said. "I've always maintained a complete list of those most likely to attempt a coup d'état. One word from me will be all it takes for my special police force to move in and eliminate that threat."

"Isn't that what Roppalo used to say to us?" Danttan asked.

* * *

"The die is cast my friends," the hooded figure known only as Citizen X said to the small group of similarly hooded associates in the private sanctuary. Everyone in the room had their hoods pulled low over their faces to completely hide facial features while audio units distorted the voices. Being unknown, even to each other, had kept them safe until now.

"The triumvirate has received our letter," X continued. "We know because they're marshalling their military forces. Our spies in the capital tell us that the military has canceled all passes and furloughs, and the troops are being deployed as quickly as possible. Meanwhile, our announcement of secession is presently being printed on every planet and moon in the Empire, and distributed before the ink is even dry. The fence-sitting days are over. All planetary governments will be forced to declare their allegiances now. Those who defy the triumvirate will need our full support, and those who support them will have to be removed from power by whatever means necessary. Long live the Society of Aligned Planets."

* * *

"Do you really think we'll be able to pull that off?" Welssica asked.

"Of course," the hooded man said. "It's the perfect operation. They'll never be expecting it, so their guard will be down. We'll make headlines across the entire SAP. When Plelillo's forces try to move in and impose martial law, they'll find the task is far more onerous then they ever imagined."

"But attacking a diplomatic yacht in GA space? Space Command won't stand for it."

"What are they going to do? We've made test runs across the border and have never even seen an SC ship. How are they going to stop us if they're never around? They're too busy consolidating the new territory they won after their war with the Milori. They've sent all their patrol ships to the other side of their space. If they started tomorrow, it would take them four or five years to get them back here. By then, our territory will be free from Empire rule and the GA will have to negotiate with us to enter SAP space."

"But what about the Clidepp warship we'll need? How do you intend to steal it?" Welssica asked.

"The *Glassama* and *Abissto* are in docks at the Olliggin shipyard for minor upgrades to their FTL drive. Although the work has been completed, the work logs show that they're each still waiting for a vital drive component. I have a contact on the inside who will provide the security schedule and the codes to unlock the bridge consoles. We'll only need eighteen freedom fighters to pull it off, plus a few bridge and engineering people. The work barges normally seat fifteen, but we can fit thirty inside the passenger area. They won't be comfortable, but the flight will only last sixteen minutes."

"You intend to steal *two* warships?"

"Might as well. We'll only get one chance to do this. After that, security will be tightened. Right now they can't conceive of anyone doing it, so their security is lax."

"What about the guard ships?

"All taken care of. There are only the two old destroyers on security duty, and they never go anywhere. They only use thrusters for minor parking orbit corrections, so our people were able to sabotage their Sub-Light and FTL engines. When the bridge crews try to engage their Sub-Light engines, the systems will report broken hydrogen fuel lines and fire alarms will sound. The fire suppression systems will then fill the combustion areas with suppressant. The FTL generators pass daily system tests, but the sabotage prevents them from actually building an envelope. Those ships won't be going anywhere until the Sub-Light engines are thoroughly cleaned and the FTL generators are repaired. The *Glassama* and *Abissto* will be light-annuals away by then."

"It sounds like you have more than one contact on the inside," the man said with a smile.

"Everyone is sick of the government on Yolongus stripping the rest of the Empire to feed their excesses. We're going to end those days forever, and the only way to do that is by separating ourselves from the government. Our new government will let *all* the people live decent lives for a change. Let's see the people on Yolongus take care of *themselves* for a while. Without access to the food grown on other planets and the ores being mined in space, they'll be begging to join the SAP in a few years."

Chapter Five
~ Jan. 29th, 2285 ~

"Commander, two work barges are requesting entrance to the yard," the com chief aboard the Clidepp destroyer *Darhmassa* said to the watch officer.

"Are they giving the proper recognition code?" Commander Plericce asked tiredly.

"Yes, sir."

"Then clear them to enter the yard, chief."

"Yes, sir.

* * *

"I told you everything was set," Welssica said from the co-pilot's seat as they received approval to enter the shipyard. "Now calm down. I got the word from Citizen X himself. He's personally arranged everything."

"I'm here, aren't I?" Currulla asked testily. "But don't tell me not to be nervous. Being nervous keeps me careful, and being careful has kept me and my people alive."

"There's our ship, the *Abissto*. Bring the barge to the forward, starboard airlock. Our man will be waiting."

Ten minutes later, the rebels aboard the barge had transferred to the *Abissto*. The other barge had reached the *Glassama* and rebels were already in control of the ship's engineering section.

The two commandeered destroyers had been staffed only by a small maintenance group since the records indicated that the engines were off-line and inoperable. The takeover by armed rebels who had practiced the assault for weeks took minutes, and no alarms were sounded.

* * *

"Commander, the *Glassama* is moving," the tactical officer aboard the *Darhmassa* said.

"Impossible. The ship is inoperable."

"Then something unknown is pushing it, sir, because its position is definitely changing and it's picking up speed."

Commander Plericce's eyes opened wide and he began stabbing furiously at the monitor by his left hand to access the DeTect image that the tac officer was seeing. When he found it, he confirmed the movement.

"Now the *Abissto* is moving, sir," the tac officer said.

"Com, contact those ships and ask them what's going on."

"The *Glassama* isn't responding to hails, sir. I tried to contact her as soon as tac said it was moving because she hadn't requested clearance. The *Abissto* isn't acknowledging hails either."

"Tac, sound GQ. Helm, pursue the *Glassama*. Com, tell the *Serissa* to pursue the *Abissto*. They are authorized to use whatever force is necessary to stop her."

As the helmsman engaged the Sub-Light engines, alarms all over the bridge began to sound.

"What's going on?" Commander Plericce screamed.

"The system is reporting a broken fuel line in each of the Sub-Light engines, sir," the helmsman said. "The automatic suppression system has responded. The problem is resolved, sir. But we can't use the Sub-Light engines."

"Then build temporal envelopes and pursue FTL."

"Uh, I tried sir. The generator won't build an envelope."

"What's the problem?"

"The computer says everything is a go, but the generator isn't activating."

"This can't be happening!" the commander screamed. "No Sub-Light *and* no FTL?"

"Sir," the com chief said, "message from the *Serissa*. She suffered problems in her Sub-Light engines and can't pursue the *Abissto*. She reports that her FTL drive appears to be down as well."

"Damn," Commander Plericce said. "This is too coincidental. It has to be sabotage. Com, get me Military High Command."

* * *

"We did it," Currulla said from the command chair on the bridge. Relief seemed to be dripping from every pore in his body.

"Of course we did," Welssica said. "I told you we would. Citizen X guaranteed it. It went exactly like he planned it."

"If he was so sure it would be successful, why wasn't he here with us?"

"We can't take even the slightest risk that he might be caught. He's far too valuable to the movement to risk his being identified, even when the risk is almost non-existent."

"I always feel better when a leader is leading."

"If he gets caught or killed, this uprising might die with him. Don't worry— at the appropriate time he'll come forward and we'll have a chance to meet him."

"You haven't met him?"

"I've spoken directly with him on several occasions, but he's always cloaked and his voice is distorted. No one knows who he is, really, and only he knows the identities of the supreme council members. It has to be that way or we'd all be in a death camp by now."

"What do we do now?"

"Now, we execute Phase Two. You pick up the rest of your crew and then set course for GA Space."

* * *

"Marcola," Sydnee said sleepily in response to a call via her CT. When she repeated it and still didn't get an answer, she realized she hadn't established a carrier. She reached over to touch her Space Command ring with her right index finger. "Marcola," she said for the third time.

"This is Lt. Carstairs. I'm acting watch officer while the Captain is in a meeting with Commander Bryant. We just detected a ship coming across the border and I'm altering course to pursue. Your name came up on the pilot rotation list. When GQ sounds, get suited up and head for the flight deck instead of going to AC&C."

"Roger, Lieutenant."

"Carstairs out."

"Marcola out."

A second later the GQ alarm sounded, followed by an interdiction operation announcement. All over the ship, crewmembers would be locking down loose equipment and running for their GQ stations. Sydnee rolled out of her bunk and stripped off her pajamas before pulling on the black, padded body suit in preparation for slipping into her battle armor. She'd worn the armor so many times during the past several months that she could have dressed in the dark.

She was out the door of her quarters within five minutes of the GQ sounding and in the flight bay in three more. She performed a quick walk-around preflight with her mechanic and then entered the craft and stowed her weapons in the pilot's locker on the shuttle's flight deck. She immediately began the checklist procedure and was ready to roll when Lt. Kennedy entered the flight deck cabin and dropped into the co-pilot's seat.

"We're good to go," was all he said. In the short time they had worked together, he had developed an appreciation for Sydnee's ability as a pilot, her intelligence, and her behavior once they had boarded the vessel to be inspected.

Sydnee checked the instrument panel to make sure the ship was sealed and then released the magnetic skids. She engaged the oh-gee drive and the shuttle lifted off the deck and began to turn in response to her movement of the controls. When they reached the bay door, Sydnee let the shuttle settle to the deck and then engaged the magnetic skid locks again as the temporary airlock bulkheads folded down around the ship. They remained like that until the *Perry* had come to a stop and the bay door was opened.

Once the small ship was away from the *Perry*, Sydnee engaged the Sub-Light engines. The other shuttle was likewise out-ship and doing the same. Sydnee established communication with the other shuttle, and within seconds of engaging their Sub-Light engines, they were approaching their destination side by side. Until now, Sydnee had only participated in inspections of freighters, and the routine had gotten a little boring. This would be her first passenger liner, and she felt a little of the excitement she'd felt the first time out.

Sydnee remained in the shuttle until the Marines checked out the situation. When it was determined that the ship was just an ordinary passenger ship and not some kind of disguised smuggling operation, she was told to disembark and join the inspection team. Before leaving the shuttle, she strapped on her pistol belt with the handgun and two knives, and clipped her short rifle to the quick-release attachment ring on her armor's chest plate. She headed for the shuttle ramp as soon as her helmet sealed.

While part of the inspection team went with the Marines to check the cargo holds, Sydnee remained with the main group. They would check the passenger rolls, looking for travelers with missing or forged documents.

All passengers and crew had already been rounded up and herded into the Grand Ballroom. No one would be allowed to leave the area until the Marines had verified that there was no one else aboard except for the few people who couldn't leave their duty posts. Their credentials would be checked without requiring them to go to the ballroom.

Sydnee was immediately delighted when she entered the Grand Ballroom. This was her first real opportunity to personally observe several species of which, until now, she'd only seen pictures in Alien Anatomy classes. The species she'd observed aboard inspected freighters in recent months— Nordakians, Cheblooks, Arrosians, Alyysians, and Wolkerrons— were all inhabitants of GA space, and although she had never seen any personally until she became a member of the Perry crew, were seen fairly often aboard space stations and in transit locations. The species she identified aboard the passenger ship were very uncommon visitors to GA space.

*   *   *

Home to three sentient species sufficiently advanced to have interstellar travel and half a dozen lesser sentient species that only enjoyed off-world travel through journeys with one of the three, the Clidepp Empire had been ruled by the Yolongi since its inception. It was the Yolongi who first introduced FTL travel in their region of space after acquiring it from an enterprising traveler from the GA, and as their travel expanded, Yolongi explorers laid claim to new territory unclaimed by other species. It wasn't long before their claimed territory included the planets of the two other species able to grasp the intricacies of DATFA, or Dis-Associative Temporal Field Anomalies, and who later developed their own interstellar cargo and passenger fleets.

Using DATFA technology, a spaceship coalesced a temporal envelope around itself that disassociated it from normal space and time. Once enclosed, the ship was no longer subject to the mechanics of Einstein's Theory of Special Relativity that stated no object could travel faster than light.

The general appearance of the Yolongi was similar to that of the urban legend 'greys' of twentieth century Earth, but since FTL development on their planet apparently followed that of Earth's, it was obviously mere coincidence. And while the 'greys' were reputed to be considerably shorter, the Yolongi were about the same average height and build as Terrans. Still, there were those on Earth who continued to insist that the Yolongi and greys were one and the same species, and had merely hidden all information about their space program's existence until they were forced to show their hand.

The other FTL shipbuilding species of the Clidepp Empire were the Mydwuard and the Olimpood. The Mydwuard had an exoskeleton, such as that of crustaceans and insects on Earth. They walked upright on two legs but had four arms with three fingers on each hand. The Olimpood were equally at home on land or in the sea and had flabby bodies which greatly facilitated their buoyancy when in the water, but which made them a bit clumsy on land. Like many species in the GA, they had two arms and two legs. While the Yolongi breathed an earth-normal atmosphere, the other two species required special breathing apparatus to provide certain gaseous elements found in their planet's atmosphere. When wearing the full, floor-length cloaks common in the Clidepp Empire, it was impossible to tell which species was present when the full hood was drawn over the head.

All three species had spread their seed around the Empire, but the Yolongi settlers had spread the furthest. Few of the Yolongi explorers had any remaining ties to the home planet of their ancestors, nor loyalty to the repressive government there.

*   *   *

Sydnee's role on this occasion was to check the papers of the travelers as they presented themselves for inspection. The Marines were still searching the ship for anyone in hiding, so the inspection team had begun their task with just a squad for support. SOP called for them to remain in full armor with weapons at the ready in case anyone refused to cooperate or became openly rebellious.

Everyone whose papers were in order was allowed to move into a smaller ballroom next door. Where the papers were in question, the traveler was escorted to a small conference room guarded by two Marines.

The translation device built into her armor's breastplate was keyed to her implanted CT, so everything said to Sydnee as she inspected documents seemed as a whisper in her left ear, and everything she said emanated from the small speaker that was part of the translation device.

The first travelers to be checked were Mydwuard. Sydnee required them to pull back their hood so she could visually compare their appearance against their passports and visas. Only one hesitated, and she discovered why when it finally complied. Its head was horribly disfigured, as if it had been in an accident and unfortunate enough to receive care from a very poor surgeon. Of course, she knew little of its biological composition and perhaps the surgeon had only done what was necessary to save its life. She had to remind herself not to apply human physiology knowledge to other species.

*   *   *

"Currulla," the rebel at the tac station called out, "we have a ship on the DeTect monitors. It's a long way off, but it might be the one we're looking for. It's headed in the right direction."

"I told you to call me 'Captain,' you imbecile," Currulla said angrily.

"Sorry, *Cap*tain."

"Better. How long before we cross paths with the contact?"

"We won't unless we change course."

"Then how long will it take us to reach the contact if we change course?"

"Roughly thirty-eight centmers, if we maintain maximum speed."

"Well, of course we're going to maintain maximum speed. Navigation, plot an intercept course for that ship."

"Okay, Currul— I mean *Cap*tain."

"The proper response is "Aye, Captain.""

"Aye, Captain," the rebel at the navigation station said as he rolled his eyes.

* * *

It took hours to check the papers of the thousands aboard the passenger liner, and the thrill of meeting six new species had worn off long before the task was complete. Once the Marines had determined that there was no one in hiding, they allowed those whose papers had been checked to return to their cabins. The dozen passengers whose papers raised some concerns had been forced to wait in the smaller ballroom until the first process was complete.

After a detailed examination of the papers again, as well as a check of information available through the *Perry's* database, all but one of the passengers were cleared to continue their journey. It was proven that the one individual was using a forged passport and wouldn't be permitted to continue further.

"What do you mean I have to turn around?" the Captain of the ship said when he was informed about the bogus passport.

"The GAC has declared that the shipping company is responsible for validating passports and visas before entering GA space," Lieutenant Resono, the senior interdiction officer aboard on this stop, said. "Failing that, the ship must withdraw from GA space and discharge the passenger outside our border."

"But it's at least ten days back to the nearest inhabited planet over the border. It'll add twenty days or more to our voyage. We'll have to refund ten percent of the ticket fare to every single passenger for the delay."

"It would seem that in the future you should check the paperwork more thoroughly before issuing passenger tickets."

"You can't expect us to know who is legal and who isn't."

"Yet that is exactly what is expected. If the paperwork appears fraudulent or expired, require the passenger to provide updated documents before accepting them for passage."

"That's unreasonable."

"Not at all. But it's your choice. This time we're only turning you back. If your company begins to show a pattern of abuse, your ships could be turned back without a check even being performed."

"You can't do that."

"Yes— we can. The GAC has ordered Space Command to put responsibility for checking paperwork on the company. It's up to you whether you wish to cooperate or not. But it would be beneficial to cooperate."

"I refuse to turn back. You must take the person into custody as you've always done in the past and return them to the border yourself if you don't want them in your space."

"With the trouble we're experiencing elsewhere, we don't have the resources to do that at this time. If you fail to turn back willingly, I'm authorized to destroy your FTL generator so you can't continue into GA space."

"You can't attack my ship. It's a violation of GA law to perpetrate an unprovoked attack on a helpless passenger ship."

"If you refuse to heed lawful orders, that's all the provocation we require."

The Captain began to sputter and stammer as he searched for words. When Lt. Resono began to receive a message on his CT, he turned slightly away, activated his CT and held up his hand towards the passenger ship's Captain.

"Resono," the Lieutenant said.

"Lt. Resono," Captain Lidden said, "we've received an emergency SOS from a Clidepp diplomatic yacht under attack by a warship. All hands are to return to the ship at once."

"Yes, sir. We'll return at once. Resono out."

Turning again to the passenger ship's Captain, Resono said, "The *Perry* must respond to an emergency call for assistance. You will wait here until we return so my Captain will be able to address your complaints."

"How long will that be?"

"Unknown. A ship is under attack by a warship."

"Raiders or rebels?"

"Also unknown. But Raiders would seem to be the less likely of the choices."

"You can't expect us to just sit here. That's even worse than going back. We might be attacked ourselves."

"You *will* remain here until we return. That's an official directive." Activating his CT as he turned from the Captain and hurried towards the exit, he said, "Attention, inspection team. Captain Lidden has issued an emergency recall in response to an SOS from a ship under attack. Return to your shuttles at once. Resono out."

Sydnee raced to the hangar deck along with the inspection team. Marines were already converging on the shuttle from every direction and Sydnee had to practically climb over their backs to get to the cockpit. There wasn't time for a preflight and Sydnee hoped that nothing had happened to the shuttle while it was unattended.

Once everyone had been accounted for and the shuttle was sealed, Sydnee moved it into position for the temporary airlock to be erected. As the bay door reached the fully open position and the green light came on to signal that the way was clear, Sydnee punched the rear thrusters control and the shuttle zipped out of the passenger ship. When they reached a point where the engines could be ignited, Sydnee touched off the Sub-Light engines and the shuttle accelerated away so fast it would have been difficult to follow with the human eye. The occupants of the shuttle felt only the briefest sensation of movement, thanks to the inertial compensation generators.

The emergency recall allowed Sydnee to bypass most of the usual safety protocols and the shuttle slid into the hangar bay's temporary airlock like a MAT arriving at a hot LZ. It was the most fun she'd had since flight training at the Academy.

Lt. Kennedy screamed as the shuttle slid to a stop just centimeters from the temporary airlock bulkhead and then worked to re-swallow his heart as the hatch closed and the bulkheads rose before Sydnee moved the shuttle to its parking slot using the oh-gee engine. As he climbed out of the co-pilot seat, all he said was, "Uh, great job, Lieutenant."

"Thank you, Lieutenant Kennedy," Sydnee said. Despite her effort, a stiff informality was the best she'd been able to achieve so far with the by-the-book young officer.

Sydnee disembarked after all the Marines had climbed down and left the area. She spotted the mechanic studying the shuttle's undercarriage as she stepped down onto the deck.

"Problem, chief?" Sydnee asked.

"I haven't found it yet, ma'am."

"Found what?"

"What it is that kept the landing struts from being twisted up like pretzels. I saw your landing from the control room and I was about to activate the emergency systems. I thought for sure you were going to crash through the temporary airlock. I can't understand why this undercarriage isn't crushed into scrap."

"I've never yet damaged a craft I was piloting, chief. You see, the trick is to always stop the ship exactly one-half centimeter above the deck and then let it settle on its own."

"One-half centimeter, ma'am?"

"*Exactly* one-half centimeter," Sydnee said with a straight face before turning and heading for the flight bay exit.

The mechanic was left scratching his head as he tried to figure out how she could have stopped the small ship exactly one-half centimeter above the deck.

Chapter Six
~ Jan. 29th, 2285 ~

Back in her quarters, Sydnee stripped out of her armor and flopped onto the bed. She couldn't stop giggling as she thought about the confused expression on the chief's face. Always stopping exactly one-half centimeter above the deck was an expression used with new cadets by one of her flight instructors at the Academy. It was as ridiculous as when a MAT flight instructor at the WCI would tell new students they wouldn't receive flight certification until they could perform a four-g reverse roll in atmo with a full complement of Marines on board. Such a maneuver was impossible with a Marine Armored Transport, but she and her fellow students had spent a lot of time trying to figure ways to accomplish it.

Sydnee's watch had ended hours ago and she wanted to roll over and go to sleep, but instead she forced herself to get up and slip into her uniform so she could go down to the Auxiliary Command and Control bridge. The emergency recall meant that they were hurtling through space to assist a ship in trouble. If they expected to arrive within a few hours, Sydnee would resist the urge to sleep, but if the problem was further away, she'd try to grab what winks she could. She would be able to learn the true situation in AC&C.

* * *

"How did they see through our disguises?" Currulla screamed at the bridge crew, all of whom were of Yolongi ancestry and currently dressed in Yolongi Space Fleet uniforms. "They stopped when we ordered them to."

"It must have been the recognition codes, Currul— Captain," the com chief said. "As soon as I sent the codes, they went silent and began building their envelope."

"Striking their temporal generator from this distance was a lucky shot," the tac officer said. "If they'd gotten their envelope up, we would never have been able to stop them."

"Stop them? We didn't stop them. We only slowed them down. They're running at their maximum sub-light speed and screaming for help."

"Let them scream," the tac officer said. "There's no one out here to help them. Even at FTL, we're days from the Clidepp border. It'll take them light-annuals to reach it at sub-light."

"Currul— Captain," the com officer said a few moments later, "I just intercepted a message sent in the clear. A Space Command Border Patrol ship is on its way here to help the diplomatic yacht."

"Space Command? Wonderful." Looking over at the tac officer, he said, "So there's nobody out here to help them, eh?"

"Well, there's usually no one out here. It must be a fluke."

"We're inside the GA border. Where else would you expect to find a Space Command Border Patrol ship? Inside the Clidepp Empire?"

"It's a fluke. Space Command only has a token force out here."

"Fluke or not, they're on their way here. Let's finish off that yacht so we can be long gone when they get here."

"We're almost in range," the tac officer said as he returned his concentration to the console readouts. "Ten, nine, eight, seven, si— Helm, hard to starboard."

"What is it?" Currulla asked, stumbling over and slurring the words badly in his effort to get them out.

"The yacht fired a torpedo at us— no— two torpedoes."

"But *we* can't be in range if *they* aren't."

"We were in pursuit, so we were closing the gap towards their torpedo while they were getting further away from the point where we would fire. We should be okay now. The torpedoes either didn't get a lock or lost the lock when we turned. They're continuing along their original trajectory."

"Should I change course to pursue, Captain?" the helmsman asked.

"Tac?" Currulla said.

"I suggest an intercept course where we minimize exposure to their bow or stern tubes. It's unlikely a ship of that size would have either larboard or starboard torpedo capability."

"Got that helm?" Currulla asked.

"Got it."

"Got it, *Captain*," Currulla said with great emphasis.

"They know we're not Yolongi Space Fleet now," the helmsman said lackadaisically. "We can stop pretending."

"We'll stop when *I* say we'll stop."

"Aye, *Captain*."

* * *

"We're coming up on their starboard quarter and we're almost in range," the tac officer said.

"Fire as soon as you get a lock," Currulla said.

"Firing now," the tac officer said calmly, then hollered, "Damn! Helm, hard to starboard."

"Again?" Currulla screamed as he sat up in the command chair and glared at the tac officer. "You said they didn't have starboard tubes!"

"I didn't think they would in that small ship. They can't be normal-sized torpedoes. Damn, the torpedoes are still pursuing us. We didn't lose them this time."

"Helm, maximum Sub-Light speed."

"Already at maximum, Currulla," the helmsman said as he twisted the joystick again. No matter what he tried, the torpedoes continued to close.

The laser array gunners weren't very accurate and three minutes later the rebel ship rocked from an explosion, then another two seconds later.

"We've been hit," the tac officer shouted.

"Oh, really?" Currulla said. "Com, find that genius of an engineering chief and ask him how bad it is."

"Captain, should we move in again on the yacht?" the helmsman asked.

"Oh, it's Captain again, is it?" Currulla growled. "No, you idiot, we can't re-engage until we know how bad our damage is. Stay on their tail, though. We don't want to get too far behind them."

Over an hour passed before the ship's engineer reported in. "It's bad, Currulla. Both torpedoes hit the forward hull section where the oxygen regeneration equipment is located. They couldn't have hit us in a worse spot. Whoever fired those torpedoes is either very lucky or knew exactly where to put 'em. The entire section is destroyed. Once we use what oxygen we have in the storage tanks that weren't destroyed, the carbon dioxide level in here is slowly going to increase until we can't breathe."

"Well, get one of the damaged systems working. That's why we hired you."

"I can't fix what doesn't exist anymore. All you have down there is a hundred tons of twisted scrap metal."

"How about the regeneration systems in the shuttles?"

"They're designed to provide air for small areas, not an entire destroyer, and for maximum benefit, the shuttle's engine must be operating. If we evacuate the ship, the shuttles will easily be able to support a fully configured load of onboard passengers— for as long as the fuel and power cells last."

"Do we have enough shuttle capacity for the entire crew?"

"No, but we can save about twenty percent."

"What are our other options?"

"Evacuate the ship."

"You said that already. What else?"

"There is no 'else.' We have a finite amount of reserve oxygen in the storage tanks. When that's gone, we begin to die. I suggest that all crewmembers reduce their activity as much as possible."

"You're telling me that the ship can't be saved?"

"No, the ship will be fine, but the people are a different matter. Everyone who remains aboard— will die."

"Damn."

"Exactly," the chief engineer said.

* * *

Sydnee managed four hours' sleep and awoke refreshed when the computer sounded her requested wakeup call. The computer never let up until the requestor was out of bed, and if they returned to the bed within five minutes, the computer renewed the wakeup messages via that person's implanted CT or ID. Having the computer talking inside their head was as bad as having a drill instructor shouting in their face. No one ever slept through a wakeup call on the *Perry*.

After a quick shower, she slipped into her uniform and headed for the officers' mess. A buttered roll would satisfy her appetite until she had time for a regular meal, and she nibbled at it as she headed to the AC&C.

Most of the off-duty bridge officers were already assembled in the much smaller version of the bridge when Sydnee entered. She nodded to the ones who made eye contact and found a spot from where she could see the large monitor at the front of the room. She didn't have long to wait as the *Perry* arrived at the last reported position of the ship calling for help. When the com chief made contact with the diplomatic yacht, the image of the ship's Captain appeared on the monitor. Everyone quieted down and listened as Captain Lidden's voice emanated from speakers in the room.

"Captain, we're here to assist. What's your condition?"

"Thank you, Captain. We were attacked by one of our own warships. We were hailed and ordered to stop, so we complied."

"One of your *own* warships? In GA space?"

"Yes, a *Bernouust* class destroyer. It was apparently one of two stolen by rebel forces from a shipyard while undergoing refits. They used the name of a third ship, one operating in our space just over the border, to disguise their identity. I believed the story that they had come to give us an escort since rebels now controlled two warships, but when they sent the recognition signals we knew they weren't who they claimed to be. The codes were changed a few days ago, following the thefts. Unfortunately we had already canceled our envelope. We then applied full power to our Sub-Light engines and tried to build a new envelope, but their ship was faster, of course, and they knocked out our temporal field generator. We returned fire and were able to damage them with torpedoes. They trailed us for a while and then left. I guess we damaged them enough that they wanted no further part of us."

"I see. Your vessel is armed then?"

"It's necessary these days, even for a diplomatic yacht. I don't see the situation improving any time soon."

"Yes, it would appear that way. Do you need engineering assistance from us, sir?"

"Our most pressing need is a ship to protect us so we can stop and make repairs. We won't know what other assistance we might need until my people can evaluate the condition of the temporal field generator."

"Very well, sir. I offer you the protection of the Galactic Alliance Space Command Light-Destroyer *Perry*. We have you on our DeTect screen and see no other ships in the vicinity. You may stop where you are and commence repairs. We'll be there in a few minutes."

"Thank you, Captain. I'll halt my ship but await your arrival before I send out our engineers."

"Understood, Captain. *Perry* out."

"*Darrapralis* out."

It appeared that the excitement was over. Since there were six hours before Sydnee's watch began, she could either get more sleep or find something else to do. She decided to catch up on her correspondence, so she returned to her quarters.

Sydnee again viewed several messages before recording her replies. The first was the most recent vid message from her best friend, Katarina.

"Hey, Syd," the image of Kat said from the monitor as the message played. "How's everything? I received your last message and I almost envy you. You may only be inspecting freighters and passenger liners, but at least you're doing something productive, and you get to fly occasionally. All I do is train. I train all afternoon, and then again all evening until it's time to go on watch. When a ship is in port, the third watch is supposed to be an easy time, and most watch commanders allow informal talk as long as it's kept low key. But as soon as I report for my watch, the watch commander begins assigning me navigation problems to solve, then grades my results. I feel like I'm back at the Academy.

I've decided that we *are* functioning as the protection fleet for Region Two Headquarters because the *Pholus* hasn't left port since I arrived at Quesann. Admiral Carver hasn't been seen in months, and the scuttlebutt is that she's off fighting an enemy of significantly greater size. But other than the repair to the *Colorado*, which I've learned she was commanding when it was hit, we've seen no proof of any action. Still, we wouldn't be training this hard if *something* wasn't going on *somewhere*. And eventually that something may wind up here at our doorstep.

"Anyway, at least we get some down time once a week, and we're permitted to go dirt-side for a few hours. Quesann is beautiful, Syd. It's kinda like a duplicate Earth, but instead of major continents with vast expanses of water, the land mass is distributed as islands, some as large as New Zealand, that dot the whole surface of the planet. Since it wasn't inhabited when Admiral Carver selected it for Region Two Headquarters, it's still almost all wilderness.

"I heard that the reason the Milori hadn't colonized it was because it was too cold for them. They like high tempera-tures. And since they had subjugated every species in their

Empire capable of space travel, there was no one else to colonize it.

"I wish that I could get a couple of weeks off and go exploring, but most of it is still off-limits because they don't know what harmful plant, insect, amphibian, reptile, marine, and animal life might exist in the uncharted areas. If Admiral Carver opens the planet to occupation by civilians, it's sure to fill quickly. Perhaps one day it will become the hub for the GA instead of Earth because it's much more centrally located between Regions One and Two than Earth.

"Have to go. Message me soon.

Katarina Somulowski, Lieutenant(jg), aboard the SC Battleship *Pholus* in Region Two, message complete."

Sydnee took a deep breath, released it, and began her reply.

"Message to Katarina Somulowski, Lieutenant(jg) aboard the GSC Battleship *Pholus* in Region Two.

"Hey Kat, got your message yesterday but I was tied up all day checking passports and visas on a Yolongi passenger ship. It was interesting seeing some of the alien species we'd only heard about at the Academy, but after the first few hours it was just a chore that had to be completed. Presently, we're preparing to assist a Clidepp diplomatic yacht that was attacked by rebels inside our border. It doesn't look like I'll be involved since we're only going to stand by as protection while they repair their temporal field generator. The rebels were gone long before we got here, so unless they show up again it's going to be just another boring watch. At least I don't have to constantly prepare courses to places we're not going. We have to stay alert when we're not in port, but it's a relaxed atmosphere on third watch unless we detect a ship coming from, or headed to, the border.

"Quesann sounds beautiful. I hope I get a chance to see it someday, but as I told you last week, there's almost no chance of getting a transfer off the *Perry*. Nobody wants to take a member of *this* crew unless they're really desperate, and Space Command HQ hasn't initiated a transfer off since the war with the Milori began and they had to send every ship they could spare to the Frontier Zone. Are they still calling it that out there now that Region Two territory has been officially annexed to the GA? I feel so out of touch here. We pick up all the news and entertainment broadcasts, but I have this strange feeling of being so detached from everything and everyone I've ever known. I thought I was prepared for a life in space, but perhaps I had romanticized it too much. Every day seems too much like the previous day.

"But hey, don't mind me. Perhaps I'm just tired and still a bit depressed over being posted to the *Perry* without knowing what I did to deserve it. Time to go. I love you Kat. You be careful out there. From what you're saying, it looks like big trouble might be brewing again in Region Two.

"Sydnee Marcola, Lieutenant(jg) aboard the GSC Destroyer *Perry*. Message complete."

When the *Perry* arrived at a position twenty-five thousand kilometers from the damaged diplomatic yacht, it found her apparently dead in space but still drifting slightly forward. As Captain Lidden reopened a dialogue with the Captain of the yacht, the yacht's nacelle-housed maneuvering engines rotated around to perform a complete braking action. Within minutes of coming to a virtual dead stop, engineers in EVA suits emerged from the airlocks on the yacht and moved towards the temporal envelope generator on top of the ship. Like a warship, the generator was housed in an armored repository. When needed, the cover slid back and the generator extended upwards until completely exposed and able to create an envelope that spread out in all directions like an expanding soap bubble. Unlike a bubble, however, the envelope wasn't spherical. It was more like a tight-fitting pouch a few millimeters thick that coated the entire hull with a network of expanding temporal anomalies.

Sydnee had just completed a message to her mom when she received a call to her CT.

"Marcola," she said.

"Lieutenant, this is Commander Bryant. Suit up. You're taking a shuttle to the disabled ship."

"But I thought it was a diplomatic yacht, sir."

"That's what they said. We're going to verify their documents. Hustle it, Lieutenant."

"Yes, sir."

Sydnee stripped off her uniform, then slipped into her body suit before donning her armor. She debated whether to bring her weapons and then decided it was better to be safe than sorry.

"You're loaded for bear again," Lt. Weems said with a smile when she reached the flight deck. "This is a diplomatic yacht, you know."

"It's my first. I didn't know if I was supposed to bring weapons or not. I was thinking of the *Santiago* interdiction tragedy. They were only supposed to be checking a harmless freighter."

Weems nodded sadly. "Well, it can't hurt I suppose. Just don't fire your weapon unless someone is trying to kill you. The GAC takes a very dim view of us shooting holes in diplomats. It would ensure you *never* get off the *Perry*."

"Not to mention prison time."

"Nah, they wouldn't send you to prison unless the dip dies. Being sentenced to spending the rest of your career on this bucket is far worse punishment."

"Jerry, you've never told me what you did to get posted to the *Perry*."

"No," Weems said, as he returned his attention to the viewpad he'd been studying when she arrived. "I didn't, did I?"

"Well?"

"A deep subject."

"Why you're here?"

"No, wells."

Sydnee frowned. "You're not going to tell me?"

"Get your ship preflighted, Syd."

"What did you do, Jerry? Did someone die? Did you shoot a dip?"

Weems looked up at Sydnee, grimaced, then turned and walked towards his own shuttle.

Sydnee stared after him for a few seconds, frowned again, then began her preflight check.

Chapter Seven

~ Jan. 30th, 2285 ~

"I've just received word that the attack on the diplomatic yacht failed," the hooded figure at the head of the table said.

"What happened?" another asked. "Was it Space Command? The plan seemed perfect."

"Our people managed to gain access to the two warships and seize them without violence, then make a successful escape from the shipyard. They located the ship carrying the diplomats while it was still in Galactic Alliance space, and it halted when they ordered it to. But somehow the yacht discovered that the destroyer wasn't commanded by Clidepp military personnel and tried to escape. Our people managed to destroy its temporal field generator, preventing it going FTL, but the yacht fired torpedoes and damaged our ship. The destroyer was forced to break off the attack when their life support systems were incapacitated.

"Where is it now?"

"They're attempting to reach an uninhabited planet in a small, out of the way, solar system before the air is too foul to breathe. They'll vacate the ship and wait for someone to pick them up."

"What about the ship? We can't just abandon a valuable resource like that."

"The oxygen regeneration equipment was destroyed, and the supply that remained in un-ruptured tanks was inadequate for the large crew we had placed aboard. When the pickup ship arrives, they'll repair whatever storage tanks aboard the damaged ship they can and refill them. Most areas of the ship will be sealed off from life support, and a small crew will attempt to pilot it back to Clidepp space. A crew of twenty should have sufficient reserves. If that proves impossible, tugs will tow it back. Once the ship is here, we can have it repaired at a planet in the outer reaches where they don't ask questions if your credits are good."

"This is a bitter pill to swallow. We invested a lot of money and effort in this plan. We were expecting the operation to be successful."

"It was successful," X said. "It was even more successful than we could have hoped."

"What do you mean? You said that all they did was damage the temporal field generator."

"Our people stole two warships from under the noses of the military and then harassed a diplomatic yacht. No one was killed in either operation, but people will understand what the outcome *could* have been. Everyone will assume that the warship could have annihilated the diplomatic yacht but chose not to. They won't give credence to Empire claims that a yacht successfully fought off a destroyer. And since no one was killed, the bleeding hearts can't scream that we committed murder. Overall, the operation was a huge success."

"Yes, I see," the second man said. "That's brilliant. Absolutely brilliant."

"Of course we still have the problem of a disabled ship in Galactic Alliance space," a third member of the group said. "What if the crew is captured before they can learn of this cover story and tell everyone what the real objective was?"

"That could be a problem," X said, "but there's little chance that Space Command will find them before we pick them up. There are only a few SC ships on patrol along our entire border with the Alliance."

The door suddenly burst in and an agitated man rushed in. "X, the military has entered the city. They've begun searching houses and beating or arresting people who resist. Several citizens have already been killed. You must leave this place immediately. You must all leave."

Citizen X rose quickly from his seat at the head of the table and said, "Yes, my friends, it is time to go. We must not be found here. We'll meet again in seven solars at the house in Reumella just after sunset. You all know your planned escape route from this location. Move quickly now."

* * *

Sydnee was on the flight deck going through the preflight procedures when Lt. Kennedy entered and flopped into the co-pilot's seat. "Take it easy today, Lieutenant," he said. "Make it smooth and gentle."

"Not feeling too good?" Sydnee asked.

"I'm fine. It's the Captain I'm thinking of."

"What about the Captain?"

"He's in the rear cabin."

"The Captain is going over to the dip ship?"

"Yeah, some protocol regulation or other I guess. Or maybe he just wants to make sure everything goes smoothly."

"Oh, at first I thought maybe our last landing was a little rough on you."

"You did scare the crap out of me. I'm lucky I didn't have to clean my underwear after that. Ya know, I've known since the first flight that you were a good pilot, but after that last trip I have to say you're probably the best I've flown with since I arrived aboard the *Perry*."

"I guess that's a compliment," Sydnee said with a grin.

"Yeah, it was supposed to be."

"Thanks."

"Just don't make a habit of coming in like you did last time."

"Don't worry. We were under orders to ignore the usual flight regs and get aboard as quickly as possible. So I did. If it makes you feel any better, I was always at the top of my flight instruction classes at WCI and I had the ship under control at all times."

"I think I knew that. It just kinda caught me off guard."

"Everybody strapped in?"

"Yeah, we're good to go."

Sydnee nodded, checked to make sure the ship was acknowledging that the two hatches were closed and sealed, then started the oh-gee engine.

"The shuttle is ready to depart, Commander," Sydnee said to the watch officer on the bridge.

"You're cleared to depart, Lieutenant. The Captain has cancelled the other ship, so you're the only shuttle going over. Bay Two on the starboard side of the *Darrapralis* will be open for your docking."

"Understood, sir. Starboard Bay Two."

Sydnee released the magnetic skids and the small ship lifted up gently before she turned it one hundred eighty degrees and moved it towards the flight bay's exterior hatch. As the ship settled to the deck, Sydnee re-engaged the magnetic skids. The Docking Controller, watching from the flight operations room, lowered the temporary airlock bulkheads around the shuttle, evacuated the air, and opened the outer hatch. Sydnee slowly moved the shuttle out of the *Perry* and headed towards the diplomatic yacht, floating some twenty-five thousand kilometers away. Although the *Darrapralis* was a diplomatic yacht, it was still not a Space Command vessel. Space Command regulations required that this minimum distance always be maintained from all non-SC ships in space because it made laser weapons largely ineffective. Once the Sub-Light engines were engaged, the shuttle would close the distance in a minute.

"Smooth enough, Lieutenant?" Sydnee said to Kennedy with a grin.

"Perfect, Lieutenant."

The hatch for Bay Two in the diplomatic yacht was wide open. Sydnee piloted the shuttle in and let it settle gently to the deck. It was so gentle that she wouldn't be sure it was completely down if the sensors hadn't shown that the magnetic skids could be engaged. She tapped the button and a red light indicated that the locks had engaged.

The bay was small compared to the bay on the *Perry*, but it could still accommodate two shuttles of the size Sydnee had flown over. One shuttle parking location was occupied by a Clidepp ship. Sydnee waited until the outer hatch had closed and the temporary airlock bulkheads raised before releasing the skids, then moved the small ship to the other location. A Yolongi officer motioned her forward as she maneuvered the vessel. When he crossed his arms with his fists clenched, she lowered the ship to the deck and engaged the skid locks again.

Kennedy jumped to his feet and left the flight deck as Sydnee powered down the craft. Seconds later she heard the sounds of pounding feet as the Marines left the ship, then all was quiet. It was peaceful on the shuttle's flight deck as she relaxed and wondered if she'd be called to do something or if she would just have to sit in the ship until it was time to return to the *Perry*.

"Marcola," she suddenly heard in her CT.

"Marcola here," she replied after touching her ring.

"What are you waiting for, Lieutenant? An engraved invitation?"

"Sir?" she said questioningly as she recognized the Captain's voice."

"Get your six out here."

"Coming, sir. Marcola out."

Sydnee leapt to her feet, pulling on her gloves as she fumbled to open the locker behind the pilot's chair. She removed the belt containing the two knives and her laser pistol and strapped it around her waist. As she pulled her rifle from the locker, she remembered Weems' words about shooting a dip and pushed it back into the locker. She then took her pistol out of the holster and looked at it as she considered whether she should leave it in the locker. She decided that she couldn't wear a pistol belt without a pistol.

As Sydnee left the flight deck, she pulled her helmet onto her head. It automatically self-sealed to the personal body armor and she was ready for anything by the time she reached the shuttle hatch.

The Marines were aligned two deep along the side of the shuttle as Sydnee hurried down the ramp and braced to attention in front of the Captain. "Lieutenant(jg) Marcola reporting, sir."

Lidden, not wearing personal body armor, looked at her, scowled, and said angrily, "It's about time, Lieutenant."

"I'm sorry, sir. My standing orders are to wait on the flight deck until summoned to leave the ship by the officer in com-mand of the Marines I'm transporting or issued new instruc-tions by the watch officer."

Lidden frowned, then turned towards Kennedy. "Lieutenant, you and your men will remain here unless I call for you."

"Yes, sir. But is that wise, sir?"

"I have Lieutenant Marcola for protection." Looking down at the two knife handles protruding from their scabbards on her belt and the flap holster holding the pistol, he added, "She seems ready for any trouble that might come our way."

"Yes, sir."

"Follow me, Lieutenant," Lidden said to Sydnee as he turned and walked towards the flight bay exit where a ship's officer was waiting.

"Welcome aboard, Captain," the officer said in Amer. I'm First Officer Sleddling."

Sydnee had set her armor's translator for Yolon but it wasn't needed.

"Thank you, I'm Captain Lidden, in command of the Space Command destroyer *Perry*. And this officer next to me is Lieutenant Marcola."

"Welcome, both. If you'll come with me, I'll take you to where Captain Surrosso and Ambassador Blethalla are waiting to greet you."

Lidden and Sydnee followed the officer and in a few minutes they were ushered into a lavish salon where the ship's Captain and the Ambassador were seated. The two Yolongi stood as they entered and introductions were made all around.

"Ambassador, may I see your credentials, please?"

"My credentials?

"I need to verify that you are who you say you are."

"What? Who else would I be? This is a Yolongi diplomatic vessel."

"Yes, sir. But I still need to see your credentials."

"I refuse, and you have no right to ask."

"I have every right. Galactic Alliance law states that diplomatic status is extended only to legitimate members of a foreign nation who prove said status when asked to present their credentials. If I don't see them, I'm required to treat the vessel and occupants as I would any other vessel. That means I must commence an immediate search for illegal contraband and persons without proper visas."

"This is preposterous," the Ambassador said. "This is an official Yolongi vessel."

"Yes, and you've stated that the vessel that attacked you was also an official Yolongi vessel. You can't both be in the right and I need to clearly establish which one is."

The Ambassador grumbled a little, then held out his left hand.

"Would you remove the data ring, please?" Lidden said as he produced a viewpad from a side pocket of his tunic.

"I can't. When a Yolongi official is issued his identity ring, a small microchip is embedded in the flesh beneath the ring. Once the ring is activated, if it moves more than half a finger length from the chip, the action causes a message to be transmitted if the wearer is aboard— or within a prescribed distance from— a Yolongi diplomatic vessel. The ring then powers down and can never be re-activated."

"Then would you touch your ring to the edge of this viewpad, please?" Lidden said as he extended it towards the Ambassador.

The viewpad issued a subdued chiming noise after a couple of seconds and Lidden pulled the viewpad back to stare at the display.

"Thank you, Ambassador. Your credentials have been confirmed. I apologize for any misunderstanding, but I was only following regulations. If I failed to ask, I could be charged with dereliction of duty and removed from command of my ship."

The Ambassador smiled. "Well, we wouldn't want that to happen. We do appreciate your rushing to assist us when we needed help."

"It's our duty to assist all vessels requesting help, regardless of nationality."

"Well, now that we have that out of the way, would you care for some refreshments while we talk?"

"Thank you, sir. That would be appreciated."

"Then come have a seat at the table and food will be brought in."

"Thank you."

"Lieutenant, would you care to remove your helmet now so you can enjoy some rare delicacies?"

"Lieutenant Marcola is required by regulation to keep her armor on at all times while aboard any vessel other than the *Perry*," Lidden said.

"But surely now that our identity has proven you're on a diplomatic vessel, that can be relaxed."

"I'm sorry, sir. It's a regulation and there is no exemption."

"Pity," the Ambassador said as he took his seat.

Lidden sat down across from the Ambassador and next to the Captain as the Ambassador clapped his hands twice and nodded towards the two guards at the door, one of whom then spoke quietly into a tiny transmitter on the back of his hand. Sydnee stood behind Lidden's chair and to the left.

"I realize it's still early, Captain," Lidden said, but have your engineers established a rough estimate of the time required to complete your repairs?"

"Right now, they're estimating six GST days. Of course that could go up or down slightly."

"Of course. Can you give us the course of the destroyer after it broke off the attack?"

"Yes, we watched it on the DeTect screens until it got out of range. Naturally, it wasn't transmitting an AutoTect signal. My tac officer will give your bridge the course information."

"Thank you. Once your repairs are complete, we'll have to see if we can locate it."

"And then?"

"If we find them, we'll attempt to take them into custody and send them to a justice court location."

"You must turn them over to us, Captain," the Ambassador said. "They are Yolongi citizens."

"Who committed a crime in Galactic Alliance space," Lidden said.

"That crime was against this ship. I won't press charges for that. We want them for stealing a Clidepp Empire warship and impersonating Clidepp military personnel."

"Their crime of attempting to hijack a ship in GA space became part of the official record when you called for help, Ambassador. It doesn't require that you press charges. In any event, I must follow regulations. If we find them and take them prisoner, our duty is clear. I'm sure the Galactic Alliance court system will consider your request for extradition according to the treaties that are currently in place."

"What of the ship?" the Ambassador asked.

"It will be returned to the rightful owners, if they want it."

"Of course we'll want it. Why wouldn't we?"

"There may not be much left if they don't surrender peacefully."

"Oh."

"Exactly."

The door opened and a small parade of six servants entered with trays. Unusually, all of the servants were Terran females. They placed their trays on a side table and began serving the three men, but one couldn't stop staring at Sydnee and Lidden.

After the food and drink was served, the women turned to leave, but one raced to Lidden and grabbed his arm saying, "Help me, please. You're Space Command. My name is Carla Taft. I was captured by Raiders twenty years ago when they seized our ship, the *Siren of Seren*. They sold me to this Yolongi. He has eighteen of us as slaves. Please help us."

The Ambassador and Captain Surrosso had jumped to their feet as the woman grabbed Lidden's arm.

A guard, who had raced from his position by the door as soon as the woman started shouting, dragged her away, but she broke free of his grasp as they reached the door and ran towards Lidden again while the other women ran to a corner of the room and cowered in fear.

The woman who had sought help from Lidden suddenly screamed and fell to the floor in pain before she could reach his side. The material near the neck of her dress was brushed aside as she writhed on the deck and a collar like the ones the Raiders used to control their prisoners was plainly visible. Sydnee noticed that the guard by the door was aiming a small blue controller at the woman. She wasn't wearing the other bracelets Raiders usually place on their prisoners, but the neck collar was enough to control anyone. The wrist, waist, and ankle bands only prevented movement. The collar was used to *correct* bad behavior.

"Stop it," suddenly emanated loudly from the speaker on Sydnee's breastplate.

The guard nearest the woman looked up, then reached for his weapon. But Sydnee, prepared for such a response, was faster. She had unsnapped the flap on her holster when the woman grabbed Lidden, but hadn't pulled her pistol. In one quick movement now, she pushed aside the flap of the holster and pulled her handgun, then fired directly into the chest of the guard trying to pull his pistol. He went flying backward and crashed to the deck where he lay motionless. Sydnee immediately swung her pistol towards the other guard, who was by then also reaching for his weapon, and fired again. That was a slightly more difficult shot since he was about five meters away, but she hit him dead center and he crashed backwards to the deck with a thud just like the first one. The time between shots had been less than a second.

Surrosso and the Ambassador had turned towards the guards when Sydnee pulled her pistol. They were in time to see their guards crash to the deck. They believed they were next. Neither was armed, so they dropped back into their chairs and covered their heads with their arms.

"Lieutenant!" Lidden yelled.

"They were reaching for weapons, sir. I had to protect you since you're unarmed."

"Me?"

"Well— us."

The woman who had been shocked was still writhing on the floor. If the collar was of Raider manufacture, she would probably be completely incoherent for several minutes, after which she would have trouble with her basic motor skills for another five minutes.

"Ambassador Blethalla, Captain Surrosso, I apologize for the rash actions of a very young lieutenant(jg)," Lidden said.

The Ambassador and Captain slowly lowered their arms and regained their composure.

"Rash actions?" the Ambassador said, his voice increasing in volume with each syllable. "Rash actions?" he said again. "She's murdered two of my guards. If I had known you would be bringing someone so unstable, I would have arranged for a room full of guards to protect me."

"You were never in any danger, Ambassador, since you're unarmed. I'm equally sure that your guards wouldn't have been shot if they hadn't been reaching for weapons. Isn't that correct, Lieutenant?"

"Yes, sir. I was only looking to protect us from possible danger."

"Captain, I will be filing a full report on this incident. You can't come aboard my vessel, kill two of my people and expect that there will not be repercussions."

"No one has been killed, Ambassador. Lieutenant Marcola is holding a stun pistol…" Glaring at Sydnee, he said, "Which she will now holster." Turning back towards the Ambassador, he continued with, "…not a laser pistol. Your guards will awaken in a few hours and be just fine. And I can assure you that they experienced far less pain than this young woman whom one of them shocked."

The Ambassador looked down at the three crumpled people on the deck as Captain Surrosso walked to one of the guards and felt for a pulse, then checked the other.

"Both have strong pulses, Ambassador, and there are no entry wounds."

Looking back at Lidden, the Ambassador said, "It doesn't matter. You attacked two of my guards."

"The Lieutenant used non-lethal force to protect our lives, which she believed were at risk. I'm not happy that she was driven to take that measure by your guards, but I'll defend her actions to the end. I think you have other issues to worry about, Ambassador."

"What do you mean?"

"We've heard for years that Yolongi officials were keeping Terran slaves, but your government has always denied it and we've never had any proof. Now I've seen it with my own eyes."

Looking towards the five women cowering in the corner, the Ambassador yelled, "You women, get out of here, and take this one with you."

"Captain," Sydnee said, "We have to free these slaves. This is Galactic Alliance space. Slavery is illegal."

"Outside this ship, it's Galactic Alliance space, Lieutenant. Inside the ship, it's Yolongi space. This is a diplomatic vessel, and since the Ambassador has presented his credentials, there's nothing I can do."

Sydney watched as the five women tenderly picked up the one who had been shocked. She was mumbling incoherently and drool was hanging from her mouth as they gently cradled her in their arms and carried her out. It was a good thing Sydnee hadn't brought her laser pistol because right then she had an overwhelming desire to see what color the insides of a Yolongi Ambassador might be.

The Ambassador smiled smugly. "Quite right, Captain. Now if you'll leave quietly, I think we can forget all about this little— incident. No one was hurt after all. As you say, my guards will be fine in a few hours."

"Yes, I think it's best that we leave, Ambassador," Lidden said.

The slaves were nowhere to be seen when the two Space Command officers left the room. Lidden lead the way to the shuttle bay with Sydnee following. Surrosso trailed along in case they lost their way or took a detour.

As they entered the flight bay, Surrosso said, "I'm sorry for the incident in the salon, Captain. We do appreciate your coming to assist us. I'll see that my tac officer sends you the information about the rebel-commanded spaceship."

"Thank you, Captain. I too regret the incident. Let us hope that future encounters will be less stressful."

Sydnee couldn't believe it when Lidden actually extended his hand in friendship and it was accepted by Surrosso. She turned away without a word and walked to the shuttle, still guarded by the Marine contingent. She didn't bother to pre-flight the craft since no one had been able to get at it while it was surrounded by four full squads, and she was anxious to leave.

Sydnee stowed her helmet and weapons in her locker and plopped into the pilot's chair to run through the takeoff checklist.

Kennedy came in just as she was finishing up and sat down without a word. He looked a little nervous and avoided eye contact with Sydnee. She was still upset and glad that he wasn't looking for conversation.

The shuttle received clearance to move to the temporary airlock area by the bay's controller, and after verifying that the small vessel was sealed, Sydnee started up the oh-gee engine and directed the ship towards the hatch.

Within minutes, the shuttle was outbound for the *Perry*. Kennedy never said a word the whole trip.

Chapter Eight
~ Jan. 30th, 2285 ~

As Sydney shut down the power aboard the *Perry*, Kennedy looked at her and said, "Good job, Syd."

It was the first time he had used her given name, and she was taken completely by surprise.

"Um, thanks. But it was just a routine flight."

"I don't mean that. I mean what you did aboard the dip ship— trying to protect and free those Terran women. Well done."

"Um, how do you know about that?"

"The Captain filed a quick report with the watch officer before we left the bay. He said in his report that he feared the Yolongi might want to ensure that no one learned they were keeping Terran slaves, so he made sure to report all the facts before we came under their guns. If they had decided to fire on us, we wouldn't have stood a chance in this shuttle. I've never wished harder for an uncomfortable seat in a MAT. At least we wouldn't have had to worry about the lightweight laser arrays they have mounted on the hull."

"Perhaps they decided they had gotten lucky with the Clidepp destroyer and that they might not come out so well with an SC destroyer, even if it is only the *Perry*," Sydnee offered.

"Maybe. But still, well done."

Kennedy jumped up and left the flight deck while Sydnee was still shutting everything down. She retrieved her weapons and helmet from the storage locker, then pushed the stun pistol into the holder/recharger unit in the flight deck locker where it belonged before shoving her laser pistol into her holster. She was glad she'd spoken to Weems before the flight. His words had convinced her to swap the stun pistol for her laser pistol before she left the flight deck of the shuttle. It was the non-lethality of the weapon which had allowed her to draw and fire without seriously worrying about the consequences. If she'd only had a laser pistol, she might have hesitated. She and the Captain might very well be dead right now if she hesitated and the guards didn't.

As Sydnee walked down the shuttle ramp, a squad of Marines blocked her path.

"Lieutenant," the company sergeant said, "we'd be honored if you'd accept the four-four-three's helmet icon. The way you took out the two guards torturing the Terran women shows what you're made of."

When Kennedy had mentioned the incident, she'd supposed he had overheard a private communication from Lidden to the *Perry* while they were still outside the shuttle, but now she realized that Lidden must have sent the report while in the shuttle cabin. Since Lidden wasn't wearing a helmet, it meant that every Marine on board had also heard.

"The honor is mine, Sergeant," she said as she accepted the data wafer. "I'll upload it as soon as I reach my quarters. Thank you."

"Oo-rah," the squad said loudly in one voice, then turned and left the bay.

After Sydnee removed her armor, she added the contents of the data wafer to the helmet's memory where several different images of her face were already stored. During inspections, the front of her helmet displayed the facial image she felt was most appropriate for the particular encounter, and it could be changed in an instant. As soon as the new image was loaded, she activated it to see how it looked.

The four-four-three's icon was the most evil-looking human skull Sydnee had ever seen. And the image wasn't fixed; it was an animated 3D vid. Steam rose from the top of the skull, and the eye sockets glowed brightly with a luminescent green color. Every couple of seconds, small flames emanated from the rhinal openings to simulate exhaling while the skull appeared to laugh maniacally. This icon wasn't for ordinary inspections. The Marines usually left their helmet fronts blank for those. This was a game mask for when the unit went into battle. Its presentation showed that she had been officially accepted as one of the team rather than simply being viewed as just another stick jockey. The presentation represented a great honor and she was appropriately pleased for having received it.

Sydnee had just started to peel off the padded suit she wore under the armor when she received a call via her CT.

"Marcola," she said after touching her ring.

"Lieutenant," she heard the fourth officer say in his capacity as acting first watch officer, "report to the Captain's briefing room on the double."

"Understood. Marcola out."

Sydnee peeled off the rest of the padded suit and pulled on her uniform. She took a few seconds to make sure she was presentable enough for a visit to see the Captain and then hurried to the bridge.

The briefing room door opened when she arrived without her even having to request admittance. It was not a good sign. Sydnee walked to the Captain's desk and braced to attention.

"Lieutenant(jg) Marcola reporting to the Captain, as ordered," she said.

Lidden looked up from his com screen and stood up. He came out from behind the desk and stood on Sydnee's right side.

"Lieutenant," he said loudly into her right ear, "you're lucky."

Sydnee didn't reply.

"You're lucky because if there was a worse place to land than this one, you'd already be on your way there."

Sydnee remained quiet but couldn't help thinking that already being posted to the worst ship in the fleet wasn't much of a consolation.

The Captain continued, this time even louder. "You were privileged to attend a meeting with an ambassador from a foreign nation, and what do you do? You shoot the Ambassador's bodyguards and make him and the Captain of the ship believe they're next. I've never been so ashamed of the actions of any officer in my command. I've filed a full report on the incident. Once SHQ reviews it, you might find yourself sitting dirt-side on some obscure moon for the rest of your time in Space Command. In any event, it's unlikely you'll ever get either promoted or posted to any ship other than the *Perry*. That's all, Lieutenant. Dismissed."

Sydnee saluted, turned on her left heel, and left the office. She didn't make eye contact with anyone on the bridge and went straight to her quarters. It was likely that the entire crew already knew the story and the bridge crew probably deduced that she had just been reamed out by the Captain. Within a few hours, everyone aboard would know.

Once back in her quarters, she stripped down to her underwear and climbed into her rack. She felt that perhaps sleep would help take the edge off what had just transpired.

* * *

Sydnee awoke two hours before her watch. She didn't feel any better than when she had gone to sleep, but she got up, showered, and walked to the officers' mess to get a meal before it was time to go on duty.

After selecting her food from the available assortment, Sydnee looked for a free table where she could eat alone. There were none to be had, but the bulkhead-mounted counter with several stools was empty, so she headed for that.

"Lieutenant, take a load off," a voice said as she passed a table occupied by one Marine officer. Sydnee looked down and saw Marine First Lieutenant Kelly MacDonald gesturing to the chair across from where she was sitting. Sydnee hesitated for a second, then sat down.

"Bad day, eh?" MacDonald said as Sydnee began eating.

"You could say that."

"I hear the Captain probably leveled both barrels."

"Yeah," Sydnee said with a grimace. "And then reloaded for another round."

"Don't let it bother you. He does that to everyone occasionally. It doesn't mean too much. He's trying to keep us on the straight and narrow."

"It might mean more this time. He told me that after SHQ reads his report I might wind up dirt-side, permanently, for shooting the two guards."

"As I heard it, they deserved it."

"Yeah, they did, but you're not supposed to give it to them because they were on a diplomatic yacht."

"I would have made sure the bastards never got up again," MacDonald said. "What's the Captain going to do about the Raider slaves?"

"He says there's nothing he can do. Inside the dip ship is considered Clidepp Empire space."

"It ain't right."

"No, it isn't. I wish Admiral Carver were here. She'd know what to do."

"Sounds like you've met her."

"Not personally. She gave a speech at NHSA when I was a senior."

"Wish I'd been there. She talked at SHSA also, but I had already graduated the previous year and was at the Marine Officer Institute."

"I have a recording of the NHSA speech on a data wafer," Sydnee said. "You're welcome to come view it sometime."

"Thanks. I will. So what are we going to do about the slaves?"

"What can we do?"

"I heard there were six of them."

"The woman who asked the Captain for help and got zapped by one of the guards said the Ambassador has eighteen female slaves."

"The pig."

"Yeah, but he's a diplomat so he's untouchable."

"The women aren't diplomats. They're not untouchable."

"But they're stuck inside what's defined as Clidepp space," Sydnee said.

"If we could get them to abandon ship, they'd be back in GA space."

"Yeah, but how do you get the Yolongi to abandon ship without firing on them and starting a war?"

"It might be worth it to get all our people back."

"There must be a way *without* starting a war."

"If you find one, I guarantee you won't have to look far for support. Every Marine on this ship will back your play."

"Thanks. I don't have a clue right now. But we have five days to come up with something. That's the minimum time they think they'll need to complete their repairs."

"Even if they can't fix their temporal drive generator, they won't leave their ship. They'll simply wait for another Clidepp ship to come get them."

"It's too bad the rebels didn't damage the ship just enough to force them into life pods. If we picked them up and brought them into the *Perry*, they'd be in GA space."

"Yeah."

"Well, I'd better get up to the bridge. Third watch will be starting soon. Goodnight, Lieutenant."

"It's Kel. Or Mac if you prefer."

Sydnee smiled. "Thanks, Kel. I'm Syd."

"Syd, you should come down to the Combat Range sometime."

"That's 'Marines Only,' isn't it?"

"Usually, but certain Spaccs have been welcomed there at times. You have a standing invite anytime you want to see how *we* train."

"Thanks, Kel. I will."

"Have a better one, Syd."

The third watch was quiet. Talk was subdued, no doubt because of Sydnee's censure by the Captain. In all likelihood, everyone supported her actions, but they couldn't say that on the bridge without it becoming part of the official bridge log record, so everyone remained mum on the subject.

Sydnee, as navigator, had nothing to do as the *Perry* simply stood guard over the damaged Clidepp ship in case the rebels came back. Usually she was assigned to a tac station once the ship came to a halt unless she was required to act as shuttle pilot, but perhaps Lidden felt she might lose control and fire on the dip ship if she was seated at a weapons console.

The yacht was brightly illuminated while work parties of engineers in EVA suits toiled to repair the generator. Since there was no nearby sun, the lights would remain on twenty-four hours a day GST until the work was complete. It made the ship an easy focus for Sydnee's attention on the huge monitor at the front of the bridge. Try as she might to develop a strategy for freeing the Terran women slaves, she continued to come up dry.

*   *   *

Two days following the incident on the *Darrapralis*, Kelly MacDonald contacted Sydnee just after she came off watch.

"Hi Syd, the range is currently available if you want to give it a go."

"I'd love to."

"Great. Slip into your armor and come on down. I'll be waiting for you."

Sydnee hurried to her quarters and donned her personal body armor before heading down to deck two, frame section twelve. She didn't bring any of her weapons.

The sign on the door said 'Marine Personnel ONLY,' but Sydnee stepped up to the door without seeking additional authorization. As the door slid open, she saw Kelly sitting on a wide padded bench just inside the room, talking to another Marine officer.

"Hi, Syd," Kelly said. "Come on in. Meet Lieutenant Aguilo. He functions as our range officer down here."

Aguilo extended his hand and said, "Martin."

Syd took the hand, smiled, and said, "Syd."

"Welcome Syd. We have the range set up for 'recruit level.'"

"Is that the lowest level?"

"Well, actually we have one lower, but we reserve that for visiting flag officers."

"Ever have one use it?"

"No, we don't see many flag officers on the *Perry*. But if we ever do get one, he or she is guaranteed to get a fantastic score on our range."

Sydnee smiled and nodded. "What's the usual average score for recruits?"

"First timers typically score in the one-hundred point range."

"Out of a possible…?"

"One thousand. It's just the newness of it all. First timers don't know what to expect and are slower to react until they get a few games under their belt and know what to look for."

"Here's your pistol, Syd," Kelly said as she held out a laser pistol.

As Sydnee took the weapon, she said, "You use live pistols?"

"It's a real pistol that's been modified. The laser pulse looks real, but it wouldn't cut through a sheet of paper. The internal circuitry has been modified to make it completely harmless. There's a red 'X' under the bottom of the grip so we can ensure someone isn't using a real pistol by mistake. Of course, if they did, alarms would sound from ten different points on the range. Come on, I'll show you the course."

Kelly led the way to an area that looked large enough to house a dozen full-sized shuttles. It was divided into two separate combat courses. The first resembled a bombed out town and the other resembled two acres of jungle. Some sort of polymer-ceramic molding process had been used to fashion buildings, trees, boulders, terrain formations, and even the enemy combatant dummies.

Noticing the expression on Sydnee's face, Kelly said, "The ship's engineers helped us remove a number of bulk-heads between old storage holds that weren't being used and reinforce the frame sections so they were as strong as before. I'll put the courses into 'exhibit' mode and we can do a walk-through."

Once in exhibit mode, all targets appeared in the open as someone approached their location. In the two-acre town, assailants appeared on rooftops, in windows, behind vehicles, and could even pop up from sewer openings. In the jungle course, they appeared from behind trees, up in the trees, from behind fallen logs or boulders, from a watery swamp pit, and even from camouflaged holes dug in the ground.

"For each hit, you get points. If you hit a vital area, you get the max points and the target drops. It won't appear again. If you don't hit a vital area, it'll drop and may or may not pop up again. You get fewer points for the non-vital hits based on the place where the beam strikes. Targets move around, so you can't depend on them appearing where you see them now. And this course differs from the old-style courses in one important way. Here, the targets shoot back."

"With real weapons?" Sydnee asked jokingly.

"Of course not," Kelly said with a chuckle. "We'd lose far too many recruits if it was *that* realistic. Their lasers do emit a beam, but it's as non-lethal as the one from your weapon. There are cameras mounted all over the course, and a computer scores any hits the targets make on your armor according to the location of the hit. The weapon is fixed in the target so the entire target has to change position to fire unless it's waiting for you to move into its sights, so you have a good chance to avoid being struck if you notice the movement or see it before it fires. Each time the target hits you, you lose points."

"So you can actually have a negative score?"

"Sure, if you're slow or a lousy shot. I don't think you're either."

"Thanks."

"If you think you're ready, we'll return to the starting line and see how you do as a first timer. Of course, you have a slight edge over new recruits."

"Do I? What is it?"

"You're familiar with wearing your armor from having been on a number of interdiction runs."

"That's true. At first I felt really clunky. But now, I don't even think about it. How come you don't use holographic projections for the enemy combatants?"

"Mainly because the projectors can give away the location. Also, the bodies of holographic images always have that sort of translucent, vapory look. We prefer the solid appearance, even if the dummy's mobility is more limited. It seems much more lifelike and realistic."

"Okay, that makes sense."

"Ready to start?"

"I'm set. Oh, wait! How much time do I have to complete the course?"

"As much as you want— up to an hour. There's a points penalty for going too slow, and it gives your enemies more time to arrange ambushes. Enemies that you only wound can move ahead to meet you again at a different place. That's all controlled by the computers based on established algorithms. But if you go too fast, you might take more hits because of rushing. It's just something you have to work out for yourself."

Kelly walked to a console table and began entering some parameters for the contest as Sydnee looked on. "The time of day is automatically set to noon for this level of play." Lightly pressing a large green button, she said, "Okay, the clock will begin as soon as you move into the range, Syd. Have at it."

Sydnee smiled and pulled on her helmet. As soon as it self-sealed to her body armor, she moved forward into the bombed-out town. She hadn't gone more than five steps when a gunman popped up on the roof of a two-story building. She caught the movement with her peripheral vision and had a bead on him before he could fire. When she fired, he either dropped or fell backwards out of sight. Sydnee was fairly confident that it was the latter. She felt really good about her first 'kill,' but things went downhill a bit fast after that. It always seemed like there were two or more gunmen jumping up at the same instant and she was kept busy firing and dodging fire. Often one gunman would hit her while she was dispatching the other.

The course ended back where it started. Kelly was at the console, waiting for Sydnee.

"Well, how did it go?" Kelly asked.

"You tell me."

"I mean, did you have fun?"

"Um, yeah, it was exciting. And challenging."

"You haven't seen anything yet. You were only getting the recruit-level combat."

"How much worse can it get?"

"You'll see."

"Come on. Give me a clue."

"Okay. There are tiny holes in the deck that eject streams of dirt while buried speakers provide noise and lights flash to simulate explosions. It gets pretty intense when you're trying to watch for assailants."

"Wow. Um, how bad was my score?"

"Your score was great. At three hundred forty-six, it's way above the average first-timer. Have you ever used a combat range before?"

"No, not a combat range. But I used to spend a lot of time on the firing ranges at NHSA and the WCI. The targets were always stationary, but I practiced my marksmanship religiously. One of my instructors at the Academy was a devotee of the quick-draw tactics and had won several competitions. He taught me everything I know, such as how to shoot from the hip. Most Space Command personnel raise the weapon to eye level before firing, but that wastes a lot of time."

"So *that's* how you beat those guards to the draw?"

"I'm sure it helped. The standard issue flap holster of the uniform makes it difficult. I prefer just a narrow strip that snaps down to hold the pistol in the holster, then moves out of the way when you need to draw your weapon quickly."

"But you managed it anyway."

"I guess I was motivated. You should have seen that poor woman and the way she was writhing in pain on the floor."

"I wish I *had* been there— with a real laser pistol. Those guards would never have attacked an innocent again."

"No you don't. It would mean you never get off the *Perry*. Or you might wind up dirt-side like me."

"Trust me. It would have been worth it."

Chapter Nine
~ Feb. 1ˢᵗ, 2285 ~

"The report from the Captain of the *Perry* is next," Admiral Moore said to the other admirals sitting around the large table in Admiralty Hall. "As far as I know, the Clidepp Empire hasn't filed a complaint with the GA Council. At least not yet."

"Nor will they, I believe." Admiral Bradlee said. "The Clidepp Empire has always denied that any of their citizens have purchased slaves from the Raiders. Now we learn firsthand that not only have those denials been false, but that at least one high-ranking member of the government has owned Terran slaves for decades. Perhaps the Ambassador felt that Captain Lidden would fail to report the shooting incident to avoid possible censure of his command. Lidden has always been a by-the-book officer, so he would report it even if he had been personally responsible."

"I wish we had a vid of the episode," Admiral Plimley said. "It's too bad it took place on the Clidepp ship instead of inside a conference room on one of our ships."

"The report is pretty complete," Admiral Moore said, "but a log vid from a perspective that allows us to see all participants to this event would ensure that we are basing our decision on precise information. However, we do have the feed from the helmet cam of the young officer involved in the shooting incident. After the Terran slaves carried food and beverages to the meeting, one broke ranks and appealed to Captain Lidden as a Space Command officer to help her regain her freedom. The guards immediately punished the woman for speaking out by shocking her through the Raider detention collar that was locked around her neck. The lieutenant accompanying the Captain shouted for them to stop their torture. The Ambassador's guards took the shout as a hostile act and started to draw their weapons. The lieutenant was faster. She drew her pistol and dropped them both before they could fire."

"Why was a junior Marine officer even in a meeting with an ambassador and a ship's captain?" Admiral Woo asked.

"Lieutenant Marcola is a Space Command line officer. Her rank is actually lieutenant(jg). She piloted the shuttle that brought the *Perry's* people to the *Darrapralis*. Let's play the helmet cam vid," Admiral Moore said as he nodded to his clerk.

"Oh no, another Jenetta Carver," Admiral Hubera moaned as the vid ended.

"What's that, Donald?" Admiral Ahmed asked.

"Don't you remember, Raihana?" Hubera said. "Carver drew a pistol and shot a freighter captain and his XO, then left both of them to die on Raider-One."

"Now hold on," Admiral Hillaire said. "If you're going to bring up ancient history, at least get your facts straight. Admiral Carver did not leave the freighter captain and his XO to die on Raider-One."

"It's okay, Arnold," Admiral Ahmed said. "I remember the incident well and had already discounted Donald's peculiar twist on the story before you spoke up. I simply didn't make the connection when he brought it up."

"It's not my 'peculiar twist.' It's the truth."

"Only as you see it," Admiral Hillaire said.

"Ladies and Gentlemen," Admiral Moore said, "Can we please get back to the issue at hand?"

"I think the helmet cam feed is detailed enough for us to understand the situation fully," Admiral Platt said.

"I don't think the young officer should be censured for telling the guards to stop torturing a Terran woman who had been illegally enslaved," Admiral Bradlee said. "Nor do I feel she was out of line for shooting them in defense of herself and her Captain. I'm just glad she didn't have a laser pistol because then we couldn't let this issue slide. The bigger issue here is that the slavery of Terrans is being condoned by a government with whom we've had diplomatic relations for decades. They've obviously been lying for that entire time. And now we're facing a time when they will turn to us for increased support if the insurgency there continues to grow. The GA council must decide if we will support the Clidepp Empire, disassociate ourselves from relations with them, or throw our support behind the rebels."

"As you say, Roger, that is a decision for the GA Council and Senate. Our role is only to notify them of this new information regarding a violation of one of our basic tenets. Slavery in the Uthlaro Dominion has been one thing. They're located thousands of light-years from here. Strictly in terms of distance, the Clidepp Empire is our closest neighbor."

"I agree that the young officer should not be punished," Admiral Platt said. "Were I there, I doubt that I could have held my tongue while a defenseless woman was being tortured in front of me. That the woman is a slave in a nation who claims they're opposed to slavery makes it all the worse. The officer was also perfectly justified in defending herself and her Captain when the guards took threatening actions. I'm sure both guards were fine after their short nap. We have no way of knowing what weapons they were attempting to use, so stunning them was the perfect defense."

"Do we have a motion?" Admiral Moore asked.

"I move that in the matter of the Clidepp Ambassador's two guards being stunned by a young officer from the *Perry*, extenuating circumstances were adequate to fully justify the action," Admiral Platt said. "I further move that no censure is warranted. Finally, I move that the GA Council be immediately notified that we now have proof that the Clidepp Empire has been condoning the slavery of GA citizens for decades."

"All in favor?" Admiral Moore said. After a quick glance around the table, he added, "let the record show that the motion has carried unanimously. Now, onto the next matter..."

* * *

"Lieutenant(jg) Sydnee Marcola reporting to the Captain as ordered," Sydnee said as she braced to attention in front of his desk.

Lidden looked up from his com screen and said, "I've just received a response to my report about the incident aboard the *Darrapralis.*"

Sydnee tensed even more. *This is it*, she thought.

"SHQ has informed me that no action will be taken against you since the Clidepp Empire has not filed a complaint. Perhaps Ambassador Blethalla was embarrassed that you were able to draw and fire faster than his two guards. In any event, you've avoided a dirt-side posting for the time being. Let this be a lesson to you, Marcola. Keep a tighter rein on that temper."

"But sir, they were reaching for their weapons."

"There's no proof that they would have used them."

"I didn't feel it was worth taking the chance, sir, especially not after we'd just learned they have Terran slaves aboard."

"Did you come to that conclusion before or after your actions?"

"Before, sir."

Lidden looked at her thoughtfully. He knew she was bright but wondered if she had really thought of that *rationalization* beforehand. Perhaps she had. "That's all, Marcola, dismissed."

Sydnee saluted, turned on her left heel, and left the office. After the doors closed, she stopped, allowed herself to take a deep breath, and then release it as the tension also drained from her body. As bad as it was being on the *Perry*, it was still a hundred times better than being posted on a remote planet or moon where she might never get a chance to fly.

It was midday, so she had twelve hours before her watch. Since she preferred to sleep during second watch in order to be fresh when she reported for duty, she headed down to the flight simulator room with the intent of spending several hours forgetting about the threat of being forever stuck dirt-side.

The room contained four flight simulators. Two units were devoted to Space Command ships and two were for Marine ships. Her certifications for all shuttle types on the *Perry* were up to date, so she headed towards one of the two Marine simulators. There was no one in the control room, but an operator was only required during certification testing. Her MAT certs were current, so it was time to play. She selected 'FA-SF4 Marine Fighter' and the console area reconfigured to resemble the appropriate cockpit. She climbed in and strapped herself down, then ran through the checklist and started the oh-gee engine to maneuver the ship for launch position. Within minutes, she was cruising between mountain peaks, with an occasional dip to treetop level, and laughing with glee at the realistic sensations offered by the flight simulators.

*   *   *

As Sydnee's watch began at midnight GST, she sat down at the navigator's console and watched the activity on the *Darrapralis*. An image of the diplomatic yacht had appeared on the large viewscreen at the front of the bridge ever since the *Perry* had first arrived on the scene. Dozens of EVA-suited engineers could be seen on the hull around the clock as they worked to repair the FTL drive. Sydnee couldn't help but wonder if any of them were slaves. The Raiders hadn't *only* enslaved women. In fact, the percentage of males to females missing after a believed Raider attack in Region One was about four to one.

For days, Sydnee had racked her brain for a way to save the slaves aboard the *Darrapralis* before it completed its repairs and continued its journey home, but short of a clandestine assault on the ship, she hadn't been able to think of a thing. And any assault on the ship would be met with resistance, so the attack would be tantamount to declaring war on the Clidepp Empire.

When Sydnee's watch duties ended at 0800, she still hadn't come up with an idea for saving the slaves and she headed for the officers' mess to have breakfast while still working on a solution.

"This chair taken?" Sydnee heard through her reverie as she pushed her scrambled eggs around on her plate. She looked up to see Marine First Lieutenant Kelly MacDonald gesturing towards the chair.

"Hi, Kel. No, sit down. I was thinking."

"Yeah, I noticed that while I was in line for chow. Must be *some* problem."

Sydnee lowered her voice when she said, "Yeah. It's the same one as usual. Namely, how can we rescue the slaves on the *Darrapralis* before it leaves for the Clidepp Empire?"

MacDonald likewise lowered her voice to keep it from being heard at other tables. "Ah, yeah. We've spent a lot of time down in Marine country talking about that one. So far, all we can come up with is a full assault to take over the ship."

"Yeah, but that won't fly."

"Why not? We know they've got Terran slaves on board. There must be something in the interdiction law books that allows it."

"There're plenty of laws that allow us to take a ship where we know they have slaves. The trouble is that it all takes second place to the laws regarding diplomatic rights. I hate it, but the Captain is right."

"So, as long as the slaves are aboard that ship, the laws of the Clidepp Empire apply to them, and our laws mean nothing?"

"That's about the size of it. Hey, that's it, Kel."

"What's it?"

"That might be the answer. We've been working this from the wrong angle."

"I don't follow you."

"I've been trying to remember everything I've learned about Galactic Law, Interdiction Law, and Diplomatic Law, but I've never looked at Clidepp Law."

"How would that help?"

"I don't know yet. The Clidepp Empire has always publicly stated that there's no slavery there, but is that part of their law, or not? What I'm thinking is that if the Ambassador has consistently violated Clidepp Empire law for twenty or thirty years, the law may automatically strip his status from him. If he's not legally an Ambassador, then he can't claim diplomatic status."

"But that only covers him. The *Darrapralis* is still a dip ship."

"Is it? Is it an official Clidepp vessel, or is it a private yacht belonging to the Ambassador and listed as a diplomatic ship simply because he's on board?"

"God, I wish we had a JAG officer on board."

"Yeah, one who was familiar with Clidepp Empire law. There's another thing that's been on my mind."

"What?"

"I've been observing the engineers working on the dip ship while I've been on watch. Heck, there's nothing else to do. So anyway, I was wondering if any of them are slaves. The Raiders took a lot more male spacers than females."

"But it's the same situation. We can't rescue them either."

"Maybe, maybe not. The Captain said the space inside the Clidepp ship must be considered Clidepp Empire space, even though the space outside the ship is GA space. When those engineers come out to work— they're in GA space."

"Wow, I never thought of that. Then we could legally board that ship as long as we remain outside?"

"It sounds right, but I'm not sure. On a planet in GA space, the planet's authority extends to one hundred kilometers above the mean surface. After that, GA law takes effect. So the question is, how far from the mean hull surface does dip law extend, if at all? If it ends at the outer plates, can we go over there and administer GA law?"

"I like it. I can have two companies of volunteers ready in an hour."

"Um, I don't think we should be too hasty. We'd better check with Milty at least. Maybe he knows about the law regarding diplomatic coverage outside the ship. And we really should have the Captain make the decision."

MacDonald's voice wasn't much higher than a whisper when she said, "Syd, I like the Captain, but I can tell you from experience that when it comes to grey areas, he stops short of anything that isn't black and white. If you tell Milty, he'll have to tell Commander Bryant, and Ben will tell the Captain."

Sydnee's voice was so low by now that lip reading was practically required to figure out what she was saying. "I don't see where we have any choice, Kel. We can't do this alone, even if we have the entire crew behind us. We might even be charged with mutiny."

"Mutiny? We're not talking about taking control of the *Perry*. We're talking about freeing slaves. Terrans who were taken prisoner by Raiders and sold to those damn Yolongi liars. Our people have been suffering for decades. We need to free them. Now, not twenty years from now."

"Okay, but we have to do this by the numbers. First, we need to see if we can find anything in Clidepp law concerning slavery. Do you have any really sharp people who can look into that?"

"I might have a few officers I can ask, including Kennedy."

"Kennedy?"

"I know he's pretty stiff at times, but he's damn sharp with the law— at least GA interdiction law. And I know he's fascinated by you."

"Me? I've known him for months and he used my given name for the first time just this week."

"Did you ask him to use your given name?"

"Um, no."

"It's that stiffness again."

"The first time we met he told me that he would call me Lieutenant and that I should only call him Lieutenant. I don't even know his first name."

"It's Everett, but everyone calls him Rett. He's a pretty good sort once you get to know him. What else?"

"Else? Nothing else. He just always acts so— distant."

"No, I mean about the dip ship."

"Oh. The rest will hinge on what we learn from studying Clidepp law. If there's no legal avenue for us, then we'll have to see if we can get support from above for a raid on the *exterior* of the Clidepp ship at a time when they have the most people outside. If any are slaves, we'll offer them sanctuary aboard the *Perry*. If there are Yolongi with them, it might turn into a shooting incident, so we have to know how solid our ground is, figuratively speaking."

"Sounds like a plan." MacDonald pushed the final forkful of scrambled eggs into her mouth, chewed quickly and swallowed. "I'll get started on my end." With that, she stood, raised her voice to a normal speaking level, and said, "Okay, Syd. I'll see you later."

"Right, Kel."

* * *

"Open," Lieutenant Mark Milton said when the computer informed him that Lt(jg) Sydnee Marcola was at the door. "Hi Syd," he said as the door opened. "Come on in. What's up?"

"Hi Milty. If you have a few minutes, I'd like to talk with you about a problem."

"Sure, Syd, but if it's about the shooting incident, I can't help you much."

"No, it's not that. The Captain informed me yesterday that I was cleared by SHQ. No further action is being considered."

"Really? Wonderful. I hadn't heard. I couldn't say anything before, but I'm pretty sure that every crewmember on this ship was behind you."

"Um, yeah. That's sort of what I want to talk with you about."

"The slavery issue?"

"Yeah."

"Well, that may be another issue I can't say anything about."

"Will you hear me out, at least?"

"Sure, Syd. Have a seat," he said, pointing to one of the chairs in his small sitting room. Although just a lieutenant, his position as second officer gave him use of the quarters normally occupied by a Lieutenant Commander. On a new ship, the quarters would be substantially larger, but even on the *Perry* it was a significant upgrade from the usual lieutenant quarters.

"Um, Milty, I don't know where to begin."

"Then begin at the beginning."

"No, that's too far back. Um, let me start with our watch last night. I spent a lot of time watching the activity on the *Darrapralis* most of the night."

"We all did."

"Yeah, but I wasn't just watching, I was trying to think of a way to help the Terran slaves."

"As the Captain told you, there's nothing we can do. Inside that ship is Clidepp space. We can't interfere."

"Yeah, but what about outside?"

"Outside?"

"Yeah. How many of those people working on the exterior might be slaves the Ambassador bought from the Raiders?"

Milty got the point immediately. "So you want to rescue any slaves that might be outside the ship's Clidepp space?"

"Yeah. Exactly."

"Interesting idea, Syd."

"Yeah, but is it do-able?"

Milty took a deep breath and released it slowly while he thought. After a couple of minutes, he said, "So what is it you're asking of me?"

"Advice."

Without hesitating, Milton said, "Go to the Captain."

Syd cast her eyes downward and her face reflected the dejection she was feeling.

"Not what you wanted to hear?"

"I was hoping for advice, not just a 'take it upstairs' evasion."

"That wasn't an evasion. It's the best advice I can give. On a Space Command vessel, or really any vessel in space or at sea, the captain is the absolute authority. They earn those positions of power and trust after years of hard work and dedication to duty. All it takes is one minor lapse in judgment to lose their command or their opportunity to achieve command in the first place. Any action you're contemplating must have the approval of the Captain in advance or you'll regret it for the rest of your career."

"I would never take any action without first seeking the Captain's approval, but I want to have all my facts straight before I approach him. I hoped I could count on you for some advice." Standing up, Sydnee said, "I'm sorry I disturbed you, sir."

As she started to turn, Milton said, "Syd, wait. I'm sorry. I didn't intend to brush you off. I thought you were soliciting my help in your plan to take over the dip ship."

"My what?"

"The scuttlebutt is that you intend a hostile takeover of the dip ship and that you're lining up people to help you."

"That's not true. I'm only trying to learn what actions are possible *and* legal. If I find something, I'll bring it to the Captain for his approval before doing anything."

"I'm glad to hear that."

"I can't believe that people are thinking I'd try some overt action without the Captain's approval."

"Sit back down, Syd. After you dropped those two guards that were torturing a Terran slave, everyone aboard ship lined up behind you. The Marines are even talking about following you into a fight to recover our people from the Yolongi if their own officers won't lead them."

"I'd be proud to lead the Marines in a recovery effort, but only if the Captain approved the action first."

"What kind of advice are you looking for?"

"Where can I find out if we're on legal ground with this? Where *exactly* does the Clidepp space end and the GA space begin with relation to that ship?"

"I honestly don't know. I've never heard of a case where such precision was required. Normally, we maintain a strictly hands-off posture with respect to dip ships. I could ask Commander Bryant if you wish."

"Only if he won't immediately tell the Captain. If my idea is absurd, I'd rather the Captain didn't know I was behind it. I'm already on his shit list. He told me after the shooting that I would probably spend the rest of my career dirt-side on some obscure planet or moon."

Milton chuckled. "Only here a few months and you've already been given the dirt-side speech, eh? You're a fast worker. Most of us were here a year before we got it."

"You got it too?"

"Everybody gets it the first time they screw up. The old man seems to think it keeps us on the straight and narrow from then on. Maybe it does."

"But mine was delivered before he sent a report to SHQ."

"I didn't see the report, but I can guarantee one thing. It was a fair and unbiased description of exactly what the old man saw. He doesn't try to color them and always reserves his personal opinion unless they solicit it. You said you were cleared, right?"

"Yeah."

"So there you go."

Chapter Ten
~ Feb. 4th, 2285 ~

"Captain, how much longer will it be before your repairs are complete?" Lidden asked the com image of Captain Surrosso.

"Our engineers have encountered more difficulties than originally expected. I've asked for a revised figure, but they say they won't know for sure until they can remove more of the damaged equipment. Unfortunately, we carry only a few engineers on the ship— just the number normally required for basic maintenance."

"Space Command has too few ships in this area. We can't continue to provide protection for disabled ships indefinitely. My superiors are pressuring me to return to our interdiction activities."

"We did request that one of our destroyers come to serve as protection, but they were denied entry into GA space."

"That's understandable. At present, we believe there are two rogue Clidepp Empire destroyers operating in our space, so we will immediately engage any that we encounter. We would hate to destroy a legitimate ship and crew while believing we're attacking one controlled by rebels."

"We could establish some sort of recognition code."

"Did you have recognition codes at the facility where the ships were being refitted?"

"You can't assume that because they got one set of codes, they'll get another."

"And we can't assume they won't. Someone had to have leaked that information."

"I'm sorry, Captain, but the repairs will take as long as they take. Please don't leave us defenseless out here."

"You're hardly defenseless. You fought off the Clidepp destroyer who attempted to stop you."

"That was a lucky shot. They outgunned us twenty to one."

"Perhaps my engineers can assist your people to get you underway sooner. I'm sure I have a much larger engineering staff than you have available on that small ship."

"The Ambassador forbids any further entry into the ship by Space Command personnel."

"Are you having engineering difficulties inside?"

"Ah, no."

"Then there's no need for my people to enter your ship. I was only offering assistance with the repairs to your temporal envelope generator. Your warships will not be allowed into GA space until we've found and destroyed the two that are already here, and we can't stay here indefinitely simply because you have inadequate engineering staff to handle your problems."

"I'll have to discuss it with the Ambassador."

"Do that, and then get back to me. *Perry* out."

"*Darrapralis* out."

* * *

"Lieutenant(jg) Sydnee Marcola reporting to the Captain as ordered," Sydnee said as she braced to attention in front of Lidden's desk.

"Do you recognize that young female, Lieutenant?" Lidden asked as he pointed to the large bulkhead monitor. The image of a young girl about age nine or ten was being displayed.

Sydnee studied the image for a few seconds before saying, "She doesn't look familiar, sir."

"That's an image of Carla Taft. She was just ten when the ship on which she was a passenger was taken by Raiders."

"The woman from the *Darrapralis*, sir?"

"The very same."

"Now that I understand the age of the image, I can see the facial similarities."

"The feed from your helmet cam has enabled SCI to positively identify five of the six women we saw. They believe they know who the sixth is, but they won't release that information until they're sure."

"Does this mean we're going to free the women, sir?"

"No. At least not yet. But I do have an assignment for you. I'm offering it to you since it sprang from your idea."

"My idea?"

"You asked Lt. Milton to define where Clidepp space ends and GA space begins, relative to the hull of a spaceship. He asked Commander Bryant, and Commander Bryant asked me.

"I've offered to assist the Clidepp ship with their repairs, and they've accepted, with the provision that we not attempt to enter the ship. I'm offering you the position of shuttle pilot for that operation."

"Of course, sir. Is there anything else I should know about the mission objectives?"

"We will attempt to have the Clidepp ship send out as many people as possible to assist in the work. When that happens, we'll try to ascertain if any are Terrans, and, if so, whether they're slaves. If they are, we shall offer them their freedom. Of course, I don't expect there will be any women among them. The women seem to be used for serving duties— and possibly— other activities."

"Yes, sir."

"Your role will be to function as shuttle pilot and nothing else. You will not leave the shuttle. Is that clear?"

"Perfectly, sir."

"SCI believes that if we can produce one former slave who will testify in court to his or her captivity, we might be able to secure the freedom of the others. Right now, it's only our word against theirs."

"But we have the helmet cam images."

"They only prove that the women are there, that one was tortured, and that the one who was shocked was wearing a Raider captive collar. We couldn't see the collar until she fell to the deck because the clothing the women wore hid their necks, so we can't be sure anyone else was so outfitted. Normally, the prima facie evidence of just one collar might be enough, but if the Clidepp Diplomatic Corps offers a rebuttal, the situation could become murky. They could say that the woman was under contract, and that the contract required her to wear a collar. Yes, I know it's weak, but they could offer that as explanation, and say that the woman was simply trying to break her contract. If we manage to get one slave away from the Yolongi, one who can testify in court, then we'll have a much stronger case that the women are being held against their will."

"I understand, sir."

"Good. You'll be notified when you should report to the shuttle bay for this mission. That's all. Dismissed."

*　*　*

"We've arrived," the navigator stated as the helmsman put the warship into orbit around the second planet from the sun.

"And none too soon," Currulla wheezed. "The air in the ship is so foul I can barely breathe." Turning to the tac officer, he said, "what else have you been able to find out about this planet besides that it can sustain life?"

"It's extremely hot and humid. A number of indigenous species are deadly, so we must be careful. I've selected what I understand to be the safest landmass, but I still suggest creating a wide clearing for a campsite as soon as we land so we can see any danger coming while we wait for the pickup ship. I've downloaded what data we have available into viewpads so everyone will know what's safe to eat and what isn't. We have testing equipment, so all liquids, even the processed ones, should be checked before anyone drinks them. I've issued instructions to the crew on what equipment and supplies we should bring down. And I recommend we begin making shuttle trips as soon as possible."

"I didn't need to hear that last part. I'm ready. Let's get outta here."

* * *

Sydnee completed her scheduled time in the simulator and reluctantly shut the power down. She wished she could spend another hour but she had to get some sleep before her watch began, so she headed to her quarters.

After setting a wakeup call time that would allow her to grab some chow before going on watch, she climbed into her rack and fell into a deep sleep.

"Okay, computer, I'm awake," Sydnee said aloud, then realized it wasn't her wakeup call. She glanced at the barely discernible chronograph on the bulkhead and saw there were almost five hours before third watch would begin, so she touched the face of her SC ring and said, "Marcola."

"Lieutenant, this is the Captain. Get down to your shuttle."

"Aye, Captain. Marcola out," she said, then jumped from her bed. In seconds, she was pulling on the padding she wore under her armor, then pulling on the armor itself. She knew that orders called for her to remain on the shuttle's flight deck, but standing orders required the wearing of personal body armor when leaving on any mission, and she would have worn it on this trip regardless of standing orders.

It had been three days since the Captain had informed her of his plan, and each night she had watched Space Command engineers shuttle over to the dip ship and work with the Yolongi engineers on the repairs. She had begun to wonder if the mission had been called off. Perhaps SHQ had ordered a halt to the plan. But now it seemed as if it was a go, unless there was something else in the works.

When Sydnee arrived in the shuttle bay, she found a half-dozen people already assembling near her shuttle. Several were Space Command engineering techs wearing EVA suits, but the other half were Marines wearing EVA suits with Space Command insignia and engineering insignia.

Marine Captain Burrows entered the bay and walked directly to Sydnee. He nodded and said, "I'll be leading this mission, Lieutenant. The Captain wanted the senior Marine there in case things go less than smoothly."

"Aye, Major. You won't have to worry about me acting like a loose cannon. My orders are to remain on the flight deck."

"I was never worried about you, Lieutenant. You're one of just two Space Command officers aboard the *Perry* who enjoy the privilege of full access to the Marine Combat Range, with my blessing. I've seen your scores. They're very impressive for a Space Command officer."

"Thank you, sir. I'm grateful for the privilege that's been extended to me."

"We'd better get on with our preparations now."

"Aye, sir."

After Sydnee completed her walk-around with the mechanic, she boarded the ship and began running through her checklist. She had just completed her work when Burrows entered the flight deck and sat down in the co-pilot seat.

"We're all buttoned up back there and ready to go."

"Aye, Major," Sydnee said as she confirmed acknowledgment that all hatches were closed, locked, and sealed.

As the shuttle exited the *Perry*, Sydnee said, "I was beginning to think this mission had been canceled."

"It took a couple of days to develop a degree of trust that we weren't going to storm the ship once we were inside their laser array umbrella. Our engineers have also convinced the Yolongi that we need every hand they can spare for the next stage. As you probably know, the generator sits in a protected repository until needed. It then extends up and out so that the envelope can be formed. The generator rises on a shaft like that used for the periscope on a submarine, but it's a single-piece shaft that extends fifteen meters into the ship. The length is required to provide the strength and absolute stability necessary for envelope generation.

"Our engineers have convinced the Yolongi chief engineer that the shaft seems to be either bent or damaged in some way and so must be removed and checked. That work is almost never done outside of a shipyard where they have the proper equipment. Since it's a weightless environment, it's possible to do it without a boom, but the shaft must be raised straight up, then laid down on the hull where lasers can be used to check that it's perfectly straight to within three microns. It will take a lot of hands to do it in this environment. This will be the best chance we have to see if they have any Terran male slaves."

It took just minutes to travel the twenty-five thousand kilometers to the Clidepp ship once the Sub-Light engines were engaged. Sydney established a parking position some twenty meters from the ship and then sat quietly as her cargo of engineers and Marines disembarked. Rather than using the one-person airlock, the flight deck was sealed from the rest of the ship and the two large hatches were opened after the pressure inside the cabin area had been reduced to zero. Sydnee was able to watch the departure and then the activity on the dip ship using the numerous onboard cameras.

Five hours later, the generator shaft had been checked and restored to its shaft housing. After the *Perry* personnel returned to the shuttle, the cabin was pressurized and Marine Captain Burrows unsealed the flight deck and entered wearily. He pulled off his helmet and then flopped into the co-pilot chair.

Sydnee waited in silence for several minutes, but when the Marine officer didn't say anything, she asked, "None of the slaves wanted to come back with us, Major?"

"There wasn't a Terran in the lot. They were all Yolongi. We did the work and wrapped it up for this watch."

Sydnee felt anger rising up inside. *All those female slaves and not one male,* she thought. *All this time wasted.*

The trip back to the *Perry* seemed to take little more than the blink of an eye. As Sydnee let the shuttle settle into its regular parking spot, she said, "Thanks, Major. I guess it just wasn't meant to be."

"We're not going to give up, Lieutenant. We'll find a way to get our people back, even if we have to declare war on the whole damn Clidepp Empire to do it."

"It's just not right that dips can flaunt the law the way they do."

"That's the way it's always been when a nation wants to protect certain diplomats. There have been cases in history where a diplomat has committed cold-blooded murder while in a foreign country. All the country could do was order them out. However, there have been a few times where, in the face of overwhelming criminal evidence, the foreign power revoked their representative's diplomatic status and allowed the government of the country where the crime was committed to arrest the former dip before he or she could flee the country. I wouldn't count on that happening in this case though. We believe the slavery issue is too systemic."

It was several hours into the third watch and Sydnee hadn't gotten a lot of sleep, so she was excused from the watch. She decided to go back to bed and try to forget her disappointment, but she couldn't sleep. After tossing and turning for a couple of hours, she got up and went to her com system. She used the Marine access code assigned to her to see if there was any free time on the Combat Range. She was delighted to see that no one had scheduled any time during the next several hours, so she booked an hour.

When she arrived down at the Range, she found the area deserted. She retrieved a laser rifle from the weapons cabinet and walked to the control console. Until now, she had been using the Basic Training setting, but for this session she selected Intermediate. She started the game and then stepped up to the start line. She took a deep breath, released it, and moved onto the 'city' course. She hadn't gone more than a meter before two enemy soldiers confronted her. One popped up through a sewer hole and the other was on a rooftop. She shot the sewer rat first and then dove forward, shooting at the roof pigeon as she fell. She saw the roof target go down, but she didn't think she scored a killing shot. As she got to her feet and began to move forward again, she scanned the windows of the buildings but kept an eye on the roof. Sure enough, the roof shooter popped up again, but this time Sydnee scored a killing shot and he dropped out of sight. When another shooter appeared, this time at a first floor window, she dove into the building and shot him while lying on the floor as he turned to face her.

By the time Sydnee reached the end of the city course, her armor was working at full cycle trying to keep her cool. She didn't even glance at her score; she just started the clock running on the jungle course and moved in.

"I saw your name on the schedule when I checked availability," Lieutenant Kelly MacDonald said as she entered the Marine Combat Range antechamber, "but it listed you as coming in several hours ago."

Sydnee was relaxing on one of the sofas and looked up. "Yeah, I couldn't sleep."

"I heard the mission was a bust. Too bad."

"Can you believe it? Not one single Terran male was sent out to help."

"Well, we don't actually know that they have any male slaves on board. The slaves might all be female." Looking up at the board in the anteroom that showed the start time, participants, level, game run time and score for each of the courses, Kelly whistled. "You went through each of the courses three times at the Intermediate level? Your scores are fantastic."

"No one else came in, so I figured it would be okay."

"It's okay— it's just— unusual. You must be dead on your feet."

"I had a compelling urge to destroy something and I decided it was better to work it out down here than wreck my quarters."

"Yeah, I've felt that urge from time to time."

"I'm better now."

"Nothing chases that urge away like killing something," Kelly said with a grin.

"The only thing I have an urge to kill is that Yolongi Ambassador. But I'll control my temper. He'll get his eventually, and we'll get our people back."

"Yeah, but I was kinda hoping it would be sooner rather than later."

"Me too."

"Got enough energy left for another walk? We can do a tandem."

"I'm not in your class. I'd slow you down."

"You're good, and you're getting better all the time. Let's give it a go, and then you can go sack out. I bet you'll be able to sleep when you try again."

"Okay, you're on."

When Sydnee got back to her quarters after going two more rounds on the Marine Combat Range with Kelly MacDonald, she could barely stand up. Her rack had never felt as good as it did when she climbed beneath the covers and said, "Lights out," but the switch picked this day to malfunction again. When "Lights out, damn you," didn't work any better, she just rolled over and closed her eyes. The light didn't prevent her from falling asleep within seconds.

* * *

"We can't keep sending the men up to the ship for more supplies, Currulla," the rebel named Thellerro said. "The air is too foul. The last group almost didn't get back out. Two men had to be carried to the shuttle. Besides, we have enough supplies to last us five years."

"Did we retrieve all the weapons and ammunition in the armory and small arms lockers?"

"We have enough to wage a small war. Since the ship was in a protected spacedock, they left everything aboard. Getting into the armory was difficult, but we managed it."

"How about medical supplies and clothing?"

"We brought down everything we could. Far more than we'll need."

"How much is that?"

"How much is what?"

"Far more than we'll need. Can you tell me how long we'll be here? We're in GA space and dependent on rescue from our own forces. I have no idea how long we'll be here, or even if we'll ever be rescued."

"We sent the distress message to our people, didn't we?"

"Yes— and they responded. But that doesn't mean we'll ever see anybody. If something happens to the pickup ship, we may be stuck here for the rest of our days. According to the database, this miserable excuse for a planet has just one thing going for it— it's just barely habitable. There are no mineral resources or agriculture settlements, and it's not of any strategic value. It's miserably hot the entire annual, there're deadly indigenous life forms, insects that attack in swarms, and it rains almost every solar. We selected it for its desolation, and we got what we were seeking. It may be our undoing."

Chapter Eleven
~ Feb. 9th, 2285 ~

Thanks mainly to the efforts of the *Perry's* engineers, the repairs to the *Darrapralis* were completed quickly once the generator shaft had been inspected. SHQ still refused the *Perry's* request to violate the diplomatic rights of the ship in order to save the women, and Captain Lidden would take no further action to free the slaves. Sydnee watched from her position at the navigator console and fumed as the diplomatic yacht built its envelope and disappeared in an instant.

Once the yacht was on its way to Clidepp space at FTL speeds, Lieutenant Milton, in his capacity as watch commander, ordered the *Perry* to return to the passenger ship they had left to answer the yacht's distress call.

"The ship isn't here," Lieutenant," the tac officer said. "This is where we left it."

Milton scowled. "Com, append a note to the pending interdiction report that the Captain violated a direct order from the senior Space Command officer aboard the ship at the time we received the distress call to remain at this location until we returned. Then send it to SHQ." To no one in particular he said, "It's their problem now. That dumb bastard will probably lose his Master's papers over this and never be allowed to captain a ship in GA space again. And the company will receive a fine so high they'll be screaming for years. But— they'll never let one of their captains violate a Space Command directive again. Sydnee?"

"Aye, sir?"

"Pull up that course heading we got from the dip ship and establish a course to the nearest world with a breathable atmosphere. Then send it to the helm. Helm, as soon as you have the course and destination, take us there at top speed. We want to find that rebel ship."

"Aye, sir" both Sydnee and the helmsman said.

* * *

"I figured you'd be here this morning," Lt. Kelly MacDonald said as she entered the anteroom of the Marine Combat Range and saw Sydnee cooling down after just finishing both range courses. "I heard that the dip ship left during third watch."

"Yes, I watched it prepare to leave and wished I was at a Laser Array console instead of the navigation console."

"We'll free them eventually. We have the proof now in the images from your helmet cam, right?"

"Yeah. Space Command Intelligence said they were able to make positive identification of five of the six."

"So the Clidepp won't be able to deny it when the GA Council presses the issue the next time. They can't just say it's a vicious rumor promoted by political rivals."

"There's no telling how long it will take to get the Clidepp Empire to fess up and free the slaves."

"But— it will happen."

"Maybe."

"Come on. Let's do a duet in the city."

"Okay. And then the jungle. You'll probably do better in the city, but I bet I beat your score in the jungle."

"I do love a challenge," Kelly said, smiling.

* * *

"Another dry hole," Captain Lidden said to his XO during their daily briefing. "No sign they were ever here."

"It's too bad the Captain of the diplomatic yacht couldn't tell us how badly the rebel destroyer had been wounded."

"Those dip ship officers were probably pissing their pants and hiding under their beds during the attack. The Captain probably got all his info from watching the logs after the rebels left."

"I suppose it's possible they headed for Clidepp space and crossed the border while we were still with the yacht."

"I doubt it. As soon as the distress call went out, every available Clidepp military ship and commercial ship near this sector's border area would have been watching for that destroyer. I don't think the rebels would have risked a crossing if they were less than one hundred percent, and the way the Captain of the *Darrapralis* talked, they were only marginal."

"So, do we keep looking, or resume interdiction efforts?"

"We keep looking until we find it, the Clidepp military announces they caught them, or SHQ tells us to stop. If the rebels get that ship repaired, they could become a more serious threat to commercial shipping than the Raiders ever were."

"You think they present a hazard to normal shipping?"

"They're trying to start a war, and I doubt they're very particular about how they do it. I think they deliberately attacked the diplomatic yacht on this side of the border in the hope that it would drag us into the conflict."

"Aye, sir. We'll stay on it."

* * *

As alarms began sounding all over the *Perry*, crew-members were rolling out of their beds and searching for clothes. Within seconds, they were running to their GQ stations.

"We've found the ship, Captain," Lt. Milton said when Lidden called the Watch Commander station.

"Is the identification positive?" Lidden asked as he glanced up at the chronometer on the bulkhead in his bedroom. It was just 0026."

"As positive as we can be from this distance, sir. The computer has identified her as a Clidepp destroyer. We're standing twenty-five thousand kilometers off her stern. She's running dark, and we're getting no indication of power."

"I'll be there in a few minutes."

"Aye, sir. Milton out."

"Lidden out."

When Lidden arrived on the bridge, he paused to look at the front monitor. They were currently in the umbra created by the planet, so the greatly magnified view of the destroyer they'd been hunting for weeks was a composite image prepared by electronic sensors.

"Where are we?" he said absently to Lt. Milton.

"We're in orbit around a planet named Diabolisto." Reading from a monitor on the arm of the command chair, Milton said, "It orbits a Type G2 Yellow MMK class V (dwarf) star once each three hundred four Earth days. The planet has a mass of 0.96 and a radius 0.89 times that of Earth, makes one full revolution each twenty-two hours and six minutes, Galactic System time, and has tectonic plate movement similar to Earth's. It has a breathable oxygen-nitrogen atmosphere with a roughly 18/82 mix and no more than three percent of non-deadly trace gases, with a mean temperature of 54 degrees Celsius."

"Diabolisto? They couldn't have chosen a much more inhospitable place in this sector if they'd had months to search for one."

"No, sir, at least not one with a breathable atmosphere."

"As I remember, it's never had a colony because it's such a miserable little mud ball."

"I heard that a long time ago a company of Marines came here for thirty days of survival training but landed on the wrong landmass. Seventy-five percent were killed by deadly indigenous life forms before they could evacuate."

Lidden chuckled. "That's probably just a campfire tale told to young space scouts, but I won't deny it's a deadly place for the unwary. Have you hailed the ship?"

"Negative. I was waiting to see what you wished to do, sir. I didn't want to alert them to our presence if they're not already aware. After I contacted you, I alerted Major Burrows for a possible assault."

Lidden nodded. "Tac, launch an IDS jamming satellite to keep our rebel friends from calling for help. Com, tell Major Burrows to assemble two full teams for a 'no atmo' assault on that ship. We have no idea how large the crew of that destroyer is, but let's anticipate the worst. Milty, who's up on rotation?"

"Lieutenants Caruthers and Bateman."

"Notify them that they should report to their shuttles."

"Aye, Captain."

"Com, hail that ship using RF in the three-to-thirty megahertz range." To Milton, he said, "I'll take over, Milty."

"Aye, sir," Milton said as he climbed down from the command chair and moved to the first officer's chair. "You have the bridge, Captain."

Thirty minutes of hails and waiting for responses produced nothing but dead air on the hailing frequencies.

Lidden lightly stabbed at a contact spot on the monitor mounted on the chair by his right hand. "Lt. Bateman, what's your status?"

"We're loaded and ready, sir."

"Good. Lt. Caruthers, how about you?"

"Buttoned up and ready to go, sir."

"Good. Launch and stand by for a command to approach the enemy destroyer."

Both officers acknowledged the order and commenced their taxi procedures as the bay controller directed them to move to temporary airlock locations near the bay's large hatchways to space.

Laser array teams watched anxiously as the shuttles approached the Clidepp destroyer. They were too far distant for their lasers to be effective but were ready if any torpedoes were launched towards the *Perry*. Fortunately, space remained calm as the shuttles reached their destination. An engineer was dispatched with two Marines, all in EVA suits, to open a shuttle bay. The bridge crew of the *Perry* watched as they succeeded in opening a small airlock and moved inside the destroyer. Eighteen minutes later, a shuttle bay hatchway opened to admit the first of the two shuttles. It took just nine minutes for the airlock to recycle and then reopen to admit the second small ship.

"The air is pretty foul," the lieutenant in command of the search reported as the Marine squads spread out. "No one could survive here for long without oxygen or a rebreather unit."

"How long can you maintain your search, Lieutenant?" Lidden asked.

"According to my armor's sensors, the built-in rebreather unit shouldn't have any difficulties for several days based on the size of the team with me, but anyone without supplemental oxygen would be unconscious within minutes."

"Understood. Proceed with caution but search the entire ship for holdouts. Be sure to check all life pods, stasis beds, and auxiliary spacecraft."

"Acknowledged, sir."

"Com," Lidden said, "cancel GQ."

Images from the helmet cams filled the front viewer of the *Perry* while the search was conducted, but no personnel were encountered. The Marines relayed images of the empty food, medical supplies, clothing, and small-arms lockers, plus the emptied armory.

"It looks like they took everything they could that wasn't nailed down," the lieutenant in command said when the search was completed. "I thought Tsgardi were supposed to be the galaxy's worst scavengers. The Yolongi could give them lessons. From the condition of the oxygen regeneration equipment, I'd say this ship isn't going anywhere under its own power, even though the engines, FTL generator, and power levels are fine. They must have been wearing EVA suits or rebreathers full time just to get it here."

"Okay, Lieutenant," Lidden said. "Good job. Wrap it up and come on home."

"Yes, sir."

Turning to Lieutenant Milton, who had returned from AC&C when GQ was cancelled, Lidden said, "Let's examine that planet in minute detail. I want to know exactly where those rebels landed."

"Yes, sir."

"You have the bridge, Lieutenant. I'm going back to my quarters. I'll relieve you at first watch."

"Aye, sir. I have the bridge. I'll get our people working on locating the rebels. Good night, sir."

"Good morning, Milty."

* * *

"Good morning, Milty," Lidden said as he returned to the bridge just before first watch. The tiredness he was feeling was clearly evident in his eyes. It had been 0518 when he'd returned to his quarters, but thoughts of the problems ahead had kept him from falling asleep so he'd only gotten one hour of sleep all night.

"Good Morning, Captain."

"What's the situation?"

"The assault teams returned without incident. We've identified the probable location on the planet where the rebels might have established their base camp. There are three large clearings filled with cargo and a dozen campfires were visible before daybreak down there. Currently, we can still see smoke rising from the same area, but it's heavily wooded jungle so most of the optical scans show only treetops."

"Did you perform an infrared scan?"

"Affirmative. We've counted two hundred eighty-six hominid shapes."

"Two hundred eighty-six? I was hoping for fewer. Well, it makes sense— given the size of the vessel they stole. They'd need a crew that size for the ship to run efficiently. They couldn't know they'd lose their oxygen regeneration equipment. They must have been in a bad way by the time they reached this planet."

"We're, uh, not going down there after them, are we sir?"

"I'm afraid so, Milty."

"They'll have our entire Marine contingent outnumbered almost three to one, sir."

"Yes, it's not a chore I look forward to."

"Can't we just leave them there? I mean, they're not going anywhere if we tow the destroyer away. Not that they could go anywhere if we didn't."

"You mean— maroon them there? I'd be willing to bet they signaled for help before they even arrived here. If we don't take them down before their comrades arrive, we might find ourselves facing triple the number, or they may even slip through our grasp. I wish we had reinforcements available out here, but we don't, and we can't wait months for another SC ship to arrive. Like always, out here it's just us."

"Yes, sir."

"Who's up on rotation?"

"For shuttles, sir?"

"No, this trip will be MATs. We can't send someone into a possible firefight in a shuttle."

"Only Weems and Marcola are certified for the new MAT-12A. We've been so shorthanded, we haven't been able to send anyone else back to Earth for training."

"We still have the two MAT-11's don't we?"

"Both ships are down for maintenance. The repair parts we've ordered still haven't arrived."

"Damn," Lidden said softly. "Com, notify Lt. Weems to report to the MAT hangar for an assault run." Looking towards Sydnee's back as she sat at the navigator's console, he said loudly, "Marcola."

At the sound of her name, Sydnee jumped up and reported to where the Captain was standing at the command chair. "Sir."

"Hop into your armor and then get down to the MAT hangar."

"Now, sir?"

"Of course now. I know you just stood a full watch but you're one of the only two pilots aboard who are certified for the MAT-12A."

"Yes, sir."

"Go, Lieutenant," Lidden said as she stood there waiting for additional instructions. "You'll get your briefing instructions by com."

"Yes, sir," she said, then turned and hurried towards the door. As she moved into the corridor, she heard Lidden say, "I'll take the bridge, Milty. You're relieved."

Sydnee may have wondered if taking all her weapons was necessary when preparing for interdictions, but there was no hesitation now. She probably would have taken more if she had had it, but the laser pistol, rifle, and the two knives should be adequate. Where she had previously only worn the two knives in her belt, she now strapped one to her left thigh and attached the other to her right calf. She had noticed some of the Marines wearing them that way and it seemed like a more effective arrangement.

"Loaded for bear again, I see," Weems said as she entered the MAT hangar.

"Are you expecting a tea party?" Sydnee said as a retort.

Weems grinned. "I'm expecting a stop and drop, then back up to where the angels cruise. This one is the real deal, Syd. It's not like boarding a passenger ship to check passports and visas. We keep our noses in our birds."

"Yes, several hundred rebel fighters is a different story entirely."

"Where did you get the number?"

"I just came off watch. There are two hundred eighty-six rebels down there. We have to either take them into custody or see that they stay on the planet permanently. That's why I'm loaded for bear. We can't just drop the Marines. We have to stay behind to evacuate them if things get too dicey."

"Yeah, I know. I was just kidding. I also have everything I was issued— plus a little more. I stowed it in the pilot's locker when I first got here. I know this could turn real nasty, but we should be okay as long as we stay in the MAT. These new ships can take a direct hit by a mortar round and shrug it off everywhere but the engine intakes and exhausts. Even the nacelles are Dakinium sheathed. It's only while the cabin hatches are open that we really have to be worried."

When the corridor doors opened and Marines came flooding into the hangar, Weems said, "Guess we'd better get our ships preflighted, Syd."

"Sure thing, Jerry. Catch you on the planet."

As Syd did a walk-around with the MAT's mechanic, Marines began lining up near the starboard hatch. For this trip, she would have a full load of forty Marines that included eight four-man fire teams, four corporals, and four sergeants. Lieutenant Kennedy was the platoon CO on Syd's ship. A similar number of Marines were lining up near the MAT that Weems would pilot. She saw Kelly MacDonald checking her people over in preparation for boarding the ship.

As soon as her exterior check was complete, Sydnee went aboard and stowed her gear in the pilot's locker on the flight deck, then began running through her checklist. She finished at about the time she heard Marines piling into the MAT, and she was sitting there trying to relax when Kennedy entered the flight deck and dropped into the co-pilot seat.

"All buttoned up, Syd. We can move out whenever you're set."

"Okay, Rett."

From the corner of her eye, she saw him react slightly to the use of his nickname, but he didn't correct her or say anything else.

After receiving taxi clearance from the hangar controller, Sydnee proceeded through the methodical steps necessary to join the MAT piloted by Lieutenant Weems. His ship was already outside the *Perry*, waiting a thousand meters off the starboard hull.

"Watch Commander, MAT-Two is in position near MAT-One and everything is go," Sydnee reported as she aligned her craft with that of Weems.

"Understood, MAT-Two," she heard Lidden say. "The rebels probably know we're here since we believe they have the portable communications and DeTect equipment that would have been stored on the destroyer. We're currently over the opposite side of the planet from their camp, so it's doubtful they could have seen you deploy from the ship. You will approach the planet in a stealthy manner according to the flight instructions we've just downloaded to your nav computer and set down in the designated clearing. The Marine officers have received their briefing instructions and are in command once the ship is down. MAT-One will be the lead ship into the LZ."

"MAT-One, acknowledged."

"MAT-Two, acknowledged."

"MAT-One to MAT-Two, engage Sub-Light-1 on zero. Five, four, three, two, one, zero."

Sydnee had already entered the speed and only had to push the engage button to start the ship moving. She felt a slight lurch before the inertial gravitative compensators kicked in, then all was smooth. Glancing down at her DeTect screen, she saw that MAT-One hadn't moved.

"MAT-Two to MAT-One. You did give the order to engage Sub-Light, didn't you?"

"MAT-One is experiencing a problem with its Sub-Light engine." She heard Weems say. "Disengage and standby."

MAT-Two was already halfway to the planet when she disengaged the Sub-Light engine and continued to move forward ballistically. She told Kennedy why she had disengaged the Sub-Light drive while she waited for new instructions.

Chapter Twelve

~ Feb. 18th, 2285 ~

Sydnee listened as MAT-One reported the engine problem and was ordered to return to the *Perry*. She wondered how long the delay would be, but it was unavoidable. They certainly didn't want to take on a camp full of well-armed rebel fighters with only one platoon. She reversed the engines to halt the ballistic flight and they floated in place.

"Do you want to make an announcement to your people, Rett?" Sydnee asked Lt. Kennedy.

"I suppose I should. They'll be wondering what's going on." Kennedy took the cabin mike and explained the delay very succinctly.

Thirty minutes later, Captain Lidden called MAT-Two.

"MAT-Two, we have a change of plans. MAT-One will not be spaceworthy for at least a full day, and possibly two, due to control issues with its Sub-Light engines. The mission is being modified rather than scrubbed. Lt. Kennedy's platoon will now perform recon activities so we have better intelligence when the other MAT is ready to head down to the planet. We've downloaded new data to your nav computer and to Lt. Kennedy's briefing computer. The new landing zone is a small clearing approximately five kilometers from the rebel camp. After you land, the Marines will deploy and carry out their new objectives. Lidden out."

Sydnee glanced over at Kennedy without a word.

"You heard the man," he said. "Punch it. I'll alert my people."

Sydnee glanced at the image on the nav screen and then engaged the Sub-Light engines.

Twenty-three minutes later, the MAT touched down in the clearing identified on the nav screen. She had come in at treetop level for the last twenty kilometers, using just the oh-gee engine for altitude and thrusters for yaw, pitch, and roll. MATs were a lot more stable with a bit of speed from the Sub-Light engines, but quiet was more important for this mission, so she'd elected to fight the tendency of the small ship to wobble for that entire twenty kilometers.

Sydnee spent several seconds flipping switches as the MAT settled into the tall grass of the clearing, then looked at Kennedy. "It's your show now, Rett."

Kennedy nodded, stood, and left the flight deck. His people were already on their feet and eager to hit the ground running as soon as he gave the word.

"Listen up," Kennedy said as he entered the rear cabin area. "This is not the assault we had prepared for. At present, this is strictly a recon mission. We'll assemble outside the craft and I want all noncoms to gather for a briefing. We're five klicks from the enemy camp, but they might have patrols out, so the rest of you will remain alert and quiet until your sergeants brief you. I want the scouts to fan out for one-half klick and report any sightings of the enemy. Now move out— quietly."

A camera mounted in the rear of the cabin area allowed Sydnee to view and hear Kennedy's instructions from her seat on the flight deck. As the Marines stealthily moved down the ramp and assembled in small groups instead of bounding down the ramp in one or two steps and racing away, she had to smile. Marines almost never did anything quietly— it was totally inconsistent with their training. From almost the first minute they arrived at boot camp, a DI was putting his or her face an inch from the new recruit's and yelling with all the force their lungs could generate. It does tend to get one's attention.

With the rear cabin vacated, Sydnee flipped the switch that would retract the ramp and seal the hatch. Being on a hostile planet, there was always the danger that a wild animal could enter the ship when no one was looking, not to mention enemy combatants. After adjusting the filtration system to step up the special misting process that would kill all insects that had entered the ship while the hatches were open, she leaned back to await whatever orders would follow. There was little chance she would be ordered out on recon patrol since her only 'jungle' training had been in the Marine's combat range aboard ship, and that wasn't even part of her official record. As for snakes, she'd never even seen one that wasn't secured in a glass-enclosed display area at a zoo or in a vid.

To keep her mind occupied, she called up the data about the planet Diabolisto that she had downloaded into the MAT's computer before they left the *Perry*. There was the usual planetary geological data and environment info, and that was followed by weather statistics and patterns. She wasn't interested in the entire planet so she narrowed the scope to just the land mass the rebels had chosen for their base.

After an hour of reading or listening as the computer read to her about the planet, Sydnee knew far more about Diabolisto than she cared to know. It was a miserable little planet with little to recommend it as a place you'd ever want to visit if you didn't have to. There were hundreds of snake, amphibian, and insect species, and even flora with poisonous bites, barbs, or stings that ranged from painful to deadly. The jungle on this landmass was home to carnivores as large as water buffalo and herbivores as large as dinosaurs. The database said that the herbivores would try to avoid contact, but if they felt threatened, they might try to stomp whatever was in their way.

"Great," Sydnee said. "Even the ones not trying to eat you will kill you if they get a chance. And this is supposed to be the safest landmass on the planet."

Tired of listening, she downloaded a copy of the file to her helmet's data storage and then shut the computer off. She had just closed her eyes when she heard a soft chime and then, "Lieutenant Marcola?" in her left ear.

"Marcola," she said as she touched her ring.

"This is Kennedy. We're setting up a CP under the tree cover. Open the lower hatch so we have access to our equipment, supplies, and ordnance. "

Sydnee flipped the switch that would open the large storage area in the belly of the MAT and said, "Opening."

"Kennedy out."

"Marcola out."

Seventy minutes later, Sydnee heard, "Marcola," in her ear and responded in the usual manner.

"This is Kennedy. Join us in the CP."

"Acknowledged. Marcola out."

After having read about all the dangerous life forms on the planet, Sydnee wasn't leaving the MAT without all her weapons and without her armor sealed. When she stepped through the airlock, the only way to distinguish her from the Marines who had gone before her was by the insignia on her helmet. After disembarking, she resealed the MAT using the exterior keypad, then walked to the CP. She knew where it was because she had watched the Marines on a vid monitor as they carried equipment into the jungle.

"It's about time," Kennedy said when she arrived in the CP, which was just a large tent with insect screening for wall panels. A sprayer was emitting a light odorless mist that killed insects on contact. At the rate the insects were entering the tent and dropping, the bugs were going to be ankle deep if they were here more than a few days. A com station occupied one corner, and several tables filled with electronic equipment took up the rest of the space.

"I had to get suited up before I left the MAT. Was it urgent? You didn't say it was urgent."

"The *Perry* has left orbit."

"What?" Sydnee said in surprise. "When? Why?"

"Another Clidepp destroyer entered the solar system. Captain Lidden hailed the other ship and they turned tail and fled while building their FTL. The Captain called to see if we were okay before they left to pursue. I told him we were fine and that they should go."

"What? Why wasn't I contacted by the Captain?"

"When we're in space, Lieutenant, you are in command," Kennedy said with an edge to his voice. "When we dock with another ship or land on a planet, I'm in charge. It was my decision to make, and I made it. The *Perry* will return shortly. Once the other ship achieves FTL, the *Perry* hasn't a chance of stopping her."

"So that's the basis for your decision— that the *Perry* will return because he can't catch a Clidepp destroyer? Well, I have news for you. If the *Perry* can't stop the destroyer, the Captain will follow it until they cross the border. We could be here for days or even weeks."

"We have adequate emergency food rations for thirty days. We'll be fine."

"Unless the rebels learn where we are."

"They're not going to learn where we..."

Kennedy's statement was cut short as the ground suddenly shook violently. The CP tent leaned drunkenly for a couple of seconds, and then one side drooped.

"Incoming," someone yelled, and the entire camp dropped to the ground.

Everyone listened for any sound that might offer a clue as to where the enemy mortar emplacement was located, but no more rounds landed.

"Com," Kennedy finally said, "Check with the perimeter scouts and see if they have the enemy spotted."

"All scouts are reporting that no rebels have been sighted."

"Then where did that mortar round come from and where did it land?"

"My ship," Sydnee yelled suddenly and jumped to her feet. The violent shaking had loosened the already soft dirt where the tent stakes had been driven into the ground, so as she pushed the tent flap aside, that end of the tent collapsed. She was already through, but Kennedy wasn't so lucky. The horizontal bar supporting that end of the tent dropped just as he reached it. It caught him in the midsection, felling his body in the doorway. He wasn't injured because he was wearing his armor, but he became tangled in tent material as more of the tent collapsed on top of him.

Sydnee was the first to reach the clearing and the first to see that the MAT was no longer where she had left it. She just stood there for several seconds staring at the hole where it had rested just minutes ago. Marines began to arrive and likewise stare at the huge crater. Kennedy, finally able to untangle himself from the tent material, arrived as well.

"Where is it?" Kennedy asked.

"See that hole?" Sydnee said, pointing. "That's where it was sitting. Now it's down there. It wasn't a mortar round. It was a sinkhole opening up. It swallowed the MAT. You can still see a piece of it sticking through the dirt that collapsed on top of it from the side walls."

"A sinkhole? Well that was a pretty dumb place to park."

Sydnee's face reflected incredulity as she looked at Kennedy, so it was probably good she had her helmet on and he couldn't see it. Her helmet was projecting a still image of her face on the front plate.

"I didn't pick this clearing, Lieutenant," Sydnee said. "If you remember, we were ordered to proceed to this exact location."

"Yeah, well, what now? How do we get it out?"

"The hull is Dakinium-sheathed so I doubt the ship is damaged in any way. If I was still inside, I could use the oh-gee engine to simply fly it out. But it doesn't operate by remote control."

"So? How?"

"If the *Perry* was still here, they could send down a tug and lift it out. So we either wait until they get back, or we dig it out ourselves."

"Dig it out?"

"Yeah, while we pray that the sidewalls don't keep collapsing and that the sinkhole doesn't get deeper or fill with water."

"I think we'll just wait until the *Perry* gets back and can send down a tug."

"While we hope that we don't need the protection of the MAT? This planet is not exactly a garden spot."

"You surely don't think we're going to dig that out without the proper earth-moving equipment."

"We don't have to dig out the entire ship. We only need to clear one of the two hatchways so I can get inside. Then I can fly it out. The dirt around it and on top won't even slow it down."

"I'll take it under advisement. Right now we have orders to perform recon activities. Once that's done, if the *Perry* hasn't returned, we'll see what we can do here. It's fortunate we emptied the cargo belly completely so we have all our equipment, supplies, and ordnance."

Sydnee grimaced because there was nothing more to say. The mission was all Kennedy had on his mind and all he was going to think about until it was completed. Sydnee could only think about having a way to evacuate in case something went seriously wrong. But as Kennedy had said, he was in command once they were down on the planet, and it was his call.

* * *

"Clidepp destroyer, this is Captain Lidden of the GSC destroyer *Perry*. I order you to heave to or face the consequences."

It was the third time Lidden had ordered the rebel-controlled ship to stop in the three hours since the chase had begun. The third warning seemed to have no more effect than the other two.

Lidden hated leaving a platoon of his Marines back on the planet, but he couldn't afford to let the stolen destroyer get away. His call to Kennedy was just a formality. He knew the young lieutenant wouldn't object to the *Perry* leaving in pursuit of the rebels. Marcola was another matter. Lidden knew she would voice her opposition to being left on the planet without support from the *Perry*, so he didn't give her a chance. Technically, she was under the command of Kennedy, so Lidden couldn't be criticized for not contacting her.

"Enough of this. Helm, cut across her bow."

"Aye, Captain."

The *Perry*, as old and slow as he was, was still faster than all the military ships the Clidepp Empire possessed. The *Perry* helmsman made a wide swing to larboard, then plotted a course that would take it directly across the rebel ship's bow. In the wet navy days, the move had been referred to as 'crossing the T.' The ship performing the move could then bring substantially greater firepower to bear against the other ship, an advantage that had disappeared when missiles appeared on ships. The move in this case wasn't to attack the slower ship, but merely to create a situation where the ship's ACS, or anti-collision system, automatically shut down the ship's FTL drive. The helmsman performed the move perfectly, but the rebel ship continued on in FTL as before.

"Damn," Lidden said, "they must have disabled their ACS when they saw us move to larboard. Helmsman, have you performed the required hours in the simulator to remain certified for an envelope merge?"

"Yes, sir. I practice it regularly, as required," Lieutenant Bronson said.

"Good, because it looks like we're going to need it."

Weapons were useless when traveling FTL. A laser beam appeared to stop as it emerged from the envelope because, in an instant, the ship had already passed well beyond that point. Torpedoes, their electronic brains already scrambled from passing through a temporal field, fell away too fast to see. An envelope merge was the only way to stop a ship traveling

FTL if that ship's ACS had been deactivated, but it was the most dangerous maneuver a spaceship could perform.

When two temporal envelopes touched, they coalesced into one, allowing laser array beams to travel from one ship to the other without passing through normal space. Torpedoes could likewise be fired at the other ship while both were in a single DATFA envelope, but it wasn't wise to have a torpedo detonate while you were in such close proximity, so only lasers were used. The danger in the maneuver came if the lead ship lost its envelope as a result of the attack and suddenly found itself at a dead stop in n-space and the second ship failed to cancel its envelope quickly enough. The resulting collision at faster-than-light speeds might destroy any trace of both ships. The tactical officer and helmsman of the pursuing ship must work together in perfect harmony to destroy the temporal envelope generator of the lead ship and halt the pursuit ship instantly.

If the attack was successful, both ships would suddenly be in n-space. If the procedure was unsuccessful and a collision didn't occur, the targeted ship would continue away at FTL while the pursuit ship tried to rebuild its envelope and renew pursuit. During the two minutes it took to rebuild an envelope, the target ship, traveling FTL, could change course and attempt to lose itself in the vastness of space.

"Tac, are you ready?"

"Ready, sir," Lieutenant Nivollo said.

"Okay, helm, it's up to you and tac."

"Yes, sir," Bronson said. "Beginning my approach."

The helmsman had brought the *Perry* around behind the rebel destroyer after they failed to stop it by crossing its bow and was now directly astern. Bronson began closing the distance slowly and with great care. All eyes not required elsewhere were watching the large monitor at the front of the bridge as the rebel ship loomed larger and larger. Bronson's practiced moves narrowed the gap between the two ships as other crewmembers licked at parched lips. Bronson kept one eye on the monitor and the other on his instrument gauges.

"Tac," Bronson said, "we'll do this on zero with a countdown from five. Acknowledge."

"Tac acknowledges. Will fire on zero with a countdown from five. Temporal generator is targeted and all is ready."

"Very good. Standby."

The minutes seemed to pass like hours as everyone watched the monitor. Not a sound could be heard, not even normal respiratory noises. It seemed like everyone was holding their breath, and everyone on the bridge flinched as from a clap of thunder when Bronson finally began his countdown.

"Five. Four. Three. Two. One. Nooooooooooo!"

Chapter Thirteen
~ Feb. 18th, 2285 ~

Sydnee wished she could remove her personal armor and relax, but she didn't dare unseal while in the open on this planet, and the only place that was completely safe was mostly buried under tons of dirt at the bottom of a hole that looked like the mother of all mortar craters. Fortunately, the padded body suit and armor allowed for the collection, processing, and dry storage of solid waste. Urine and perspiration were collected, purified, and available for re-absorption, so thirst wasn't a problem, but sustenance would be if she couldn't remove her helmet. If a wearer was feeling fatigue, the armor could provide concentrated doses of vita-mins and energy nutrients through a small feeding tube in the helmet. It was the same tube used to provide recycled water, but while it gave the body what it needed most, it wasn't a long-term solution.

In the hours that followed the opening of the sinkhole, the Marines had erected a couple of portable shelters. They weren't air-conditioned or even dehumidified, but they had the misters that kept the insect population near zero. One end of one shelter housed the food preparation area, and there were even a few tables and chairs, although most took their meals standing up, then put their helmet on and went outside because it was cooler with their armor sealed. The Marines had also erected an enclosed lavatory/latrine where they could wash, clean the waste system in their armor, and for a few minutes feel like a human instead of a robot, even if those few minutes were like sitting in a sauna.

The CP tent had been re-erected, and the spray from the misting device seemed to be keeping it clear of insects, but Sydnee wasn't taking any chances. Besides, the armor was keeping her fairly cool in a miserably hot and humid environment.

"Lieutenant," the com operator said, "I was receiving a message from the *Perry*, but it cut off in mid-sentence. Now they're not responding to hails."

Kennedy was out with a patrol group, so Sydnee knew the com operator was talking to her. She walked over to the console. "What did the message say, corporal?"

"The *Perry* reported that the rebel destroyer had refused to respond to hails. They had cut across their bow in a failed effort to trigger the vessel's ACS. The com chief said they were about to attempt a different maneuver."

"An envelope merge?"

"He didn't say. Or at least that part of the message didn't get through."

"Oh no," Sydnee muttered.

"What?"

"Uh, nothing corporal. Keep trying to reestablish contact."

"Yes, ma'am."

Sydnee had an image in her mind of a two-ship collision that left little of the two vessels recognizable. She knew she mustn't articulate her thoughts to anyone except Kennedy, but a collision was the only reasonable explanation for the loss of communications. The MATs don't have FTL, so they would have been unable to go check on the *Perry* even if the small ship had been available. Sydnee couldn't help but think of all the friends she had made on the ship, friends whom she might never see again, and hoped that there was some other explanation for the communication blackout.

She tried to turn her thoughts to something else, but the possible fate of the *Perry* crew refused to leave her mind completely, and all she managed to do was dredge up more unpleasant memories. She had been a young girl when her father died at the Battle for Higgins and she hadn't known him well because he always seemed to be away from home.

But she remembered how happy she was every time he returned on leave and the wonderful days the five of them had together until it was time for him to leave again. Her mother was a different person then and had never gotten over the loss. She sometimes seemed to blame Space Command, but she knew that her husband was simply doing his best to help safeguard their lives and freedoms. Sydnee believed that she had remarried again not out of love, but merely because she was seeking family stability. Curtis, Sydnee's stepdad, had a good job and was a good provider, but he had always been a little distant with Sydnee and her sister. Perhaps part of that was because the two girls had always clung too tightly to the memory of their real father and hadn't allowed him to get too close. Her brother, Sterling, had been a little closer to his stepdad. That might have been because he was the youngest and had fewer memories of their real father. Sydnee hadn't heard from her brother in four years, and her messages were always returned as undeliverable.

Thoughts of the possible fate of the *Perry* also led Sydnee to think about her friend Katrina. Her last three messages to Kat remained unanswered. She knew from news reports that things were heating up in Region Two, so it might simply be the result of a communication blackout on personal correspondence during military operations, but it might be something far worse.

Their own situation appeared to be as serious as anything being faced in Region Two. If the *Perry* never returned, they'd be marooned on this planet with hundreds of potentially hostile rebels until another SC ship could rescue them in a few months. The rebels most likely had communications equipment, but Sydnee couldn't know if they were aware that their rebel rescue ship had arrived in the system, then beat a hasty retreat when it spotted the SC destroyer. The IDS jamming satellite dropped by the *Perry* would have prevented any communication unless the rebels also had basic RF equipment. If they did know about the arrival of the rescue ship, they'd blame SC for now being marooned here.

The situation looked worse and worse as the pieces seemed to drop into place. No way off the planet, no relief from the dangers of flora and fauna, and a dangerous enemy who had shown an eager willingness to use deadly force to further their goals. No, it didn't look good at all.

"Lieutenant," Sydnee heard through the microphone mounted in the chest plate of her body armor, "that ground is unstable. I wouldn't get too close to the edge."

Sydnee looked down and was shocked to discover that she was standing a meter from the sinkhole edge. While she had been thinking, she had apparently been wandering around the base camp and former clearing. She looked towards the speaker, Sergeant Booth, one of the squad leaders, and gave him a thumbs up, then stepped backward.

*   *   *

"Report," was all Captain Lidden said to the tac officer as he struggled to his feet. His seat belt should have been buckled before the tactic was attempted, but it had been several years since the *Perry* had engaged another ship in battle and his mind had been preoccupied with the details of the maneuver. There was no sensation of movement when going to FTL and little when the Sub-Light engines were engaged, so it was easy to forget that the ship could be subjected to such violent movements. Lidden had been thrown forward out of his chair, winding up against the solid base of the helm console chair. He didn't think anything was broken, but he had definitely wrenched his back and might have seriously bruised some muscles.

The helmsman, thrown completely over the console, was trying to get to his feet near the forward bulkhead where a darkened front monitor was offering no information about the space around them or the condition of the ship. Other crewmembers were likewise trying to get to their feet. It appeared that all had been lax about wearing their seatbelts on this occasion. A few were groaning as if suffering from broken bones.

"We've struck the other destroyer, sir," the tac officer said as he regained his feet and checked his instruments. "That's all I know at present. The entire hull sensor grid appears to be off-line, including all vid units, and we seem to be bleeding atmosphere at a prodigious rate. Engineering will have to assess the damage and provide a more accurate report."

"What of the other ship?"

"Unknown, sir. Our DeTect grid is down. I fired the forward laser array as Lt. Bronson reached zero, or at least what I expected to be zero. I realized as I depressed the fire button that he was in fact saying 'no.' It would appear that the action of the rebel helmsman was enough to make me miss the shot, sir. They might have continued in FTL while we dropped our envelope. Or they could be floating nearby."

"What happened during the maneuver?"

"As we neared the rebel ship, it suddenly performed a larboard roll along the center axis of the ship with a yaw to larboard. We made contact with her starboard hull as the ship shifted position in front of us. The collision had to have caused massive damage to that ship."

"And it appears they did a good amount to us as well."

"Their helmsman must have realized what we were doing, sir, and attempted to foil our effort to destroy their temporal generator by moving its relative position," Lt. Bronson said as he moved to retake his seat at the helm. "He probably assumed we would drop our envelope immediately."

"Why did we collide, Bronson?"

"It's, uh, my fault, sir, and I take full responsibility. I lost my concentration for just a moment when the other ship moved as it did. When we collided, I was thrown over the console. Damage to the ship must have been responsible for cancelling our envelope."

Lidden grimaced. "Com, tell engineering that I need an initial assessment."

"Aye, Captain," the com chief said. A few seconds later he said, "Done, sir."

"Com, notify the Marines we left on Diabolisto that we've suffered damage during pursuit of the rebel ship and that our return will be delayed. Tell them we'll update as we have more information."

"I'm sorry, sir. The transmission relays are down. I have internal communications only."

"Not even RF?"

"No, sir. I'm unable to transmit any signals on the RF bands or the IDS band. I'm also not receiving any signals."

"Report that to engineering."

"Yes, sir."

"Okay. Listen up, people. We need information. We need to know everything we can learn about that other ship. We must know if a spread of torpedoes is about to be launched in our direction, if our temporal generator is intact, and if our Sub-Light engines can be used. Anything you can do to assist the engineers must be done. We need to find a way to contact our people on Diabolisto. We know we're too far for RF communications to reach them for years, even if we could send a signal, but there must be a way."

"Sir?" the com chief said.

"Yes, Chief."

"I remember hearing that when Admiral Carver broke the light speed record, her onboard systems shorted out so they lost all communications. She allegedly reported that if they'd had a tug or shuttle on board, they would have been able to contact the *Prometheus* with the communication system aboard the small ship."

"Yes, Chief. That's true. Excellent. Contact Chief Wallomi and have her send a message from one of our small ships to our people on Diabolisto and then one to Simmons Space Command Base informing them of our problem."

"Yes, sir."

As the Chief turned to his console, the senior Engineering officer, Lieutenant Knudsen, contacted the Captain.

"Lidden."

"Sir, the news is bad. After impacting the other ship, we slid along its hull, damaging our hull from the keel up to deck eight. At least eighty percent of the frame sections along the larboard side have sustained some damage. The lower three decks are open to space and will require a major repair effort to restore use of those sections. We're shutting down all life support systems on the three decks as we determine that there are no survivors trapped down there."

"Those decks should have been cleared when we went to GQ."

"Yes, sir, and we haven't found anyone yet. I just wanted to be absolutely sure before I shut down life support."

"How much longer to complete the verification, Lieutenant?"

"We're almost done with the areas that aren't open to space. We should have the three decks sealed off within fifteen minutes."

"Was the Marine hangar bay damaged?"

"I'm afraid there isn't much left of it. The three MATs and two tugs down there are just a pile of scrap metal now. They'll never fly again, even if someone could manage to squeeze onto the flight deck."

"I thought that new MAT was supposed to be indestructible."

"The outer skin can't be damaged by laser fire and is resistant to damage from explosions, but that doesn't include being crushed between two large vessels. The Dakinium sheathing is probably in perfect condition; you just can't get into an eighteen-meter-thick ship that's now two meters thick."

"How about the shuttle bays?"

"The larboard shuttle bay is almost as bad as the MAT hangar. The shuttles were all destroyed."

"What about the starboard bay?"

"I don't imagine it sustained any damage at all, sir."

"How many shuttles are available there?"

"None, sir. We've only used that bay for incoming visitors. Our shuttles all operated out of the larboard bay."

"Wonderful," Lidden said with a grimace. "Do you think it's possible to access the communication system in any of the small ships?"

"I think it would be far better to utilize our limited resources in getting the *Perry's* main system operational. And even that must receive a lower priority to getting the ship sealed and the propulsion systems operational."

"Surely there must be some portable IDS gear available."

"That sort of equipment was all stored in the Marine holds down on deck two. Deck two is pretty much gone, sir."

Lidden took a deep breath and then expelled it quickly, his frustration evident. "Very well, Lieutenant. Carry on."

"Aye, sir. Knudsen out."

"Lidden out." To the com Chief, Lidden said, "Forget about using the MATs or shuttles for communications, Chief. The ships were all destroyed in the collision. We won't be sending any messages from there. Any other ideas?"

"Negative, sir. That was all I've come up with up so far."

Lidden took another deep breath and released it slowly before saying, "Com, have Lt. Weems come to my briefing room."

"Aye, sir."

Weems arrived on the bridge twenty-three minutes later and was admitted to the Captain's briefing room as soon as he approached the doors.

"Lieutenant Weems reporting as ordered, sir," Weems said as he braced to attention in front of the Captain's desk.

Like the rest of the ship, this compartment was small by modern standards. A plain, office-sized desk molded from a plastic composite material took up a full third of the space and left barely enough room behind it for a chair. As with the rest of the ship, the metal bulkheads were merely painted rather than having been surfaced with any of the many available decorative coverings found in the new ships.

"Lieutenant," Lidden said. "I need someone to perform a special task, and you're it. We're dead in space at present, our communications are down, and the hull sensor grid is unavailable as well. I need to know what's going on outside this ship. Specifically, I need to know what happened to the rebel ship involved in the collision. To that end, I want you to find a couple of volunteers to assist you, suit up, and take a walk around outside. Take a vid unit and record everything of interest. Our engineers are going to be busy inside for a while, so any images you can get of the hull damage would be useful, but the primary mission is to spot the rebel ship and determine if it poses a threat to us. Understand?"

"Completely, sir."

"Good. When you select the people to assist you, avoid anyone who is involved with, or indispensable to, the current interior efforts."

"Yes, sir. I have a couple of people in mind whom I'm reasonably sure aren't indispensable in the current repair effort."

"Who?"

"Lieutenants Caruthers and Stiller, sir. If one is occupied, I can substitute with Lt. Bateman."

"Fine. Track them down and head out."

"Aye, sir."

* * *

As the evening briefing began in the CP tent, the noncoms and officers assembled around a table where a holographic mat had been rolled out. It was currently displaying an image of the rebel camp. The images, taken by an oh-gee camera that circled the rebel encampment slowly at low altitude, provided incredible detail. Using the same technology as personal armor, the cameras were almost invisible to the human eye when they projected the scene from the opposite side on the side facing an observer. No one would ever spot a camera unless weather conditions were just so. If the unit passed through fog or mist, the wake might be seen, but otherwise there was only a slight rippling effect when it moved.

"The situation does not appear good," Lt. Kennedy said.

Sydnee resisted the urge to roll her eyes, despite the fact that while wearing the helmet no one could see her real face. Rolling her eyes was a bad habit she had developed in her teen years. It always annoyed her mother, so she had used it freely when they argued, but since entering the academy, she had struggled to unlearn it. While the behavior might have been understandable in a teen, she knew it was unacceptable conduct by an adult and totally inappropriate for an officer in Space Command.

"As we can see from the map, the rebels have dropped supplies in three clearings in relatively close proximity. Their camps are all beneath tree cover, but infrared scans show they're distributed over the entire area. The clearings contain incredible stockpiles of ordnance, so they must have taken every weapon in the ship other than the torpedoes and laser arrays. We're safe from lattice weapons and primitive weapons in our armor, but these suits won't withstand a direct hit by a mortar round or having a grenade land in our lap. And the rebels have significantly more powerful weapons than mortars. I saw a stockpile of shoulder-mounted missile cases larger than our MAT. As I see it, we have two options. We can either try to destroy their ordnance stocks, leaving them to rely only on light weapons, or get the hell out of here before one of their patrols ventures out this far."

Kennedy paused as if expecting dissenting views, but noncoms don't offer opinions to a commanding officer unless asked for it, and Kennedy didn't ask. Sydnee was an officer, but she wasn't a Marine, and it wasn't her place to speak up in the meeting.

"As you've probably heard," Kennedy continued, "the *Perry* is not responding to hails. When we entered orbit around this planet, the *Perry* dropped an IDS jamming satellite so the rebels couldn't make outside contact. That restricts us as well, but before leaving the area, Captain Lidden said they would drop a relay satellite out beyond the jamming range. We can send an encrypted RF signal in the three-to-thirty-megahertz range and the relay will pass it on to the *Perry* on a set IDS frequency. Signals will return via the same route. Since we're not receiving any responses to messages, we must assume that either the *Perry* is incapable of responding, or the relay has been damaged or disabled. Without the MAT, we can't go up and check, so we have no communication with the outside.

"Our standing orders were to perform recon activities until the other platoon reached the surface, so I don't want to initiate an action without specific orders, but we have to face the fact that we might be on our own down here. I'll wait another forty-eight hours before I make a final decision on this matter. I don't believe we can afford to wait any longer than that. Dismissed."

Sydnee waited until the CP tent was clear before making direct contact with Kennedy. Most of the features of the personal armor were available by optical activation since a wearer's arms might be otherwise engaged. She stared at the 'activate' link on her helmet's heads-up display and winked. The full display popped up and she selected the 'communicate' option. When the display listed everyone within transmission distance, she selected Kennedy's name. As she stared at it and winked, a signal appeared in his helmet with her name and facial image. When he accepted the call, her helmet indicated that he was online and the connection was private.

"Rett," she said, "I think we should attempt to free the MAT while we're waiting for the *Perry* to contact us."

"It's a waste of time and effort, Syd. As soon as the *Perry* returns, a tug will lift the MAT out of that sinkhole."

"But what if the *Perry* doesn't return? We need to get away from this location."

"The *Perry* is going to return. They're just in a dead zone or something and can't contact us."

"Rett, there are no dead zones with IDS unless the signal is being jammed."

"Maybe that's it. They've jammed the signal around the ship so the rebels they're chasing can't call for help."

"But why would they begin jamming *during* a transmission."

"Perhaps the rebels jammed the signal to stop the *Perry* from calling in more ships."

"And perhaps the *Perry* was destroyed. The last message indicated that they were about to attempt an envelope merge. Do you have any idea how dangerous that is? One tiny little error on the part of a helmsman and the ships could collide. That's why helmsmen are required to practice that maneuver religiously in the simulators to keep their certification current."

"I refuse to believe that the *Perry* has been destroyed," Kennedy said.

"A commanding officer cannot afford to ignore *any* possibilities. Surely you must have heard that at the Academy."

"What I remember hearing is that a commanding officer cannot afford to take his people into battle when they are bone weary, as they would be if he allowed himself to be talked into committing them to a worthless cause just before an attack."

"Worthless cause? Uncovering our transportation so we can get out of here, not to mention protection from the enemy and this planet's hostile environment, is a worthless cause?"

"Yes, because there's no way we're going to dig that ship out by ourselves. We'd need massive earth-moving equipment before I'd even attempt it. Have you been out there in the past couple of hours, Syd?"

"No."

"Well, I have. The ship is now completely covered with dirt that's fallen from the side walls."

"That doesn't matter. We know it's under there. We just have to dig it out."

"With what? All we have are a few small trenching shovels."

"The dirt is loose. We can make some simple shovels and buckets from the local flora. We fill the buckets, raise them to the top of the hole using vines for rope, then dump the dirt in the jungle so it can't fall back in."

"No, I'll need my people fresh if we're to attack the rebel camp and destroy their ordnance supply in two days. End of discussion, Lieutenant." Kennedy switched off his connection as a statement of finality.

Sydnee left the tent and walked to the sinkhole. In the moonlight she could see that Kennedy had been truthful. More loose dirt had fallen into the sinkhole and covered the small section of the MAT's roof that had been protruding above the dirt's surface since the initial collapse.

"We are so screwed," she said to herself. "We're outnumbered ten to one by armed rebels on a hostile planet, the *Perry* must have been destroyed, and we don't even know if they reported dropping us off on the surface here. If they did report it, it could be months before anyone comes to look for us. If they didn't report it, we could be here for years. I wonder how many of us will survive if that's the case. I wish I'd paid more attention in Alien Anatomy classes. I don't even know which of the local animal life and vegetable matter is safe to eat. Or what might be looking at us as its next meal. Hmm, I wonder if that info is in the planet database file I was reviewing in the MAT."

Chapter Fourteen

~ Feb. 21ᵗʰ, 2285 ~

"Here's the situation," Captain Lidden said to the senior staff assembled in the bridge deck conference room aboard the *Perry*. "As you know, we struck the rebel destroyer we were pursuing. Both of us are seriously damaged. Originally, I believed that their FTL generator hadn't been struck, that their collision damage was less serious than ours, and that they had gotten away. But Lieutenants Weems, Caruthers, and Stiller walked the hull, taking images of our exterior damage and surrounding space. A portable DeTect unit has indicated that the rebel ship is floating some fifty thousand kilometers from here. If we had damaged their FTL generator, they would be very close, so I'm speculating that while we didn't damage their generator, other damage, such as an inability for an envelope to remain coalesced, has caused it to shut down. If the envelope cancellation wasn't an automatic response to serious damage, they certainly would not have chosen to stop so close to us. But as close as they are, they're out of our reach.

"The Marine hangar bay and our larboard shuttle bays were both destroyed in the collision, along with all shuttles, MATs, and tugs. Our only intact MAT is back on Diabolisto, which is another serious problem. Those people have been left without support in a highly dangerous situation. Our communications are down, so I can't even contact them to amend their orders. My last instructions were for them to perform recon duties until the other platoon joined them. I can only hope their commanding officer, in response to loss of contact with the *Perry*, pulls back out of danger until we can get the ship repaired and return to the planet. Speaking of which, Lieutenant Knudsen, where do we stand with repairs?"

"We've completely sealed off the lower three decks to minimize loss of atmosphere, but we still have numerous leaks we're attempting to plug. My people are currently working to seal punctures in the larboard hull and to minimize life support depletion in those areas we're unable to seal quickly. This ship is about as badly damaged as any ship that has been through a major battle and survived. We can't turn our attention to other issues until we've stopped the loss of atmosphere."

"And when will that be?"

"I don't know, sir. It could take as long as a month for a full halt. We're naturally attacking the worst leaks first and will work our way down the list until the ship is once again sealed."

"At what point can you put some people to work on propulsion and communications work?"

"When we reach a point where I know the leaks are sufficiently under control to ensure the crew will survive. We're still a long way from that point."

"Without communications we can't call for help, either from Space Command or even a passing ship," Lidden said.

"As you know, sir, this destroyer class had two communication arrays mounted on the hull— one at the bow and one near the stern. They were in protected depressions on the keel and very safe during normal interdiction operations, but both were completely crushed in the collision. Our most serious problem on this ship has always been a lack of spare parts for most repairs, so we've gotten pretty good at fabricating whatever we need from newer and older similar systems. But repairs sometimes take ten times as long as they would on a new vessel where parts are immediately available. Plus, recently fabricated units don't have the reliability of new and fully tested components. Further, this ship is so far past its prime that new components won't always work with the older equipment in which we try to install them, and sometimes they cause even more of the older components to fail because of tolerance disparities."

"Best guess, Lieutenant. When will we have communications restored?"

"The absolute earliest would probably be forty-five days, sir, but it's more likely to be sixty days."

"So the bottom line is that for two months we'll be adrift without communications?"

"Yes, sir. I'm afraid so. At least I can *almost* guarantee that life support will function properly during that time. For a while I wasn't so sure."

"There's another issue that must be considered, sir," Commander Bryant said.

"What's that, XO?"

"The rebel destroyer might not have been the ship sent to help the disabled destroyer. Its captain might have simply decided to lend his support to the effort. Another ship entirely may have been sent to help the first destroyer. It may even be bringing equipment to repair or replace the oxygen-generating equipment with the intent of getting that other ship operational. The first ship was only put out of action because of a loss of interior atmosphere. Its propulsion and weapons are still fully operational. Not only would our people on the planet face a worse situation with additional rebel support personnel, but we might also lose the first destroyer to the rebels."

"Or," Lieutenant Milton offered, "the ship tasked to help the rebels on the planet might divert to help this one first. If the second destroyer gets operational before we do, they might just decide to finish us off."

"Or," Lieutenant Weems said, "we might even be spotted by a Raider ship. I know the Raiders aren't attacking shipping anymore, but one could decide that a helpless SC target is too tempting to pass up."

"Yes," Lidden said. "We're not in a very enviable position here. We'll just have to prepare as best we can and hope our repairs are completed in time to defend ourselves and help the people we left on Diabolisto."

* * *

During the two days Kennedy allowed before making a final decision regarding an attack, scouts moved into the jungle in the morning and didn't return until nightfall. They reported seeing mammals, amphibians, and reptiles in the jungle, but none attacked and, unless venomous, they appeared to pose little threat. Most scurried away when approached, but some just stood their ground or remained perched in trees, staring at the strange two-legged creatures.

"We'll move out as soon as images from the observation vid unit show that the camp has retired for the night," Lt. Kennedy said to his noncoms and Sydnee as the briefing began. "During the past two days, our scouts have mapped the best approaches to the target and everyone has downloaded those images into their helmet's storage memory. We'll travel as a single group until we get within a klick of the rebel encampment, then divide into attack teams and proceed to our targets. The jungle between here and there is thick and the going will be hard, so stick to the mapped route.

"By the time we arrive, most of the rebels should be asleep. We know from observation that their military discipline is lax. They've only been posting a few sentries at each of the clearings, and several of them have fallen asleep within an hour of the nearby camp going quiet. We suspect they still believe themselves to be alone on this planet, so they haven't been very alert to the possibility of an attack.

"Each attack team will move to their forward position near their target and await the signal to proceed. When everyone is positioned, I'll alert you to have your people move in and neutralize the sentries. When they give the 'all clear' signal, the rest of the team will move in and place Corplastizine charges on the designated ordnance stockpiles. As soon as your charges are placed, pull back to the team's attack point and wait for the rest of the team to join you. Once all team members have reassembled, report in and head for the designated rendezvous point.

"When all teams reach the RP, I'll blow the charges and we'll hightail it back to our camp. With luck, the rebels will be in complete disarray and won't pick up our trail. If anything goes wrong, notify me as soon as your people are clear of the stockpiles. I'll blow the charges in your clearing and we can use the explosions as a diversion to cover our escape into the jungle.

"With two hundred eighty-six of them and just forty-two of us, we're seriously outnumbered on this planet. I want this operation to remain as stealthy as possible until the detonations. If you're cut off, do your best to get to the RP or back to camp. Even if they have night vision equipment, they'll have a tough job trying to find us in the jungle and will probably wait until daybreak to try to pick up our trail. Any questions?"

Sydnee did her best to hold her tongue, but in the end, she couldn't. Her mouth had gotten her into trouble with instructors more than once during her first year at the Academy, and she had finally managed to rein it in. But Kennedy wasn't an instructor. Even if he was in command here, he was still, like her, just an O-2. "Are you going to strike this camp and move it to a new location much further away before the attack?"

Kennedy looked at her, surprised that she had spoken up in front of the noncoms. "We're five klicks away from their camp. That's five klicks of dense jungle. It will take us several hours to reach their camp and several more to return. We'll have plenty of time to strike the camp and move further away when we return if we think they're following our trail."

"When we return from an exhausting, six-hour trek through five klicks of almost impassable jungle?"

"We'll have plenty of time."

"What about the fighter craft?"

"There's no sign of any fighter craft in the holo images."

"That's just it. We don't see any sign of tugs or shuttles either, but we know they had to have them in order to bring their supplies and all that ordnance down to the surface. They certainly didn't bring it down with hot air balloons. Their ships have to be under camouflage somewhere, perhaps well away from the camp."

Being a pilot, Sydnee tended to think of ships first, where Kennedy, as a Marine, thought of enemy troop size, ordnance, and supplies first. He'd been so pre-occupied with planning the attack that he'd never even given the absence of spacecraft a thought.

"I doubt they have any fighters," Kennedy said. "When ships go into a yard for repairs or refits that require the crew to be taken off, the fighters are sent to planetary locations for storage or maintenance activities."

"That's the way *we* do it, but it may be different for the Clidepp military," Syd said. "As an example of our differences, we also clean out the armory when the entire crew is taken off the ship and the ship is turned over to a civilian workforce. I doubt the rebels would have had access to the amount of military ordnance they brought down with them if it hadn't been aboard the destroyer they stole."

"You might have a point, Lieutenant," Kennedy admitted. "What's your suggestion?"

"Take an extra day to strike the camp. Bury what we can and camouflage the rest in areas where the rebels are unlikely to look. Following the attack, head off in a different direction than this camp so we don't lead them back here where they might find our supplies. Once they know they're not alone on this planet, we can't operate in the open anymore. They *will* be hunting us, and they'll be searching for us from the air. And if the raid is successful, they're really going to be pissed. If they don't pursue, we can circle around and come back here, but if they do pursue and pick up our trail, we won't be leading them to our lifeline on this planet."

"Okay, good suggestions, Lieutenant. We'll delay for an extra day and use the time to break down the camp. We'll bury as much of the supplies as we can and cart the rest off to a ravine we discovered where it can be stored and camouflaged. Each man will carry a thermal blanket for immediate use. Any other suggestions? Anyone?"

No one spoke up so Kennedy said, "Okay, let's get started tonight so we can get some sleep before we head out tomorrow."

Within ten minutes, the camp was alive with activity as Marines began hauling cases and boxes to the ravine while others began digging trenches to hide the ordnance that wasn't needed for the upcoming raid. Sydnee wished she had been able to convince Kennedy to devote this kind of effort to uncovering the MAT. They could have raided the rebel camp and then been a hundred kilometers away before the rebels managed to quench the fires. On foot, they'll be lucky to make several kilometers in that time.

By morning, the camp had been reduced to just the CP tent and equipment, and personal equipment and effects. All other traces of their short habitation had been erased through camouflage techniques. Just before they left on the raid, the CP tent would be struck and packed for transport. For now, Kennedy wanted someone manning the com gear in case a message came from the *Perry*.

Marines were asleep in every conceivable location where they wouldn't get stepped on or tripped over. Since everyone had to sleep in their armor, it would have been a waste of time to create any sort of bed from the bushes around them. Sydnee needed rest also, but she first walked to the clearing to take one last look into the sinkhole. The MAT was completely covered and there was no indication of what, if anything, was buried beneath the dirt that continued to fall from the sidewalls as the crater expanded. It seemed as if the depression had gotten deeper, but Sydnee hadn't taken measurements when it occurred so it was just conjecture. She hoped the small ship would still be accessible when they were able to attempt retrieval.

* * *

Sydnee awoke in darkness. She heard commotion all around her and at first was fearful, but then she realized that she had turned off the display inside her helmet in order to fall asleep in the morning hours because sunlight was filtering through the overhead canopy of tree branches and leaves. Even after activating the display, it was dark, but not so dark that she couldn't make out the shapes of Marines around her as they completed their final packing in preparation for the long trek ahead. She adjusted the helmet for optimal vision and everything suddenly illuminated. A faint red glow in the HUD reminded her that the image she was seeing was an enhanced composite view from the helmet cam and sensors.

On Earth, a five-kilometer hike, or even run, could be enjoyable when done in shorts on a decent day, but the journey ahead of them wasn't going to be pleasant at all. The new armor was lightweight compared to the old, but it was still dead weight. When weapons and other essential gear were factored in, each Marine would be carrying roughly fifty extra pounds. It would have been much worse if not for the four oh-gee sleds they'd used to ferry gear to the camp from the MAT. They had been invaluable in transporting the heavier loads for concealment in the ravine and were now being packed with food, com equipment, medical necessities, and other supplies in case they couldn't return to this location. The one-meter-wide by two-point-five-meter-long sleds could be adjusted to float up to a meter and a half above the surface with loads as great as a metric ton.

The sleds were being loaded with the heaviest cargo to minimize the weight the Marines would have to carry rather than the bulkiest items, so a couple of Marines would work in tandem to transport lighter but more cumbersome loads such as the CP tent poles. The Marines had tested inflatable tents in an effort to eliminate the poles and make for easier setup, but they hadn't held up well under combat conditions. No fabric was ever lattice round and laser proof, so one errant shot was all it took to collapse the tent on the occupants. Self-sealing membranes didn't work effectively, so the Space Marines still carried poles for the large flexible-material tents. The poles were the lightweight, expandable type though. Each team member carried a thermal blanket outside their pack, sealed in a watertight package. The blanket wasn't much thicker than a workman's drop cloth and was so light that the weight added almost nothing to the load.

The packing was complete and the platoon was almost ready to move out when Kennedy got a message from one of the forward scouts watching the rebel camp using the surveillance vid units. Kennedy immediately gave the order to strike the CP tent and the platoon was on the move within fifteen minutes.

As they stepped into the jungle, everyone heard Kennedy say, "All external speakers should be off. Group chatter is restricted to Com 1. Com 2 is for communications between myself, the noncoms, and our scouts. Understood?"

A chorus of voices could be heard saying, "Oo-rah." Just as with Sydnee's private communication with Kennedy, any member of the platoon could communicate privately with any other, or any small group such as a fire team, and many would discuss personal observations as they traveled.

Unlike most of the platoon members who had either been out on recon or on patrol in the area around the camp, this was Sydnee's first venture into the jungle. She thought she was prepared for the trek, but it was unlike anything she had ever experienced before. Travel through the wooded areas wasn't too difficult, and climbing up steep slopes using ropes strung by the lead scouts was challenging, but walking through swamps where they were completely submerged at times was more than she had expected. The armor was sealed and each person remained perfectly dry, but she found it very disconcerting the first time the person ahead of her disappeared below the water line and she realized there was no one else visible ahead of her at that moment.

As Sydnee slipped below water level, she experienced a moment of panic in the dark, murky water, but then an outline of the person ahead of her appeared on the inner faceplate of her helmet. She kept following that outline until she was rising out of the muck and she saw that the platoon members ahead of her were all visible again.

"If I wanted jungle warfare I would have joined the Marines," she grumbled aloud to herself as they stepped out onto somewhat dryer land again.

"Stow it, Marcola," she heard Kennedy's voice say and only then realized that her direct com link was open. "Until the *Perry* returns, you *are* a Marine."

Sydnee silently cursed herself for not noticing that the Com 2 transmit link was open *and* for opening her big mouth. Then she smiled at her mistake.

By the time the platoon reached the point where the teams would split off and head for their designated targets, the forward scouts were reporting that the nine rebel sentries had stopped patrolling and found comfortable places to lie down. Most of them appeared to be asleep. The scouts gave each team leader the location of the sentries in his target area, and the team leader confirmed the assignments to his squads. Having all communications contained within the sealed helmets meant that no sentries could ever hear voices where none should be.

On a signal from Kennedy, the teams activated the invisibility feature of their armor and moved to their forward attack position to await the signal to proceed. The invisibility feature of the armor didn't conceal Marines from their comrades. The suits appeared as a solid mass to the helmet sensors of other Marines.

Kennedy didn't waste any time once the three teams were in place. Silently, the teams moved into the darkened clearings and neutralized the sentries. Most never awoke from their slumber until they were struggling to take their last breaths. The element of surprise had always been the most powerful weapon in a military organization's bag of tactics. The sentries were so sure that no one was going to attack the camp that they had totally relaxed their guard. It was a fatal mistake.

With little chance of discovery, the Marines could take their time planting the Corplastizine charges on the designated stockpiles. When the powerful charges were ignited, there would be little left of the materials in the clearing. The rebels might not even be able to find enough of the sentries to understand that they had been attacked by an outside force, but that would be the only explanation for the stockpiles in all three clearings being destroyed simultaneously by explosions.

Since no alarm had yet been raised at the rebel camp, Kennedy waited until all teams arrived at the rendezvous point before he triggered the Corplastizine. As the night seemed to turn into day briefly and the ground shook violently, the platoon knew that the stockpiled ordnance was just a memory. What remained would only be so much useless trash.

The platoon withdrew quickly along their planned route. They didn't leave any more nosily than necessary, but their departure certainly wasn't as stealthy as their approach had been. Nor did it need to be. Small secondary explosions were still reverberating off the trees around them as they melted into the jungle.

From their original base camp, the rebel encampment area had been almost due north according to the planet's magnetic poles, so Kennedy chose east for their withdrawal. If the rebels were able to track them, the cached supplies should remain secure for future access. The oh-gee sleds made a tremendous difference. In swampy areas, they glided above the surface pulled by a tow rope while the Marines waded in and walked along the bottom. The low weight of the armor, combined with a certain amount of buoyancy from air trapped inside, made travel in the water less difficult than it would have been otherwise, but occasionally they encountered mucky areas that offered no footing and so had to be circumvented.

At one point, Sydnee heard someone say on Com 1, "Oh shit, I've picked up a hitchhiker. I don't know if it's trying to eat me or make love to me. Can someone help?"

Sydnee managed to locate the speaker, who was just emerging from a submerged walk through the swamp. There was an enormous creature atop his helmet that looked like a cross between an octopus and a squid. Long tendrils were draped around the Marine's helmet and upper torso.

The Marine behind him placed her laser rifle almost against the creature's main body sitting atop his helmet and fired once, careful not to hit the Marine or anyone else. The creature slumped and began sliding off as the gripping tendrils lost their power to remain in place.

The Marine grabbed it before it hit the ground. "Anyone know what this thing is?" he asked.

"I think it's called a Grepper," Sydnee said. "Or at least it's a member of that family. Supposed to be good eating, if you like squid," she said with a grimace that no one could see.

The Marine stuffed it into a large, empty plastic sack that he pulled out of his backpack. "I like my calamari cooked in seasoned tomato sauce," he said. "We'll check it out later."

In four hours, the platoon managed to cover only four kilometers of jungle owing to the fact that it was all swamp. The way in had been planned for the easiest going, so it had been mostly dry, wooded land and small ridgelines easily scaled. Sydnee supposed Kennedy hadn't told the scouts to plot an escape route.

The platoon was just exiting a swamp area when a scout detected aircraft approaching.

"Everyone pull their thermal blanket over their heads and keep still," Kennedy ordered.

In seconds, the platoon was sitting or squatting, motionless, as three shuttles appeared overhead just above treetop height.

Chapter Fifteen
~ Feb. 27th, 2285 ~

The three shuttles, each floating on a silent cushion of oh-gee waves, slipped through the sky above the canopy of green provided by the trees. They passed the platoon slowly, then stopped for a few seconds before returning to hover directly above the Marines.

Suddenly, a hatch opened on each shuttle and someone threw out smoke grenades that landed around the Marine perimeter.

"Everybody up," Kennedy yelled, "and move out. On the double."

Within a second, everyone was on their feet and trying to put as much distance as they could between themselves and their former location as fast as they could. The shuttles disappeared as two fighters took command of the sky overhead.

Using the smoke as their target, the fighters fired missiles into the area. The Marines, clear of the former area by just a narrow margin, dropped to the ground and hoped the fighter pilots were well trained, or at least accurate.

The attack didn't last long and ended when the fighters were out of rockets. Whether the pilots were good or only just lucky, the platoon was the winner when no one was hurt. As the aerial fighters left the area, Kennedy yelled, "Everybody up and moving, now. They might decide to come back."

The dark, acrid smoke from the explosions hung in the humid air like a morning mist, blotting out what little sunlight managed to pierce the treetops, but the helmet sensors enabled the Marines to run without fear of crashing into an obstruction or falling into a ditch. They were exhausted from their night's activities, but the attack gave them new strength. They were at least two kilometers away when the scouts reported that aircraft were approaching.

The shuttles didn't seem to be hunting this time. They just came straight in and hovered above the treetops. The growth was too thick to allow them to land, so when the hatches opened this time, instead of smoke grenades being tossed, it was ropes, which enemy combatants then used to lower themselves to the ground.

"It's going to take them awhile to pick up our trail in all that smoke, so let's cover some ground," Kennedy said, as he stepped into a swamp and was almost instantly up to his waist in filthy water.

"Marcola?" Sydnee heard coming in over Com 2. She recognized the voice as belonging to Kennedy. "Marcola," she replied.

"How did they find us? We were hidden under thermal blankets. They shouldn't have been able to spot our heat signatures from the air. What kind of thermal imagers do they have in those military shuttles?"

"I don't know what the Clidepp military has, but I imagine it's just standard equipment. The reason might be that thermal blankets were used. It doesn't get cold here overnight, so the surrounding vegetation stays warm. The instruction wafer that came with my armor said that the personal body armor blocks all thermal readings produced by a warm body while the exterior skin mimics the temperature of the surroundings. Perhaps they saw forty-two cold spots where they expected to see none. It might not have been body heat readings but the absence of all heat that tipped them off."

"Why didn't you call that to my attention earlier?"

"I assumed you read the instructions that came with your new armor and were prepared for thermal scanning from the air."

"You knew what I intended to use the thermal blankets for."

"I *suspected* what you intended, but you didn't share your plan. I assumed that you had read the armor instructions and that my assumption was wrong."

"Kennedy out," he said brusquely.

"Marcola out."

On Com 1, Sydnee heard Kennedy say, "If we detect shuttles overhead again, do *not* cover yourself with the thermal blankets. Let the armor handle the cloaking. Kennedy out."

The platoon had covered another two kilometers when a scout watching the rear reported that the rebels had left the drop zone and were following their trail. It seemed impossible that the Marines could pick up the pace, but they did, in spite of the fact that the going seemed to have gotten more difficult.

Slogging through a swamp was never fun, but knowing that someone was trying to catch up so they could kill you provided a lot of incentive to hurry. Although Kennedy had originally opted for maximum distance from the target over an unobtrusive retreat, he ordered the lead scouts to blaze a path where they would leave the least evidence of having passed. On Diabolisto, that meant slogging through every watery morass near their intended path. They also changed directions several times, although every step took them further from the rebel encampment.

* * *

"Reports from the *Perry* are overdue, sir," Commander Plummer reported to Captain Brookings, the base commander at Simmons Space Command Base, "and we're not receiving responses to our outgoing messages."

"When was their last report?" Brookings asked.

"On the 18th, sir."

"Nine days, eh. Is there any suggestion that this might be related to the diplomatic ship encounter?"

"None, sir. The *Perry* had assisted the diplomatic yacht in making its repairs and had then gone in search of the destroyer that attacked it. In his last message, Captain Lidden reported locating the ship in orbit around Diabolisto. It wasn't responding to challenges and appeared to be derelict. Lidden reported that there was obvious damage to the destroyer's forward larboard hull, but the Sub-Light engines and the FTL drive appeared to be undamaged. He was sending Marines over to investigate. That was the last report we received."

"It would seem that the ship wasn't a derelict after all." Brookings snorted. "Lidden's an excellent officer— too good to be stuck aboard a ship like the *Perry*. I know he wouldn't have moved in closer than twenty-five thousand kilometers until he knew the destroyer was in fact derelict, or at least impotent, but the destroyer could have suddenly come to life and engaged the *Perry*."

"The Clidepp reported that two destroyers were stolen from their shipyard, sir. It's possible that the second destroyer showed up while the *Perry* was engaged with the first."

"Yes. The *Perry* is only a light destroyer, and an old one at that. Two modern destroyers might have been too much for them. That damned old bucket should have gone to the scrap yard decades ago. It's barely been adequate for interdiction work. It's not up to fighting even one modern military war- ship, let alone two."

"If they really wanted to keep it in service, they should have assigned it duty such as guarding the entrance to the Mars shipbuilding yards or something. It doesn't belong any- where where it might have to fight."

"We'll have to send someone to investigate. Who do we have available in that sub-sector?"

"No one."

"No one?"

"The *Perry* was the only SC warship in his sub-sector and, in fact, his entire sector because he was operating just a few days' distance from the border. If this was solely a search and rescue mission, we have a number of ships we could send, although it would take them months to arrive. But since there's a possibility of encounters with enemy warships operating in GA space, we can't send unarmed or lightly armed vessels. As for warships, we have the two light destroyers that are presently serving as a protection force for this base and seven others that are out on patrol. The warship closest to the *Perry* is the light destroyer *Pellew*. He could reach Diabolisto in about ninety-six days at top speed."

"Three months?"

"That's the best we can do, sir."

"Very well. Order the *Pellew* to proceed immediately to the last reported position of the *Perry* and commence a search for the ship. I'll notify SHQ that I've changed the *Pellew's* patrol route in order to deal with this situation."

"Yes, sir."

*   *   *

"The *Abissto* reached Diabolisto and established a camp on the surface," the hooded figure said. "The Captain of the *Glassama* went to see if he could render assistance and was spotted by an SC destroyer. They tried to escape, but the Spacc ship was faster. It pursued them and tried to merge envelopes in order to destroy their FTL generator, but the helmsman on the *Glassama* attempted an evasion maneuver. The two ships collided."

"Did anyone survive?" another hooded figure asked.

"Eighteen of our people were crushed in the wreckage and twelve more are missing and presumed lost when sections of the ship were opened to space. The Captain reports that their FTL generator is intact, but the damage to the hull makes travel at FTL impossible because the ship can't maintain a cohesive temporal envelope. They lost their starboard maneuvering engine and two starboard stern engines in the collision, but they can manage with just the larboard engines for the time being. They're presently sitting fifty thousand kilometers from the Spacc ship and the Spaccs have made no effort to close the distance, which leads the Captain to assume that the Spacc destroyer is much worse off. He wants to know if they should commandeer the Spacc destroyer for our use or destroy it."

"Commandeer a Space Command vessel in GA space?" the second figure asked in surprise. "Is he insane? X, that would constitute an act of war against the GA. So far all we've done is violate their space."

"The Spaccs probably consider the attack on the diplomatic yacht an act of terrorism or they would not have attempted to merge envelopes. I doubt that they feel any allegiance to the Clidepp Empire. I would have expected them to simply chase our ship back across the border if not for the attack."

"We don't want to start a war with the Spaccs," a third said. "We'll have enough to do just bringing down the Empire."

"I agree. I sent a message telling the Captain not to initiate any action but told him he can respond if the Spaccs attack again."

"What of the ship we sent to assist the *Abissto*?"

"The freighter is still underway. The *Glassama* was already in GA space, so they decided to assist if they could."

"So now we have two ships and crews that must be rescued."

"The freighter will have tugs. As soon as they reach the *Abissto*, two will hook up and tow the ship across the border while the crew boards the freighter. Then other tugs from the freighter will do the same for the *Glassama* if they haven't been able to restore their drive."

"I think we should help the *Glassama* first. Let's tow it away from the Spacc ship before its idiot captain decides to start a war with the GA."

"Very well. We just have to hope that the freighter gets there before the Spacc vessel completes its repairs or we may yet have to teach Space Command not to meddle in our affairs, even when they occur in their space."

* * *

"Give us an update, Lieutenant Knudsen," Captain Lidden said to the senior Engineering officer. The entire senior staff was assembled in the conference room on the bridge deck.

"Yes, sir. Since our last meeting, we've made a little progress..."

"*A little?*" Lidden said, interrupting.

"Yes, sir, a little. As I've reported previously, and as we all know so well, the *Perry* is so far past its prime that proper parts are no longer available. Virtually *everything* requires fabrication to some extent. We don't have the luxury of time for proper testing and burn-in periods as we go, so some fabricated components fail soon after installation or don't even work initially. We're trying to cobble together complex systems from complex components that were never intended to perform the tasks we're asking of them. Everyone aboard ship who isn't absolutely required for some other task is assisting in the repairs. I have about half of our people working on hull repairs, with the rest allocated to engine power restoration and electronic systems."

Lidden nodded. "What's the situation with the engines?"

"As I've reported previously, the larboard maneuvering engine is gone— ripped away during the collision. The two lower stern engines were damaged so extensively that they are scrap, but we're using what parts we can salvage to repair the upper two. The starboard rotating engine is intact but was completely isolated from bridge control when the lower decks were crushed. We're trying to reroute the system pathways and reestablish control of the engine. The FTL generator is intact, but the damage to the hull prevents use because we can't establish a proper temporal envelope until the hull is shaped like a hull instead of a twisted pile of scrap metal. And it likewise suffers from the loss of bridge control."

"Do you have an estimate for when we might have some sort of propulsion available?"

"We might have minimal sub-light in six days using the starboard maneuvering engine since sub-light doesn't require a proper hull shape."

"What about FTL?"

"I estimate two months."

"TWO months? Two MORE months?"

"Captain, following the collision the three lowest decks were twisted scrap. We're attempting to cut away the wreckage and rebuild the hull down there. We're not trying to make it look pretty, just enclose the space. A DATFA envelope isn't like an air bubble. It doesn't assume a more or less predetermined shape. It follows the contours of the ship, so there are some basic design requirements. If a ship tries to go FTL without a cohesive envelope, it can be ripped apart in an instant and have its parts scattered over a light-year of space. It would be as devastating as having a hundred torpedoes explode inside the hull at the same instant."

Lidden took a deep breath and exhaled it slowly. "What about communications? We left forty-two of our people on Diabolisto. If the almost three hundred rebels on the planet learn that they're there, they could be in great danger. They must be wondering why we haven't communicated with them."

"I have a small group working on communications. I can assign more people if you want me to take them off the hull repairs."

Lidden thought for a moment before saying, "No, we need propulsion even more than communications. If the rebel destroyer repairs their vessel while we're helpless, they might attack us. We must have sensors and basic maneuvering capability so we can bring our intact torpedo tubes and laser arrays to bear. The lives of the hundreds aboard the *Perry* must take a higher priority than the forty-two we left on Diabolisto."

* * *

"Well?" Currulla asked the officer in charge of the search when the shuttles returned. "Did you find them?"

"We think so," Suflagga said.

"You *think* so? Either you did or you didn't."

"We found— something. We couldn't get a good read on it from the shuttle, but there was *something* below us. We almost overflew it but the man on the scanning equipment asked for another pass. There were strange, grey— *spots*— on the ground that offered no heat readings."

"Terrans are warm-blooded creatures like us. They would have looked yellow on our equipment."

"I know, but they could have been masking their body temperature somehow. Anyway, we dropped some smoke and got out of the way so the fighters could pepper the area. After they finished, we went back. Because of the bombing, the vegetation was still burning. We couldn't get any kind of read, so we landed some of our people. They had to wait until the smoke finally dissipated, but they didn't find any bodies."

"So your assumption was wrong?" Currulla asked.

"They did find indications that something had been there and had left in a hurry."

"Was it the ones who attacked us, or just some big animals that live in the jungle?"

"That's what we don't know yet," Suflagga replied. "I put our best trackers on the trail we found and sent everyone else in support. They'll call in when they learn something. I know that big jungle animals didn't destroy our stockpiles."

"That had to be Spaccs. Who else could have pulled off a raid like that? We saw their ship on the DeTect equipment when it entered orbit and then heard them when they hailed the destroyer. They must have boarded it and determined that we were down on the surface. But I don't understand how they could have landed a force without us seeing it."

"They probably approached from behind the planet and flew so low that we couldn't pick them up on our equipment."

"But the vessel left orbit days ago."

"They needed time for recon and to plan their attack."

"They left their people behind?"

"It would seem so. It was a very effective tactic. We never expected anything like that."

"Yes, they really caught *us* napping," Currulla said. "Literally."

"I doubt that will happen again. Everyone is now aware that we're not alone on this planet and that sleeping on guard duty can be the very last dumb thing they ever get to do. How bad was the damage?"

"They knew what they were doing. We lost all our major ordnance. All we have left is small arms and the fighters."

"Fighters that are now out of rockets and bombs. Those crazy pilots shot everything they had. The rest was in one of the cargo areas that were destroyed."

"At least they have their laser weapons."

"Useless in this jungle. You can't see a target to hit it. The overhead vegetation is too thick."

"So they're effectively grounded?"

"Yeah, there's no sense sending them up. Except..."

"Except?"

"The Spaccs may not know we have no rockets or bombs left," Suflagga said. "We can rig up some dummy weapons for the fighters so that from a distance it will look like they're armed."

"What good will that do?"

"If the Spaccs see armed fighters overhead, it might keep them on the run until we find a good ambush location."

"We can just keep the trackers on their trail. That will keep them on the run."

"But it wears down our forces. That jungle is a miserable place. Better to wear the Spaccs down while our people prepare the ambush."

"Yeah, okay. That makes sense. Where will this ambush take place?"

"I don't know yet. We'll send the shuttles up to snap images of the terrain. Once we have decent maps, we'll be able to pick the ideal place. Then it's simply a matter of driving them into the trap."

"It might not be so simple if they discover they're being driven."

"We'll keep it subtle. They'll never know they're walking into a trap until we spring it. And once we spring it, they'll all be as dead as the sentries they killed."

"Don't underestimate them. They're professional soldiers, not like most of *our* lot."

"For twenty-four years I was a professional soldier for the Empire. I know what I'm doing."

* * *

"Mom, have you heard from Syd lately?" Sheree Marcola asked as she sat down to dinner in their New York home.

"I got her usual weekly vid message," Kathee Deleone said absently.

"This week?"

"Yes. Uh, no, come to think of it. The last one I received was about three weeks ago. Today is the day it usually arrives. Maybe there's one in the queue. I haven't checked my mail today."

"I didn't get one last week or today," Sheree said. "I wonder if something's wrong."

"What could possibly be wrong?" Curtis Deleone asked. "She's not out in Region Two fighting in this ridiculous war with her hero, Admiral Carver. She's safe and sound right here in Region One. Rather than getting shot at on a daily basis by grotesque-looking aliens, she's checking passports, visas, and shipping manifests. She's doing what she wants, and she's as safe as she could be. That's what you want, right? One thing you can be absolutely sure of— no one is going to be trying to kill your baby while she's on simple Border Patrol duty."

Chapter Sixteen
~ Feb. 27th, 2285 ~

"Have we lost them, Sergeant?" Kennedy asked the noncom with the rear guard team.

"Negative, sir. We've slowed them a bit, but their trackers are good— real good. It takes them awhile sometimes, what with the false trails and backtracking we've done, but they keep at it until they find our real trail. The good news is that we've widened the distance between us by about another kilometer. I doubt if they'll hear any incidental noise from the platoon now. And if we can keep this up until dark, we'll have a good chance of getting away."

"How fast are they moving? We've been at this for almost eight hours straight and we need a break."

"I wouldn't recommend more than ten minutes, sir. Every-one will stiffen up and we have a lot more swamp to cover before dark."

"Okay, Sergeant. We'll stop at the next clearing for ten minutes."

"Oo-rah."

Adrenaline had kept everyone at maximum effort since the raid. By calling a ten-minute rest, it might seem that Kennedy was more or less declaring that the immediate danger was over, so he stressed that the rebels were still close on their heels. Marines immediately dropped their backpacks and then dropped themselves into the tall grass where they were standing.

Sydnee had never felt so exhausted as she dropped her backpack to the side and then fell backwards next to it. As she disturbed their nesting area, a flurry of insects took flight all around her and then slowly settled again. She hoped she would find the energy to move again when the ten minutes were up. At that moment, it didn't seem likely.

"Okay," Kennedy said over Com 1, "I want everyone on their feet and ready to travel in sixty seconds. The rebel band is still tracking us and they're coming on strong. I don't have to tell you what will happen if they catch up. Let's be long gone when they arrive at this spot."

Sydnee assumed that everyone had turned off their helmet's transmit capability on Com 1 because she didn't hear any moans, groans, or comments. It was good that her own transmit circuit was off because she couldn't help groaning a bit as she climbed to her feet and grabbed the backpack. She shooed off a handful of insects and then slung it onto her back using the left strap. The weight nearly toppled her as she twisted to get her right arm into the other strap because she hadn't planted her feet properly, but the load suddenly became weightless as someone behind her grabbed the pack. She was able to get her right arm into the strap and settle the pack on her back before she felt the weight return. She turned and gave the Marine a thumbs up for the assist. He responded in kind.

As the platoon moved out, Sydnee fell into line like before. The hours seemed to pass like days as they traversed every swamp and marshland the scouts could locate along their general route. More than once it seemed like they were passing through a swamp they had already crossed, but that was just because they had all begun to look alike. Most creatures they encountered moved away from their path, but some seemed to defy them to attack. The scouts usually gave a wide berth to anything large enough to be a problem. To make the situation even more miserable, it began to rain off and on. Sometimes it was gentle, while other times it seemed like they were walking beneath a waterfall.

Just before the grey of evening gave way to the dark of night, they could see a distant ridgeline of low hills. Kennedy ordered the scouts to head in that direction and the platoon altered course by forty degrees to the right. It would be great to get out of the swamp for a while. Although their personal armor kept them dry, slogging through boggy wetlands and swamps required five times the effort required for crossing jungle and ten times the effort expended while moving through normal forested areas. Climbing hilly terrain couldn't be any worse than what they had been through so far.

As they changed direction, rain began to fall with an intensity previously unseen. The heavy rain slowed them even more and it took hours to reach the long narrow range of hills.

News that one of the scouts had identified a depression in the side of a hill was greeted by optimism when the lead scout speculated that an overhanging ledge might provide a respite from the rainfall overnight and requested permission to back-track to check it out. Kennedy told him to continue his regular assignment and ordered a fire team to check out the depression.

The rest of the platoon dropped their backpacks and their bodies and listened in on Com 1 as four Marines made their way to the identified depression. When they reported that the depression was actually the entrance to a narrow fissure, Kennedy ordered them inside to see if it might be large enough to provide shelter for the night.

Almost immediately after entering the fissure, the fire team reported that it widened to a narrow cave after a few meters. As they further explored, they continued to report no contacts with any sizable indigenous life forms, although they said that the volume of insects was prodigious.

The exploration took about half an hour and the final report was that it appeared dry and safe. At the extreme reaches, the team had found a large domed area suitable for overnight habitation. Kennedy immediately ordered everyone inside. The weary Marines picked up their backpacks and entered the cave, then followed a twisting, torturous path to where the explorers had found the large chamber.

The cave would have been perfect but for the insects and the one wall where water was running down in rivulets. Fortunately, the water was collecting in a pool that seemed to drain off by itself so the rest of the cave was dry, if a bit humid. Scattered rocks sat on sandy soil with a loose, granular feel. The best part was that the cave had to be at least twenty-five degrees cooler than outside.

Sydnee selected a spot near a sidewall where she'd be out of the way, kicked the loose rocks away, and dropped her pack for just the third time since the raid. She was suddenly more tired than at any time she could ever remember. Adrenaline had kept everyone going throughout the day, but the sense of temporary safety now would cause the adrenal glands to slow the production, and they would begin to react to the exhaustion they were all feeling.

Before the platoon could rest, they had to prepare their camp. Two Marines took a small holo-projector to the front of the cave and had the unit assemble an image of a rear wall from selected shots of the sidewalls. When it was complete and looked acceptable, they activated the unit. From outside, the fissure no longer looked like a fissure. To anyone more than a meter away, it would appear to be just a half-meter depression in the ridge wall. The projector would adjust the image to conform to the proper lighting from outside and the winding path to the bivouac area meant that no light would be visible from behind the projection.

Inside the domed area of the cave, Marines were unpacking the four oh-gee sleds after the main floor area had been cleared of loose rocks. Several of the misting devices used to control insects had been started and the air had begun to clear almost immediately. Within minutes, the insects that hadn't managed to get out of the cavern area were dropping to the floor. Within ten minutes there wouldn't be an insect left alive in the cave unless it happened to be immune to the spray.

Other Marines were setting up a food preparation area. It would be the first meal they'd had since leaving their former camp almost twenty-four hours ago, and although prepared from emergency ration packs, no one doubted that it would taste like some of the best food they'd had in weeks. Hunger would do that to a person.

Kennedy walked over to where Sydnee was sitting and plopped down next to her. She heard on Com 2, "I'm glad you're with us."

"You are?" she replied after activating her transmit feature from the menu with a wink of her eye.

"Of course. We could have gotten stuck with Weems."

"Lieutenant Weems is an excellent pilot," Sydnee said, trying to keep the edge out of her voice. She was once again glad she was wearing the helmet so Kennedy couldn't read her face and see the anger there. "He would have gotten you down just as safely as I did."

"Of course he is and would have, but he doesn't spend much time in the gym anymore. I doubt he could have kept up with the platoon today. We would probably have had to carry him or leave some supplies along the way so he could ride on one of the oh-gee sleds. You kept up great today because you work out regularly."

"Uh, thanks, but I'm sure Lt. Weems would have surprised you."

"If you say so."

"I do. It would have been nice to have a few dozen oh-gee sleds, though. I've been thinking about that all day as we slogged through the swamps. We could have made better time getting away from the rebel camp."

"The Corps tried to come up with something awhile back. In the end, they decided that the idea was impractical. The equipment just wasn't stealthy enough."

"Not stealthy? The oh-gee process is totally silent."

"The oh-gee part wasn't the problem; that's noiseless. The problem was the propulsion. Any kind of jet or even thruster makes far too much noise where total silence is required."

"I wasn't even thinking of self-propelled. If we had a bunch of sleds, we could have given one to each fire team. Only one member would then have had to slog through the swamp while the others rode. Pulling an oh-gee sled is almost effortless because there's no resistance from the ground to overcome, and the one acting as a draft animal could have switched with the others every thirty minutes or so."

"Yeah, it could work. Of course, none of us expected to be in this situation. We intended to use the MAT to land near the rebel camp with a force large enough to capture them in a surprise raid. I hope the *Perry* returns soon so we can finish the job here and get off this planet."

"Rett, you have to face facts. The *Perry* might not be coming back. If everything was well with them, we'd have heard back by now."

"Maybe. Or maybe it's just some space anomaly that's preventing us from receiving their messages."

"If they were sending and not getting replies, they'd be here by now to check on us. It has to be that they *can't* come. I think we should circle back to the rebel camp."

"Go back? What for?"

"If I can commandeer a shuttle, we'll at least have a chance of surviving down here."

"Absolutely not. My scouts have reported that there are about seventy rebels behind us. If we circle back, we'll have seventy rebels behind and two hundred in front of us. I don't intend to be caught between two rebel forces. Besides, they have those fighters we saw. They'd be after you before you could get away. One rocket is all it would take to shoot you down."

"We'd have sabotaged their fighters before taking the shuttle."

"Syd, there are almost three hundred rebels who must, by now, have a burning desire to see every one of us dead. To return to their camp would be the most foolhardy thing we could do."

"That's just it. They'll never expect it. They believe we're still out here somewhere, and be unprepared for another assault."

"I already went way outside my instructions when I order-ed the attack, but I had to make sure the rebels could never use that ordnance. However, we got away clean, and I don't intend to stick my head into the lion's mouth a second time."

"Rett, it's our only chance. Without a shuttle, we'll spend the rest of our days slogging through swamps until the rebels catch us or this planet kills us. That is if we don't run out of food first."

"We just have to evade the rebels until the *Perry* comes back. They wouldn't desert us."

Sydnee rolled her eyes, glad Kennedy couldn't see her face. "No, they would never desert us, but they might not be able to return. Why can't you understand that the *Perry* might have been destroyed?"

"By a bunch of rag-tag rebels? Never. Why, that bunch couldn't even commandeer a diplomatic yacht."

"Then why are we running?"

"I, uh, don't want to lose even one Marine. I know we could defeat them in a fight, but we might be bloodied. And for no reason. Once the *Perry* returns, we'll mop them up with less chance of anyone being killed."

Sydnee knew that she wasn't going to change Kennedy's mind— at least not yet. If the *Perry* failed to return in the days ahead, he might begin to accept that it wasn't coming back. Sydnee believed their best chance for survival lay with commandeering one of the small ships the rebels had acquired with the destroyer. If she could get a tug, she might even get the MAT out of the sinkhole. Tugs were all engine, except for a small flight deck, and would have no trouble getting the MAT out of the hole if they got to it before it got too covered with dirt. The weight of the dirt wasn't a problem, but it could prevent the tug from locking onto the MAT with its magnetic skids. For that matter, Sydnee wasn't even sure if the tug could get a magnetic grip on a Dakinium-sheathed ship.

"Listen up, everyone," Staff Sergeant McKenzie announced on the Com 1 frequency. "The bugs appear to be dead. At least there's nothing flying around in here. Everyone can remove their helmets and even strip off their armor if they aren't scheduled for guard duty."

Within seconds, most of the helmets were off. After days of living like sardines in a can, the Marines couldn't wait to strip down to shorts and tees. A few put on fatigues, but many opted for the simpler look. Kennedy didn't insist on proper military decorum and settled for shorts and a tee himself. Because of the rough surface on the floor of the cave, almost everyone wore combat boots. Sydnee opted for the soft-soled boots all SC personnel wore aboard ship.

While the armor was designed for long-term wear under emergency conditions, it did have shortcomings. It contained nutrient packs that were replaceable without removing the armor, recycled all water waste to drinkable condition, and provided for solid waste storage, but it left a lot to be desired in comfort. Although everyone was delighted to be free for the present, they didn't waste time in seeing to the cleaning and care of their armor for its next use. A small unit that could clean and dry five padded bodysuits at a time was set up. Although specially treated not to absorb body oils and odors, the padded bodysuits did need to be cleaned occasionally.

Cleaning functions were intended to be performed aboard the MAT where the armor could be completely removed, but that hadn't been possible since landing on the planet. While at the original camp, they had risked removing their helmets only for eating, and then only in the CP tent or one of the shelters where the insect misting devices killed all insects. Sydnee had once contemplated the agony of having an insect or insects buzzing around inside her helmet if she had to remove it and then replace it while outside.

Thin gravity-shielding cloth, like that used in gel-comfort beds, was used for bedrolls. Suspended as much as a quarter of a meter above the bedroll, depending upon their weight, the Marine would float in complete comfort as the normal gravity field curved over the bedroll and again took hold to keep him or her from floating too high. While encased in armor, no comfort would be derived from using the bedrolls, but once they'd stripped it off, the bedrolls made a world of difference.

"That's much better," Kennedy said, as he settled atop his bedroll after cleaning his armor, taking a turn inside the portable shower, and grabbing some chow.

"Almost makes you feel human again," Sydnee said.

Looking at Sydnee's food plate, Kennedy remarked, "Are you actually going to eat that thing?"

"You mean the Grepper?"

"Is that what it's called?"

"I think so. I'm pretty sure that I heard it was a delicacy on some planets, but I didn't know where it came from. Sergeant Booth put it into the alien food analyzer and it tested safe, so he skinned it, cut it up, and rolled the pieces in flour before frying them."

"How does it taste?"

"It has a consistency kinda like chicken, with a slightly fishy taste. It's good. Want to try a piece?"

"No thanks, I'll pass. After spending most of the day in swamps, the last thing I want is something that tastes fishy."

Following a brief lull in the conversation during which time both officers managed to partially fill the void in their midsections, Sydnee said, "I wonder how the rebels on our trail are making out."

"Corporal Jenkins reported they've bedded down for the evening. They have some kind of insect-control device, but it's apparently not a hundred percent effective in the open. Jenkins said he could hear a lot of cursing and slapping from his vantage point."

"This cave has to be like a luxury hotel compared to being out in the open. We lucked out."

"Yes, we really did luck out. I don't know how much longer we could have continued to run from them tonight. There are no decent maps of this area, other than basic topographic stuff, so I was just trying to put as much distance between us and the rebels as possible to ensure they couldn't see lights or smell food from our camp. I never expected to find a cave that was so ideal for a camp."

"Too bad we can't lay over for a few days and rest up."

"Yes, but the rebels will be scouring the landscape for us. Their trackers are good. They'll find our trail once it's light. We'll have to get up early and be ready to pull out at day-break."

"Couldn't our scouts create a false trail that leads away from this area?"

"Our rear guard tried that twice today. The rebel trackers saw through our attempts and were back on our real trail in no time."

"If we can't shake them, what are we going to do?"

"We have no choice," Kennedy said. "We run until we find a good, defensible position, then set up an ambush and hope we can change their minds about pursuing us."

"I doubt if we'll find a more defensible position than right here. We're protected from air attack, can't be outflanked because there's only one entrance in, and the walls provide better protection from ground attack than anything we're likely to find."

"The single entrance is the problem. They could blow the ridge above us and collapse it on the entrance, burying us alive."

"We supposedly destroyed all their heavy ordnance. Without mortars, they'll be limited to hand grenades. What-ever damage they do can be undone later with our Corplastizine charges."

"We don't know that they have no mortars. There may have been small stocks elsewhere that we didn't spot, or even stored in one of the shuttles."

"I still don't think we'll find a more defensible position. You really should try this Grepper, Rett. It's delicious."

* * *

"Well?" Currulla asked when Suflagga finished taking the reports from his people in the field.

"The Spaccs keep changing direction. We've set up ambushes in two locations and then had to shut them down when the Spaccs went in another direction."

"They discovered your traps?"

"No, they weren't close enough. It's as if they have no real destination and are just wandering around."

"To what end?"

"I don't know. They might be hoping to divide our forces."

"They're succeeding. We have seventy men on their trail and another seventy setting up ambushes. That's half our force here, and the ones that are left are only support personnel. They'd be useless for tracking or ambushes. And they're so out of shape they'd collapse if you asked them to walk even two kilometers through that miserable jungle."

"I know, I know."

"We can't keep our people chasing Spaccs around this planet forever."

"I know, I know."

"You have to end this quickly."

"I know, I know."

"What are you going to do?"

"I don't know."

"You said you were a professional."

"The ambush plan is all I have."

"You only had one plan?"

"Our ordnance has been blown to hell, my *battalion* is composed mostly of farmers and store clerks, and the enemy isn't following a rational withdrawal route after a highly successful strike against us that has demoralized the camp. My options are limited."

"Your job is to locate and kill the swine that attacked us and murdered our men. I suggest you find a way to do that or I'll find someone who can."

"If I can get them in our gun sights, we'll kill every last one. And I'll bring you their heads."

"Please," Currulla said a little squeamishly as he raised his hand with the palm facing Suflagga, "no severed heads."

Chapter Seventeen
~ Feb. 27th, 2285 ~

Sydnee awakened to the sounds of people moving around. She opened her eyes and was shocked for an instant to see the roof of the cave high overhead; then she remembered where they were. She pulled back the light thermal blanket, sat up, then stood. The first order of business was use of the portable latrine curtained off from the rest of the cave.

After emerging relieved and refreshed, she took a good look around. She was surprised to see that no one was packing up. She saw Kennedy at the com station and walked over to stand next to him. "I thought we were leaving at daybreak," she said.

"Change of plans. I decided to follow your idea."

"Really," she said, her eyes opening wide. She wondered what had gotten him to change his mind. "When do we leave?"

"We're going to stay, as you suggested last night."

"Oh, I thought you meant we were going to grab a shuttle."

"C'mon, Syd. That idea is nuts. They know we're here now and will be on high alert. We'd never even get close to their ships."

"Have you at least identified their location so we know what they have?"

"Yeah, we've been watching their camp using the two surveillance cameras we left there. We found where the ships are parked. It's about a kilometer from the area where the supplies were dropped. I guess the supplies used up all the cleared space so they had to park the ships at the next available clearing. They have three shuttles, one tug, and two fighters. The distance from the main camp is the reason we didn't spot them before our raid."

"Too bad, that would have been the ideal time to commandeer one."

"Spilt milk."

"What?"

"That's something my Mom always said about things that couldn't be changed because they were in the past. It's best not to think about them."

"Your Mom obviously wasn't in the military."

"Why obviously?"

"Military people must always continue to review past incidents, their own and those of others, to make sure they don't make similar mistakes in the future."

Kennedy's face contorted slightly. He obviously didn't like to be reminded that he had somehow failed to consider every aspect of the raid on the rebel camp. "Get some rest and forget about the damn shuttles," he said as he turned and walked away.

Sydnee watched his back for a few seconds and then turned towards the food preparation area where Marines were queuing up for breakfast. She hurried to get in line.

* * *

"Well?" Currulla said as he walked over to the table where Suflagga stood staring at a holo-map.

"They're in there somewhere."

"You mean you haven't found them yet?"

"My people have traversed this entire jungle area during the past two days. They could not have gotten past us, yet the trackers arrived at the ambush point without ever seeing a single sign of them."

"Perhaps they were air-lifted out."

"NO," Suflagga said vehemently. "They're there. They're still there."

"Where?"

"I— don't know."

"Up in the trees perhaps?"

"Don't be ridiculous."

"Underwater, in the swamp then? Perhaps they have a secret base under there."

Suflagga glared at Currulla for a second before saying, "Don't be ridiculous. We just missed them somehow. They must have some new kind of camouflage. It's like they just disappeared. We've searched for them from the air, but we haven't seen any of those strange cold areas, or any indication of body heat except for our own people; we've been able to identify every one of *them*."

"But your best trackers were following their trail."

"They lost that after the all-night downpour we had two days ago. It wiped out all trace of the trail."

"So what do we do now?"

"I don't know."

"Is this the great twenty-four-year military leader speaking?"

"Look, this isn't some garden variety smuggling group. This has to be an elite group of Space Command's finest troops. How they happened to be on that destroyer, I don't know. But we're up against the best Space Command has."

"Or perhaps your people aren't as good as you thought."

"My people are good. I trained them myself, and we were chosen for this mission by X. If you had been able to stop that diplomatic yacht like you were supposed to, you would have seen a model board-and-secure operation. We practiced for a full month. Only twenty of the personnel in this operation are mine. The rest involved in this disaster are yours, and most couldn't find their lunch in a paper sack."

"My people aren't warriors trained for jungle operations. They've only been trained for ship operations. So I ask again, what now?"

"The only thing to do is go back to the place where we lost their trail and try again. They *have* to be somewhere between that point and where we set up the ambush."

* * *

When the large monitor at the front of the *Perry's* bridge suddenly came on, a cheer went up on the bridge. The bridge crews had been sitting at their stations day after day with nothing to do, so some indication that things were getting fixed was cause for celebration. Unfortunately, the monitor went dark again after a few seconds. Just as depression started to set in, the monitor came on again. And this time it stayed on. Milty waited for five minutes, just in case, before calling the Captain, who wanted to be kept abreast of all developments regardless of the hour.

"Captain, I'm sorry to disturb you but I wanted to report that the main monitor has come on. We have eyes again, sir."

"That news is worth being awakened for. Can you see the other destroyer?"

"Yes, sir. It's still sitting where it's been since the day of the collision."

"No sign of any other vessels?"

"No, sir. She's alone."

"Okay, Milty. Anything else to report?"

"No, sir. All consoles are still down except for the main monitor functions at the tactical station."

"Okay, Milty. Keep an eye out for any other vessels. Goodnight."

"Goodnight, sir."

"Good morning, Milty," Captain Lidden said as he entered the bridge at 0740 and walked to the command chair. "Have there been any changes since you reported earlier?"

"Lieutenant Nivollo has tested the sensor system, sir. About sixty percent of the grid appears operational at this time. Space off the lower larboard hull is still black, as expected, but the rest of the ship's exterior sensors seem to be back on line, although neither the AutoTect nor DeTect systems are online yet."

"At least we can see our adversary," Lidden said as he looked at the large image of the rebel destroyer on the main screen. "It appears she didn't get off much better than us."

"No, sir. Her damage appears to be pretty extensive. I doubt she'll be going FTL anytime soon."

"I'd almost be tempted to put a couple of torpedoes into her if our tubes were operational, but we have to go by the book. She didn't use deadly force against us, so we can't use it against her."

"Yes, sir. But they could have killed all of us with that crazy helm maneuver. "

"That might have been the act of one person, operating without the approval of the commanding officer."

"Yes, sir."

"Okay, Milty, I'll take over. Get some chow."

"Yes, sir," Milty said, climbing down from the command chair. "You have the bridge, Captain."

* * *

"Give me an update on efforts to find Citizen X," Gustallo Plelillo, Premier of the Clidepp government, said as he enter-ed the office of Weislis Danttan, the Minister of Intelligence.

"No change. The army has been arresting people on every planet but has learned nothing so far."

"Then they're not arresting enough people."

"They're picking up everybody who has ever spoken out against the central government. The camps are filled with screams from day to night, and the blood is being carried out of interrogation rooms in buckets. If anyone knew, they would talk. We've even tried drugs where pain didn't work. It made no difference. They simply don't know who Citizen X is."

"Kurrost," Plelillo said loudly.

Kurrost Mewaffal, the Minister of Public Information sat up straighter and said, "Yes, Gustallo."

"We need a new information campaign. We want to paint Citizen X as a crazed renegade hiding behind the people and ourselves as beneficent leaders who only want to end the terrible suffering of our people."

"We're already doing that."

"Well, step up the effort then. And— increase the reward of a hundred thousand credits to a hundred million for the identity and location of this Citizen X. There's always some-one in the know who will sell their own mother for a few credits."

"A hundred million credits is a lot more than a few. It could break the treasury."

"I didn't say pay it. I said offer it. The individual who turns in Citizen X will quietly disappear. After all, if they know his identity, they have to be working for him."

"They'll want immunity from prosecution before they speak."

"Then simply give the informant to Weislis's people if you believe the traitor has the information."

"If word gets out that we did that, we'd never get anyone to turn again."

"Then make sure that no one finds out. Do I have to think of everything?"

* * *

"The plan is working perfectly," the hooded figure said. "The more the army cracks down on the civilian population, the more the fence-sitters give up their tenuous perch and finally adopt a position. And the overwhelming choice is the rebellion."

"X, did you plan it this way?" one of the others asked.

"Knowing how the central government on Yolongus works, and has always worked, it was an obvious course for events to follow."

"So you planned for people to be hurt in order to force others to make up their minds?"

"I expected it to happen because on Yolongus dissension has always been met with brute force. I didn't want it to happen, but I've always known that the situation had to devolve to this point before our rebellion could advance. The central government wasn't simply going to surrender power, and there was no mechanism in place for a peaceful transition because those in power were never going to step down willingly. Their heavy-handed techniques were expected and, in fact, necessary to give our movement the grassroots support it needed."

Citizen X stopped for a second, then continued with, "My friends, I'm no happier than any of you that our people are being hurt, but from the moment we began this initiative, there was never any question that we would arrive at this point. People can adapt and become complacent in almost any situation, but change is inevitable.

"Governments, even supposedly benign ones that claim to be representative of the people, if left alone, tend to usurp more and more citizenry rights and freedoms until the situation reaches a breaking point where excessive taxation and unreasonably low standards of living force the masses to take drastic action. As the divide between rich and poor widens, discontent increases proportionally. If there is no mechanism in place for real social change, the populace is forced to violently pull down governments propped up by powerful and excessively wealthy individuals and enterprises. That's the way it's always been. A pendulum can only swing so far, and then it must swing back. Our pendulum has almost reached that extreme point in its arc. As it begins to swing back, the wealthy who own the souls of the so-called public officials are going to resist firmly. We must help our people throw off the yoke of oppression and free them from the tyrannical rulers that have enslaved them for decades."

"You make it sound so easy," another hooded figure said, "but this campaign is just starting. Many will suffer and die before we achieve our goal."

"Yes, that's true. But nothing worth having ever comes easily. And freedom for all the people of this nation is worth having. What we must ensure is that the government we install remains ever responsive to the needs of the people instead of just the wealthiest one-percent. That's perhaps the most difficult challenge ahead. When the lessons of this rebellion become murky in the memories of our people, those in power will again begin stripping power from the masses in order to again shift the wealth of the nation to those moneyed enough to have bought the loyalties of politicians. They'll do it slowly, insidiously, and patiently as they attempt to subvert a government where the power should rest with the people. Unless we want to go through this agony again every few centuries, we must find a way for people to bloodlessly take back the power we have only lent our political leaders for a short time. Government officials must be the guardians of power for the people, not mindless lap dogs to rich over-lords."

* * *

Sydnee awoke to the sounds of activity in the cavern. They had enjoyed four days of almost carefree rest and the muscle aches of the first couple of days were just a memory. She was no longer startled when she awoke and saw the domed cavern ceiling overhead.

Sitting up, she looked at the activity going on around her. She motioned to a PFC passing back and asked, "What's going on?"

"The LT has decided it's time to move on, ma'am. We pull out at sundown."

"Okay, thanks."

The PFC said, "Oo-rah," and returned to his task of packing up some of the gear and carrying it to an oh-gee sled. Sydnee sauntered over to the mess table and looked at the imitation scrambled eggs made from dehydrated powder and bacon made from soy flour and chemicals. It was amazing that the food from emergency rations packs could taste so close to the real thing when there was the time and the hot water necessary to prepare it properly.

"Move it, Syd," she heard from behind her. "We pull out in twelve hours, and we want this place to look as it did when we arrived."

She turned to see Kennedy standing behind her. "I heard," she said. "Where are we headed?"

"East."

"Why?"

"Why not?"

"I mean, why move at all? This cavern has been great. Why don't we just stay here until the rebels stop looking for us?"

"They passed us by a couple of days ago, then returned and made another, slower pass. Our scouts are watching them and report that the rebels don't seem disposed to giving up. Their shuttles have just returned them to the starting point for the second time. They've spread out and they're making a third search, far more thorough than the last. Someone is driving them to find us and I don't think he'll give up until they do. So we'll take advantage of their slower progression on this pass to put some distance between us."

"Rett, isn't it better to stay holed up in here where we're hidden and are less exposed to fire if found than to break out into the open where they might see us?"

"Look, I'm no more anxious than anyone else to start trudging through swamps again, but we're rested, and the rebels have to be exhausted after searching for days. This is our best time to make a run for it and try to put so much distance between us that we won't have to worry about them again."

"But how do they know we haven't already gone? Why are they assuming we're still in this area?"

"I don't know, Syd."

"Isn't not knowing enough to make us tread more carefully? Are we on a plateau from which we can't descend? Is there something impassable ahead, like an un-scalable cliff wall? There has to be a reason why the rebels keep searching this area for us after already completing two passes."

"I've already made the decision that we go. We pull out in twelve hours. End of discussion."

* * *

"We've found them," Suflagga announced proudly that evening when Currulla entered the operations tent.

"It's about time. I just learned that we lost an eighth man to one of those enormous swamp monsters that grab you and pull you down, then seem to just disappear with their victim. Are you sure it's them?"

"Yes— almost."

"Which is it?"

"On the second pass through the area, I had our people drop motion sensors every kilometer. We've had a few stray hits since then, probably from wildlife in the area, but we're now tracking approximately forty targets. If it's not them, then it's an unusual herd of animals."

"Why unusual?"

"Because they're walking single file."

"What now?"

"It's dark, so we'll keep monitoring them until dawn and then prepare our ambush."

* * *

"It's not right, Sterling," Sheree Marcola said to her brother. "You haven't even spoken to Sydnee in more than four years. I keep telling her that I haven't heard from you because I know how devastated she'd be if she knew we talked every week."

Sterling Marcola stared at the image of his sister on the vid phone for a couple of seconds before saying, "You know how much I opposed her decision to join the military."

"And because of that you cut yourself off from your sister? You should have seen how happy she was the day she graduated from the Academy."

"I saw."

"How?"

"I was at the graduation ceremony."

"What?"

"I sat alone up in the grandstand."

"I thought you were in Switzerland at the time."

"I was, but I flew in to see her graduate. As opposed as I was to her joining Space Command, I couldn't miss her graduation."

"And you never told any of us, you awful thing. Why didn't you sit with us? We had four tickets for seating down near the stage."

"I didn't want her to know I was there. I'm really proud of her accomplishments, but I can't support her desire to be in Space Command. Dad was always away when we were small, and then he died out there in space. What kind of a life is that for a woman? What about a family?"

"It's a difficult life for anyone, man or woman, but the job is important. We all miss dad, but I'm proud that he fought to make the galaxy a safer place for all of us. And it is. The Raiders are a thing of the past."

"Now you sound like Syd."

"If you're so proud of her, why did you stop calling her and refuse to accept her calls?"

"I'd always hoped she would come to her senses and drop out of the Academy. When she didn't, I just— I don't know."

"Syd doesn't quit once she's made up her mind to do something. She never has. You should know that as well as anyone. She's your big sister."

"There's a first time for everything. Maybe being stuck in a boring assignment until she's met the service requirements for her education will convince her to quit."

"Sterling, Syd will never quit. She might change her direction slightly at times to improve her chances of accomplishing the goal she's set, but she *never, ever* quits."

Chapter Eighteen
~ Mar. 4ᵗʰ, 2285 ~

Although Sydnee remained perfectly dry when encased in her protective armor, slogging through bogs and swamps to hide the trail quickly grew tiresome. She was a pilot, not a ground pounder, and longed for even the briefest of rides through the sky at mach-five to forget the misery of this march. The four-day layover had been great but hadn't been long enough. As she trudged through mud and mire she wondered if any amount of time away from the morass would be enough to make her forget the experience.

They hadn't covered more than three kilometers from the cave when Syd heard a shout come over Com 1 and saw commotion ahead. Suddenly, one of the Marines, about the sixth ahead of her, disappeared below the water line in the swamp. A second later, the Marine in front and the Marine in back disappeared as well, but they seemed to dive under, where the first had seemed to be pulled under. "Something's chewing on my leg," Syd heard clearly over the com.

A flash that made the filthy water seem to glow was visible for a second, and then a series of flashes created a light show beneath the surface. During that time, the first Marine appeared briefly above the water before being sucked down again. More flashes could be seen in a light show that lasted at least two minutes while strings of curses and profanities from multiple voices were delivered over Com 1 and seemed to reverberate in her head. Everyone rushed to where the three Marines had gone under but could do nothing but watch an ever-widening froth of bubbles appear on the surface. Occasionally a human limb encased in armor broke the surface, then disappeared again, and once, something that looked like the belly of a crocodile, appeared for just an instant then slipped beneath the muddy water again.

"What's going on," Kennedy shouted on Com 1 several times, but the only answer to his demands were grunts, groans, and more strings of curses as the water continued to churn and bubble with an increasing ferocity.

Finally, the water began to calm and all three Marines involved in the situation regained their footing.

"We're okay," one said.

"What happened?" she heard Kennedy ask.

"Some of the local wildlife wanted to play, sir. We convinced it that we weren't in a playful mood."

"What was it?"

"Don't know, sir," another said, "We'll drag it ashore—when we make shore."

Several hundred meters ahead, Syd climbed up onto dry land and got a look at the thing that had tried to eat PFC Riley. It was as long as a giant anaconda on Earth and had two stubby legs, like those you might find on a lizard, attached along every meter of its twelve-meter body. Its head was as large as that of a great shark and, like a shark, had rows of serrated teeth. The PFC's armor hadn't been damaged, but it wasn't because the creature hadn't tried.

"Anyone know what it is?" Kennedy asked.

"I'll check the alien database," Sydnee said.

"You have an alien database that covers Diabolisto?"

"I downloaded all files pertaining to Diabolisto into the MAT's computer before we left the *Perry* and then added it to my helmet storage before I left the MAT," Syd said as she scanned the DB using eye movements. "That's how I knew what the Grepper was. Ah, here it is. It's a Lampaxa Vorheridine."

"Lampaxa Vorheridine? My Latin was never very good. What does that translate to?"

"Um, nothing. It wasn't named by an Earth scientist. According to the database it was named by a Cheblookan aboard a freighter when it stopped here looking for fresh food. His friend was killed by one as they searched the swamp for Greppers. After the hunting party killed the creature and determined that it was safe to eat if processed properly, the Cheblookan reportedly named it after his mother-in-law, Lampaxa Vorheridine. He said it sort of reminded him of her, even though they look nothing alike."

"Then it's good to eat?" Sergeant Booth asked.

"The DB lists it as perfectly edible, but gamey tasting."

"I can fix that with some of my special Cajun crawdad sauce. Some of you guys help me load this thing onto an oh-gee sled."

As they started to move it, the creature began twitching. A few laser shots to the head was all it took to quiet it down again. Once the creature was secured on the sled, the platoon moved out.

By dawn, the platoon was weary from trudging through jungle swamps and Syd was wondering if they would ever find dry land again as they proceeded east on the trail blazed by the lead scout. The thick overhead canopy of tree branches and leaves provided full cover from the air, and the rear scout, who was now holding position roughly three kilometers behind the platoon, reported that he hadn't seen or heard any sign of the rebels in hours and that the trail being left by the platoon was faint. Kennedy decided to order a stop in a section of jungle that was mostly dry and Marines dropped their packs and then themselves where they stood. They would find no nice dry cave in this area, and breakfast would be served cold from emergency ration packs. The Lampaxa Vorheridine would have to wait until they had a proper camp set up.

* * *

"We're almost ready to spring the trap," Suflagga said to Currulla. "Thanks to the motion sensors we dropped, we know exactly where the Spaccs have stopped after traveling all night. We're assuming they have made camp and intend to remain there to rest up."

"And they're still headed directly for the trap you established?"

"No. They changed direction twice, forcing us to select a new ambush each time, but we've always found a new place. The current ambush point isn't as ideal as the others, but it'll work. It's pretty much an open area and they'll have a ridge line on their right flank with a sheer wall of rock that will block any chance of escape." Pointing to a location on the holo-map, he said, "The map indicates that the rock wall is seventy meters high and almost vertical, so it eliminates any chance of escape in that direction."

"So it's un-scalable?"

"Un-scalable without oh-gee ascent packs or climbing gear. And if they attempt to scale the wall, even with ropes, they'll be exposing themselves to fire from every one of our people."

"How do you know they don't have oh-gee ascent packs?"

"If they had them, they'd have used them to evade pursuit. We don't have them and neither do they."

"That wall won't remain on their right. They'll turn and head for it so they have it against their backs."

"I'm counting on it. All other escape routes will be cut off because my people will close in on the other three sides."

"By putting them near a wall like that, you lose the advantage of using the fighters. They can't get near enough to attack the Spaccs without hitting the wall."

"Without rockets, they're of no use anyway."

"They still have their laser canons."

"We have all the laser weapons we need. My people will decimate the Spaccs without air power."

"How are you going to trap them if they're not on the move?"

"We're going to drive them into the trap by dropping every available man who can hold a gun behind their position and prodding them forward."

"I've told you that the men still in camp would be no good in a ground action. They're ship people."

"When the Spaccs see a force of a hundred men coming at them, they'll move quickly enough and in the direction we want. They won't know if the men are professional soldiers or cabin boys."

"My men are not cabin boys," Currulla said angrily.

"I didn't say they were. I was only drawing a contrast between professional soldiers and the least offensive profession I could imagine."

"A hundred men?" Currulla said, calming down.

"Yes, it will take several trips with our three shuttles. I don't need them to fight. I only need them to drive the Spaccs into my trap. I already have a hundred fifty men positioned in front and on their left flank. When the Spaccs move into the trap, the flanking squads will close any avenue of retreat. Then we just pick them off until every last one of them is dead."

"And what happens to my people?"

"Once we spring the trap and have the Spaccs pinned down, your people can return to the shuttles and be back here in time for their afternoon tea social. As you've said, they'd be no good in fight; they'd only get in the way. I have more than enough people to handle the Spaccs. We'll have them outnumbered four to one without your *ship* people, and they'll be under our guns before they realize how we've trapped them."

"Where will you be?"

"I'll remain at the command post and direct the action from here."

"Shouldn't you be out with your people?"

"My place is here at the command post."

"Yes, it is much safer here."

"I'm not here because it's safer," Suflagga said, his nostrils flaring slightly. "From this location I can better coordinate the action."

"Of course," Currulla said lightly, knowing that his tone would irritate Suflagga even more.

Suflagga glared at him for a moment and then turned his attention back to the holo-map.

* * *

"Bravo-Leader, this is Charlie-One."

"Go ahead, Charlie-One," Kennedy said to the scout who was watching their rear.

"Three shuttles have just dropped about fifty enemy soldiers between your position and mine. They're about one klick behind you. They're standing around as if they're waiting for more people before they move out."

"You think they're headed our way?"

"That would be my guess."

"Roger, Charlie-One. Keep me informed. Bravo-Leader out." To the platoon, Kennedy said, "Everyone up. We have enemy combatants massing on our rear. We're moving out in five minutes."

The oh-gee sleds had been loaded before everyone not on guard duty tried to get some sleep, so there was little to do in preparation for resuming their withdrawal. When the five minutes were up, the platoon moved out, quietly but not completely stealthily. Since it appeared that the enemy already knew of their location, they didn't waste time trying to conceal their trail.

"Bravo-Leader, this is Charlie-One. The three enemy shuttles have dropped another group. You have about one hundred combatants on your six."

"Roger, Charlie-One. Hold back and keep me informed."

"Charlie-One. Affirmative. Out."

On Com 1, Kennedy announced, "There are approximately one hundred enemy soldiers to our rear and they're headed this way. They apparently know where we are, so we won't waste time covering our trail. We have to make some time, people, but don't panic. We have a good lead and they won't catch us as long as we keep moving."

Sydnee, as an officer, was monitoring both Com channels and had heard the reports from the scout. She rolled her eyes at Kennedy's speech, then immediately scolded herself silently for doing it. Since everyone was wearing their helmets, no one saw her slip. She wondered what expressions their hidden faces wore while wishing again that they had never left the cave.

Over the next three hours, they jogged east, all the while keeping the ridge line on their immediate right. If they strayed north, they'd be in swamp or bog. The area along the ridge was higher and drier, allowing them to make better time.

"Bravo-Leader, this is Alpha-Two."

"Go ahead, Alpha-Two," Kennedy said to one of the two advance scouts.

"It's a trap. I can see troops up ahead on the far side of a clearing. They mean to catch us out in the open."

"How many do you see?"

"Just three, but there have to be more hidden in the jungle cover ahead."

"What's the terrain like?"

"As flat as my little sister's chest. There's hardly a pebble to offer cover."

"Roger, Alpha-Two. You and Alpha-One return to the platoon. Bravo-Leader out."

"Oo-rah. Alpha-Two out."

"Platoon halt," Kennedy said on Com 1, then looked first towards the east and then south. "People, we've been tricked. The rebels have been pushing us towards a trap. They're both behind us and in front of us. We can't turn north because we'd be easy targets in the bogs, so we're going to head for the ridge to the south and dig in. Let's move it."

Knowing that there was a force of a hundred enemy soldiers behind them was bad enough, but knowing that perhaps an equal number were waiting ahead put new vitality into everyone's step.

Sydnee managed to keep up but was out of her element and knew it. She wasn't afraid of a fight but preferred to do it from the cockpit of a fighter or the bridge of a ship. And she was real tired of wearing the confining armor. She longed to slip naked between the sheets of her rack aboard the *Perry* for a good night's sleep after a deliciously hot shower. But this wasn't the time for daydreaming, so she focused her full attention on keeping up with the man in front of her.

They reached the vertical face of the ridge without incident and began preparing for the fight that everyone knew was coming. There was a meter-and-a-half-deep trench against the face of the rock, which appeared to have been cut by rain runoff from the ridge. It was dry at present and provided sufficient cover so that no one would be exposed to direct fire.

* * *

"Damn, damn, damn," Suflagga uttered as he stared at the holo-map.

"What now?" Currulla said as he entered the tent. "Another setback? Did you lose them again?"

"No, we know where they are," Suflagga said through gritted teeth. "They're just not where I want them to be."

"Didn't a famous general or other once say that 'in combat, you can't always expect the enemy to do exactly what you wish him to do?'"

"That was General Verimilla. He said, 'When you believe an opponent has just two options, he will always surprise you with a third.'"

"Yeah, that's the one I was thinking of."

"Well, in this case, it's true. The enemy has done the unexpected. Instead of proceeding into our trap, they've turned south towards the ridge. You can see it here," Suflagga said, pointing to the ridgeline on the holo-map.

"But you said the mountain was unscalable."

"It is, without special gear— which I've been assuming they don't have."

"So perhaps they have that gear after all."

"No, it's more likely that they discovered our ambush somehow. I had expected them to fall back towards the ridge after they had gone further east. Once we sprang the ambush, their numbers should have been greatly reduced, and the ridge there offered a lot less protection than the area they're in now. Now we'll have to dig every one of them out like ticks." Pointing to the map he said, "There's only one open space against the ridge in that area and the Spaccs are probably on the south side. If they are, they've probably taken positions in this trench."

"So your people will have to cross a hundred meters of open ground to get to them?"

"Yes."

"That's exactly what you were planning for the Spaccs, wasn't it— to fire on them from concealed positions as they crossed a hundred meters of open ground?"

"Yes."

"Then it would appear that you have a serious problem."

"Yes."

*   *   *

"Charlie-One to Bravo-Leader."

"Bravo-Leader."

"There's something strange going on out here. The rebels who were dropped between us, and who then made the push to drive you east, have fallen back and are being picked up by shuttles. Rebels from the group that was in front of you have moved west and established front-line positions along the north side of the open ground directly opposite the ridge wall. Some then filled in the area on your left flank that was just vacated. We were trying to rejoin the platoon, but they closed the gap too quickly."

"How many would you estimate remain on our left flank and in positions facing us?"

"Best guess at this point would be about a hundred-twenty."

"Do you see any ordnance?"

"My vid unit caught sight of two mortars being set up about fifty meters behind their front line, and every soldier facing you seems to be carrying a sack with four RPGs in it."

"Roger, Charlie-One. Stay outside the perimeter and keep feeding us intel. Bravo-Leader out."

"Oo-rah. Charlie-One out."

Kennedy stood up and looked at the tree line across the rocky, open ground. It seemed as though he could see a little movement in the woods, but there weren't any clear targets. He dropped to the ground again so as not to present too inviting a target.

Lying in a ditch, even one that wasn't dry, would have been preferable to racing through a jungle if not for the certainty that a large force was preparing to attack their position. Sydnee tried to think of more pleasant times, but the image of her MAT at the bottom of the sinkhole kept invading her thoughts, so she concentrated on thinking about its recovery and the best ways to dig it out since they didn't have a tug or shovels and she didn't expect the *Perry* to return.

. She was working on an idea to tunnel down a few meters from the MAT and then go horizontally toward one of the two hatches. She'd seen a number of old prison movies where inmates tunneled out using only spoons or sticks. She knew they could do it if they tried. She just hoped the work would go faster than that of the Count of Monte Cristo, the protagonist in Alexandre Dumas' classic story that illustrated the abuse of political power, and the retribution served up by an oppressed individual. She tried to remember how long it had taken Edmond Dantès to escape, but she couldn't place it exactly. She thought it might have been about fifteen years because his former lover had a teenage son when he had returned to confront her.

Suddenly, a loud whooshing noise from her external microphone was followed with a shout of "incoming," on Com 1. A second later, a loud explosion high up on the cliff face behind them shook the ground and rained bits of dirt and rock on them. Lattice rounds began bouncing off the wall behind them and laser shots momentarily seared the rock.

The lattice and laser fire lasted for several minutes, during which a half dozen mortar rounds landed in the clearing in front of them or against the rock face behind them. Then everything went silent.

"What's happening?" Sydnee heard someone ask on Com 1.

"Easy, Adams," Sydnee heard Sergeant Booth say. "They're just trying to rattle us into deserting these positions. Everybody okay?"

"No one hurt over this way, Sarge."

"What the heck were they doing with the mortars?" someone else asked. "They were dropping them all over the place out there."

"I think they have some people who have never fired a mortar before," Sergeant Booth said. "They're trying to learn how to use them as they zero in locations in the open area."

"Jeez," someone said. "They wait until a battle to learn how to use a mortar? Give me one; I'll show them how to use it."

"I think their ordnance is a little low," Sergeant Booth said, "thanks to our visiting their camp. They probably couldn't afford to waste any of it until they had a chance of it possibly being— useful."

"So what are we gonna do, Sarge?" someone asked.

"We're going to do whatever the LT tells us to do, when he tells us to do it. Now pipe down."

Sydnee didn't know if Kennedy was listening in on the Com 1 chatter or if he had turned it off. It seemed like he would have said something to calm everyone if he'd heard the conversation. He was lying immobile on his back in the ditch roughly five meters from her position. "You okay, Rett?" she asked on Com 2.

"Yeah, I'm okay."

"Okay. I thought you might have been hit."

"Nope. I'm fine. I'm just waiting to see what they attempt next now that they know we won't run away in a panic and give them easy targets."

The next overt act occurred some twenty minutes later. A section of the wall behind the platoon suddenly blew apart.

"Mortars," someone yelled on Com 1.

"No— RPGs," Sergeant Booth yelled. "Keep your heads down."

Rocket-propelled grenades weren't as deadly or as accurate as mortar rounds, but the armor wouldn't protect anyone who was struck by one.

The RPG attack lasted for twelve minutes. Like the first barrage, it failed to dislodge the Marines. Towards the end, the rebels were experimenting with firing the RPGs into the air like mortars in an attempt to land them in the ditch. They had come close, but so far no one had been injured.

Kennedy looked up and down the line of his command, then squatted on his knees and said, "Okay, people, we're not going to get out of this lightly, but I think they may have fired a good amount of their RPG arsenal and now is the time to counterattack. Rather than sit here until they get lucky with those RPGs, we're going to charge their line. This new armor may not stop mortars and grenades, but it'll stop lattice rounds and laser fire, so once we start moving, we keep going until we're in their ranks. Burn down everyone who doesn't want to surrender. Everyone get ready because we're going to charge their line on the count of five. One, Two, Three…"

When Kennedy reached five, he stood up, but no one stood with him so he dropped to his knees again.

"I said move out on five," Kennedy yelled, "Now move it. We're attacking their front line."

When nobody moved to this repeat order, Kennedy lost his temper. "I said we're going to attack. Now, people."

When no one moved to the latest order, Kennedy reached up and removed his helmet in anger, then screamed for everyone to move as he rose up on his knees.

Sydnee was surprised when Kennedy stood up without having said anything first, then dropped down again, but she couldn't believe her eyes when she saw him remove his helmet, scream something, and rise up on his knees. She yelled, "Rett, stay down. They can see you," but he apparently couldn't hear her because he had removed his helmet. She activated the speaker on her armor's chest plate and yelled again, "Stay down."

Thinking she was countermanding his orders, Kennedy yelled angrily, "Don't listen to her. I'm in command here and I'm ordering you to get up and charge that enemy line."

Sydnee realized then that Kennedy must have turned off his Com 1 channel and forgotten to turn it back on. Perhaps the chatter was breaking his concentration as he tried to formulate a plan. But before Sydnee could correct his misconception about her shouted words, a three-round lattice rifle burst hit Kennedy. The first round bounced off the armor on his shoulder. The second round struck his skull and cut a groove of skin off the back of his head. The third round entered his ear hole, skidded around the inside of his skull, and exited through his right eye.

Kennedy's body stayed upright for a couple of seconds as muscles contracted in position, then fell over as the muscles relaxed. He would live, technically, for perhaps another minute while blood poured out of his ear and eye socket, but he was essentially dead when he hit the ground.

Sydnee lay where she had been all along and stared in horror at the scene. This was the first human death she had witnessed. Combat training was intended to prepare a military person for this event, but the first death was always a shock. She stared at the lifeless body for what seemed like minutes.

Chapter Nineteen
~ Mar. 5th, 2285 ~

Staff Sergeant McKenzie had witnessed the death and scrambled over to Kennedy's side. He felt for a pulse on the side of Kennedy's neck but knew there was no chance even as he checked. Even if Kennedy hadn't died almost immediately, they had no doctor or access to medical facilities. He would certainly have died before they could get help.

Sydnee shook herself mentally and crawled over to Kennedy's body. She removed the thermal blanket from his backpack and, working together with McKenzie, wrapped the body in it.

As they finished, McKenzie said on Com 2, "What do you want to do now, ma'am?"

"There's nothing we can do. We'll just leave him like this for now. I'm sure we have a few body bags on one of the supply sleds."

"I mean about the platoon, Lieutenant."

"The platoon?"

"Yes, ma'am. You're next in line for command."

Sydnee was taken completely by surprise, but she tried not to show it. She wasn't a Marine and had never anticipated being expected to assume command, so she hadn't given any thought to commanding the platoon before that moment. But she was now the senior officer— in fact, the only officer. The Academy taught cadets deemed worthy of command that when they found themselves in command, they must always act decisively and never allow subordinates to see any signs of indecision.

Sydnee's field combat training was limited to the summer of her third year at the Academy, but she had studied every major battle fought by Earth forces. She quickly formulated a simple plan in her head.

Sydnee took a deep breath and said, "Yes, Sergeant, that's true. Well, we can't just sit here and let them pound us to pieces, so we'll have to take the fight to the enemy. I'm switching to Com 1."

On Com 1 Sydnee said, "Listen up, people. Lieutenant Kennedy is dead and I'm taking command. I don't know about you, but I'm tired of sitting here on my arse while they pound on us, so we're going to take the fight to the enemy. Our armor will protect us from lattice and laser, so once we start moving we keep moving so they can't target us with mortar or RPGs. We're going to execute a breakout along our entire front line and attack with a Highland Charge towards the western half of *their* front line. That's the side on our left flank. That might make some of their front line break ranks to reinforce their defense on that side. Then, when I give the word, we pivot and head for the eastern half of their front line. They have us outnumbered about four to one so don't spare the ammo. The more we put down on our charge, the easier the mop up will be. Are you ready?"

A chorus of "Oo-rahs" filled Com 1.

"Then we go on five. Let's put on our game faces."

Sydnee pulled up the icon given to her by the four-four-three and posted it on her helmet's outer SimWindow. The evil-looking human skull would continue its maniacal laugh on the front face of her helmet until she cancelled it.

"Ready? One, Two, Three, Four, Five."

As Sydnee said 'Five,' every Marine jumped to his or her feet, leapt out of the trench, and began racing towards the enemy. Some Marines were playing a soundtrack of a maniacal laugh at full volume, while others were simply yelling for all they were worth with the volume on their chest plate speaker set to high. All had the animated icons showing on the faceplates of their helmets and they appeared every bit a frenzied horde from hell. Lattice rounds bounced off their armor while laser hits were absorbed and dissipated. The

Marines kept up a steady rate of fire as they ran towards the enemy.

As the charge began, the rebel forces tried to use their RPGs on the charging mass. Some fired directly at the Marines while others fired into the air as they had practiced. Neither tactic was truly effective. The RPGs fired directly at the Marines mostly passed over their heads or through their ranks. The ones fired into the air were so off target as to be completely ineffective.

Time seemed to slow down for Sydnee. All around her, lattice rounds were bouncing off armor, creating a blizzard effect of spent steel rounds, while the laser shots emanating from both sides in the conflict created a sort of surreal light show.

A bit more than halfway across the open plain, Sydnee yelled, "Wheel right!" Everyone suddenly pivoted and began racing toward the other half of the enemy's front line. Sydnee's prediction had been correct. Rebel soldiers on the rebel left flank had deserted their positions to reinforce the western end of the line. The second move by the Marines caught them by surprise, and when they stopped to reverse direction they became easier targets for the charging forces.

As the Marines reached the three-quarter point in their charge across the open area, the rebel line before them began to crumble. Many of the rebels, seeing that their weapons were having no effect on the Marines, jumped up and deserted their positions, dropping their weapons as they ran towards the rear in search of safety from the charging forces. The rebel diehards simply died hard, still firing their weapons as Marines overran their positions and ended their fighting days forever.

Being outnumbered four to one meant that the Marines weren't looking to take prisoners, but they allowed the fleeing rebels to continue their flight unmolested as they mopped up the ones along the entire front line who continued their fire. Marines were professionals but not saints, so a few may have taken some relish in dispatching a part of the rebel force that had been chasing them for days and had killed their commanding officer. When the firing on the front line ended, a couple of Marine squads on each end of the line mopped up the rebels still firing from their positions on the flanks, while the remainder of the Marines continued their charge toward the rebel rear positions until they reached the mortars.

As the scout had reported, there were only two mortars set up, and the stockpile of fresh rounds found nearby was pitiful by any measure. It was understandable why the earlier use had been so judicious. The destruction of the stockpiles in the three clearings at the rebel camp had to be responsible for the lack of ordnance and ammunition.

"Lieutenant Marcola?" Sydnee heard on Com 2 as she stood looking at the mortars.

"Marcola," she said.

"All resistance has ended, ma'am," McKenzie reported.

"Did we get hurt bad?"

"We lost two, both from hits by RPGs. No other injuries, thanks to the armor."

"Who did we lose?"

"PFC Pineta and Private Hotaling."

Sydnee had spoken to Pineta a couple of times but only knew Hotaling from having seen her during interdiction stops."

"I'm saddened by the loss of two fine Marines. I suppose we should be grateful it wasn't worse. Did we take any prisoners?"

"Negative, ma'am. Those who didn't run away wanted to fight to the death. At least that's the way it seemed to us."

"Okay, Staff Sergeant. Let's wrap it up. Collect all the enemy weapons and place them in a pile so we can destroy them with a Corplastizine charge before we leave. Then load our three dead onto the oh-gee sleds. We're not leaving them here for scavengers. We'll find a place to bury them far enough from here that the Yolongi won't disturb them but where we can recover them at a later time."

"Aye. Ma'am. What about the enemy dead?"

"How many are there?"

"My tally is sixty-three. I guess about a hundred ran away."

"There's nothing we can do for them. Leave them where they are. If the rebels want them, they can come get them. They have several shuttles."

"Aye, Ma'am. We're on it."

McKenzie started issuing orders and Marines near Sydnee picked up the mortars and ammunition and headed back towards the clearing. Sydnee tagged along, trying to develop a plan for what to do next. Ordering the charge had been easy. She believed it was what Kennedy had been trying to do, although he never should have removed his helmet.

As Sydnee reached the clearing and saw the Marines piling up the weapons, she hit on a plan.

"Staff Sergeant McKenzie," she said on Com 2.

"McKenzie."

"I've decided we shouldn't destroy the mortars and ammunition. Load them on one of the sleds instead."

"Aye, ma'am."

"Bravo-Leader, this is Charlie-One."

"Go ahead, Charlie-One."

"Ma'am, the last of the rebels seems to have passed our position. They're running like Lucifer hisself was after them. I bet they don't stop until they reach their original camp."

Sydnee chuckled. "Understood, Charlie-One. Bravo-Leader out."

"Lieutenant," Sydnee heard McKenzie say on Com 2, "we just found a large cache of food supplies about fifty meters behind their front line."

"Great. Let's put a hot meal together." Looking up at the sun, she added, "It's just about lunchtime."

"Here, ma'am?"

"Yes, I feel as though I haven't eaten in days."

"But what about their fighters, Ma'am? Won't they send them to attack this position?"

"I don't think we have to worry about them, Staff Sergeant. They had us pinned down for hours. I expected their fighters to show up and blow us away, or at least try to bring the cliff face down onto us. The fact that they didn't has to mean just one thing: they don't have any rockets left."

"Unless they were holding them in reserve."

"We were the greatest threat they were likely to find on this planet. They would have used them if they had them. We can thank Lieutenant Kennedy's raid on their camp for that."

"But what about their lasers?"

"They didn't have a clear shot at us while we were in the ravine against the cliff wall."

"But we're exposed out here now."

"True, but even if they show up, I don't think we need worry. We've just seen how totally ineffective the small arms lasers are, and I suspect the same would be true for the more powerful lasers on the fighters. Even a ship's laser array can't harm a MAT, so I don't think we have to fear the fighters if they have no rockets left."

"Aye, ma'am. I'll get my people working on a meal."

"Bravo-Leader out." As Sydnee uttered the sign-off, she was surprised that she had adapted to command of the platoon so quickly. *Must be the training*, she thought.

* * *

"A rout?" Currulla said, his lips contorted in anger.

"Their action wasn't expected," Suflagga said. "They charged our position like unthinking wild animals."

"A child's domesticated Flommbo will defend itself if trapped and in fear of its life. Didn't they teach you that in the military?"

"If we had had fighters, we could have wiped them out. We just didn't have the necessary ordnance."

"No, I think it was the necessary leadership that was missing. You should have been out there with your people instead of being holed up here unable to see what was going on and give timely orders. You call yourself a military leader?"

"I remind you, we were fighting the best the Spaccs have to offer. I don't know what such an elite fighting force was doing on a destroyer in this backwater area, but I can't be expected to beat Space Command's finest troops with farmers and hotel clerks who run from danger."

"And what will you do now when they come after us again?"

"What? They're not going to come after us again. They've been running away for days."

"Running away? Space Command's elite fighting force? I'll remind you that they could have killed us all while we slept that first night, but instead all they did was destroy the ordnance and supplies we removed from the *Abissto* and then withdraw."

"They killed our sentries."

"Avoiding detection until their mission was complete was probably a necessary part of the operation. I'm beginning to think they wouldn't have harmed anyone if you hadn't posted guards around the supplies. They tried to withdraw without harming anyone else, but your pursuit eventually cornered them and they had no choice but to fight."

"Then what makes you think they'll come after us now?"

"Did you kill any of them?"

"Yes. I received reports that at least thirty were killed."

"Thirty of forty-two? And twelve of them routed your troops?"

"Well— the reports may have been exaggerated."

"If you managed to kill *any* of them, we might see them again very soon. You've probably heard that military people get very angry when you kill their comrades— a sort of honor code that makes them consider their comrades as brothers."

"If they come at us, we'll defend ourselves."

"With what?"

"The ones who ran away will eventually return here. If they're cornered, they'll fight, just like a domesticated Flommbo."

"But what will they fight with? We have no ordnance and our force is made up of 'farmers and hotel clerks,' to use your words."

"I'll whip them into shape and we'll use rocks and clubs for weapons if we don't have enough guns."

"I'm sure that will be most effective against Space Command's elite troops." Currulla turned his back on the military man and walked away without seeing the enmity in Suflagga's eyes.

* * *

Within an hour, the tent formerly used for a CP had been erected and misting devices had killed all insects inside. Those that managed to sneak inside as people entered or left dropped to the ground within seconds. The Marines were able to cook the food in the open, then bring it into the tent where everyone could remove their helmets to eat without having swarms of insects trying to crawl into their ears or up their noses. Sydnee had searched the database and found an entry for preparing the Lampaxa Vorheridine. It stated that the reptile was safe to eat if its poison sac was first removed. *Sort of like Terran Blowfish whose ovaries and liver must be removed for food preparation*, Sydnee thought. She'd tried Blowfish once while at the WCI. It was tasty but not worth the chance of dying if it wasn't properly prepared. The process for preparing the Lampaxa Vorheridine seemed like a safer bet.

Sergeant Booth followed Sydnee's directions for removing the head by cutting it off at least six centimeters behind the eyes and then sniffing the trunk to see if the poison sac had been broken while killing it. The database said there would be a smell like ammonia if the poison sac had been punctured. It seemed okay, but after skinning a small sample, he processed it through the alien food analyzer. It came back as perfectly safe for human consumption, so he set about skinning the rest of the nearly twelve-meter creature and began slicing it up to become part of their meal. A couple of Marines, including the one who was attacked, passed on the offer to try some, but that was understandable. The rest of the platoon came back with statements that it tasted a lot like pork sausage and sought seconds or thirds.

"What next, ma'am?" Staff Sergeant McKenzie asked. "A nap, perhaps?"

Sydnee looked at him but couldn't tell if he was joking or being insubordinate, so she let it slide. "No, no nap. At least not yet. As soon as we've eaten and relaxed for thirty minutes, we'll pack up and head back the way we came."

"The way we came, ma'am?"

"Yes, but we'll avoid the swamps and jungle as much as possible. There's no need to hide anymore. It didn't work the first time anyway. They've found some way of tracking us. When we leave here, our destination is the cave where we laid up for several days. We'll spend a few more days there while we prepare for the next stage."

"Which is?"

"Still in planning, Staff Sergeant."

"Aye, ma'am."

* * *

"What's so urgent?" Currulla said to Suflagga as he entered the command shelter.

"They're headed this way."

"Who, the Spaccs?"

"Yes. We're picking up signals from the motion sensors we dropped a few days ago."

"Dammit. They're probably coming here to wipe us out for killing their people. How many are coming?"

"We seeing thirty-nine separate signals, but that can't be accurate because our people killed thirty. Perhaps they were reinforced."

"Or perhaps your trained soldiers lied. They were probably too busy running away to get a true picture."

"I lost a lot of good people in that fight," Suflagga said angrily. "Don't dishonor their memory."

Currulla was about to say something in response, then thought it better that he hold his tongue. Instead, he asked, "How many did we lose?

"We don't know yet. We won't know until the survivors all get back here. Some of your farmers scattered in every direction when the Spaccs counterattacked. We may lose even more of them to this planet's wildlife because I was told they dropped their weapons when they fled. So far, the shuttles have located and picked up about fifty, but the others seem to run and hide when the shuttles approach. They might believe the shuttles are manned by the Spaccs."

"Wonderful. When do you think the Spaccs will arrive here?"

"I don't know. I would have expected them to make camp after their victory because we know they hadn't slept all night."

"If they didn't sleep last night, they'll have to rest up before they attack."

"Yes," Suflagga said. "That gives us at least a day to prepare."

"Not that we have anything to prepare with."

* * *

The platoon was able to make much better time on the trip back to the cave because they weren't trying to hide their trail. The scouts were out all the way, checking the trail ahead and guarding the rear.

At one point Alpha-One contacted Sydnee to report finding a strange piece of electronic equipment. Sydnee had her hold position until they reached her.

"What do you think it is?" Sydnee asked Sgt. Autumn Kolter about the tiny piece of black silicon she was hiding in her hand.

"My guess is either a tracking device or a motion sensor to detect and report movement."

"Well, we know now how the rebels placed us. Either someone was tagged at some point or this unit reported our movement past this point. Did you see any others?"

"None yet, ma'am, but I haven't been looking for them. They're tiny, but I'll keep my eyes open for more. They're kinda hard to spot though. I only identified this one because the moon glinted off it while I was wearing my low lux goggles."

"Good work, sergeant. This clears up a mystery. Better get out on point again."

"Aye, Ma'am."

As Sergeant Kolter left, Sydnee summoned the platoon's radioman. "Ever see anything like this, Walsh?" she asked as she held it out.

Cpl. Walsh took the chip and examined it. "Yes, ma'am. They sell these in security equipment stores for special event protection. It uses ground vibration to report any motion."

"How does it report?"

"Just a plain tone signal on a set frequency. Nothing fancy."

"Can you tell me what frequency it uses?"

"I can once I have my equipment set up. Usually these are simply dropped on the ground and each one employs a separate frequency. They act like a sort of sensor net. They're cheap and only last a few weeks before they use up the stored charge once the package is opened. They can't be recharged, and they're biodegradable with exposure to sunlight."

"I need to know what frequency this one is sending."

"No problem once we're in the cave, ma'am."

"But I don't want the rebels to know about the cave."

"The signal from this thing is so weak it won't give us away once we're inside, and I can store it in a small non-conductive pouch until then so the rebels will see it wink off and think the person has passed out of range. They don't send position information, so they won't know that it's been moved anyway. Location is determined by the receiver only through careful parceling of the units in a set order as someone walks along. "

"Very good, Walsh. Block its signal and check it out when we're in the cave."

"Aye, Lieutenant."

It was almost midnight when the platoon reached the cave. It had been almost thirty exhausting hours since anyone had slept, but they set up camp while the mist devices killed the insects. Once the cave was clear of flying bugs and the holo-projector was concealing the entrance, the ones who hadn't pulled guard duty removed their armor and cleaned it in preparation for its next use.

Sydnee was ecstatic at being able to peel off her outer skin, as she had begun to think of the armor. She had been hit dozens of times by lattice rounds and lasers during the charge, and she knew she owed her life to the equipment. Still, it was a delight to shed it for a while.

The Marines had filled their bellies before they left the battle site, so while a few with hollow legs wanted more sustenance, most spread their gravity-shielded bedrolls on the floor of the cave once their chores were done and dropped off to sleep.

While Sydnee relaxed on her bedroll, she thought about Kennedy. As Kelly MacDonald had said, he was a little stiff at times, and Sydnee had seen how intractable he could be at others, but he was a good Marine and a good person. She would miss him, and she would never be able to forget the horrible way he had died. Fortunately, he hadn't suffered very long. She also thought about Pineta and Hotaling. She hadn't known them well, but they had been under her command when they died so that sort of made her responsible. The manner of their death was horrific, but there wasn't really a good way to die in battle. She knew she would remember the sight of the dismembered bodies, torn apart by RPGs, for the rest of her life.

Sleep finally pushed all conscious thoughts from her head, but Sydnee would relive the battle in her dreams for many nights to come.

Chapter Twenty
~ Mar. 10th, 2285 ~

Four days of rest and plentiful food had recharged the internal batteries of the Marines. Some were even getting a little antsy from sitting around, so Sydnee approved requests from two squads who wanted to venture out as a hunting party in search of fresh food. Everyone had enjoyed the Lampaxa Vorheridine, but it was just a memory now and they wanted something fresh as opposed to dining on the emergency meal packs.

Sydnee had no idea how long they would be there and preferred to save the meal packs as backup anyway. But before she allowed them to leave, she uploaded a copy of the Diabolisto database about the planet to each Marine's helmet information storage chips so they would be able to identify edible and inedible flora and fauna and avoid danger. Each group took an oh-gee sled in case they were successful and the load was heavy.

After the hunting parties left, Staff Sergeant McKenzie said, "I hope you know what you're doing Lieutenant. If they run into a company of rebels, they may not be able to handle them."

"I think they'll be okay, Staff Sergeant. We're a long way from the rebel base, and their more militant ones stayed at their positions and fought until their end. The ones who ran away won't want any more trouble with the GA Space Marines."

"How long do you intend for us to remain here, if I might be permitted to ask?"

"I can't think of a better place to be until help arrives, can you?"

"Uh, not really. I was just wondering if you had worked out the details of the plan you mentioned."

"Pretty much. We're going to attack the rebel camp."

"Attack the rebel camp?" McKenzie said, his eyes opening wide.

"Yes. I wanted to have everyone rested and ready for the hike."

"Ma'am, there is still a large force there. If they had two-hundred-eighty something at the start, they must still have over two hundred. What do you hope to accomplish, ma'am?"

"I want to steal, or perhaps I should say recover, one of the small ships they stole from the Clidepp military. We may be on this planet for a very long time and we'll need some transportation. Should the rebels get transportation off the planet, they'll most likely take the shuttles with them. If we've taken one and secreted it somewhere, we'll have both transportation and access to space around the planet after they're gone."

"You think someone is coming to pick them up?"

"I'd put money on it."

"I think I'd have to agree. They must have sent distress messages to the rebels back home while they were on their way here."

"And there's another thing. If the *Perry* doesn't return, we'll have to go search for the IDS jamming satellite the *Perry* dropped and shut it down so we can send a message to Space Command. If the *Perry* has been destroyed and hadn't informed anyone that we'd been left down here, this could be our permanent home if we can't get a message out."

"The thought of remaining here for the rest of my life doesn't appeal to me, ma'am."

"Yes, in a few months it's going to get hot here."

"It gets hotter?"

"Sure. We're in mid-winter right now. Tourist season."

"I'm sure the travel agents would have trouble finding anyone who wanted to book a tour to Diabolisto, mid-winter or spring."

"It certainly wouldn't top my list of choice travel destinations."

* * *

"The freighter we sent to pick up our people on Diabolisto has been held up at the border," Citizen X said to the other cloaked opposition leaders present at the clandestine meeting. "The Spaccs have changed their policy regarding illegals trying to enter their space. Rather than simple internment pending return to Clidepp space, the GA now requires the ship to return and drop them off before proceeding back to GA Space for another inspection. The military has seized upon this as a way to inspect all outbound ships because they have the excuse that timetables will be less affected if all passports, visas, and travel papers are checked before the ship leaves Clidepp space. As a result, the queue of ships waiting for clearance grows daily. Any ship refusing to wait and trying to leave Clidepp space without an inspection will be fired upon and possibly destroyed."

"Barbarous," one of the leaders said.

"They can't possibly continue to hold ships once the queue grows to an unmanageable size," said another. "The reason for simple spot checks in the past was owed to the impossible task of checking all ships."

"Our fight for independence is having an effect on all space travel. But there's a positive side. Although our freighter has been forced to wait for clearance, the tactics of the Empire are helping to sway citizens to our cause. The screams from the shipping companies about delays are like a mere whisper when compared to the shouts from angry travelers."

* * *

"We still have no word from the *Perry*," Admiral Platt said to the other admirals at the regular meeting of the Admiralty Board. "Captain Brookings, base commander at Simmons Space Command Base, has ordered the *Pellew* to the last reported position of the *Perry* to begin a search, but it'll be months before it reaches the sub-sector."

"Even with the acquisition of Region Two," Admiral Plimley said, "it sometimes seems that our territory is shrinking because of the FTL speed improvement, but then something happens to bring you back to the realities of just how large our space really is."

"The Uthlaro armada should be reaching Quesann any day now. It was imperative we send Admiral Carver every ship we could. That naturally included everything capable of Light-9790. The fastest ship assigned to the Border Patrol fleet is only capable of achieving Light-225."

"Even my Light-9790 transports have predominantly been traveling to Region Two. Every ship has been filled with ordnance and supplies in support of the fleet located there," Admiral Ahmed said.

"The situation in Region Two is critical, and I'm sorry to say that, at this time, we cannot spare any resources from that effort to search for the *Perry*," Admiral Moore said. "If Admiral Carver is victorious, we may begin to free up a few more ships for border operations, but it will take years to realign our forces and resume normal operations. Owed to the tremendous size of Region Two, our fastest ships must be concentrated out there."

"I do hope some calamity hasn't befallen the *Perry* that has left them dependent on help arriving in less than two months," Admiral Bradlee said.

* * *

"Mom, it's been five weeks since Syd's last message," Sheree Marcola said to her mother at dinner. "I'm really worried. It's not like her not to call. There's something wrong. There has to be. Before this, I got at least one message every single week. Have you heard from her?"

"Not since early last month. Don't worry, dear. If something had happened to her, Space Command would have notified us. They're probably just doing some secret military thing or other and communications have been blocked until it's over. I went through that many times with your father."

"How can I not worry? This isn't right. If she knew she would be blocked from sending vids for an extended period, she would have prepared us. Is there somebody we can call?"

Kathee Deleone looked at her husband. "Curtis, do you know someone we can call?"

"I'm sure it's nothing, dear. She's in the Border Patrol—that's border, as in boring. Nothing ever happens in the Border Patrol. They don't fight wars, don't shoot at other ships, and never get shot at themselves. It's not like she's out fighting in Region Two where she might actually get injured. They've probably just had a com failure in that old ship she's on. She's probably lounging on her bunk right this minute, staring up at the overhead and cursing that old ship and its ancient com equipment."

"But do you know someone you can call to find out? It would put our minds at ease to know she's okay and that it's simply a technical problem."

"Oh, alright. I have a few friends in Space Command Headquarters. I'll place a call tomorrow and see if one knows anything about a problem with the *Perry*."

"Thank you, dear."

* * *

Captain Lidden stared up at the overhead from his bunk and cursed the ancient com equipment on the *Perry*. They had been floating almost helplessly in an area of space that saw little traffic, and even if freighters or passenger ships were nearby, the *Perry* couldn't contact them and request assistance. Also, the engineers hadn't yet been able to restore control to the starboard Sub-Light engine or two remaining stern drives. Every available man was being used outside the ship, trying to repair the damaged hull so that an FTL envelope would coalesce around the ship, but it was an overwhelming task. It would probably take six months of intensive effort in a shipyard, and they were trying to do it in space with an enemy ship floating nearby that might come to life at any moment.

In his entire career, Lidden had never felt so impotent as he had every minute of every day since the collision. It was taking all of his inner strength to remain calm in the daily status meetings. He knew that everyone was giving a maximum effort, but he wanted to scream at somebody just to get it off his chest.

He was especially worried about the people he had left on Diabolisto. One young lieutenant in command of a platoon of Marines operating without orders or guidance from more experienced commanders wasn't a good scenario. And then there was Marcola. She was probably completely disorientated in that Marine environment. A young female pilot, essentially fresh from the WCI, thrown in with forty rough and tough ground-pounders sounded like a recipe for disaster. Lidden hoped they weren't being too rough on her.

Then again, he'd heard that she'd been invited to use the Marine Combat Range following the incident on the diplomatic ship. So perhaps she was a little tougher than she appeared to be. Lidden had never been able to learn why she'd been assigned to the *Perry*, and it would continue to bother him until he did.

In addition to being worried for his people, Lidden was scared for himself and his future. What scared him most was that the rebels may have detected the presence of the Marines on the planet. It had been his call to send them down alone when MAT-One suffered engine problems. If he'd known that other destroyer was going to show, he never would have ordered MAT-Two to continue with the mission. If the platoon has been attacked on Diabolisto, Lidden might be court-martialed and booted out of the service. Where would he go? What would he do? He knew that he probably couldn't get a job as a freighter captain. Most of the freight companies had grudges against him for holding up their shipments while thorough interdiction operations took place. He might find that *no one* would hire him. If they stripped him of his pension, he'd have nothing.

Lidden sighed, turned off the overhead light, and rolled over to see if sleep would claim him.

* * *

The hunting parties returned with something that looked a little like a water buffalo, and a ton of leafy vegetables, nuts, berries, and tubers. They said they had confirmed that all were safe to eat by locating the item in the Diabolisto database, but Sydnee forbid anyone to eat anything until it had been verified safe by the alien food analyzer.

A few hours later, the platoon was feasting on roasted buflo, the actual DB name for the buffalo-like creature, baked tubers, and fresh salad with nuts and berries.

After dinner, Sydnee called for attention and informed the platoon that they would be attacking the rebel base camp the following evening. Everyone appeared a bit incredulous, but no one challenged her decision. She laid out the operation, made sure that everyone knew the objectives, and then closed the briefing. She estimated that they could easily reach the camp if they weren't slogging through swamps and bogs as they had done to hide their trail after the initial operation. They would move out at dawn, leaving most of the gear in the cave. Sydnee had decided that it would be their base of operations until they left the planet.

Sydnee tossed and turned for hours but finally fell asleep. Taking over after Kennedy was killed had been a spontaneous act, but planning and executing a new operation burdened her with great anxiety. She'd tried to plan for every contingency, but she knew it was impossible to predict every possible outcome of every action. She finally fell asleep wondering how Admiral Carver did it. Sydnee was making herself a wreck just worrying about commanding thirty-eight Marines. How did the Admiral manage to sleep knowing she was responsible for hundreds of thousands of Space Command and Space Marine personnel, not to mention the trillions of civilians relying on her to protect them?

When Sydnee was awakened by movement in the cave the following morning, she wished she could cancel the operation and go back to sleep, but she knew that wouldn't be prudent if she was to continue commanding the respect of the platoon. Instead, she jumped up and busied herself with the preparations. Somewhere between awakening and completing the preparations for leaving, she managed to grab some chow and slip into her armor.

At 0700 the platoon left the cave and headed west toward the rebel base camp. The two Alpha scouts were out ahead and two Charlie scouts behind. They would notify Sydnee of any danger ahead or if anyone was trailing them, but she never received any calls. At one point, she tested Com 2 by asking them to respond just to ensure her com system was operational.

The platoon walked all morning, sticking to solid ground as much as possible and never worrying about leaving a trail once they were several klicks from the cave. At noon they stopped briefly to eat a meal of leftover buflo meat and greens, then started walking again.

As the sun disappeared over the horizon, the platoon was just a kilometer from the rebel base camp. Sydnee had used the oh-gee vid units to survey the rebel camp and finalize her plan. The platoon ate a cold dinner and rested up prior to moving to their attack positions.

At midnight, Sydnee had the platoon head for their planned attack point. She then left with Sergeant Pedro Morales, who had been the advance scout known as Alpha-Two during the withdrawal, for their attack position.

After a wide sweep around the encampment, Sydnee and Morales moved stealthily through the trees on the north side of the camp to the clearing where the small ships were kept. Following the first attack, the ships had been moved closer to the camp and now sat in one of the areas that an ordnance stockpile had occupied. Sydnee spotted her target and pointed it out to Morales.

By 0030, everyone was ready and in position. Sydnee gave the order to commence, and the sky lit up as several Corplastizine explosions rocked the area at the south side of the rebel camp. Sydnee hoped every rebel in the camp was, at that moment, picking up their weapons and heading towards the explosions. Sydnee and Morales reached the ship she intended to take, but a large stack of boxes blocked the hatch. They put their weapons down and began working furiously to clear the hatchway. As they moved the last large crate, Sydnee heard, "Stop right there or die." Sydnee froze, as did Morales next to her. She turned her head and saw a man holding an RPG launcher on his shoulder. It was aimed at them and he had his hand on the trigger. All he had to do was squeeze, but that would probably destroy the small ship as well.

When the man spoke again, Sydnee glanced at a readout inside her helmet and saw that he was speaking Yolon. The translation circuitry converted the words to Amer and she heard, "Back away from the ship. Leave the weapons on the ground where you put them and don't make any sudden moves."

Sydnee no more wanted to see the small ship destroyed than the man with the RPG launcher on his shoulder, so she and Morales slowly moved away.

When they were clear of the ship, the Yolongi said, "Who are you?" He shifted his own position slightly so that if he fired, the RPG couldn't hit any of the parked ships.

"Space Marine Corps," Sydnee said after turning to face the man and activating the speaker on her chest plate with a wink of her eye at the correct entry in the helmet display. The translator automatically spoke her reply in Yolon.

"I thought so," the man said.

"Who are you?" Sydnee asked.

"I am Colonel Suflagga, late of the Empire's Green Guard. I've been waiting here every night for you to come. I knew you'd either come to destroy the ships or try to steal them. You didn't seem to have any transportation of your own, and it's the only thing of value we have left after your raid. I'm glad you came early. I'll be able to get some sleep tonight."

With her speaker off, Sydnee said on Com 2, "Sergeant, are you behind me."

"Just off to your five o'clock, Lieutenant."

"Good, when I make my move, I want you to dive to the ground at your three o'clock. Got that?"

"Oo-rah."

"What are you doing on this planet?" Suflagga asked.

"You should know that. We're here to take you into custody for violating Galactic Alliance space and performing terrorist acts."

"You spent days running away. That's no way to take someone into custody."

"We have to wait until our ship returns. We have no intention of standing guard over several hundred prisoners without a place to house them. If you hadn't pursued us and forced us to fight, your force would be a lot larger than it presently is."

"You murdered dozens of my people."

"We didn't murder anyone. You boxed us in and forced us to respond or die. The Marine Corps doesn't teach its people to accept death without a fight. Your people were lost to you when they chose to attack us without the proper ordnance."

"We had the proper ordnance until you destroyed it."

"Hence the reason for destroying it. Are you going to fire that thing or put it up?"

To Morales, Sydnee said, "Get ready, Sergeant."

Suflagga couldn't believe his ears, but he had learned everything he wanted to know. Without another word, just a sneer, he tightened his grip.

"Now," Sydnee said as she pushed the flap of her holster aside and pulled her pistol with one swift movement. As the pistol cleared the holster, she fired, her shot striking Suflagga in the lower abdomen almost immediately.

Reaction to the shot rocked Suflagga back slightly. He had already squeezed the trigger on the RPG launcher, but the delivery wasn't as quick as a laser.

Sydnee would never know if her shot had caused Suflagga to 'pull' his shot, or if he was simply unfamiliar with the weapon and the manner in which you had to brace yourself when firing it. In any event, the grenade passed high over her right shoulder on its way to the wooded area behind her as she dove for the ground on her left. A large tree suffered the effect of the blast, but it was far enough from their position to have no effect on the ship or the people in the clearing.

Suflagga was still standing, but he had fired his one shot and didn't have the strength to reload. His face mirrored the disbelief he felt when he was shot. As Sydnee and Morales climbed to their feet, Suflagga fell to his knees and then collapsed face down into the dirt.

Morales raced to retrieve his weapon, but it wasn't necessary. Suflagga wasn't moving.

"Quickly, Sergeant, let's get into the ship. That explosion is sure to attract the attention of somebody and we want to be long gone before they get here."

With the obstructions removed, the hatch opened fully. Sydnee was in the command chair, studying the controls, by the time Morales had retrieved her rifle, climbed in, and closed the hatch.

The controls of the ship were different than anything she had ever flown, but she was able to get the oh-gee engine started and lift off. After a few seconds on the controls, she began to get a feel for the vessel.

"Bravo-Leader to Bravo-One, what's your status?" Sydnee said on the prearranged com frequency once she had figured out the ship's com system and entered the encryption code.

"Bravo-Leader, this is Bravo-One. We've completed our mission and are returning to base."

"Understood. Bravo-Leader and Alpha-Two are airborne. Continue monitoring the established frequencies. We'll be in touch. Bravo-Leader out."

"Good luck, Bravo-Leader. Bravo-One out."

"Uh, Lieutenant? If I'm reading this crazy display right, it looks like someone is coming after us."

Sydnee glanced at the display. "You're right, Sergeant. It looks like they got the two fighters up. Strap in. Things might get very serious very quickly."

Chapter Twenty-One
~ Mar. 12th, 2285 ~

The small ship was already straining to climb away from the planet, so there was nothing further Sydnee could do to hasten their departure. The fighters had much greater speed in atmo.

"I wish we'd taken a fighter," Morales said wistfully.

"Shuttles and fighters don't have FTL capability."

"Yeah, but tugs don't have lasers and rockets."

"True. It remains to be seen which is more important right now."

"They'll be on us in another two minutes."

"Maybe," Sydnee said. "We've just passed from the planet's sensible atmosphere. From this point, fighters quickly lose the speed advantage they have from aerodynamic design."

As Sydnee operated the controls, an invisible envelope began to coalesce around the tug.

"They're almost on us, Lieutenant," Morales said after a tense minute of watching the monitor.

"They haven't had a shot yet because of their angle of climb through the atmosphere. It's going to be close, though. If they can get free of the planet and line up on us before our envelope is built, they could puncture our hull, or worse. Whatever you do, don't remove your helmet."

The next sixty seconds were nerve-racking. As Sydnee engaged the FTL drive, two laser shots passed over the bow. A second later, the small ship disappeared from the view of the fighter pilots.

"Wow, that was close," Sydnee said. "I was beginning to think we wouldn't make it."

"We're lucky they missed us with those shots."

"Did they?"

"Well, yeah. Of course. Why? Were we hit?"

"No, we weren't hit. I just don't know if they missed us. Those shots may have been an attempt to get us to stop. Fighters don't normally carry the electronics that would allow them to determine if a ship is building an FTL envelope. And you can't see one. They may have thought that by firing across our bow we'd heave-to and allow them to stop us without damaging this ship. You can remove your helmet now. The air filtration system seems to have removed any insects that might have been in here."

As Morales removed his helmet, he said, "So they should have *targeted* us?"

"I would have, given the same situation," Sydnee replied as she set her helmet on the deck next to her chair.

Morales chuckled. "You shoulda been a Marine, Lieutenant. You have a Marine's attitude towards warfare."

"I almost did apply to the Corps."

"What stopped you?"

"Um, I think it was Admiral Carver."

"The admiral stopped you from applying to the Corps?"

"Not directly. I was just so inspired by her that I decided on Space Command instead of the Corps. I want to be just like her. And— my dad was Space Command. He died at the Battle for Higgins just before Admiral Carver arrived and saved the station. I know that if she'd been able to get there quicker, he would have lived. I want to have that chance to save others aboard a ship or station."

"Marines save people too."

"I know, and I'm not trying to diminish anything that the Corps does or has done. I simply think I can be better positioned to help if I command a battleship rather than a battalion. The Corps serves a vital role, and I've been proud of my association."

"Okay, I can live with that, even though I can't imagine my life without the Corps. And I have to say that you're the fastest draw I've ever seen. You drew and hit that guy back there before he could even pull the trigger on the RPG launcher. I'd heard about your quick draw, but it has to be seen to be believed. If you hadn't had to dive out of the way, I bet your shot would have been spot in."

"You saw me draw?"

"Yeah. I had to know what was going to happen so I could decide on my next move if you hadn't taken that guy out. I was looking over my shoulder as I dove for the ground. That's how I knew you missed hitting him in the chest."

"I hit where I was aiming."

"Then why didn't you go for the kill shot? He was trying to kill *us*."

"I did. A Yolongi's heart is in his pelvis. He was dead the second my shot reached him. It just took his brain a few seconds to register it."

"His heart was in his pelvis? That sounds like a bad joke, or an insult. Where did you learn that?"

"Alien Anatomy classes at the Academy. I never expected that anything I learned from those classes would prove to be useful information, but it sure paid off today."

"Then what's in a Yolongi's chest?"

"His womb sack."

"Womb sack?"

"Yes. Yolongi females sit on the chest of their mates and deliver one or more fertilized eggs into the male. Then the male cares for it, or them, until it's time to wean. The womb sack is a little like the pouch on a kangaroo, except the baby kangaroo is already born when it makes its way into the kangaroo's pouch."

"Whoa. Talk about learning more than I ever wanted to know about the Yolongi."

Sydnee smiled. "Everything you know about an enemy is useful."

"I guess. Uh, where are we headed, Lieutenant?"

"We're going to the last reported position of the *Perry* to see if we can discover what happened to them."

"Ah, now I understand why you wanted the tug instead of a shuttle."

"Yes, FTL made the decision. I have to know what happened before I send a message to Space Command."

* * *

"Captain, we're picking up a contact on the DeTect. It's headed directly this way."

"How far away, Milty?"

"Maximum distance— about four billion kilometers. It appears to be traveling about Light-75. It should be here in just under three minutes."

Lidden looked up at the chronograph in his bedroom. It indicated that the time was 0428 GST. "Sound GQ. I'll be there in two minutes."

"Aye, Captain," Lt. Milton said as he nodded to the tac officer.

In seconds, crewmen were rolling out of their racks and jumping into their clothes. The ship, whose corridors had been as quiet as a church a few minutes before, was suddenly as busy as a department store during their annual one-day, ninety-percent-off sale on women's shoes.

Lidden made it to the bridge and relieved Lieutenant Milton before the DeTect'ed vessel arrived. As he climbed into the Command chair, the tac officer said, "Unknown vessel will reach this location in thirty seconds."

All eyes on the bridge not otherwise engaged turned toward the large monitor. A half-minute later a freighter came to a halt some seventy thousand kilometers off the starboard beam. Lidden was glad they stopped there rather than on the larboard side or the stern because the sensor grid on those quarters was still mostly unavailable.

There was little doubt that the ship was of Clidepp origin. It was too far away to get an image that could be used for matching it to one in the database, but the ship was definitely Mydwuard in design.

"It doesn't appear to be here for us, Captain," Milton said from the XO chair.

"No, Milty, it doesn't. Let's see what she does now that she's here."

The freighter remained where it had stopped for more than an hour, then moved towards the damaged Clidepp destroyer controlled by rebels.

"I guess she wanted to see if we made any kind of move in response to her arrival before she showed her true colors," Lidden said to Milton.

"Well, there's no doubt now."

"It could be worse. I don't see any weapons showing on that freighter."

"There are none visible," Milton agreed. "What now, Captain?"

"We wait to see what *they* do. We're still not in a position to act the aggressor."

"Captain," the tac officer said. "I'm DeTecting another vessel headed directly this way. It just came on the monitor. Range is roughly four million kilometers. Speed is Light-75. ETA is three minutes."

"All of a sudden this area of space seems very popular," Lidden said to Milton. "If we'd been able to get a message out, I could hope that it was someone coming to assist *us*."

* * *

Sydnee halted the small ship a hundred thousand kilometers from the group of three ships. She didn't cancel the tug's DATFA envelope because she wanted the ability to make a quick getaway if the ships weren't friendlies.

"It looks like two destroyers and a Mydwuard freighter," Sydnee said to Morales. "One destroyer looks a lot like the *Perry*, but it's too— short. It has the right length but doesn't have enough decks."

"That's the *Perry*," Morales said. "There can't be two old buckets that look that much alike. All the other ships in his class went to the scrap dealers decades ago."

"But what happened to the lower decks?"

"Maybe that's why they never came back to get us."

"I'll contact them and verify that Space Command personnel still control the ship before I move in."

After ten minutes of hails, Sydnee gave up. "No one is responding. I wonder if anyone is left alive over there."

"Maybe we should get a closer look."

"Yes, let's go look at the keel."

*   *   *

As Sydnee moved the small vessel closer and lower, she slipped off the working part of the sensor grid and the *Perry* lost her image on the monitor.

"The tug was moving in slowly, but I can't see it anymore," the tac officer said. "There was no sign of mounted weapons."

"Do you think they're a salvage operation, Captain?" Milty asked.

"I don't know," Lidden said. "I saw no company markings on the exterior. Com, find out if Engineering has people outside."

"Aye, Captain," the com chief said. A few seconds later he reported, "Engineering states that no one is scheduled to be outside until the next watch."

"Then tell them to get someone suited up and out on the hull so they can report what the sensor grid isn't."

"Aye, Captain."

*   *   *

"Wow," Sydnee said. "Would you look at the damage to the keel and lower larboard decks. No wonder the *Perry* didn't respond to my hails. Her two communications arrays are completely gone."

"What do you think happened, Lieutenant?"

"The last message we received said that cutting across the bow of the Clidepp destroyer hadn't worked to cancel their envelope and that they were about to try a different maneuver. The only maneuver I can think of is an envelope merge. If it's not executed properly, the two vessels can collide. I think the *Perry* collided with the other destroyer. That has to be it with the freighter."

"Do you think there's anyone left alive inside? And how do we tell them we're out here?"

"I can think of only one way."

* * *

"Sir, look at the monitor," Milton said to the Captain who was busy reading a report on the small monitor near his left hand while they waited on word from the Engineering personnel suiting up to go outside.

"What's it doing?" Lidden said.

"It looks like it's waiting to be invited in."

The tug was sitting just outside the starboard shuttle bay, its nose pointed towards the *Perry*. Lidden debated for a minute and then said, "Com, tell the Marine commander that we need two squads of armed Marines at the starboard shuttle bay on the double, then tell Flight Operations to open the hatch and let it in."

"Aye, sir."

"Milty," Lidden said, "go greet our guests. But use extreme caution until we know that they're unarmed and what they want."

"Aye, sir."

* * *

The bay controller had to reposition the bulkheads of the temporary airlock to their maximum size to accommodate the tug because it was twice as large as a shuttle. As the hatch rose out of the way, Sydnee piloted the tug into the bay.

As the outer hatchway closed and the transparent airlock bulkhead retracted out of the way, Sydnee released the magnetic skids and moved the small ship to a parking area.

Once properly aligned, she let the small ship settle to the deck and engaged the magnetic skids again.

Morales headed for the tug hatchway while Sydnee completed the orderly shutdown of all systems. As the hatch opened, Morales stared into the barrels of the thirty rifles pointed at the opening. "Whoa, guys, I surrender," he said with a smile. "We come in peace."

"Who's with you, Sergeant?" First Lieutenant Kelly MacDonald asked.

"Lieutenant Marcola, ma'am."

"Who else?"

"That's it, ma'am. Just the two of us."

"Okay, people, at ease," she said to her squads. As Sydnee appeared in the hatchway next to Morales, MacDonald said with a smile, "Welcome back, Lieutenant."

"Thank you, Lieutenant. I'm happy to be back. It looks like you had a bit of trouble out here."

"Sydnee?" she heard from the door as Milton entered the bay."

"The prodigal daughter has returned," Sydnee said as she walked down the ramp. "I see you've been doing a little redecorating since I've been gone."

"Yeah. Just don't joke about it in front of the Captain or he'll bite your head off. Literally."

"Envelope merge went bad?"

"Yeah. The Clidepp destroyer helmsman tried to keep us from hitting his temporal generator and twisted his ship just as we were about to merge envelopes. We don't know which ship was more badly damaged because we've been dead in space since it happened. Come on, we'd better get you up to the bridge before the Captain comes down here to see what's holding us up."

"Catch you later," Sydnee said over her shoulder to MacDonald as Milton hustled her out the door.

"How did you find us?" Milton asked as they rode the lift to A deck.

"I went to your last reported position. Failing to find you there, I began a standard grid search. We got lucky and DeTect'ed the three ships on just the third pass."

"The Clidepp destroyer took us on a merry chase when we tried to catch him. The Captain did everything he could to get them to surrender peacefully and finally gave up when it became apparent that wasn't going to happen. The envelope merge was the final option. It was either that or give up. The Captain doesn't like to give up."

"We thought you folks were dead and we'd be stuck on Diabolisto for the rest of our days."

"So you stole a tug?"

"I needed to know what happened out here."

The doors to the bridge slid apart to let the two officers enter as they stepped into the sensor area.

"The tug was piloted by Lieutenant Marcola, sir," Milty said as they crossed the bridge to the command chair.

Lidden turned and looked at Marcola. "I'm surprised to see you out here, Lieutenant."

"Yes, sir."

Lidden took a deep breath before saying, "In my briefing room, Lieutenant." Sydnee stepped out of the way as Lidden climbed down from the command chair. "Milty, you have the bridge."

"Aye, sir. I have the bridge."

Sydnee followed Lidden into his briefing room and stood in front of his desk while the Captain took his seat behind it.

"Okay, Marcola, tell me everything."

Over the next twenty minutes, Sydnee related the high-lights of everything that had happened since they left the *Perry* in the MAT. "That's pretty much it, sir."

"And you're saying that Lieutenant Kennedy decided on his own to attack the rebel base camp?"

"He believed that destroying the stockpiled ordnance was imperative when we lost contact with the *Perry*. He feared that the rebels might have intended to use the ordnance to start a civil war within the Clidepp Empire."

"And after he was killed, you took command and led an attack against the rebel forces."

"They had us pinned down, sir. They left us no choice. We were forced to fight."

"Because you killed six of their sentries during the attack on their camp."

"We didn't have stun weapons, and Lt. Kennedy believed our safety lay in a stealthy operation."

"And then you planned another raid, and killed a senior officer when you stole the tug."

"We created a diversion to distract everyone in the hope we wouldn't have to kill again. Colonel Suflagga wasn't fooled and discovered what we were doing. He was about to kill Sgt. Morales and myself when I acted, sir. He left me no choice. I recorded the entire attack with my helmet cam."

"Lieutenant, would you like to transfer to the Marine Corps?"

"What?"

"I asked if you'd like to transfer to the Marine Corps. You seem to think you're a Marine officer rather than a Space Command officer. Your job was to ferry a platoon of Marines down to the surface of a planet, not lead charges through enemy fire and play deadly quick-draw games with retired military officers."

"I only did what I felt was necessary for the survival of myself and my people, sir."

"They're not *your* people, Lieutenant. They're Marines. From this time forward, you will leave Marine operations to the Marines. Am I clear?"

"As crystal, sir. But what happens if I'm again the only surviving officer?"

"We'll just have to make sure that doesn't happen."

"Yes, sir. Sir, I'd like permission to return to the planet and bring back the platoon."

"How many do you think you can squeeze into that tug?"

"Um, only about eight per trip, but I'd like to retrieve the MAT. Then I can bring everyone home in one trip."

"Negative. We need the tug you brought because it has an IDS transmitter. We haven't been able to report to Space Command since the collision." Lidden sighed and said quietly, "We'll get those people off the planet, Marcola. I promise. Go get some rest. You've had a far rougher time of it than we have. You need some down time. You're off duty until notified."

"Yes, sir."

"Dismissed."

Sydnee left the Captain's briefing room and crossed the bridge without making eye contact with anyone. She knew they all wanted to question her, but she wasn't in the mood just then.

Once in her quarters she quickly stripped off the armor and headed for the shower. As she relaxed in the warmth of the hot spray, she felt almost at peace for the first time in weeks. Thoughts of Rett Kennedy's death and the deaths of the others on both sides would haunt her for some time to come, but for now, for just a few hours, she would do her best to forget the pain and misery she'd experienced on Diabolisto.

Wanting to forget and actually forgetting are quite different things. Sydnee's sleep was restless and troubled as her unconscious mind refused to relax its tight grip on the recent memories.

Chapter Twenty-Two

~ Mar. 12th, 2285 ~

"You look terrible," Kelly MacDonald said in the officers' mess that afternoon.

"Thank you," Sydnee replied.

"Couldn't sleep?"

"Barely. I seemed to sleep fine while I was on the planet. Perhaps I was just so exhausted at the end of each day from crawling through swamps that I would have slept through a GQ drill. I was happy beyond words to climb into my rack this morning, but mostly all I did was toss and turn for seven hours. Every time I fell asleep, I saw Rett die again. Seeing the bodies of the rebels didn't bother me half as much. I suppose I might have felt they deserved it for killing someone close to me."

"You and Rett were close?"

"Um, no, not in the way you mean. I meant that we were comrades in arms, not lovers. As you once said, Rett was a little stiff— and at times he was intractable— but overall he was a nice guy just trying to do his best in a difficult situation. He was a good Marine, all the way."

"Yes, he was. He'll be missed."

"Do you know why he was here? Aboard the *Perry* I mean."

"He would never talk about it, but I heard that it had to do with an incident on Earth. Allegedly he was hurrying to a staff meeting and bumped into a visiting general."

"That's all? He bumped into a general?"

"He was carrying a pitcher of scalding coffee at the time."

"Oh."

"Yeah. I heard that his transfer orders were in his hands within an hour, and he was off the base and on his way to the *Perry* in two."

"Wow."

"Yeah. This is the brass's dumping ground. Land on someone's shit list and you wind up on the *Perry*."

"I still have no idea *why I'm* here. I didn't spill a pitcher of coffee on a general— or an admiral. I didn't repeat sordid stories about a superior officer. I didn't have people under my command die from negligence. I didn't do any of the things that I've heard others did, or were simply *accused* of doing, to wind up here."

"You'll probably find out eventually."

"I hope so. I really want to know who I pissed off so much that Supreme HQ would ship me off to a space-going gulag."

* * *

"Marcola," Sydnee heard in her left ear as she sat on her bunk a few hours later thinking about the people she had left behind. She touched her SC ring and said, "Marcola."

"This is the Captain. Come to my briefing room. Lidden out."

"Marcola out."

Sydnee jumped out of her rack and straightened her uniform, then checked her appearance in the mirror. Satisfied, she hurried to the bridge. She crossed to the Captain's briefing room without stopping for conversation and stood at the door until it opened.

"Lt.(jg) Marcola reporting to the Captain as ordered," she said as she braced to attention in front of his desk.

"At ease, Marcola." Gesturing to an overstuffed oh-gee chair he said, "Have a seat."

It was the first time she had been invited to sit in the briefing room and she didn't know what to make of it, but she did as ordered, sitting stiffly on the front edge of the chair.

"Relax," Lidden said. "When you're invited to sit, you're not in trouble."

Sydnee sat back in the chair and tried to relax, but none of her previous visits to this office had been exactly cordial.

"This command owes you a debt of thanks. By bringing that tug to us, we were able to contact Simmons Space Command base and apprise them of our situation and location. It lifted a great weight from my mind. The *Pellew* had been sent to search for us, but by now his captain has been informed of our status. He will proceed directly here to assist us, but unfortunately he won't arrive here for two months. I say unfortunately, because I believe the situation will worsen substantially in that time."

Lidden paused for a couple of seconds, then said, "Would you still like to return to Diabolisto?"

Sydnee wasn't sure she heard right, so she hesitated.

"There'll be no repercussions if you request to remain here."

"Um, yes, sir. I would like to return to the planet. As I said, I think we can retrieve the MAT now that we have a tug."

"Since the MAT doesn't have FTL, there's no way you can return the Marines to the *Perry*. It might be best for everyone to remain on Diabolisto anyway."

"Sir?"

"The *Perry* is even more badly damaged than might appear from outside observation. When the lower three decks were crushed, control systems were damaged so severely that we may not be able to get them functional again unless we get the *Perry* to the Mars shipyard. Following the collision, there was some concern that we might not even get life support systems operational again, but our engineers have done wonderfully under extremely trying conditions. The main issue seems to be that the *Perry* is so old that its systems just won't integrate with the replacement parts in inventory that were sent to us but weren't needed until now and so were never tested with the old systems.

"Presently, we're sitting fifty thousand kilometers from a Clidepp military ship held by rebels. A freighter has arrived, apparently to assist in their repairs, but we cannot allow the destroyer to leave before the *Pellew* arrives. All tac officers and watch commanders have standing orders to prevent that from happening. If there are any indications that they're attempting to build their envelope, this ship will immediately fire torpedoes with the intent to stop or even destroy the rebel ship.

"I probably don't have to tell you what the consequences could be. We're essentially dead in space. If we fire on the destroyer, they could turn and attack us. Without the ability to maneuver, we may just be a sitting duck. We do have about fifty percent laser array capability. If the rebel ship comes closer than twenty-five thousand kilometers, we'll use it to our best advantage, or we'll use it for knocking down her torpedoes. But if they determine where our weaknesses are, they can maneuver to our weak side and destroy us.

"I'd like you to go back to Diabolisto and look after those people. Your chances of survival are better there. If you can raise the MAT, you'll all be able to join the *Pellew* when it arrives. They'll know we left people on the planet and will come to find you."

"Do you really believe the *Perry* will be destroyed, sir?"

"I hope not, but it's very possible. We have to do whatever it takes to keep that destroyer from getting away, despite the fact that we're ill-equipped to respond to an attack on this ship."

"But why not just let it go, sir? Let the Clidepp Empire worry about it. I'm sure that all the rebels want now is to get out of GA space."

"We can't just turn our backs on a terrorist act that occurred inside GA space. It's our job to do whatever we can to bring these people to justice. There is no second option."

"Yes, sir."

"A return to Diabolisto must be voluntary, Marcola."

"Yes, sir, I volunteer. May I ask a favor?"

"You may ask."

"I'd like to take Sgt. Morales, Lieutenant Weems, Lieuten-ant Caruthers, and Lieutenant MacDonald with me."

"That tug only has four seats on the flight deck."

"Yes, sir, but someone can sit on the deck at the rear and strap themselves to the rear bulkhead when we reach the planet. Now that we know where you are, a direct route is only three hours."

"Why Weems and Caruthers?"

"We went to a lot of trouble to get this tug. I don't want to just leave it if we resurrect the MAT. Weems can pilot either ship, and Caruthers can at least fly the tug if needed."

"Very well. You can take them if they volunteer to go. Weems, Caruthers, and MacDonald are all O-2 like yourself but are all senior to you in time in grade. However, given that you were in command when you left the planet, you'll con-tinue to take the lead. I've had engineering prepare some shovels for digging the MAT out and several oh-gee sleds with an open-topped box for transporting the dirt. As the box is filled, a remote control will allow you to raise it up over the lip of the sinkhole and dump it away from the hole. They'll be mounted on the hull so they won't require any of your limited interior space. "

"Yes, sir. And speaking of limited interior space, I'd like to bring as many emergency food packs as we can fit into the tug's engine areas, the exterior tool boxes, and the oh-gee sled boxes. We should have at least three months' worth because I don't know what's going to happen to the rebels there. We destroyed a lot of their supplies and we might have to share our food when their ride doesn't arrive."

"Very well. Is that all?"

"Um, yes, sir."

"You'll leave as soon as your team is ready and the food is loaded. Carry on."

"Yes, sir," Sydnee said as she stood up, braced to attention, then turned to leave.

"Good luck, Sydnee," Lidden said before she passed through the door.

She stopped, smiled, and said, "To you also, sir."

"Let me get this straight," Lt. Weems said, "the Captain has authorized your voluntary return to Diabolisto, and you requested that we accompany you?"

The three officers she had requested— Weems, Caruthers, and MacDonald— were sitting with Sydnee in the conference room on A Deck.

"Yes. I need help recovering the MAT from a sink hole, and I need at least one more pilot. Two would be better in case something happened to one of us."

"What could happen?" Caruthers asked.

"We're going to try to recover a MAT from a very deep sinkhole on an alien planet with dangerous indigenous life forms. I'd say a lot could happen. But this mission is important. We left people down there and we need to recover them."

"I'm ready," MacDonald said. "I expected to be there already."

"We all hold the same rank. Who's in command?" Weems asked.

"Given my experience with the situation on the planet, the Captain has named me to lead the team."

Weems looked at Caruthers and said, "You have a problem with that? You're senior in time in grade."

"No problem. It's a simple, straightforward recovery project of very short duration."

"Um, not exactly," Sydnee said.

"What's that mean?" Weems asked.

"The Captain wants the team to remain on the planet until the *Pellew* arrives in two months."

"Two months?" Caruthers said in surprise. "Why should we wait on the planet for two months if we get the MAT out? Isn't the planet a miserably hot mud ball?"

"What I'm about to say now is confidential. You can't tell anyone."

Sydnee looked at each and held their gaze until they nodded.

"The Captain expects to engage the rebel destroyer at some point. I believe he doesn't expect the *Perry* to survive."

No one responded for a full thirty seconds. Finally, Weems said, "I'm not really surprised by that information. I've had my doubts that the *Perry* would survive an encounter while in this condition. So the Captain is using this as an opportunity to save part of the crew?"

"I believe so. If he had more ships available, I believe he would send all non-essential personnel to Diabolisto. He seemed to be looking for excuses. He even said that if I got the MAT out, I couldn't use it bring the platoon back here."

"That's not an excuse, it's true," Caruthers said. "The MAT doesn't have FTL."

"No, but the tug does. I could fill the MAT with Marines and then tow it here using the tug."

"Uh, that's true. I wasn't thinking of it like that. Ya know, I can't say that I've felt very useful lately. We sit on the bridge and stare at the big monitor all night, watching for any sign of life from that destroyer. I know the tac officers have standing orders to fire on the destroyer if it starts to move or build a temporal envelope. Those instructions are posted in the pass-down log."

"So, assuming we get the MAT out," Weems said, "and don't attempt to bring the platoon home, where do we stay? I mean, we don't want to be near the rebel camp after having attacked them twice and killing so many when they attacked."

"We found a nice little cave where we can live in relative comfort. We'll stay there."

"Cave? Relative comfort?"

"Relative to living in the open. Outside, the insects are so bad that you have to keep your armor sealed at all times. I don't know how the Yolongi do it. They have no armor, just ordinary fatigues. They must have some insect spray or something to keep the bugs off."

"Or they have a natural immunity."

"Whatever," Sydnee said. "The cave is also about twenty-five degrees cooler than the outside temperature and a lot drier because it's always raining on that planet. I need your answers now. If you don't want to go, I'll find someone else."

"As I said before, I'm in," MacDonald said.

"I'm in," Weems said.

Sydnee looked at Caruthers with anticipation written all over her face.

"I'm thinking, I'm thinking."

"I understand if you'd rather not go. You'll have to be fully suited up in your personal armor every time you leave either the cave or one of the ships, and while the cave is much cooler than outside, it's still hot and humid. I can ask Lieutenant Bateman to go instead."

"Bateman? There's no way he'd go voluntarily. He'd have to leave the love of his life behind. His girlfriend works in Engineering. Oh, alright, I'm in also. At least it'll be something different to do."

* * *

As the tug neared the planet, Sydnee said, "Sgt. Morales, you'd better strap yourself to the bulkhead during reentry and landing, just in case."

"Aye, Lieutenant."

Morales, as the lowest-ranked member of the group, was naturally the one without a seat, but he wasn't uncomfortable. He had rolled out a piece of anti-gravity cloth and floated a dozen centimeters above the deck during the entire three-hour trip, using his backpack for a backrest. Sydnee occupied the pilot chair while Weems rode as co-pilot. MacDonald and Caruthers occupied the two rearward-facing jump seats behind the pilot seats.

To hide their return to the planet, Sydnee entered orbit on the far side. She continued dropping the small ship lower and lower as they approached the sinkhole location to ensure they couldn't be observed by line-of-sight tracking equipment. They were at treetop level by the time they reached the site of the original camp.

"There it is," Sydnee said. It was too dark to see anything through the tug's windows, but sensors provided a clear image of the ground contours on the monitors. "It looks like it's expanded a bit more. I've selected another clearing nearby for the tug."

"Are we supposed to dig this out by ourselves?" Caruthers asked. "I thought we'd have Marines to help with this phase."

"The cave is about twenty-five kilometers from here. Once I make contact with them, I can arrange to pick a few up to help with the recovery."

Once positioned over a nearby clearing barely large enough to accommodate the ship, Sydnee slowly reduced power to the oh-gee engine and the ship began to settle.

As the ship touched down on the ground, Sydnee said, "I checked the ship configuration database while on the *Perry*. We won't be able to use the magnetic skids to lift the ship because of the Dakinium skin. The designers included annulus fasteners, like those used on cargo containers, at eight key points for lifting the ship. Any one of them can be used to lift a fully loaded MAT without damaging it so we only have to dig down, uncover one, and hook up. But two connection points might be better if we factor in the weight of the dirt covering the ship.

"I wouldn't recommend going outside until daybreak, but if you must, stay close to the ship. There are a lot of dangerous creatures out there. And remember, keep your armor sealed at all times."

"Why don't we start work tonight?" Caruthers said. "We can set up portable work lights and get a jump on the effort."

"We're only five kilometers from the rebel camp. They'd be able to see the glow from the lights and might come to investigate. "

"Oh, right."

"It's less than an hour to dawn here," MacDonald said, "even though the GST time is 2021."

"Yes," Weems said, "Let's relax a little and formulate a plan while we wait for the sun to rise. Syd, how far down is the MAT, and how much dirt is covering it?"

"I haven't been here since the first days on the planet, so I don't know if it's fallen farther, but the top surface was about ten meters down. I imagine there's at least a meter of dirt on top. It was almost completely hidden just after the collapse, and dirt was continuing to fall from the sidewalls. At least the dirt should be fairly loose because it had to crumble to fall in."

"Unless it fell in large chunks," Caruthers said.

"Assuming that the MAT is buried under a meter of dirt—" Weems said, "in fact we probably should assume two meters— and that we don't know its angle or position, finding those annuli could be difficult."

"Yes," Sydney said, "Since they're made of Dakinium, like the frame and sheathing of the hull, a magnetometer won't give us a reading. Dakinium soaks up most energy directed at it."

"Most energy?" MacDonald said, "What kind of energy doesn't it soak up?"

"I know that visible light in the four-hundred to seven-hundred-nanometer range is reflected back. I don't know what else it doesn't eat, but I read that it absorbs microwaves, x-rays, and gamma rays."

"Interesting," Weems said. "What does it do with the energy it absorbs, Syd?"

"I don't know if it stores it somehow or dissipates it, but I read that as energy excites the atoms, the molecular strength increases, making it more resistant to force."

"So the more you try to alter it through the release of energy, the stronger it becomes?"

"Exactly."

"No wonder lasers and plasma torches have no effect. The material is actually fighting back when you attempt to damage it."

"Yes, that's the way I understand it."

"So what's the plan after we recover the MAT? Just sit back and wait out the inevitable?"

"I've been trying to think of a way we can help the *Perry*. I have an idea, but I have to think on it a bit more. It might be construed as being in violation of the orders I received from the Captain."

"If it helps the *Perry* survive a fight with the rebel ship and saves our shipmates," Weems said, "a court-martial would be worth it. Besides, what's the worst they can do, sentence you to the *Perry*? If the idea is sound, relinquish command to me and I'll do it."

"Let me think on it a little more. Hey, it looks like it's getting light outside."

"Great," Caruthers said. "By the time we get our armor on, it should be light enough to see without needing portable lights."

Within thirty minutes, the group had left the tug and they were on their way to the sinkhole clearing. It was getting light quickly, but they walked in darkness beneath a canopy of leaves that blocked most light until they reached the clearing.

"I think we have a problem, Syd," Weems said as they arrayed themselves along the shore of the small lake in front of them. Water lapped at their feet.

"But that was empty when we got here, wasn't it?" MacDonald asked.

"Probably not," Sydnee said. "The ground contour radar doesn't see water."

Chapter Twenty-Three
~ Mar. 13th, 2285 ~

"Great," Caruthers said. "A difficult job just became almost impossible. We didn't bring any portable pumps, and I left my swim fins back on Earth."

"Perhaps not so impossible," Sydnee said with a smile. "It might actually help."

"Help? How could it possibly help for the MAT to be submerged at the bottom of a twenty-meter-deep lake?"

"Look at the physics. We have a submerged craft filled with trapped air. That gives it a certain amount of buoyancy. It's not like a shipwreck where water has filled the craft and displaced the air. Perhaps the only reason the MAT isn't already floating on the surface is that the extra weight of the dirt on top is holding it down."

"Yeah, that's right," Weems said. "It has to have a certain amount of buoyancy, and that *has* to assist our efforts to get it raised."

"But it's still twenty meters down, buried beneath a meter or more of dirt," Caruthers said.

"That's twenty meters to the bottom," Sydnee said. "The top should only be about ten to twelve meters down."

"And the dirt? Do you know how much wet dirt weighs? You have to add the weight of the dirt and the weight of the water it absorbed. We're going to break our backs shoveling the dirt off the MAT."

"Dirt has a certain buoyancy underwater also. And we don't have to shovel it off. We might be able to simply kick it out of the way. This isn't a tragedy; it's a cause for celebration. We might be out of here in hours instead of days."

"I'll believe it when I see it."

"Then let's get started so you can become a believer," Syd said. "First, let me download the images of the MAT that I got from the *Perry's* database into everyone's helmet storage. You can call them up and study them when you have a few minutes. They'll help us locate the annulus fasteners."

The download took only a few minutes. Once everyone could see the diagram with the fasteners, they had a better understanding of what had to be done.

Holding up a three-meter aluminum pole she had been carrying, Sydnee said, "I brought these poles along to help us probe the depth of the dirt, but now we can use them to stir the dirt out of the way and feel for an annulus once we determine where the edge of the MAT is located. When we find one, we dig it out enough to get a rope on it. When we have two located, we'll fasten a cable to each and bring the tug over. As soon as the cable is hooked onto the tug, we lift the MAT free."

"You make it sound so easy," Caruthers said.

"Yeah, I like to think positive."

"Me too. I'm positive it's not going to be that easy."

Sydnee chuckled. "We'll see. Let's give it a go. Who wants to be first?" When no one spoke up, she said, "Okay, I'm first."

"I'm second," MacDonald said. "We'll show these big, strong men how it's done, Syd."

"I'll go third," Morales volunteered.

"Fourth," Weems chimed in.

"I'll take clean-up position," Caruthers said, "if the big, strong women aren't able to find their annulus with a pole and both hands."

Sydnee stepped into the water with two ropes tied around her waist. One rope was for attaching to an annulus, and the other was her safety line. As soon as she stepped over the edge of the hole, she began to sink slowly towards the bottom. The water was as dark and murky as the swamps they'd traversed when withdrawing after the attack on the rebel camp, but the armor's sensors helped considerably. They projected outlines on the SimWindow faceplate so she at least had an idea where the sinkhole's walls were located.

When Sydnee touched down, she announced it on Com 1. "It's pretty murky, as you know, and the ground beneath my feet is really soft. It's like the muck in the bogs. I'm beginning my probe."

After about ten minutes of carefully feeling her way along, Sydnee's pole sank deeper than expected.

"I've found an edge. I don't know which edge it is, but I'm going to work my way along it in a southerly direction until I find a corner."

To allow maximum useful interior space, the MAT was shaped like a big, square brick with rounded corners. Stubby wings could be extended out from the body to help improve stability in atmo operations, and were automatically retracted when the ship's power systems were shut down. The annuli were located near the corners of the craft.

It took a half hour for Sydnee to feel her way along and find a corner of the ship, pushing the pole into the muck until she met resistance or the pole went deeper than it should. It took another half hour for her to dig down and find the annulus, then tie a cord around it.

"Okay, one down," Sydnee said. "Pull me up."

As Sydnee's helmet cleared the surface, she said, "It's nice to see daylight again. It's like working in a dark closet down there."

Weems extended his hand to help her out, but just as they were about to make contact, Sydnee was suddenly jerked backwards into the water. The hand she had extended to Weems was the last thing they saw as a froth of bubbles appeared on the surface.

"Syd," MacDonald shouted on Com 1, "What's happened?"

"Something's grabbed me and is trying to eat me," Sydnee shouted back. "I think it's a Lampaxa Vorheridine. I'm trying to get to one of my knives, but it's wrapped itself around me and my arms aren't free."

Without a word, Morales grabbed a line and tied it around his waist. He pulled a knife from the scabbard on his left leg and jumped in where Sydnee had disappeared. A second later he felt the creature beneath his feet, then felt its jaws clamp on his right leg. The next thing he felt was Lt. MacDonald landing on top of him.

Weems and Caruthers watched as the froth of bubbles grew ever wider and the water on the surface swirled in irregular patterns. On Com 1, they could hear the heavy breathing of their three comrades, as well as the grunts, yells, and strings of cuss and curse words as the three fought the creature. Then, finally, the noise abated and the bubbles began to dissipate.

"If there's anyone left up there, will you pull us up?" Weems and Caruthers heard. They pulled on the lines attached to Sydnee and Morales, and four tightly intertwined bodies appeared at the surface. It took all of their strength to drag the bundle ashore.

"Are you okay, Syd?" Weems asked.

"I think so. I'll know for sure when you get this thing off me."

"You okay, Kel?" he asked Lt. MacDonald.

"When you get us unwrapped, you can tell me."

"How about you, Sergeant?"

"I think so, sir, but for a while there it felt like Saturday night in the barrio. I think this thing is dead, but its teeth are still locked on my leg."

Starting from the tail, Weems and Caruthers were able to slowly untwine the creature from Sydnee, MacDonald, and Morales, but not before it showed that it wasn't quite dead at least three times.

On the third time, Morales plunged his double-edged blade into an area ten centimeters behind its head and rocked it back and forth a few times until the head was almost severed from the body. The trunk was almost a half-meter thick at that point, and it took some doing to sever all the nerves. When the jaws relaxed, he pulled it off his leg and stood up. "Man, I wouldn't want to meet one of those things when I wasn't wearing my armor. A person wouldn't stand a chance."

"You know it," MacDonald said. "Even with the armor, I don't know if one person could handle it. I was beginning to think that the *three* of us were over-matched." Turning to Sydnee, she said, "You called this thing a Lampaxa Vorheridine. You've seen one before?"

"Yeah, one of them tried to eat PFC Riley while we were trying to elude the rebels. It took three to subdue it, just like today. It's delicious, by the way, if we haven't punctured its poison sac. It tastes like pork sausage."

"You ate one of these things?" Caruthers said, making a face as he stretched it out on the shore to its full twelve-meter length.

"Well, not by myself. The platoon ate one. Everyone came back for seconds and thirds."

"But it's a snake."

"Sort of. But it tastes good and we have to save the emergency food packs for emergencies. We'll take it with us to the cave when we go. Sergeant Booth did a great job with the other one."

Caruthers made another face and then sighed. "I may regret my decision to come here if I have to eat snake at every meal."

"There're lots of other things to eat," Morales said. "We found a squid-like creature that was good, and there're tons of larva and grub worms everywhere."

"Okay, enough. If you want me to be able to help, stop making me sick."

Syd and the others were all grinning behind their helmets. Teasing Caruthers provided a sort of release from the tension of the deadly struggle with the creature.

"Okay, who's next?" Syd asked. "I think Morales and MacDonald should sit this dance out."

"I'll go," Weems said, then hesitated. "Uh, do you think there are any more of those things down there, Syd?"

"I'd say no, but I can't know for sure. Just remember to stay calm. In two encounters, the creatures haven't been able to bite through the armor."

"Oh, that's reassuring."

Syd smiled. "You'll be okay. I tied the one rope to the annulus I found. From the feel, I'd have to say that it's the larboard bow annulus. Follow the rope down and when you reach the bottom, walk about three meters to the right before you start probing for the edge, then just follow along until you find the corner."

"Got it. Wish me luck."

"Luck, Jerry," she said as she tied the two ropes around his waist.

Weems jumped in, followed the tied rope down to the MAT, then walked to the right and began his probing. It only took twenty minutes to find the corner and then another half hour to locate and tie a rope around the annulus.

Weems had carried on a nervous conversation almost the entire time he was underwater, but as he finished tying the rope on the annulus, he felt something coil around his body and he began screaming.

Sydnee and Morales quickly grabbed ropes and tied them around their waists, but as they prepared to jump in, Weems said, "Hold it," between huffs and puffs. "Everything is okay. I got wrapped up in my safety line and thought it was one of those monsters attacking me. Sorry."

In ten more minutes, Weems was ashore and breathing normally. "I'd rather face an armada of Raider destroyers in a scout ship than have one of those things attack me. I've always had a thing about snakes."

"Well, you did good," Sydnee said. "We have the two annuli marked and now it's just a matter of attaching the cable and we can lift it out. Why don't we grab some breakfast first? We're way ahead of schedule. "

"Sounds good to me," Weems said. "I need a cup of coffee and a reason to get out of this tin man suit for a while."

It took all five of them to pick up the Lampaxa Vorheridine and carry it back to the tug, where it was secured to the two oversized oh-gee sleds on the hull that had thankfully not been needed for ferrying dirt.

The cramped cockpit of the tug wasn't an ideal mess, but it did allow them to remove their armor during breakfast. They dined in the padded bodysuits worn under the armor. Afterwards, the group returned to the sinkhole to complete their mission. Morales took on the task of replacing the ropes with lifting cables and had everything hooked up in less than thirty minutes. Weems left to get the tug as Morales was pulled from the water-filled sinkhole.

In twenty minutes, the tug was hovering overhead. The lifting cable was attached to the hook on its keel and Weems took up the slack slowly, then began adding power to lift the MAT.

"It's not coming up, Syd," Weems said on Com 1. "I'm worried that the strain on the cables will snap them."

"So much for buoyancy," Caruthers said.

"There must be something holding it down," Weems replied. "Was it jammed in the sinkhole, Syd?"

"I don't know, Jerry. We didn't have a tug, so we never tried to raise it. You know, I wonder if all this water in the hole came during one of the deluges this planet experiences. Do you think it could be suction holding it down?"

"I don't know. I only know it isn't moving."

"Try rocking it."

"What?"

"You know, applying power and then backing off and then applying power again. Keep doing it in a steady pattern. It might help break the suction if that's the problem."

"Okay, I'll give it a go. Everybody better back away in case this cable snaps."

Weems started applying power and then backing off but never so much that the cable became loose. On the fourth application of power, the tug began to rise a little and then a lot. The MAT suddenly appeared on the surface, bobbing like a cork. As Weems pulled the craft free of the sinkhole, the water began to recede faster and faster. After about thirty seconds, a whirlpool action was noticeable, and in five minutes the sinkhole was completely drained.

Weems ferried the MAT over the treetops and brought it to another large clearing a few kilometers further from the rebel camp. After setting the stern of the ship down carefully, he gently lowered the bow as he moved ahead slightly. When the MAT was solidly on the ground, he released the cable and returned to the small clearing.

"Mission accomplished," Weems said as the others cycled through the tug's airlock.

"Good job, Jerry," Sydnee said. "In fact, you did so good that we might even forget about that safety line thing."

"You wouldn't tell anyone about that would you, Syd?"

"Well, I might be bribed. What did you do to wind up on the *Perry*?"

Weems looked away. "I'd rather be the butt of jokes for getting tangled in the rope."

"Okay, Jerry," she said, "If that's the way you want it." But she knew she'd never tell anybody about his getting tangled in the rope and thinking it was one of the Lampaxa creatures. Perhaps Jerry also knew she'd never tell anyone about the rope incident, which is why he would still not tell her what grievous faux pas he had committed in the past to earn a berth on the *Perry*.

Weems piloted the tug to where the MAT was resting and everyone disembarked to check out the ship. It was filthy on the outside, but that would change as quickly as the weather. The next rainstorm, which wasn't far off from the look of the sky, would leave it looking like new.

Sydnee entered the security code and the ramp extended as the hatch opened. Everything seemed fine so far. Within five minutes everyone had cycled through the airlock. There were a few things that hadn't been properly stowed, and they had wound up against the rear bulkhead when the ship was lifted up on end, but otherwise everything seemed perfect. The real test would naturally come when Syd activated the power systems and oh-gee engine, but for now everyone simply wanted to relax in the spacious, insect-free environment of the MAT. Compared to the cramped cockpit of the tug, the rear compartment of the MAT was like a grand ballroom.

After two hours of rest and a lunch made from emergency meal packs, it was time to continue their tasks. Weems left to pilot the tug and Sydnee moved onto the flight deck of the MAT. She proceeded through the checklist slowly and with utmost care. Everything tested fine, so she started the oh-gee engine and raised the MAT slowly as a driving rain began to fall. At a hundred feet, she advanced the throttle and the ship moved forward with increasing speed.

It took just ten minutes to reach the distant landing area that Sydnee had selected from surface maps. The rain had passed through the area already and the sun was shining brightly. The group spent an hour camouflaging the MAT so it wouldn't be easily spotted, then boarded the tug and flew to a tiny clearing not far from the cave.

Weems moved the tug slowly in against the trees and let it settle to the ground, then cut the engine and sat back. "Three more chores," he said to Sydnee. "We camo this ship, disable it so that no one can grab it like you did, then load that overgrown snake-lizard monster into the oh-gee sleds. Then we can head to that cave of yours. I'm dying to see it."

"I hope I haven't oversold it," she said with a smile.

"I'm sure you haven't. Let's see— decorated in a 'primitive' motif but free of insects, just slightly cooler than a sauna, and one large master bedroom that accommodates forty-two. That about it?"

"That's about it. Still want to go?"

"Syd, I wouldn't miss it for anything."

As they approached the cave, Weems said, "I don't see a cave along here."

"That's the idea. Watch and be amazed. And don't drop dinner."

Sydnee led the way into the cave, walking through the holo projection that simulated a solid wall without even slowing. The others followed as Weems said, "Very clever. I never would have guessed there was a cave here."

"The rebels didn't guess it either. They searched this area twice and walked right past it."

When the group reached the large domed area, the misting devices were working and the cave was free of insects but also people. The lights came up automatically.

"Where is everyone?" MacDonald asked as she looked around.

"I don't know," Sydnee said. "It looks just as it did when we left to grab the tug. Everyone's packs are still here. Even the thermal blanket is still here in the spot where I slept. I sure hope the others are safe. They were only supposed to create a diversion so I could steal the tug, then hightail it back here."

"Could they have been captured by the rebels? Or killed?"

"I can't imagine them being captured. During the battle, the rebels who ran away dropped everything they were carrying. I guess they wanted to be able to run faster. The ones who stayed to fight never left at all. We destroyed all the weapons at the site, except for two mortars that we kept for our own use, so we've pretty much reduced the armaments of the rebels to whatever they could find lying on the ground."

"So what do we do, Syd?" Caruthers asked. "Wait here, or go recon the rebel camp?"

"Um, let's wait here. Perhaps they went hunting for food."

"All of them at once?" MacDonald said.

"Let's just give them some time. If they're not back by dark, we'll reevaluate the situation."

"Okay, where do we bed down?" Weems asked.

"Rett and I slept over there," she said, pointing, "so I guess that's O-country. The noncoms were sleeping there and there, and everyone else just picked a spot wherever they felt most comfortable."

The officers all dropped their things in O-country and Sgt. Morales dropped his pack where he had been sleeping before. Within seconds, all were stripping their armor off.

After everyone had cleaned their armor in preparation for its next use, the newly arrived officers were trying to determine if they'd be more comfortable in tee shirts and shorts in the humid cave or wearing their fatigues. For now, tees and shorts won out.

Morales pulled the two carts filled with food packs and topped with the Lampaxa over to the food preparation area. As he prepared to cut off the head, Sydnee came over to look on. She watched as he removed the head carefully and then sniffed for the scent of ammonia. Smelling none, he said, "Smells okay, Lieutenant. I guess my killing cut was far enough back to avoid the poison sac, but I'll run a piece through the alien food analyzer just to be sure."

Ten minutes later the verdict was in. The Lampaxa was safe to eat. Morales had already made good progress skinning it and washing the trunk in preparation for slicing it up. Weems watched him work, fascinated that Morales could work so nonchalantly on such an alien creature. He exhibited no more distaste than someone might who was carving a rib roast on Earth.

When the Lampaxa had been cleaned and wrapped for storage, Morales packed most of it into one of the large collapsible coolers the platoon had brought with them. The other coolers were filled with vegetables, fruit, and what was left of a buflo the hunters had brought back a few days earlier.

"Lieutenant," Morales said loudly. "I mean Lieutenant Marcola. There's quite a bit of food here. It doesn't seem like they'd have to go hunting for more."

Sydnee walked to the mess area and looked in the coolers. "Yes, there's certainly enough food that they didn't need a reason to get more. If they haven't returned by tomorrow morning, you, Lt. MacDonald, and I will leave for the rebel camp. If a recon shows that our people have been captured, we'll work out a plan for freeing them. As I recall, we left quite a bit of Corplastizine buried at our original camp. We may have to make a trip there to get it."

"Aye, ma'am. Give the word and I'll be ready."

"Oo-rah."

"Oo-rah."

Chapter Twenty-Four

~ Mar. 14th, 2285 ~

Dinner in the cave consisted of Lampaxa steaks and the green, red, and yellow vegetables found in the coolers, with nuts and berries for dessert. Sgt. Morales grilled the steaks while Sydnee and MacDonald steamed or washed the vegetables and Weems and Caruthers washed and checked the berries, and shelled the nuts. Beverages were prepared from powered packages of fruit drinks.

"You were right, Syd," Weems said as they finished eating. "The Lampaxa does taste like pork. How about it, Vince?"

"Not bad," Caruthers said. "It's a lot better than I expected. I suppose I eventually could even get used to the sight of it. I'm not so sure about catching them on a regular basis if you have to jump into a swamp and engage in a fight to the death every time."

"That probably means it should be treated as a delicacy," MacDonald said with a smile, "and expected only when the meeting has been accidental, although I know a few Marines who would look upon it as sport and probably try to arrange contests like the alligator wrestling events on Earth— one man or woman, one knife, one Lampaxa."

"I know I'm not looking for a rematch with the species anytime soon," Sydnee said.

"You did great, Lieutenant," Morales said. "You probably didn't even need us to assist."

"If you and Lt. MacDonald hadn't assisted, I'd probably still be at the bottom of that sinkhole. Thanks, by the way."

"I think Lampaxa wrestling should definitely be considered a team sport," MacDonald said. "At twelve meters, it definitely has the edge."

"So what's your idea to save the *Perry*, Syd?" Weems asked.

"It doesn't matter. It wouldn't work without the support of the platoon, and we don't even know their status."

"Assuming that we find them, and that they're alive and healthy, what's the plan?"

Sydnee looked around the table. All eyes were on her. "Okay, I know it's crazy and an almost impossible task, but it's all I can come up with."

When she paused for longer than expected, Weems said, "Well?"

"I— I thought we might commandeer the *Abissto*?"

"What's an abissto?" MacDonald asked.

"I think it means *thrasher* in Yolon, but it's also the name of the Clidepp military destroyer in orbit around this planet."

"But that ship's a derelict, isn't it?" MacDonald asked.

"When it attacked the dip ship, a lucky shot or two destroyed the oxygen regeneration equipment. The atmo in the ship slowly soured and the crew barely made it here. I guess their last act was to strip the ship of everything of military value. But— they couldn't remove the torpedoes and couldn't remove the exterior-mounted laser arrays. The FTL drive and the Sub-Light engines are fully functional. So the ship is just as deadly as any other Clidepp destroyer, assuming the people in command know what they're doing."

"But it takes a huge number of highly trained people to operate a destroyer."

"It does take a lot of highly trained, intelligent people to operate a destroyer in day-to-day operations, but we're talking about a three-hour trip in FTL. Just the presence of a second ship might get the rebel-held destroyer to surrender. They won't know how many people we have on board, or what our fighting condition or capability is, so they'll have to assume the worst. We three command officers can handle tactical, helm and command. The Marine radioman can handle communications. Kelly and her people can handle the gunnery. The torpedo system is self-loading once the safeties have been removed. We only need one person in there to keep an eye on things in case there's a problem. That's six men, one for each torpedo room in the bow, stern, and amidship.

"We don't need cooks, medics, stores clerks, or even engineers. I'm sure the platoon has a few people who are good mechanically in case we have a problem."

"You make it sound so easy," MacDonald said. "That's probably what the rebels thought. And we saw how that turned out."

"I admit I've simplified things a bit. The most difficult part, aside from translating the Yolon signage to Amer, will be training the Marines as laser gunners, but that should only take a couple of days if the ship's simulators are any good. We'll have to remain in armor the whole time we're on the bridge and bring the MAT with us for sleeping accommodations, but I'm so used to the armor by now that it feels like a second skin at times. Depending upon the air quality in the *Abissto*, we may have to return to the MAT every few hours just to replenish our supply. Hopefully, the rebreather unit in the suits will be able to pull enough oxygen from the air in the destroyer even though you can't breathe it directly because of the CO_2 levels."

The group sat looking at one another for several minutes as they thought. Weems finally broke the silence with, "Ya know, if we could just get the ship to where the *Perry* is, we could get all the additional help we need."

The statement was greeted by a few smiles.

"Okay, I know the *Perry* is considerably understaffed to begin with, but given what's at stake, I'm sure we could borrow a few engineers to help with problems aboard the *Abissto*. They might even be able to rig some sort of an air regeneration system. At the very least, we can fill the *Abissto's* supply tanks from the *Perry's* supply. Right after the collision, it was touch and go with life support because so much of the ship was bleeding atmo, but once the hull was sealed, life support was fully restored and the air supply tanks are at maximum levels."

"Yeah, it could work," Caruthers said, "*if* we can get the ship to where the *Perry* is sitting. And *if* the ship is automated enough to be run from the bridge by just the three of us. And *if* the platoon wants to go along with us— we have to remember that this isn't sanctioned by the Captain so it should be limited strictly to volunteers. And *if* the platoon is even available and not captured or dead."

"Do you always have to play devil's advocate, Vince?" Weems asked.

"What can I say?" Caruthers said with a smile and a shrug. "It's my natural comfort zone."

"If we do this," Sydnee said, "I agree that everyone involved must be a volunteer."

"I don't see where we have a choice. We know how bad off the *Perry* is. It's not even close to what Space Command calls fit for duty. The crew can't possibly fight off that rebel ship if it's made fully operational. We might make the difference."

"It's getting late," Sydnee said. "Do we stay here or go to the MAT?"

"Go to the MAT?" MacDonald said in surprise. "Why should we go there? The heat and humidity aren't really that bad here."

"I was thinking more along the lines of safety. If we stay here, we have to do sentry duty in shifts. If we go to the MAT, we just seal ourselves in and no one can sneak up on us."

"I vote to stay here," Weems said. "I'll take the first two-hour watch."

"I'll take the second," Caruthers said.

"Third," Morales called out from where he was wrapping up the leftover food and storing it.

"I'll take fourth," MacDonald said.

"Guess that leaves fifth for me," Sydney said. "Okay, guys, I'm beat. That wrestling match with the Lampaxa really wore me out, and the work of camouflaging the MAT pretty much finished me off for today. Good night."

Within ten minutes, everyone except Weems was floating slightly above their bedroll and on their way to the deep sleep that often comes after an exhausting day. He retrieved his rifle and found a place in the shadows from which he could watch the entrance, then dimmed the lights in the cave.

* * *

"One of our lookouts has spotted a force of Spaccs," the radioman reported to Currulla when he came to the communications tent.

Awakened in the middle of the night by the urgent summons, Currulla was still a little groggy with sleep and wasn't in the best of moods. "Spaccs? How many?"

"The lookout reports seeing about forty or fifty."

"Headed this way?"

"No. The lookout said they seemed to be going out of their way to go around us."

"Thank Lullelian for that. The Spaccs don't *have* to go around us here if they don't want to. They could walk right through the middle of the camp and we couldn't stop them. We thought we had a chance against them once, but that armor they wear makes them almost invincible. Lattice rounds bounce off and laser hits have no effect at all. And if lasers won't hurt them, shovels and rocks certainly won't. I've had enough dealings with them to last me a lifetime. If Suflagga had listened to me, we wouldn't have lost a quarter of our people. The Spacc mission must have been just to destroy our ordnance. Once they accomplished that, all they wanted was to be left alone. Suflagga refused to drop it— and now he's dead as well. The fool." Currulla realized he was rambling and shut his mouth.

"So we do nothing?"

"Haven't you been listening to me just now? There's nothing we can do. Just pray they continue to leave us alone. Any word from command yet?"

"Nothing. It's been weeks since we learned that a freighter was coming to pick us up. Now I get no replies to anything. Do you think the rebellion is over and our cause is lost?"

"Our cause will never be lost, but Citizen X might have been caught and everyone has gone into hiding. We won't know until we either get a message or we get off this miserable planet from hell."

* * *

Captain Nesadeedis, Captain of the *Glassama,* had been waiting impatiently for the Captain of the freighter *Furmmara* to arrive but managed to disguise his impatience when the visitor was finally escorted into the A Deck conference room.

"Welcome to the *Glassama,* Captain Pouurricas," Nesadeedis said.

"Thank you, Captain. I've just received a message from the council. They've asked me for an update on the situation here. How are your repairs progressing?"

"We've managed to adhere to the projected schedule. It takes time to rebuild a ship in space without access to the necessary parts."

"And you expect to be under power and on your way back to Empire space within ten kalins?"

"Yes, as planned."

"Very good. I admit that I don't like sitting here in GA space. Did you observe the arrival and departure of that Space Command tug?"

"Yes, of course. We DeTect'ed it as soon as it came in range."

"What did you make of that?"

"What do you mean?"

"Where do you think it came from?"

"I would have to say that it came from Diabolisto."

"Yes, we felt the same. It supports the decision to come here first. It would seem to suggest that Space Command has a presence there."

"I doubt it. If they had any other ships in this area, they'd already be here."

"Why?"

"Why would they be here? To help the Space Command destroyer we collided with."

"Perhaps they don't need help."

"I don't follow you, Captain Pouurricas."

"Perhaps the Space Command ship is not as badly injured as you suppose. Perhaps its role right now is just to observe you."

Nesadeedis stared at Pouurricas without replying. He was obviously deep in thought.

"Have you noticed the frequency of IDS transmissions from the Spacc destroyer?"

"Frequency? There haven't been any."

"And what does that tell you?"

"It's obvious. It means that their communication systems are still down."

"Then how did that tug know where to find them?"

"Uh, I don't know."

"Perhaps Space Command has some new communication system we know nothing about. They were the ones who developed the IDS, the AutoTect, and the DeTect systems, after all. Perhaps they have a new method of communicating. Hyperspace has many different layers."

"What are you driving at?"

"We've been unable to contact the crew of the *Abissto* since their original call for help. You reported that when you arrived at the planet, there were Space Command ships in orbit. Since your collision with the Spacc destroyer, you've been unable to detect any communications, yet a mysterious tug arrives and departs from and to an unknown location. There are obviously forces at work here that are unknown to us. We are beginning to feel uncomfortable about this situation."

"Space Command only has a few ships in this entire deca-sector. We only saw one at Diabolisto because that's all there was."

"Then what of the tug? Why did it remain just a few worllies and leave again. If the destroyer was as badly damaged as you believe, why didn't the tug tow it away?"

"You believe they're fully functional and just waiting to see what we do?"

"Yes, or perhaps waiting for a task force from the Empire to arrive. Perhaps Space Command doesn't want to create an international incident unless absolutely necessary. You reported how hard and how long they tried to get you to stop. Normally, Space command gives just one chance to stop and then performs the envelope merge procedure."

"Some of your points have merit. So what does the council suggest?"

"That you accelerate your repairs to whatever extent possible and get back to Clidepp space. Don't fire on the Spacc ship unless provoked."

"We're already following that line of thought. But if they fire on us, we'll respond."

"The council accepts your right to defend yourself, but they must fire the first shot. So far, neither side has used a weapon and the collision can be attributed to a miscommunication."

"And what of the crew on Diabolisto?"

"The council acknowledges that they are lost to us. It doesn't want either of us to further provoke the Spaccs by even going there to check up on them."

"There were almost three hundred of our people on that ship."

"The Spaccs won't harm them if they don't resist. When we've won this war with the Empire, our people will be repatriated."

"Very well. But if the Spacc destroyer so much as fires a shot across our bow, I'll destroy him."

* * *

Caruthers leaned back against the wall where Weems had spent his two hours on guard duty and yawned. It was going to be difficult to keep awake for another hour, but he had developed little mind tricks over the years when his duty schedule had been extended without notice.

He was concentrating on stifling a yawn when he heard a noise in the cave entranceway. He stopped everything, including breathing, and strained to hear the slightest of noises. When he heard what sounded like footsteps on gravel, he said loudly, "Lights, full illumination." The lights position-ed around the cave immediately went to full brilliance. Then he shouted, "Who goes there?"

The noises had stopped when he raised the lighting level, and he heard just one word.

"Buttercup."

"What? Who are you?"

"Wrong answer. Put your weapon down and walk toward the cave entrance or we come in shooting."

Sydnee had awakened in time to hear the security recognition signal and the threat of violence. "Petunia," she said loudly.

A few seconds later, Staff Sergeant McKenzie walked cautiously into the dome. Seeing Sydnee, he lowered his weapon and brightened considerably. "Lieutenant, it's great to see you. We thought for sure you were gone after those fighters took off after you. It was cloudy, but we saw flashes of light from their guns."

"I guess I'm tough to kill, Staff Sergeant. Their first shots went wild and we went FTL before they could zero in on us. We didn't see any light flashes after that."

"Lieutenant MacDonald, ma'am," McKenzie said as she stood up and he recognized her. "Then the *Perry* is okay?"

"It's damaged but still somewhat intact," MacDonald said. "We didn't lose anyone, but the ship took a real pounding."

McKenzie looked at Caruthers and nodded. "Sir, sorry for the threats. When you didn't return the correct recognition word, I didn't know who was in here. I thought you might be Yolongi."

"No problem, Staff Sergeant. I wasn't aware a recognition system had been created."

"That's my fault," Sydnee said. "It slipped my mind."

"Did you come back to get us, Lieutenant?"

"Um, not exactly, Staff Sergeant. I'll fill you in tomorrow. Where have you been? I ordered you to come back here after the attack."

"We're just returning from the original campsite, ma'am. When we thought you and Morales had bought it, I decided we'd better pick up our reserve of Corplastizine charges. My intent was to blow those two fighters to pieces so they couldn't attack any more of our people when rescue finally came. It's a long trek to the original camp. We started back last night, found a place to lay up when dawn broke, then continued our travel after sunset."

As they talked, the rest of the platoon had entered the cavern. Some were scrounging around the mess area, looking for something to eat, while others just dropped onto their bedrolls.

"There's fresh Lampaxa if anyone's hungry," Sydnee said. "Sgt. Morales cleaned it and sliced it, so it's all ready to cook."

"You bagged a Lampaxa?" McKenzie said. "Anybody get hurt?"

"No one was hurt. Sgt. Morales and Lt. MacDonald jumped in to help me after I was attacked. The three of us were able to turn the tables on the Lampaxa. He wound up on the dinner table instead of me."

"Ma'am, did you check to see if the poison sac was ruptured after you killed it?" Sgt. Booth asked.

"Sgt. Morales verified that it didn't have the ammonia smell, and just to be sure, he ran a small piece through the alien food analyzer."

"That's great. I've been hoping we'd find another one of them critters. What happened to the head?"

"It's in the waste barrel," Morales said.

"Man, don't throw away the head; I'm starting a collection. I'm thinking about a new group insignia."

Sydnee smiled as Booth hurried over to retrieve the enormous head from the trash.

"Where were you attacked, Lieutenant?" McKenzie asked.

"In the sinkhole at the original camp. It was filled with water."

"Yes, we saw that. I guess we'll never recover the MAT now."

"All taken care of. That's why I was in the water. We managed to recover the MAT this morning. It's too bad you had already left the camp area. We could have saved you a long walk. I tried to contact you but I didn't get a reply."

"We didn't have the radio with us because our trip was unplanned, and the helmet transmission/reception is no more than five kilometers. Where is the MAT now, ma'am?"

"Far from here, securely locked, disabled, and camouflaged. The tug I stole is nearby though."

"Then why aren't we leaving?"

"It's long story. Get some food and rest. We'll discuss it at length in the morning."

"Aye, ma'am. Goodnight."

"Goodnight, Staff Sergeant."

Chapter Twenty-Five

~ Mar. 15th, 2285 ~

Breakfast consisted of powdered eggs, biscuits, jam made from local berries, and, of course, spicy Lampaxa patties. At the rate it was disappearing, the twelve meters of Lampaxa wouldn't last the day, but there were no doubt plenty more available for people willing to risk their life by jumping into the right swamp.

Following breakfast, the officers and noncoms held a conference to discuss the options.

"So you want to take the Clidepp destroyer to where the *Perry* is sitting in space to help protect it from attack?" McKenzie asked Sydnee.

"Yes. It won't be easy, but I'm confident we can do it. We have a bridge crew able to handle the ship if the systems are automated enough to be operated without constant engineer involvement and enough Marines to act as laser array gunners and torpedo guidance specialists."

"But you said the ship has no atmo."

"It has an atmosphere and artificial gravity. It's simply that the CO_2 concentration is too high for anyone without supplemental oxygen because the oxygen regeneration equipment was destroyed by a torpedo from the dip ship."

"So we'd have to wear our armor at all times, and then run back to the MAT every so often to refill."

"Essentially, but the rebreather units built into our armor will pull some oxygen out of the air, extending the time between refills."

"And that's it?"

"Well, not all of it. The Captain told me that the *Perry* might very well be destroyed in any engagement with the rebel ship because they can't maneuver properly with one side-mounted engine and two stern engines destroyed, not to mention fire control and the sensor grid systems being so severely damaged. He told me we should remain here on the planet until someone comes to pick us up. There's a possibility that anyone who participates in my crazy idea might be court-martialed for disobeying orders."

"I never received any such orders from the Captain," McKenzie said. "Did he order all officers to remain here?"

"No," Weems said. "We were only ordered to accompany Lt. Marcola to Diabolisto and make an effort to recover the MAT. She was named as commander of the operation."

"Then it would seem that the only one here who could be court-martialed for not remaining on the planet is Lt. Marcola."

"Thank you, Staff Sergeant, for pointing that out."

McKenzie chuckled. "Sorry, ma'am. I certainly don't mean that anyone wants to see you court-martialed. Nothing could be further from the truth. I only meant that the rest of us have nothing to fear in that regard. It must be your decision alone."

"Everyone's involvement must be their decision alone. This is strictly voluntary. Even if you aren't risking a court-martial, you'll be risking your life if you come. If you remain here, you'll be safe."

"Begging your pardon, ma'am, but I don't think we could live with ourselves if, while our comrades were fighting and possibly dying aboard the *Perry*, we chose to stay safe. I'll put it to my people, and anyone that chooses to remain here, can do so, but I'm confident that everyone is behind you a hundred percent."

"I thought you'd feel that way, but I wasn't sure about every member of the platoon. Okay, assuming that everyone supports this idea, we'll begin preparing immediately. We have no idea when that other rebel destroyer will attempt to move, but we have to be ready. Getting there an hour late won't do at all. We're going to want some fresh food with us, so let's do some foraging this morning and be off-planet by sunset. Let's gather as much of the fresh vegetables, nuts, and berries as we can. I don't want to look for any Lampaxa, but if we can take down a couple of buflo, we'll have fresh meat for a week."

"I'll put the issue of involvement to my people, then send my hunters out," McKenzie said.

"Hold off on the buflo for a few hours. We saw some small herds near where we left the MAT. It'll be easier to transport them in that area than trying to get them to the cave."

"Aye, ma'am. Should I send people out for the other items?"

"Yes. And the rest of our people should begin packing up if everyone supports this crazy idea of mine."

"Aye, ma'am. We're on it."

"That's all for now, Staff Sergeant."

"Aye, Lieutenant."

As McKenzie left, Weems said, "Syd, what about the Yolongi rebels on the planet?"

"What about them?"

"Do you intend to just leave them here?"

"We can't take them with us. It might make an *almost* impossible task impossible."

"We can't leave them here to die."

"We didn't maroon them here; they did that to themselves. They have the foodstuffs they scavenged from the destroyer and some light arms to scare away the predators. They should be fine until the *Pellew* arrives. Now, let's pack up, guys. We have a lot of work ahead of us before we even get off the planet."

The fresh food foragers returned before lunch, loaded down with the leafy vegetables the platoon had been eating and an oh-gee sled overloaded with berries and nuts. The mess people had to set up two more of the large, collapsible refrigeration units to hold everything. It was good that the newcomers had brought two more sleds with them.

The platoon left the cave pretty much the way they'd found it, except someone had scratched 'The 4-4-3 was here first, as always' on the wall. For the RP, Sydnee selected an open clearing a few kilometers away where the MAT would have enough room to land. The platoon would head there with Lt. MacDonald while the other three officers headed for the tug. They would retrieve the MAT and meet the platoon.

As the tug descended into the clearing where the MAT was located, Sydnee suddenly sent it upwards again and landed it a hundred meters away.

"What going on?" Weems said curiously.

"Look at the MAT."

Caruthers and Weems stared out the windows.

"What is that?" Caruthers said.

"I'm not sure, but I know it wasn't there when we left."

"Then park this thing and let's go look at it," Weems said.

As the three officers walked towards the MAT, the huge green and brown object lying across the black thirty-five-meter-long vessel shifted position. All three instinctively stopped and took a step backwards.

"It's alive," Weems said.

"Yeah," Caruthers agreed, "but what is it?"

"According to the alien database," Sydnee said as she read the description associated with the image, "it's called a Milossa Wayn."

"A Milossa Wayn?" Caruthers repeated back. "Sounds like a cookie."

"Yeah, well this cookie can weigh up to sixteen tons and reach a length of seventy meters."

As Caruthers took another quick step backwards, he said, "Is it dangerous? Is it going to attack us like that Lampaxa?"

"The DB says it's a herbivore, but it will attack if provoked."

"What's it doing on the MAT?" Weems asked.

"Maybe it thinks it's an egg," Caruthers said, "and it's trying to hatch it."

Weems chuckled. "Yeah, and out pop forty baby Marines in full personal armor."

"He might be right, Jerry," Sydnee said.

"I am?" Caruthers said, "I was only joking."

"I know, but your joke is as good an answer as anything I can come with. It looks like it's sitting on a nest. Perhaps it built a nest atop the MAT."

"Since yesterday?"

"How long does it take?" Sydnee asked him.

"I don't know."

"I don't either, but while some animals on Earth take a long time to make it just so, others simply find a convenient place and plop down."

"Well, that's definitely not a convenient place for us," Weems said. "If we could take off, we could simply dump it off with a roll."

"But that would mean getting inside first," Caruthers said. "That thing could stomp us without breaking a sweat. I don't think our armor would protect us."

"Any ideas, Syd?" Weems asked.

"Just one, but I hate to do it."

"We have to do something. The Marines will be waiting on us. We can't wait until that thing goes for a dinner break or potty break or something."

"I don't think it has to go for a dinner break," Caruthers said. "Look."

Sydnee and Weems turned towards the creature. A long neck, perhaps ten meters, was stretching towards a nearby tree. A second later, the small head opened its mouth, then closed on a branch. As the head dragged along the branch, it stripped off everything except the bark.

"So much for going for dinner," Weems said. "What's your idea, Syd?"

"We shoo it off."

"Shoo it off?" Caruthers said. "Like that's gonna work. If you even get near enough to that thing for it to notice you, you'll be flatter than one of those Lampaxa patties we had for breakfast."

"I didn't say we do it personally. I was thinking of using the tug."

"Yeah, that might work," Weems said. "As long as you don't let it get you in its jaws."

"Me? You're the tug jockey. I'm the MAT pilot. Besides, my job is more dangerous than yours."

"How do you figure?"

"While you're distracting that thing with low-level buzzes, I have to get inside the MAT. Once I'm in, I just roll it as you suggested and dump her off."

"Her?"

"It must be female if it's sitting on the nest."

"Not necessarily. The males in some bird species on Earth share the nest sitting and, in some cases, do most of it."

"This is all very interesting," Caruthers said, "but could we please do something? I hate standing out here in the open. What if her, or his, mate comes along?"

"Okay," Weems said. "Let's do this." Looking at Caruthers, he said, "You with me or Syd?"

"Uh— "

"Go with Jerry," Sydnee said. "The fewer people moving about on the ground, the better."

The creature hadn't even seemed to notice Sydnee yet, so she squatted down where she was and watched as the two men ran for the tug. It took just minutes for Weems to get the tug airborne. He began his efforts by flying in a tight circle above the MAT. The tug, as large as the MAT and mostly power plant, was impossible to miss.

Sydnee waited until the creature's full attention seemed to be on the tug, then sprinted for the MAT. As she reached the vessel, she dove under the belly and waited to see if she had attracted any attention. The creature seemed oblivious to her presence, so she crawled out to where she could access the keypad. She entered the code to keep the ramp from extending, then opened the airlock door. The creature suddenly let out a loud howl.

Sydnee dove back under the ship. Peering out, she could see that the creature's head was looking into the airlock. Perhaps it was wondering why part of the egg had cracked open and nothing came out.

Another pass by the tug pulled the creature's attention away again. Sydnee crawled out from under the vessel and leapt up for the open airlock. She managed to reach the bottom edge and then struggled to pull herself in. She was glad once again that she wasn't wearing the old armor that weighed about a hundred pounds.

As she climbed to her feet and pressed the button to close the hatch, the creature heard the noise and its head appeared at the opening a second before the hatch closed the last few centimeters. Sydnee breathed a sigh of relief and reported her progress to Weems.

"Okay Jerry, I'm in. Clear the area."

"Roger, MAT-Two. Tug-One pulling back."

Sydnee went through the checklist, then started the oh-gee engine. She raised the ship just half a meter and rolled it gently in a full circle to dislodge the creature. When she was upright again, she applied power, but the craft wasn't rising as it should."

"MAT-Two, you have a passenger."

"The Milossa Wayn?"

"Affirmative. It's got your starboard skid in its jaws and is hanging on."

"Damn," Sydnee said. "I was trying not to injure it."

Sydnee lowered the MAT almost to the ground and then did what Weems had done at the sinkhole. As she raised and lowered the craft repeatedly, the creature had contact with the ground and then didn't. Perhaps it got tired of the action, or perhaps it opened its mouth to get a better grip. Whatever the reason, the vessel suddenly sprang into the air as the creature's weight was released. At a hundred meters up, she leveled off.

"MAT-Two, you're good to go."

"Wonderful. Let's head to the RP."

The Marines hadn't arrived at the rendezvous point when the two ships reached the location, so the three officers performed a close examination of the MAT. The only apparent damage was to the one landing skid.

"Not too bad," Weems said, "considering how that thing was hanging on to its egg."

"I can't believe it bent it," Caruthers said. "I thought this thing was supposed to be indestructible."

"I guess the skids can't be made of Dakinium because of the requirement that they lock down magnetically to a deck."

"Ah, right," Caruthers said, "and Dakinium has no magnetic properties, which is why you knew we'd have to use the annuli to raise her. Got it. So the skids are just plain old steel or something."

"Well, the damage appears minor," Sydnee said, "and shouldn't stop us from locking down to a deck when we need to."

"There's no telling how long we'll be here," Weems said. "Let's wait inside in the A/C without our armor."

"Sounds good to me," Caruthers said.

Sydnee nodded her assent.

The Marines arrived about an hour later. While most worked to stow everything in the large storage hold beneath the MAT's cabin deck, Weems ferried a hunting party to where a large herd of buflo had been seen. They returned an hour later with three of the large beasts, already dressed and hanging from the hook beneath the ship. Before the Marines boarded the MAT for the short trip to the original camp, the three carcasses were added to the equipment and supplies stored in the MAT's hold.

It took several hours to locate, uncover, and carry the equipment left behind during the first raid to the MAT, and stow it in the storage hold. Sydnee stayed in the ship the whole time in case another sinkhole opened. None did.

The final trip was to recover the bodies of the three Marines killed in the skirmish with the Yolongi. They had been buried far enough from the battle site that the Yolongi shouldn't have found them. The graves had been covered with rocks to prevent scavengers from digging up the remains.

Once the bodies were loaded gently into the storage hold, the MAT was at last ready to head to the *Abissto*.

Sydnee planned to leave the planet as they had arrived, on the side opposite the rebel camp so the Yolongi equipment couldn't detect the departure. With Weems and Caruthers following in the tug, they made orbit without a problem and then plotted a course to link up with the damaged Clidepp military ship.

When the two small ships reached the *Abissto*, Weems slipped the tug in close to the destroyer at the shuttle bay the *Perry* had used to gain entry. Caruthers, now in an EVA suit, passed through the airlock and maneuvered to the ship using the suit's jets. He entered the standard access code established by the Marines who had preceded him here and a personnel airlock hatch popped open. About ten minutes after he entered the airlock, the bay's main hatch began to slide open.

Weems piloted the ship into the bay's temporary airlock and engaged the magnetic skids. As the airlock process completed, the temporary transparent bulkheads slid up and out of the way. Weems moved the small ship to a parking area as far from the hatch as possible. Sydnee was going to need all remaining space to park the MAT.

"MAT-Two, stand by," Sydnee heard Caruthers say. "I'm having a little trouble getting the temp airlock to enlarge to the slightly larger size needed for the MAT."

"Roger. MAT-Two standing by."

Eighteen minutes passed before Sydnee heard, "Okay, MAT-Two, the airlock bulkheads are in place and I'm opening the hatch. Stand by."

"Roger, MAT-Two standing by."

Sydnee could see the hatch rolling back. It didn't stop until it reached its maximum aperture.

"MAT-Two, you are cleared to enter," Caruthers said.

"MAT-Two entering the bay."

Ten minutes later, Sydnee guided the MAT to a parking position in the bay and let it settle to the deck, then engaged the magnetic skids. The indicator light turned green, meaning that the connection was solid and the ship secure in that location.

Sydnee flipped the switch for the annunciator system in the rear cabin as she watched the vid monitor. "The MAT is down and locked. As you've already been told, the atmo in the ship is heavy with CO_2, so you must remain suited up at all times and must use the MAT's airlock to exit and reenter. Welcome to the *Abissto*."

Sydnee ran through her shutdown checklist as Kelly MacDonald's voice blared on the overhead speaker. Sydnee turned the volume down so she could concentrate.

By the time Sydnee had finished her work on the flight deck, the rear cabin was empty of Marines. She donned her helmet but left her weapons in the locker. It was a relief not to have to carry the rifle and pistol. Her knives were still strapped to her legs, but she never gave them a second thought anymore until they were needed. They were just *there*.

The corridors were brightly lit and nothing looked amiss, but Sydnee knew that she dare not take her helmet off as she made her way to the bridge by following deck plan layouts mounted on most of the bulkheads.

Weems was at the tactical station when Sydney entered the bridge, the Marine radioman was at the communication console, and Caruthers was at the helm. All were trying to translate the Yolon words and symbols into Amer. The visual translation assistant built into their helmets came to their aid in a way not previously anticipated. They found that all they had to do was focus their attention on any relevant symbols or text. The helmet then identified where they were looking and translated the Yolon to Amer. After that, the Amer translation immediately replaced the Yolon on the inside SimWindow in their helmet whenever that text or symbol would have been seen. It made having to wear the helmet at all times less of a burden.

Sydnee climbed into the command chair and began studying the monitors and controls available to the captain or the watch officer. The equipment was pretty much the same as found on any SC ship, but the operations were unique and they had to be known perfectly so that no mistakes were made when seconds mattered at the distant RP.

It had been a long and busy day, so no one was at their best and it seemed to take longer than it should have to grasp some of the intricate procedures. After several hours of experimentation, Sydnee decided to call it a day.

Just before they left the bridge, she said to Weems, "Jerry, did you check the CO2 levels?"

"Yes, I did that as soon as we came on board. It's as we suspected. You can't breathe without an EVA suit or personal armor, but there's enough oxygen in the ship for the rebreather units to let someone in armor function for hours. I think we're feeling so tired right now because the oxygen density has slipped a little."

Sydnee checked her instruments. While not dangerously low, the oxygen in her armor was significantly reduced from an optimal range. The suit would probably have sounded an alarm within a half hour.

"We must remember to have a full recharge just before we reach the *Perry* in case our appearance alone spurs some sort of action on the part of the rebel destroyer."

* * *

Despite some seemingly early success in learning the ship's systems, it was still more than seven frustrating weeks before the four officers felt comfortable discussing a planned departure date.

"Are we in agreement then that other than the air regeneration system, the ship is battle worthy, and that our crew is *finally* capable of basic, though limited, warship operations?"

"I'd like another week of emergency procedure drills, Syd," MacDonald said, "but I know we can't spare the time. For all we know, the *Perry* has been destroyed and the rebel-held destroyer is long gone. I've been chomping at the bit, eager to get going but knowing that we needed more time to prepare. It sounded so easy in the cave, but the practical application has been something else again. I know my people can now function perfectly as laser array gunners and torpedo guidance specialists, but if something goes wrong that requires an engineer, things fall apart quickly."

"There's little we can do about that," Weems said. "We have no real engineering talent to draw on. We're essentially pilots and ground-pounders. Where are the biggest mistakes likely to occur?"

"In the torpedo rooms," MacDonald said. "We have no problem removing the safeties and monitoring the equipment as it automatically loads torpedoes, but if something jams or the electronics sense a dangerous condition, the system locks up until the condition is resolved. We've been through dozens of drill simulations and my people always take forever to locate and resolve the problem. The biggest difficulty is the language. I don't mean Yolon versus Amer. I mean the engineering language we hear after our translation devices have done their job. We just don't have a clue what the computer is talking about sometimes. Engineers have their own language."

"Every profession develops their verbal shorthand," Sydnee said, "including Marines and pilots. There's no doubt that some engineers are badly needed, but we just don't have any. Perhaps when we get to the *Perry*, we can borrow a few before any trouble starts."

"I'm hoping that just the idea of a two-destroyer-to-one advantage will get the rebels to surrender," Caruthers said.

"That would be great," Weems said, "but perhaps just a bit optimistic."

"So, let's put it to a vote," Sydnee said. "Go or no go?"

"Go," Weems said.

"Go," MacDonald voted.

"Uh, go," Caruthers practically whispered.

"And I say go," Sydnee said. "With the present crew we may never be as prepared as we'd want to be, but the *Perry* needs us, if it still lives. Do we go now or in the morning?"

"I've had my people training all day," MacDonald said. "They'll be a *lot* better after eight hours' sleep."

"We all will," Caruthers said. "We've been going night and day lately because of the urgency. Let's get a good night's sleep."

"If we can sleep," Sydnee said.

Chapter Twenty-Six
~ May 6th[th], 2285 ~

"The *Glassama* has raised her temporal generator," Lieutenant Nivollo, the third watch tac officer aboard the *Perry*, said. "She's attempting to build an envelope."

Lt. Milton sat up straighter in his chair at the news. "Fire two torpedoes. Attempt to destroy the temporal generator."

The tac officer, well aware of the standing order, had already prepared two torpedoes for launch at the ship. "Torpedoes away."

"Com, sound GQ," Milton said.

Instantly, alarms began sounding all over the ship and crewmembers were rolling out of their rack and trying to jump into their clothes.

Since no one was yet in the torpedo guidance centers located along the center line of the ship, the tac officer on the bridge would guide the torpedoes. The target had already been painted into their electronic brains, but a guidance specialist was always standing by in case the situation changed or the target moved. Passing through a temporal field disrupted a torpedo's guidance brain, but with an inbound torpedo, the disruption would occur an instant before impact and so couldn't affect the flight.

"Impact of first torpedo in— ten seconds," the tac officer said. "Envelope is still fifteen seconds from completion. Eight, seven, six, five, four, three, two, one."

Captain Lidden arrived on the bridge in time to see the detonation on the large monitor. For an instant, an intensely white light whited out the sensors. The grid was restored just in time to see the second torpedo reach the target area and detonate. Another bright flash was seen, then the screen was all white again until the sensors stabilized.

"Sitrep," was all Lidden said.

"The rebel ship began to build an envelope, sir," Milton said. "In compliance with the standing order, I ordered that two torpedoes be fired at the temporal generator."

"Very good, Milty. I'll take it."

"Aye, Captain, you have the bridge," Milton said as he climbed down from the command chair and moved to the XO's chair. A second later, he was forced to vacate the XO's chair as Commander Bryant arrived on the bridge. Without another word, he turned and headed for Auxiliary Command and Control two decks down and two frame sections further towards the stern.

Over the next few seconds, the entire bridge watch was relieved as the more experienced first watch arrived and assumed their duties. The third watch crew joined Lieutenant Milton and the second watch crew in AC&C.

* * *

Captain Nesadeedis, the rebel in command of the *Glassama*, was in shock. He had planned to leave the area in the early morning hours of Galactic System Time because he expected the third watch crew of the *Perry* to be less than alert. He only needed two minutes to build his envelope and be gone, but the *Perry* had reacted within seconds of his temporal generator being raised and the process initiated.

"Damage reports," Nesadeedis screamed.

"We were struck twice," the tac officer said.

"I know that you idiot. Where were we hit and how bad is it?"

"Both torpedoes exploded in the area of our temporal generator. I'm not getting any sensor readings at all from that part of the ship."

"The FTL controls aren't responding at all," the helmsman said.

"Dammit, why weren't those torpedoes shot down?" Nesadeedis screamed. "Aren't all gunners at their posts?"

"The torpedoes came in tight over our stern, Captain," the tac officer said. "None of the gunners had a shot. The rear laser arrays were destroyed in the collision. We have no protection on our stern."

Nesadeedis cursed himself silently. He had known his stern was facing the Spacc ship but hadn't wanted to reposition before raising the generator because it might alert them to what he was planning. He thought he could create an envelope and be gone before a third watch crew got permission from a sleeping captain to fire on the *Glassama*.

"Can you at least tell me if we're breached?" Nesadeedis screamed at the tac officer.

"All sensors are down in the area of the strike. A visual inspection will have to be made."

"Engineering reports that there are serious breaches in the sail," the communications crewman said. "They're attempting to seal off that area."

"Can we maneuver?" Nesadeedis asked.

"No damage to the two larboard stern engines or the larboard maneuvering engine."

"Then let's teach that Spacc not to start things he can't finish."

"Captain, Captain Pouurricas, asks to speak with you."

"Put him on my chair's left monitor."

As the monitor lit up with the image of Pouurricas, Nesadeedis picked up the handset to speak privately.

"What's happened? My people report that you were struck by torpedoes."

"The Spacc ship fired on us."

"Why now?"

"I attempted to build an FTL envelope. As soon as I raised my generator, they fired. It was a totally unprovoked attack."

"I warned you that they were only watching and waiting."

"And I warned you that if they fired on us, I'd destroy them."

"If they wanted to kill you, they would have fired a full spread of torpedoes, followed immediately by another full spread of torpedoes. They're only trying to keep you from going FTL. If you had allowed my tugs to tow you away when we got here, as ordered by Citizen X, your temporal generator would be fine."

"Our repairs were almost complete. There was no need to be towed away. And you can't know that they wouldn't have attacked if I agreed to your plan. They might have fired on us the second your tugs hooked up. I wanted to be at full readiness when we moved. Now we are. They have attacked us and I intend to destroy them. Will you assist?"

"I won't attack a Space Command vessel in Galactic Alliance space that didn't try to kill you."

"Then stay clear, because I will. *Glassama* out."

* * *

"The *Glassama* is beginning to move, Captain," Lieutenant Rocovich, the first watch tac officer said. "But there's something strange about her turning arc. I think her starboard maneuvering engine isn't operating."

"What's your assessment of the temporal generator?"

"The angle isn't very good, so the sensors aren't getting a clear picture, but I have to say that if we didn't clobber it, she'd probably be long gone. Perhaps she's coming to pay us a visit to return the favor."

"Yes, that would be the only reason for turning." Tapping the ship-wide com button on his chair's left arm, Lidden said, "Attention all crewmembers. The rebel ship is turning around, which can only mean one thing. She's about to attack. Stay alert and good shooting."

Lidden, the bridge crew, and the crew in AC&C watched as the *Glassama* began to make a slow circle around the *Perry*.

"Helm, keep our bow pointed at the *Glassama* no matter how she moves."

"Aye, Captain," the helmsman said as he used the starboard maneuvering engine to swing the *Perry* at the same rate as the *Glassama*.

The rebel ship continued its circling action from twenty-five thousand kilometers out while the *Perry* turned like a boxer watching his opponent in the ring and anticipating a jab. When the *Glassama* had completed a full circle on the same plane as the *Perry*, it made another that was perpendicular to the first.

"What do you think she's doing, sir?" Commander Bryant asked.

"My guess would be that they're looking us over and evaluating our ability to fight. They're searching for weaknesses. We don't want them to see our larboard hull or keel, so we'll keep turning with them. Perhaps they'll think we just want to always have our bow tubes pointed at them."

After circling the *Perry* twice, the *Glassama* stopped moving with her bow pointed towards the *Perry*.

"He doesn't know if we're seriously wounded or not," Lidden said to his XO. "He wants to attack, but he's unsure of our condition and that's making him nervous. He has a group of rebel fighters willing to die for their cause, but most are probably untrained in space combat. While he knows his people will do anything he says, he also knows he's facing a ship filled with highly trained military personnel who know their job and will follow orders to the letter."

* * *

"What do you think, Borressi?" Nesadeedis asked his XO.

"I think he's ready for action, has all his people at their battle stations, and is only waiting for us to make the first move."

"Of course, but what do you think of his ability to respond to an attack?"

"The profile is different than the one shown in the alien ship registry file for that class of SC light destroyer. It has to be the result of the collision. How that altered profile affects his ability to maneuver during battle and what weapons he can rely on are the only questions. He didn't let us get a look at his larboard hull, but we know how badly mangled our starboard hull was, so he had to have suffered at least similar damage."

"Yes, but as you said, he's not going to let us see it."

"If we feign an attack to his starboard side, then alter course at the last minute to pass him on his larboard side, we might get a quick look if he's having trouble maneuvering quickly."

"But we're having trouble maneuvering quickly ourselves. That move might give him more tactical information that he can use against *us*."

"It's the only way I can think of to get a look at his larboard hull. We can simply assume that he lost all his torpedo tubes and laser arrays on the larboard side, but that could be a fatal assumption."

* * *

"He doesn't seem too eager to attack, sir," Bryant said to Lidden after fifteen minutes had passed without any move-ment from the *Glassama*. "Or do you think he found a flaw in one of his own systems and they're trying to repair it?"

"He's just trying to think of an attack strategy that will allow him to destroy us without being destroyed himself. He may have been dismayed that we were able to follow his earlier movements and always keep him in our bow gun sights. When he does move, the attack will be fast and furious, and there may not be any pauses until one of us is out of action."

Another fifteen minutes passed before the *Glassama* started to move.

"Here we go," Lidden said. "Everyone make sure you're strapped in."

* * *

The rebel ship turned to follow a course that would have it pass five thousand kilometers off the *Perry's* starboard side at SubLight-1 speed, or one thousand kilometers per second. The tactical station was fully manned. Each of the four tac people sat outside a large circular console monitoring a quadrant of the ship, while the lead tactical officer sat in the center opening. A holo-image of what each seated tac person was seeing and responding to floated over each of the four so the lead tac could watch and direct their actions.

Just seconds before passing the *Perry*, the *Glassama* still hadn't fired any weapons, but it suddenly swerved to a new angle and passed on the larboard side.

* * *

"He had to have gotten a good look at us that time," Lidden said. "He'll probably attack our larboard side now. Everyone be ready."

* * *

The rebel destroyer turned after passing astern of the *Perry* and then headed back again. Its course would clearly take it along the *Perry's* larboard side.

* * *

As soon at as the *Glassama* reached Sub-Light-1 speed, it launched a full volley of eight torpedoes from its bow tubes, followed by two from the undamaged tubes on its starboard side at the *Perry*.

"Helm, one-hundred-eighty-degree roll," Lidden said quickly.

The roll left the *Perry* 'belly up' in relation to its former position, but there was no belly up in space and the roll was the quickest way to turn the ship so the *Perry* was ideally positioned to repel the torpedoes as they bore down on the ship. While the starboard laser array gunners began focusing all their weapons on the *Glassama's* incoming torpedoes, the *Perry* launched torpedoes from both tubes in its starboard hull. Where the rebel ship was a Destroyer, the *Perry* was only a Light Destroyer and couldn't hope to match the fire-power of the larger ship. Their only chance lay in superior training and experience on the part of the commander.

* * *

The *Perry's* laser array gunners managed to knock out all ten torpedoes from the rebel ship's first volley while the

Glassama's gunners knocked down both of the *Perry's* torpedoes.

The *Glassama* immediately turned to begin circling the *Perry*, firing from all useable tubes as they came to bear. The *Perry* returned fire just as quickly.

Space between the two ships was filled with missiles of death streaking towards specific target points on both ships, but the *Glassama's* advantage in weapon numbers slowly began to decide the outcome of the battle.

The laser gunners on both ships did their best, but torpedoes began to sneak through each ship's laser protection umbrella as the battle raged on.

Aboard the *Perry*, damage control parties were trying to be everywhere at once. Torpedo strikes had opened huge holes to space on decks five, seven, and eight. The secure rooms along the center axis of the ship, as well as the fire control centers, the bridge, and AC&C were still secure, so the *Perry* crew was able to continue fighting.

The story was the same on the *Glassama*. Several torpedoes from the *Perry* had opened huge rifts in the fabric of the hull.

* * *

"Damn Spaccs," Nesadeedis said. "Even with our better maneuvering capability and superior weapons numbers, they're inflicting almost as much damage on us as we are on them."

"Perhaps we should pull back, Captain," his XO said. "We can still be across the border in two weeks if we make use of the *Furmmara's* tugs."

"Pull back? Never. I've vowed to destroy him and we shall."

The XO bit his tongue to keep from saying what he was thinking.

"There," Nesadeedis said, waving at the large monitor. "We scored another hit. We'll crush them yet."

* * *

"We can't keep trading volleys, Captain," Bryant said. "They're bigger and can outlast us unless we strike something vital."

"I agree, XO, but what choice do we have? I didn't want to engage them, but we have a duty to see they don't make it across the border."

"I know, sir. I just feel so helpless. We can't even communicate with them and ask for a cease fire."

"Their Captain wouldn't agree anyway. He wants us dead and believes he can accomplish that and still live himself. We have to prove him wrong."

The *Perry's* bridge suddenly shook violently as a sixth torpedo reached its hull. If everyone hadn't been belted in, they would surely have been flung around.

"Com, get me an updated list of the damaged areas."

"Aye, Captain."

"That last strike seems to have taken out one of the bow torpedo rooms, sir," the lead tac officer said. "All sensors there are down."

"They're killing us meter by meter, Captain," Bryant said.

"We'll keep fighting as long as we're able, Ben."

"Yes, sir."

"Captain, another ship just appeared on the DeTect monitor. It's headed this way and should arrive in about three minutes."

"A tug?"

"Too big, sir."

"We know it's not the *Pellew*. They won't be here for more than a month. It must be someone coming to help the rebels. Tac, keep your eyes on it and be ready to target it as soon as it's in range."

"Aye, sir."

* * *

"The DeTect system shows that there's a lot of activity there, Syd," Weems said from the tac station aboard the *Abissto*. "One ship seems to be almost stationary while the other is circling. The freighter is still there, judging from size alone, but it's fifty thousand kilometers away. I hope we're not too late."

"I know the Captain is defending the *Perry* to the best of his ability, and from everything I've heard, that's considerable."

"How do you want to handle this, *Captain?*" Caruthers asked form the helm.

Syd tried to sound a lot more confident than she felt as she said, "Let's do what Admiral Carver did at the Battle of Vauzlee. Take us on a counter clockwise circle outside the action. We know how badly damaged the *Perry* was. That means that the circling ship is the *Glassama*. Establish a speed that will keep us near her."

Sydnee picked up the handset on the left arm of the command chair and announced, "Attention everyone. We're about to enter the battle zone. The action will be concentrated on the larboard side of the ship initially. This is what we've trained for over the past weeks. Let's make Captain Lidden and the crew of the *Perry* proud. Send these rebel bastards to hell. Captain out."

"Oo-rah." The Marine Radioman said loudly.

"Oo-rah," Weems said quietly.

"Oo-rah," Sydnee said loudly to Weems. "Say it like you mean it, from the gut."

Weems yelled, "Oo-rah," and smiled.

Sydnee smiled back, then returned her attention to the large screen as Caruthers shook his head.

Several minutes later, the ship's sensor system allowed them to see the battle on the large monitor. As Caruthers canceled the envelope and applied full power to the Sub-Light engines, the *Abissto* surged ahead. The gravitative inertial compensators weren't as good as those on Space Command vessels and everyone felt a hard lurch as the engines kicked in, but the sensation subsided quickly.

* * *

"That unknown ship is a Clidepp destroyer, Captain," the tac officer said.

"Clidepp? Their military was ordered to stay out of GA space."

"It's coming from the direction of Diabolisto. It might be the other rebel destroyer."

"Damn it. How did they get that thing operational? I thought the oxygen regeneration equipment was totally destroyed."

"But the engines weren't damaged," Bryant said. "Perhaps they were able to rig something up using equipment from a shuttle."

"Tac, target that ship as soon as it gets into range. Marcola reported that the platoon killed a number of rebels on the planet, so the ship has to be undermanned. That's our advantage. Perhaps we can knock them out before they even get involved."

"Aye, sir," the tac officer said as the ship was again shaken by a torpedo strike.

* * *

"The *Glassama* is really pounding the *Perry*," Caruthers said. That last strike hit in the area of the stern engines. That might have taken them out completely. The maneuvering engine on the starboard side is probably all they have left, if that's even operational."

"Damn," Weems said. "The *Perry* just fired six torpedoes at us."

"Us? Damn, they think rebels command this ship. And they have no com system so we can't tell them not to fire." Sydnee was quiet for a couple of seconds, then said, "Well, if we can't tell them who we are, let's show them. Jerry, target the *Glassama*."

"Aye, Captain. Targeting and firing all forward tubes."

The exhaust trails from the torpedoes could be seen emanating away from the *Abissto* while light rays from laser arrays flew at the torpedoes fired by the *Perry*.

* * *

"Captain," the tac officer aboard the *Glassama* said, "the *Abissto* just arrived and fired a full spread of torpedoes."

"The *Abissto*? I thought their oxygen regeneration equipment couldn't be repaired."

"They must have found a way. It's definitely the *Abissto*."

"We'll beat this Spacc ship yet. Extend my personal welcome to the *Abissto*."

* * *

"The *Glassama* extends their Captain's personal welcome to the Captain and crew of the *Abissto*," the radioman on the bridge said smiling.

"He does?"

"He probably doesn't yet realize the torpedoes we just launched are aimed at him," Weems said.

"He'll know soon enough," Caruthers said. "I'd say about five seconds."

* * *

"WHAT? The torpedoes are coming at *us*?" Nesadeedis said. "What are those idiots doing?"

Picking up the handset, Nesadeedis screamed, "All gunners, fire on the torpedoes coming from the *Abissto*."

"Tac, target the *Abissto*. Someone else must have managed to commandeer her. Maybe it's Empire forces."

* * *

"The *Abissto* is firing at the *Glassama*?" Lidden said incredulously.

Activating the ship's annunciator, he said, "Attention all crew. The *Abissto* is firing at the *Glassama*. Do not fire on the *Abissto* unless I tell you differently."

"Who the hell is in that ship?" Lidden said as he leaned back and watched the large monitor.

* * *

"I think our secret is out, Syd," Weems said.

"About time," she said. "At least none of the *Perry's* torpedoes got through. Does that mean our gunners are good?

Or that the *Perry's* tac and guidance people are bad? Well, no matter. Let's go get the *Glassama*."

The battle raged on, with each ship firing for all they were worth until Weems suddenly shouted, "Syd, the freighter is making a beeline for us."

"The freighter? What does she think *she's* going to do? Wait a minute, didn't the Tsgardi and Milori once use a freighter to attack an SC ship by hiding torpedoes in freight containers. Yeah, I think it was the Lisbon. Well we're not going to fall for that one. Helm, break off the attack on the Glassama and position our bow towards the freighter. Target her spine, Jerry. Break her in half."

"Aye, Captain," Weems said with a grin. "Two char-boiled pieces of freighter coming up."

The torpedoes from the *Abissto* reached the freighter just as the ends flew off four containers and torpedoes emerged. While the *Abissto's* torpedoes were breaking the freighter's link sections into pieces, the *Furmmara's* torpedoes were streaking toward the *Abissto*.

"Gunners controlling the starboard arrays," Syd announced over the ship's annunciator system, "the freighter has just launched torpedoes at us. Knock 'em down."

It was a tense few minutes as the four massive missiles bore down on the *Abissto*. The Marine gunners got three, but a fourth hit the starboard side amidship. The explosion rocked the ship and scrambled a number of sensor systems.

"Syd, the weapons console just went dead," Weems said.

"Completely?"

"I don't know about the laser arrays, but the torpedo system is totally off-line."

"Can you fix it? I mean, reboot it or something?"

"On the *Perry*, maybe. On this ship, I don't know where to begin. I think this is one of those 'lack of engineers' problems we discussed earlier."

"Damn, and things seemed to be going so well with my first command."

"What do you want to do?"

"With no real offensive weapons, I can only think of one thing. Com, clear everyone out of the torpedo rooms on the double. They have two minutes to report to the secure rooms amidship and strap in."

"Aye, Lieutenant, I mean Captain."

"So, what are we going to do, Captain?" Caruthers asked.

"What's our speed?"

"Presently Sub-Light-One-Point-Five."

"Take us up to Sub-Light-Ten and aim directly at the *Glassama's* stern as if we're doing an envelope merge."

"An envelope merge? No, you mean to ram her."

"Yes. I felt that ordering 'ramming speed' would be a bit too melodramatic."

Caruthers took a deep breath and released it slowly, then entered the ordered speed and set a course that should have them arrive at the same point in the circle as the *Glassama*. "I've wanted off the *Perry*, but this isn't the way I expected to go."

Syd picked up the handset and began addressing everyone on board with, "Attention all crewmembers. One of the torpedoes from the freighter took out part of our weapons control system. I know of only one way to end the *Glassama's* ability to carry on the fight and save everyone still alive on the *Perry*. We're going to ram the ship. If you're not already in one of the fire control centers or Secure rooms, get there now. And everybody strap in.

"Thank you for your efforts here and on the planet. It's been an honor to fight alongside you and lead you through part of this struggle. No one could ever ask for a more loyal, dedicated, or professional group of fighters. Thank you for your service to our nation. I hope that all of us survive the next few minutes, but if we don't, no one will ever be able to say we failed to set the bar high when the time came for us to show what Space Command and the Space Marines were made of. Thank you. Oo-rah."

"Oo-rah," her three comrades on the bridge shouted.

* * *

"Sir, the *Abissto* stopped firing after being hit by a torpedo from the freighter. Now she's increased her speed tremendously and is cutting across the circling path they were following."

"Where are they going?" Lidden asked. "Are they pulling out?"

"It seems that if they were pulling out, they would be headed away from the circle, not through it."

"Where's the freighter?"

"She's broken up into pieces that are tumbling around all over the place."

"Sir, I think the *Abissto* means to ram the *Glassama*," the tac officer said excitedly.

"What?" Lidden said as he looked up at the large monitor. For most of the battle, the monitor had projected sensor images of the *Glassama*. The only time they couldn't see her was when the rebel ship was in a sensor-dead zone.

As Lidden and the bridge crew watched, the *Abissto* appeared directly behind the *Glassama*, moving many times faster. In just the time it took to blink, the *Abissto* impacted the *Glassama*, her bow crumpling against the better-reinforced engine section of the lead ship. Following the impact, each ship appeared to be as much as fifty meters shorter and fused so tightly together that they could never be separated without a complete disassembly of the respective stern and bow sections.

"Wow," the tac officer said as he stared at the image. I think the Clidepp military can remove those two names from its ships' registry."

"Ladies and gentlemen," Lidden said in a crew announcement, "I think we can stand down and concentrate on making our repairs. The brave crew aboard the *Abissto* have saved our lives this day. Let's hope at least some of them survived and we get a chance to thank them one day, whoever they might be.

Chapter Twenty-Seven

~ May 6th[th], 2285 ~

The crew of the *Perry* had barely begun seeing to emergency repairs when the tac officer said, "Sir, we have two more ships on the DeTect monitor. They're headed this way."

"What now?" Lidden said incredulously. "Okay com, sound GQ."

Throughout the ship, crewmen looked up from what they were doing, grimaced, and then ran for their GQ stations. Within sixty seconds, gunners and guidance specialists were at their consoles and strapped in, while non-essential personnel were strapping themselves down in Secure rooms.

The seconds ticked by as bridge personnel watched anxiously for the unknown ships to appear.

Two SGC Scout-Destroyers suddenly appeared on the large monitor and came to a stop twenty-five thousand kilometers distant. For the Scout-Destroyers, it was an unknown situation so they had to play it safe, but for the crew of the *Perry*, it was simply a beautiful sight.

Lidden announced the arrival of the two GSC ships, cancelled GQ, and ordered everyone to return to their emergency repair duties.

An hour later, a shuttle left each of the Scout-Destroyers and approached the *Perry*. Knowing that a visit was imminent, Lidden had an ensign standing by in the starboard shuttle bay to let them in. When the shuttles had completed their parking procedures in the bay, the ensign escorted the visiting officers to the bridge.

Lidden was still on the bridge but gestured to the two visiting officers to follow him into his briefing room.

Normally he would have been working at his desk during first watch, but the mountain of reports he would have to file could wait until the *Perry's* life support problems were resolved. The ship was bleeding atmo from eight torpedo strikes, and it was nothing short of a miracle that it was still holding together. None of the strikes had occurred at key structural points.

"Captain Lidden, I'm Commander Galeway, Captain of the *Missouri*, and this is Commander Parney, Captain of the *Rhine*."

"Welcome, gentlemen. Your arrival was most unexpected."

"We've been trying to reach you since we left Mars but haven't received any responses," Galeway said. "We feared the worst."

"We lost all communication ability when we collided with the *Glassama* during an attempted envelope merge."

"We were fully briefed on the situation out here but were informed that you were in contact with Space Command in February."

"One of my officers ferried a Marine platoon down to Diabolisto in a MAT since we don't have any Marine pilots onboard. The *Glassama* showed up while our Marines were still dirt-side. The rebels aboard the stolen ship saw us and immediately left— FTL. In order for us to have even a chance of catching her, we couldn't wait to recover our people. I contacted them and they reported all was well. The pilot remained dirt-side to perform an extraction, if necessary, while we left to pursue the rebel-held ship. We expected to return within a few days, but the situation worsened considerably due to the collision.

"When we failed to return or contact the people on Diabolisto, my pilot managed to commandeer a tug from the rebels on the planet, then track us here. We briefly had communication ability using the com system in the tug. But the Marine officer in command of the platoon had been killed in action and my pilot had assumed command, so I sent the pilot back to Diabolisto to hold things together there until the

Pellew arrived. That ended our ability to communicate with anyone. All of the shuttles, tugs, and MATs we had aboard were crushed in the collision, and the holds where the Marine's portable communication gear was stored were crushed as well. On top of that, we've had enough electronics problems to fill a computer with reports."

"I see. You say that your SC *pilot* took command of a platoon of Marines? That must be an interesting arrangement," Galeway said with a chuckle. "In my experience, most Marines have a cavalier attitude towards SC pilots. They usually refer to them as 'pampered flyboys.'"

"Well, there's an unusual bit of history there. Following a tense incident aboard a diplomatic ship where she gunned down two of the Ambassador's guards, the Marines made her an unofficial member of their team."

"Two guards? She? Even more interesting. Well, it looks like you've been pretty busy out here, sir. After taking on a destroyer and an armed freighter, I'm amazed you survived."

"I wish I could take credit for our survival, but that must go to whoever was commanding the *Abissto*. Our initial wounds were crippling, and we were in no condition to fight a major battle. We were about finished when the *Abissto* arrived. She attacked the *Glassama*, destroyed the freighter when it launched torpedoes against her, and then rammed the *Glassama* to end its attacks on us. We owe the Captain our lives. I hope he and his crew survived."

"The *Abissto* contacted us as soon as we arrived. The Captain told us you had no communications capability and that we'd have to shuttle over."

"You spoke to the Captain? Who is he? Is he Clidepp military? How did he know we had no communications?"

"The Captain identified herself as Lieutenant(jg) Sydnee Marcola of the GCS *Perry*. Isn't she one of yours?"

Lidden's jaw dropped at least an inch before he regained his composure and said, "Marcola? Yes, she's one of mine, but I thought she was still on Diabolisto."

"You mean she's the one who took command of the Marines and then stole a tug from the rebels?"

"The very same."

"I'd very much like to meet her."

"I'm sure there will be an opportunity for that in the coming days. Right now, there are more important matters to discuss. Will you see to searching the *Glassama* and whatever pieces of the freighter remain to recover anyone who might have survived?"

"Of course. We'll make arrangements to take care of that as soon as we return to our ships. What else can we do to assist you?"

"We could use any engineers you can spare to help us with our emergency repairs. The *Glassama* did a real number on us, and we're losing atmo at every point where we were hit."

"My chief engineer was organizing his people when I left. All he needed was an invite."

"Which points to another problem. I could use a portable com system on the bridge with a relay mounted to the exterior of the ship."

"Done. I brought a system with me. It's in the shuttle."

"Wonderful. Excuse me a second," Lidden said as he notified his com chief to have someone retrieve the system.

"What else, Captain Lidden?" Galeway asked.

"There are so many things we need that I don't know where to begin, but first, I'm curious about your arrival here. I thought all new Light-9790 warships were going to Admiral Carver's command."

"They were until a few months ago."

"What happened a few months ago?"

"Oh, that's right. You've been pretty much in the dark out here. Sir, I'm pleased to announce that the war in Region Two is over. Admiral Carver soundly defeated the Uthlaro armada almost two months ago. That ended the Tsgardi, Hudeerac, Gondusan, and Uthlaro pact to take over our territory. In fact, we have an even larger territory now because Admiral Carver annexed the Uthlaro Dominion, in addition to the former Tsgardi Empire, and parts of Gondusan and Hudeerac space for their active participation in the attempted usurpation."

"My God, that woman is amazing."

"That she is. There's never been anyone like her. Anyway, no ships coming out of Mars after February 1st could possibly reach Quesann before the Uthlaro arrived, so the order to send all DS ships to Region Two was suspended pending the outcome of the battle. Knowing the dangerous situation you were facing, SHQ ordered us here to assist. There's another DS ship on its way here and should arrive in a day or two."

"What kind of ship?"

"A Quartermaster ship."

"Why are they sending a DS Quartermaster ship here?"

"It's the second design of a planned series they've been working on for a while. It's fresh out of the yard and had just begun its space trials, but I understand they're sending it here to retrieve the *Perry*."

"How is a Quartermaster ship going to retrieve the *Perry*? We need a reclamation ship, or several tugs."

"The new Quartermaster vessel is a ship transport for older ships with limited speed. The entire front of the ship opens to reveal a vast cavern of a hold capable of holding up to five destroyers. It can even hold a battleship. Once the *Perry* is secured inside, the front will be sealed and the ship is then capable of Light-9790 speed. It'll have you back to Mars in less than sixty days, barring any other course diversions."

"Two months instead of two years. Amazing."

"Yes. These new DS ships have revolutionized space travel."

"The *Perry* looks older every day," Lidden said.

"Judging from the outside appearance, I would have to guess that the Mars yard won't repair him. When we first saw you, we figured this was a dead hulk. I think he'll finally be retired and scrapped."

"Like me," Lidden murmured.

"What's that, sir. I didn't catch it."

"It's not important."

"Lieutenant(jg) Marcola reporting to the Captain as ordered," Sydnee said as she braced to attention in front of Lidden's desk on the morning following her return to the *Perry*. The MAT was safely parked in the *Perry's* starboard shuttle bay, and the three bodies had been taken to the ship's morgue.

"At ease, Marcola," Lidden said. Gesturing to a chair facing his desk near the corner, he said, "Have a seat."

This was the second time she had been invited to sit in the Captain's briefing room and she sat down without the stiffness of her first time.

"How's your arm?"

"Um, it's feeling a bit better, sir. I was lucky to be wearing my armor when the belt in the command chair broke. The doctor said that I probably would have lost the arm otherwise when it got caught between the two monitors mounted on the chair's left side. The armor prevented any broken bones and I only dislocated it at the shoulder. I should be fine in a few weeks."

"That's good. Now—what have you got to say for yourself?"

"What do you mean, sir?"

"I told you once that when you're invited to sit, you're not in trouble. Do you remember that?"

"Yes, sir."

"Well, forget it. You're in trouble up to your ears."

"Yes, sir," Sydnee said as she sat up straighter and her back stiffened.

"Didn't I order you to stay on Diabolisto?"

"Not exactly, sir. You really only asked me if I would volunteer to go back to Diabolisto. You did— suggest— that

I remain there until the *Pellew* arrived, but after we recovered the MAT, I came up with an idea for helping the *Perry*."

"You came up with this idea on your own? No one else put it in your head."

"It was my idea alone, sir. The others were under my command and I ordered them to assist me. They bear no responsibility for my actions."

"I've already spoken to the others involved. They agree that it was your idea, but all state that they supported your idea a hundred percent and returned willingly."

"Sir, no one else received any instructions from you related to remaining on the planet, so I alone should be punished."

"Do you feel that you should be punished?"

"Well— although you didn't specifically order me to stay on Diabolisto, I knew that was what you wished. I would have stayed, but once the idea of using the *Abissto* occurred to me, I felt that we could make a real difference. At the very least, you would have radio communications again. And I thought that if the *Glassama* was facing *two* destroyers when her repairs were complete, she'd never attack. We just arrived a little too late because we had to learn how to operate a ship from a foreign service and train the Marines in the use of the laser array weapons and torpedo systems."

Lidden took a deep breath and released it slowly, then said, "I would look exceedingly foolish if I charged you with disobeying an order I never specifically stated. I'm in enough trouble as it is for getting my ship wrecked and then shot to pieces. Captain Galeway of the *Missouri* believes the *Perry* won't be repaired. He thinks the weapons will be removed and the ship will finally be sent to the scrap dealers."

"Scrapped? What about the crew, sir?"

"I don't know yet. All I know for sure is that a vessel transporter is coming to get the *Perry*. I imagine we'll transfer to either one of the Scout-Destroyers for the trip back to Mars or perhaps the transport ship has quarters available for the crews of ships being transported.

"Marcola, I've never learned why you're on my boat, and I don't know if anyone will listen to me after the things that have happened, but I'm going to do my damndest to get you transferred to another ship."

Sydnee was shocked. "You don't want me on the *Perry*, sir?"

"I read your report regarding the death of Lieutenant Kennedy and how you took command and defeated the rebels who attacked the platoon. I also read of your actions when you commandeered the tug and when you worked to recover the MAT. Everything you wrote has been corroborated by the reports filed by others. Sergeant Booth has uploaded images of the head of the Lampaxa that attacked you while you were in the submerged sinkhole and images of the other one before it was butchered. I can say that I wouldn't want one of those things chewing on me, yet you immediately volunteered to go back to Diabolisto. And finally, there's your incredible accomplishment in bringing the *Abissto* to our rescue."

Lidden softened his voice as he continued. "Sydnee, before I knew who was captaining the *Abissto*, I told Galeway that we owed that person our lives. When I learned who was in command, I began to think about your time on the *Perry*. You haven't been here long, but your continued contributions to this ship have been extraordinary. There is no doubt in my mind that everyone aboard this ship owes their life to you and the people who supported you.

"Your being here has to be a mistake. You don't belong here. You belong on a first-rate ship of the line where your initiative, intelligence, and bravery can better serve the people of the Galactic Alliance. If you can be posted to a ship that doesn't carry a stigma of ineptitude, I have no doubt you'll be able to advance as you should and make a better contribution to the service.

"It's not that I don't want you on the *Perry*, if there is to be a *Perry* in the months ahead; it's that being here is a disservice to you, Space Command, and the people of the Galactic Alliance."

"Thank you, sir. And I would tell you if I had even a hint of knowledge as to why I was sent here."

"I believe you, Sydnee. I've recommended that you and the others who assisted you receive commendations for everything you've done. I've also forwarded a report to the Promotions Selection Board strongly suggesting that you be considered for early advancement to the rank of Lieutenant. It's still too soon in your career for such advancement, but it'll be in your file when you are eligible."

"Thank you, sir."

"Oh, and one other thing. The *Glassama* apparently had better success in stopping the *Darrapralis* than the *Abissto* had. Perhaps they had gotten the new codes or something. Anyway, the crew of the *Missouri* found eighteen female human slaves in the *Glassama* while looking for survivors. They're a bit banged up from the battle, but all will recover."

"That's wonderful news, sir. And the Ambassador?"

"He wasn't on the *Glassama*. I'm sure that information regarding his fate will come out at some point."

"Yes, sir.

"Sydnee, thank you for your service to the *Perry* and her crew. Dismissed."

Sydnee stood, braced to attention, and said, "It's been my honor to serve under you, sir."

Lidden smiled as she turned and left his office. He believed she had a bright future ahead of her. Then he thought about his own future and wondered if he'd be booted from the service or assigned to a post on a small base that no one ever heard of. He knew that if he was offered the choice, he'd take the base posting. The service was his life.

Sydnee flopped onto her bed when she returned to her quarters. With communications restored through the portable equipment, her mail queue had filled up with vids, some bearing dates that showed them to be several months old. But she didn't feel in the mood to start dealing with her correspondence just then. Learning that the war in Region

Two was over had come as a blow, but seeing several messages from Katarina dated after the final battle made her glad that her best friend was safe. She had always held out hope that while the war was raging, she might find an opportunity to transfer from the *Perry*, but now that the opportunity might be within her grasp, she didn't know if she really wanted to transfer. She had made a number of wonderful friends aboard the *Perry*.

She decided she would just have to wait and see what the fate of the ship would be and what would happen to the crew if the *Perry* went to the scrap yard.

Besides, she thought, smiling, she still hadn't discovered what Jerry Weems had done to deserve being sent to the *Perry*. She couldn't *possibly* leave without learning that.

~ finis ~

*** *Sydnee's exciting adventures continue in:* ***
Clidepp Requital

Watch for new books on Amazon and other fine booksellers,
check my website - www.deprima.com
or
sign up for my free newsletter to receive email announcements about future book releases.

Appendix

This chart is offered to assist readers who may be unfamiliar with military rank and the reporting structure. Newly commissioned officers begin at either ensign or second lieutenant rank.

Space Command	Space Marine Corps
Admiral of the Fleet	
Admiral	General
Vice-Admiral	Lieutenant General
Rear Admiral - Upper	Major General
Rear Admiral - Lower	Brigadier General
Captain	Colonel
Commander	Lieutenant Colonel
Lieutenant Commander	Major
Lieutenant	Captain
Lieutenant(jg) "Junior Grade"	First Lieutenant
Ensign	Second Lieutenant

The commanding officer on a ship is always referred to as Captain, regardless of his or her official military rank. Even an Ensign could be a Captain of the Ship, although that would only occur as the result of an unusual situation or emergency where no senior officers survived.

On Space Command ships and bases, time is measured according to a twenty-four-hour clock, normally referred to as military time. For example, 8:42 PM would be referred to as 2042 hours. Chronometers are always set to agree with the date and time at Space Command Supreme Headquarters on Earth. This is known as GST, or Galactic System Time.

Admiralty Board:

Moore, Richard E.	Admiral of the Fleet
Platt, Evelyn S.	Admiral - Director of Fleet Operations
Bradlee, Roger T.	Admiral - Director of Intelligence (SCI)
Ressler, Shana E.	Admiral - Director of Budget & Accounting
Hillaire, Arnold H.	Admiral - Director of Academies
Burke, Raymond A.	Vice-Admiral - Director of GSC Base Management
Ahmed, Raihana L.	Vice-Admiral - Dir. of Quartermaster Supply
Woo, Lon C.	Vice-Admiral - Dir. of Scientific & Expeditionary Forces
Plimley, Loretta J.	Rear-Admiral, (U) - Dir. of Weapons R&D
Hubera, Donald M.	Rear-Admiral, (U) - Dir. of Academy Curricula

Ship Speed Terminology / Speed

Ship Speed Terminology	Speed
Plus-1	1 kps
Sub-Light-1	1,000 kps
Light-1 (c) (speed of light in a vacuum)	299,792.458 kps
Light-150 or **150 c**	150 times the speed of light

Hyper-Space Factors

IDS Communications Band	.0513 light years each minute (8.09 billion kps)
DeTect Range	4 billion kilometers

Strat Com Desig	Mission Description for Strategic Command Bases
1	Base - Location establishes it as a critical component of Space Command Operations - Serves as home-port to multiple warships that also serve in base's defense. All sections of Space Command maintain an active office at the base. Base Commander establishes all patrol routes and is authorized to override SHQ orders to ships within the sector(s) designated part of the base's operating territory. Recommended rank of Commanding Officer: **Rear Admiral (U)**
2	Base - Location establishes it as a crucial component of Space Command Operations - Serves as home-port to multiple warships that also serve in base's defense. All sections of Space Command maintain an active office at the base. Patrol routes established by SHQ. Recommended rank of Commanding Officer: **Rear Admiral (L)**
3	Base - Location establishes it as an important component of Space Command Operations - Serves as homeport to multiple warships that also serve in base's defense. Patrol routes established by SHQ. Recommended rank of Commanding Officer: **Captain**
4	Station - Location establishes it as an important terminal for Space Command personnel engaged in travel to/from postings, and for re-supply of vessels and outposts. Recommended rank of Commanding Officer: **Commander**
5	Outpost - Location makes it important for observation purposes and collection of information. Recommended rank of Commanding Officer: **Lt. Commander**

Sample Distances	
Earth to Mars (Mean)	78 million kilometers
Nearest star to our Sun	4 light-years (Proxima Centauri)
Milky Way Galaxy diameter	100,000 light-years
Thickness of M'Way at Sun	2,000 light-years
Stars in Milky Way	200 billion (est.)
Nearest galaxy (Andromeda)	2 million light-years from M'Way
A light-year (in a vacuum)	9,460,730,472,580.8 kilometers
A light-second (in vacuum)	299,792.458 km
Grid Unit	1,000 light-years² (1,000,000 Sq. LY)
Deca-Sector	100 light-years² (10,000 Sq. LY)
Sector	10 light-years² (100 Sq. LY)
Section	94,607,304,725 km²
Sub-section	946,073,047 km²

The two-dimensional representation that follows is offered to provide the reader with a feel for the spatial relationships between bases, systems, and celestial events referenced in the novels of this series. The reader should remember that GA territory extends through the entire depth of the Milky Way galaxy when the galaxy is viewed on edge.

The millions of stars, planets, moons, and celestial phenomena in this small part of the galaxy would only confuse, and therefore have been omitted from the image.

D

The following map shows the position of the planet Diabolisto and Simmons SCB near the Clidepp Empire border relative to the core planets of Region One.

Should the maps be unreadable, or should you desire additional imagery, .jpg and .pdf versions of all maps are available for free downloading at:

www.deprima.com/ancillary/maps.html

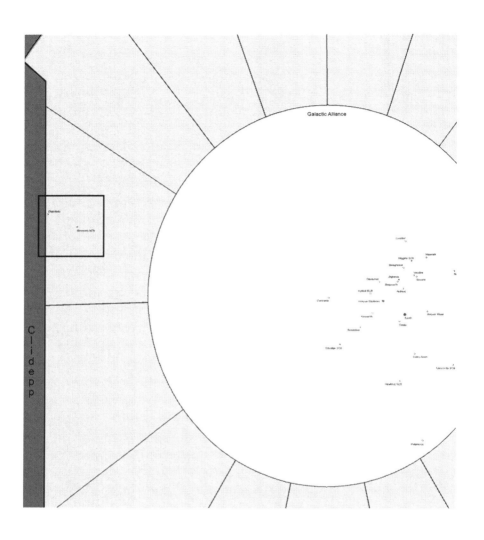

Made in the USA
Middletown, DE
22 October 2016